# THE YEAR
# OF ICE

06/29/02

For NANCY
WITH ALL BEST
WISHES,

*[signature]*

BRIAN MALLOY

# THE YEAR
# OF ICE

ST. MARTIN'S PRESS ✖ NEW YORK

Design by Philip Mazzone

ISBN 0-312-28948-0

First Edition: July 2002

10   9   8   7   6   5   4   3   2   1

In loving memory of my brother,
Thomas Michael Malloy, a stand-up guy

# ACKNOWLEDGMENTS

My deepest thanks to Teresa Theophano and Keith Kahla at St. Martin's Press for taking a chance on me.

Thanks to all who helped with the early drafts: Josip Novakovich, Emilie Buchwald, Jerod Santek, Dale Gregory Anderson, Liz Petrangelo, Don Sommers, and Bonnie MacDougal. Special thanks to the members, staffs, and boards of the Loft Literary Center and Open Book.

I am deeply grateful for the love and support of Terrence Straub. Heartfelt thanks to all my family and, in particular, to Dorothy McRee, Dorothy Malloy, Robert Bader, Phyllis Malloy, James and Holly McRee, Corrie Alicea, Michael Malloy, Denise Malloy Hubbard, and John and Lisa Rogers.

Thanks, too, to my wonderful friends John Flanigan and Michele Zurakowski, Nic Mattera, Dan Stringfield, Deb Leavitt and Anne Phibbs, Gerry Tyrrell and Kevin Reuther, Peter Farstad and Paul Melbloom, Sherrie and Brad Beal, Norajean Flanagan, Terri Foley, Scott Cantor and Chris Forbes, Carol Skay, Pat Malone, Annie Roberts and Karen Wright, Pat Cummings, Karen Kelley-Ariwoola, Kirby Bennett, Bunny and Earl Anderson, John Blaylock and Karen Nickel, Matt Halley and Mike Larson, Art and Barb Straub, and of course, Cat Thompson. Thanks for not laughing at me when I said I wanted to be a writer.

Thanks to the new friends I have made at Readerville and the *Poets & Writers* Speakeasy. Special thanks to Anne Ursu and Gretchen Moran Laskas for their encouragement.

My love from this side of the veil to Thomas Joseph Malloy, Hugh McRee, Jim Smith, Jeff Scott, and Paul Illies, gone too soon.

An extra-special dog kiss right on the lips to Pepper, Cerberus, Max, Maggie, and Lucy, good dogs all.

Often the effects of late spring and early autumn frosts upon tender plants growing outdoors can be prevented by simple, inexpensive, easily applied precautions or by prompt treatment in the early morning after a cold snap.

—The Wise Garden Encyclopedia

# THE ABSOLUTE STILLNESS
# OF THE WHITE

January 1978

Aunt Nora always says that people can still surprise you. I never got what she meant by that until last fall. I mean, Floyd Anderson always seemed normal enough. He's an old Swede who has been our neighbor for as long as I can remember. He's always had a good word for everybody. He always told the same jokes, always talked about the weather, and always kept his sidewalk clean as a whistle even during the worst snowfalls. You could set your watch by Floyd Anderson.

Then he began wearing a pyramid on his head right around Halloween. He bought it at one of those hippie shops on the West Bank, where all the sixties burnouts live. They sell them in stores that are full of body oils and incense and rolling papers and

bongs. Floyd's pyramid's not a hat; it's this kind of dumb-ass thing
that's supposed to make you, like, calm or happy or some weird
shit like that. It wasn't until a couple of weeks after he got it,
when the thermometer dropped below zero, that he'd put a hat
on underneath it. I'd watch him from my bedroom window,
shoveling his walk, covered from head to toe against the windchill, the dull brass of the pyramid reflecting the winter sun.

His wife left him about three weeks ago. They'd been married
almost forty years.

Dad said, "Makes you think." But he was wrong; it didn't
make me think. Not much does. I'm not proud of it or anything,
I'm just telling the truth.

When I see Floyd at Red Owl, where I bag groceries after
school, he smiles at me and says, "You really have to get one of
these." He means his pyramid. "I feel psychically healed. It'll bring
you peace."

Floyd's not lying. Rumor had it that he'd wanted to leave his
wife but never had the nerve.

"I don't think so, Mr. Anderson," I always tell him.

"You don't know what you're missing," he says as he grabs his
bag of Kellogg's Corn Flakes and Del Monte pudding cups from
me. "Don't know what you're missing," he says again, like I
hadn't heard him the first time.

Once he's out the sliding doors, Lorraine, the checker who
works with me at register three, says, "Is he seeing anyone, do
you know?"

I look at her like she's mental. "You mean Floyd Anderson?"

Yes, Floyd Anderson, she nods, showing me her black and gray
roots.

"You're too good for him," I tell her.

She sighs and says under her breath, "Let me be the judge of
who I'm too good for, thank you very much."


Lorraine gave up on my dad around Labor Day. He kept telling
her he wasn't ready to start dating yet. Dad's a good-looking man

and what they call in my biology class an endangered species: a
single middle-aged man. He had to stop going to a Catholic support group for people whose spouses died 'cause the widows
wouldn't leave him alone. They'd call him at all hours, sometimes
drunk, and once he stopped answering the phone, they'd ask me
for advice:

"What does he like to do?"

"What's his favorite meal?"

"Would he like to go to a Northstars game, do you think?"

I'd just stare at the receiver, feeling a little sorry for these
women who'd been cheated out of a husband so early in life. Out
of loyalty to my mom, who died in a car accident, I'd tell them
that Dad had a girlfriend and to stop calling our house. But they
didn't, not until Dad broke down and paid the extra money for
an unlisted number.

When that happened, they started dropping by with little gifts
for him. Now he has to go down the basement or hide upstairs
in his room anytime the doorbell rings. It's my job to put the
widows off his scent. A lot of them bring ties, something Dad
doesn't need—he works day shifts at the Highland Park Ford
plant—and I wonder if all these male presents used to belong to
the dead husbands.

"I never see your father at church anymore," one of the widows said to me, a brightly wrapped box of cuff links in her shivering hands.

I had Dad's permission to say whatever I needed to to get rid
of them. I told her, "He's converting."

With her teeth chattering—I never let the widows inside—she
asked: "To what?"

"Islam." We were studying world religions during fourth-
period history.

The next time she showed up at the door, she was wearing
one of those veil things over her face and had the Koran with
her.

Okay, so she didn't show up in a veil with the Koran. She
never came back at all; I think I kind of freaked her out with the

Muslim stuff. But as Aunt Nora says, "Any story worth telling is worth exaggerating."

The smart widows bring something for me. One gave me a twenty-dollar gift certificate to Positively Fourth Street, a record store and head shop near the U. To these women I'm polite, but no more encouraging.

"He's out on a date."

"He's gone on a vacation with his girlfriend."

"He's engaged."

Mom's funeral had to be held on my sixteenth birthday. To compensate, Dad gave me a hundred bucks. I still have it stashed in my sock drawer, along with the money I make at Red Owl.


I've been thinking about Mom a lot lately 'cause the second anniversary is coming up. For example, I remember my first day back on the school bus after her funeral. A really weird girl, Laurie Lindstrom, tried to be nice to me. Laurie always read books about horses and had no friends. Her parents had been murdered when they were camping up on the north shore. A motorcycle gang beat them to death as part of some weird initiation for new members. It made the national news, and somebody wrote a book about it that's being turned into a TV movie of the week. Far as I know, Laurie hasn't gotten any money from it.

She'd sat next to me on the bus and said, "I know how hard it is to lose your mother. I got a postcard from mine two days after she died."

I tried to imagine what it must have said.

>*Dear Laurie,*
>    *Aiiiiiiiiiiie! Help us! For the love of God, HELP US!*
>                                    *Love,*
>                                    *Mom*

Or maybe:

*Dear Laurie,*
*    Daddy and I are being hacked to death by satanic bikers.*
*Wish you were here.*

*                                        Love,*
*                                        Mom*

I told her, "Thanks."

"If you ever want to talk—"

"Thanks," I told her again, my voice a NO TRESPASSING sign.

I don't see Laurie much now that I don't take the bus to school anymore. Tommy, my best friend since I was a little kid, got a '71 Dodge Challenger and picks me up every morning when he can get it started. It makes a *blub-blub-blub* sound and stalls out whenever he makes a right turn. Still, it's very cool. Tommy and I belong to a clique that wears flannel shirts, smokes Camels, and goes to keggers every weekend. As members of the class of '78, we've already been counseled to go to vo-techs after we graduate this June so we can learn a trade. Tommy's gonna be an auto mechanic; I haven't decided what I'm gonna do.

Dad wants me to go to the U—they have to take any idiot with a high school diploma or GED in the General College program. In four years I'd graduate with a general degree and begin a general life. I told Dad that I'd think about it, but last week he told me: "Oh, you're going, young man. Don't think you're not going." Dad hates his job; he has for as long as I can remember. Some weeks he drank himself sick because he couldn't face one more day at the plant. When he was drunk he'd say, "That god-damn plant's killing me."

He wants me to get an education so I can get a higher-paying job of my own to hate.


Tommy says that General College is a waste of time, I should go to Dunwoody with him and become an electrician or draftsman or something. Or cooler yet, go to Brown Institute over on Lake Street and get a job in radio. We're lined up at one end of Van

Cleve Park waiting for the kickoff. Most Sundays we play Snow Football with some guys I guess you'd call our friends. I've dragged Tommy here every week for a month, even though he'd rather be inside cranking tunes and smoking weed.

"I dunno," I say. "It's only January. I got time."

Tommy tells me that he's already applied to Dunwoody Institute. He's making plans for his future, even if I'm not. While we wait for the kickoff he pushes his long dirty blond hair behind his ears. He looks like one of the Allman Brothers, except with normal-colored skin.

The ball flies at us and I catch it, but it's frozen and slick and it pops out of my hands like a wet bar of soap. The challenge of snow football is possession; that's what makes it so much better than regular football.

"Shit!"

Jon Thompson's already made it down the field and snags the ball, bad news for my side. The good news is that I'm six-two and weigh 185 pounds so it's easy for me to knock him on his ass. On the way down I hug him hard; Jon's a fox. He's got these really big eyelashes and hair that's the same color as chocolate. You could say that I'm in love with Jon. So I just lie there on top of him. This is like the only time I can get away with it without people shitting their pants.

"Get offa me," he says.

"Okay, tough guy," I tell him and I slap the side of his head. I do this for two reasons, really. First, 'cause if I smack him, nobody will guess that I want to pick him up in my arms and kiss him really hard, right on his lips. And second, he's got to be reminded that I'm tougher than he is. Wolves do this all the time to keep order in the pack. I'm the alpha; he's the beta. That's the way it always has been and that's the way, uh-huh, uh-huh, I like it, uh-huh, uh-huh. If anybody knew I liked KC and The Sunshine Band I'd have to drop out.

We wait for the snap and Tommy says, "One of these days somebody's gonna beat the crap outta you."

I shrug and say, "Nobody here."

Tommy looks around. "Nah, I guess not. But someday, somebody will."

Rick Foley falls back with the ball and I pound into Jon Thompson again. This time he doesn't yell at me to get off him, he's afraid to. He just waits quietly for me to get up. I smile and wink at him. He thinks I'm being a jerk, but my wink is sincere. And it's a thrill, maybe the only one I'll ever get to have.

Wherever Jon is on the field, I'm soon on top of him. He feels like heaven underneath me. We don't say a word to each other and he never looks me in the eye. It's easy to pretend that he's in my bed and that I'm holding him.

Tommy notices that I won't cut Jon a break. He says, "You got it in for that guy, or what?"

I choose what.


That night, alone in my bed, I pile up the pillows and hold them in my arms. Here, Jon Thompson's in love with me, his head on my shoulder and my hand stroking his cool chocolate hair. I kiss the fabric of the pillowcase and squeeze Jon tighter. We talk about the game. He tells me how much he loved being tackled by me. If people only knew, he says and laughs. I laugh with him and then I kiss him again, but harder this time.

He pulls away and holds my head in his hands. He looks at me like he's gonna cry and he says, I love you, Kevin. I'll love you forever. Promise me you'll never leave me.

Don't be mental, Jon, I'm never gonna leave you. I love you.

He puts his hand on my cheek, and that's when I hear the scraping of Floyd Anderson's shovel against the sidewalk. We've only had a dusting but Floyd spazzes out if there's even one speck of snow on the concrete. Somebody might slip in front of his house and sue him, and then he'd lose everything, and then what'd he do?

I leave Jon alone on my bed and look out the window at Floyd. He's in his blue snowsuit, and the snowflakes sparkle in the light of the streetlamps. He's resting, or maybe he's *reveling in the absolute stillness of the white* like Mom used to do. Or maybe he's receiving secret messages from the CIA through the pyramid on top of his head. He doesn't budge for a minute, maybe two, and then the *scrape, scrape, scrape* begins again, echoing off the houses and apartment buildings and making the Bartochevitzes' dog Max bark.

I go back to my bed and Jon's gone; the stack of pillows is just a stack of pillows. I stare at the ceiling for a long time, blankly, the same way Mom used to stare when she'd sit out on the front stoop in her ugly plaid coat and watch the snow fall. She'd be out there for hours, not budging an inch. When I do fall asleep I dream of snow. Of the absolute stillness of the white.


There's a widow at the front door when I leave for school in the morning. She's one of the regulars; her name's Jackie Shaw. You can tell that she used to smile a lot. She has these really deep crow's-feet like the canals on Mars that we're studying in science class. Rick Foley thinks that Martians made them, but he can be a big fucking burnout 'cause he's done way too many drugs. Still, it'd be cool if there were Martians. Maybe on their planet guys can marry guys.

"Why, good morning, Kevin," Jackie Shaw says, sweet as you please. "I just wanted to drop these off for you boys. I bet you don't get many hot breakfasts these days."

Steam comes from the box she hands me.

"They're cinnamon rolls with real cream icing," she tells me. "Just the thing to warm you up."

"Thanks."

She looks past me, into the sitting room. "Is your father at home? Maybe he'd like me to make a pot of coffee to wash these down with."

Dad's upstairs getting ready for work, but I don't tell her that. Instead I say, "Dad had an early shift today. He's left already."

Her face falls a little bit, but then she rebounds. "Well, *you* enjoy those then. Would you let your father know I stopped by?"

I hear the *blub-blub-blub* of Tommy's Challenger. In exactly three seconds he will honk the horn twice.

"Yeah. Thanks, Mrs. Shaw."

*Beep! Beep!*

This is when Mrs. Bartochevitz opens her front door and yells at Tommy for blasting his horn. I think she waits there for him.

"Do you have to do that?" she shouts at his car.

In exactly five seconds Mrs. Bartochevitz will put her hands on her hips and scream across the street at me.

"That's my ride," I tell Mrs. Shaw.

"Does your friend *have* to do that?" Mrs. Bartochevitz wants to know.

I wave in Mrs. Shaw's direction and jump in Tommy's car.

"What's that?" he asks, pointing at the box.

"Cinnamon rolls," I tell him. The love potion of widows.

Exactly two years ago, this very minute, everything was normal. I walked the halls oblivious to Jon Thompson and his chocolate hair. Mom was alive and at the Midway Target, getting paper towels and laundry detergent, and a bag of Old Dutch ripple potato chips for me. The house smelled like lemons and my father was busy stacking palettes of cardboard stock against a plant wall. Exactly two years ago, twenty minutes from now, Mom's car slid off East River Road, rolled down an embankment, and crashed into the ice covering the Mississippi. Exactly two years ago, one hundred and forty-three minutes from now, my teacher told me to report to the school nurse's office where I found my Aunt Nora waiting for me. She said I should come live with her.

But right now, I'm late for English Lit.

I see Jon Thompson in the hallway and I say hey. He looks at me weird and says, "Hey." He keeps walking but I reach out and touch him on his bony shoulder. He stops and turns toward me, maybe waiting for another smack. Guys are always pissing on each other's trees; it's like we can't help it.

I say, real casual, like I'm asking what time it is, "Any parties this weekend?"

"Haven't heard," he tells me.

I look at him. What do you say to the boy that you love when you aren't supposed to love boys? Everything that I can think of sounds faggy to me.

"Okay," I say.

He frowns. "If I knew of any, I'd tell you," he says, all defensive-like.

"It's cool, man," I say, and I bolt, down the hall and away from him. Away from his deep brown eyes with the big cow lashes. Away from his scrawny shoulder that makes my hand shake like I'm a spaz or something.

Class has started by the time I get there. I sit on the white side of the room next to Rick Foley, who's nodding his head in time to a tune only he can hear. He smiles at me; he's drawing a pair of biker-chick boobs in his notebook and the teacher thanks me for being so kind to stop by. His name is Mr. Hayes, a.k.a. Fey Hayes, the faggiest teacher at Northeast High. He looks like he's sixty and in pain. All the time.

He turns back to Donnell White, who is black, one of the many new kids from Chicago and Gary, Indiana, who're starting to freak out the teachers. "We speak proper English here, Mr. White," he says, "not urban slang. I seriously doubt that our country's greatest poet would appreciate your interpretation of his crowning achievement."

Donnell doesn't say anything.

"Try again," Fey Hayes tells him, and Donnell begins reading "Stopping by Woods on a Snowy Evening" out loud.

" 'My little horse must think it queer . . .' "

We all laugh.

Fey Hayes shakes his head. "Why is that necessary?" he wants to know. "The horse is used to a certain way of doing things, and on this night the routine is set aside. It's queer. Not the norm. Is that so difficult for you to understand?" He sighs, hanging his head. "I see that people of your generation fail to appreciate the conflict between free will and social obligation."

Donnell can't go on; he's laughing too hard and tears roll down his cheeks. Fey Hayes shakes his head and calls on me. "Mr. Doyle, would you please do the honors?"

"What page are we on?" I ask, shuffling through my copy of *Contemporary American Poetry.*

Barely opening his tight faggy mouth, Fey Hayes tells me, "Page thirty-four. Begin at 'he gives.' "

I search the page and find where Donnell left off. " 'He gives his harness bells a shake to ask if there is some mistake.' "

Fey Hayes stops me. "Is there some mistake, Mr. Doyle?"

I look up from my book. "No."

Fey Hayes is staring a hole in my head. "He's stopping on purpose?"

"Yeah."

"Why would that be?"

"To watch the woods fill up with snow."

Fey Hayes tilts his fey head. "Is that the only reason he's stopping?"

I look back at my book and read ahead a little bit. "Yeah, I guess so."

"So when Frost writes, 'The woods are lovely, dark and deep, But I have promises to keep, And miles to go before I sleep,' do you suppose he moves on or does he stay where he is?"

I don't know.

Fey Hayes knows that I don't know. So he says: "Now tell me, Mr. Doyle, why would you stop to watch the woods fill up with snow?"

Exactly two years ago this very second everything was normal. In five minutes, exactly two years ago, nothing would ever be again.

Dad's been watching me closely all night, afraid I might freak out or something. Neither of us has said boo about the second anniversary. Once in a while the phone rings and somebody offers us their condolences. None of Mom's relatives call, they're all still in Ireland, except for my Aunt Nora. Aunt Nora doesn't call; Dad wouldn't give her our new phone number.

We stare at the TV. "You're awfully quiet tonight," he says to me.

I grunt.

"Anything the matter?" he asks, hoping I'll say no.

"Nah."

When the doorbell rings, it's Jackie Shaw, not the pizza guy. She couldn't have timed this any better if she'd tried. Normally Dad would be upstairs in his room waiting for the all clear. She spots him as she sticks her head past me and through the doorway.

"Pat!" she squeals, not believing her own eyes. "They've been working you much too hard down at the plant!"

"Jackie," Dad says, like he's just learned how to talk. He stands up, and looking at the floor he says, "Come on in out of the cold."

Jackie Shaw's throwing off more heat than our furnace. "Thank you, thank you! I just wanted to drop this off for you boys," she says, a pie plate covered with Reynolds Wrap in her hands. "I hope you like pecan."

The bell rings again, and Jackie shoots a nasty look at the door. When she sees it's the pizza guy and not some other widow, she beams and says, "Oh, *no*! Not *pizza*! You two need a good home-cooked meal. Let me fix you something nice."

Dad's still standing; his hands in his pockets. He says, "Really, Jackie, you don't have to do that. Why don't you sit down and have a slice with us."

Jackie shakes her head no, but she's saying, "Oooh, a piece of pizza sounds like just the thing. It's bitter out there."

As if God himself—the Old Testament one—could get her to leave.

I pay the pizza guy with the twenty Dad gave me and I keep the change, a tradition of ours since Mom died. Dad's been a lot nicer to me since it happened, you can tell he's really trying hard. I'll put his change in my sock drawer with the rest of my money.

Jackie Shaw slips out of her black coat and she's wearing a black dress, nylons, and heels in spite of the fact that it's ten below out. The war paint's on extra thick; she's on the hunt tonight. She sits on the couch right next to Dad and tsk-tsks.

"You look tired, Pat," she says as she pets Dad's hair into place.

"I'm fine," Dad tells her.

She sighs and folds her hands in her lap. Her nails are flaming red and it almost hurts to look at them. She says, "It was two years ago today, wasn't it?"

I see Dad wince from where I sit across the room. He nods and Jackie pouts.

"You poor—"

"The pizza's scrump-dilly-icious," I say.

Dad winks at me. "I didn't know how hungry I was," he says.

We've eaten all the pizza, half the pecan pie, and drunk a pot of Sanka and still Jackie Shaw won't budge.

I've got no choice so I say, "Good night." I can't think of one more thing to say to this woman and neither can Dad. I don't want to leave him alone with her but I can't keep my eyes open another second.

"You sleep tight, Kevin," Jackie Shaw says to me with a smile, like she thinks she's my mom or something.

I just look at her like she cut one and head upstairs. The treads creak beneath my feet, old and tired. When I pull the door open to my room, Jon Thompson's waiting for me in my bed. I smile, then he smiles too. He pats the mattress and says, room for two. I pull off my clothes and goose pimples are all over my skin, so I jump on the mattress and pull the covers over us, hard. We play, tickling each other and wrestling a little. We laugh and make out and then laugh again. After the usual lovey-dovey stuff, he asks me about Mom.

What was she like, Jon wants to know.

I tell him that she was small and timid and scared of her own shadow.

Did you love her, Jon asks as he runs his fingers through my hair.

Yeah, I guess I did. She was really quiet. She never said too much. But she always told me I was becoming a very handsome young man. Dad never says that. Dad never says much of anything.

Jon holds me tighter. Dads don't say that kind of thing, just

Moms. It must have been very hard for you, losing her the way you did.

Yeah, it was pretty weird.

What do you mean?

The thing is, I whisper to Jon, I never got to see her after she died. There was too much damage. I had to say good-bye to a closed casket. Anybody could have been in there. Maybe it was empty and they just threw her in a Dumpster behind the funeral home, who knows? That's what they did with the dead cats at the animal hospital I used to work at. People would come in, all upset with their dead cats, and they'd pay like twenty bucks for us to take the bodies. But I only took them as far the Dumpster out back.

Jon hugs me hard and says that Mom's in a better place now. At peace.

Do you really think so?

Of course, Jon says, and then he kisses me lightly on my lips.

I hope she's at peace.

I know she's at peace, he sighs in my ear. I love you so much, he tells me in a soft breath.

I love you too. More than I can say.

Downstairs I hear the front door creak on its hinges. Somehow, Dad's gotten Jackie Shaw to leave.


Jon Thompson's standing next to my locker. I don't know how to look at him anymore. I'm afraid that he'll guess that I love him. But then I'm afraid that if he's like me, I'm not giving him enough clues to figure it out. This bites the big one.

"Party Saturday," he tells me.

I look just past him. "Where?"

"Debbie Polanski's. Her parents are in Bemidji till Monday."

Jon's being nice to me 'cause he's afraid I don't like him. And if I don't like him, Tommy and Rick Foley and everybody else won't like him either. If I weren't in love with him, I'd feel sorry for him. But I am, so I don't.

"Cool," I tell him.

He smiles that smile at me, the one that makes me breathe really fast, and says, "Catch you later."

" 'Kay."

I bolt to Dutch class. We only have Dutch at our school 'cause one of our teachers is from South Africa. And it's not really Dutch she speaks; it's Afrikaans. I'm late. *Ik ben laat.* Like ten minutes *laat.*

When I get to class, our teacher, Mevrouw Bergsma, says, *"Meneer Doyle, wat leuk!"* (Mr. Doyle, how nice!)

I sit next to Tommy, who's in his usual position, slumped back with his arms crossed and his legs spread really wide. Like he's pissed off. Mevrouw Bergsma doesn't like us to sit like that, she says it's too aggressive.

*"Ik ben fucking bored,"* he whispers.

*"Jammer."* (What a shame.)

Mevrouw Bergsma claps her little pink hands and says, *"Mevrouw Kooiman ontmoet Mevrouw Kees in het Vondelpark."* (Mrs. Kooiman meets Mrs. Kees in Vondel Park.) Mevrouw Bergsma looks at me and says, *"Kevin, wat heeft Mevrouw Kees bij zich."* Now I'm really lost.

"Well," I say.

*"Ja?"*

*"Mevrouw Kees heeft . . ."*

*"Heeft wat?"*

". . . stuff. Some stuff."

She sucks her lips between her teeth. I make her do that a lot. "Did you even read the assignment?"

*Nee, ma'am. Mevrouw Shaw komt by met a pecan pie. So I studeert nix.* "Yeah."

*"Echt? Waar werkt Mevrouw Kees?"* (Really? Where does Mrs. Kees work?)

*"Nederland?"* (Holland?)

The smart kids laugh at me, but I shoot them a look and they shut up fast, not wanting their asses kicked.

Mevrouw Bergsma gives up and moves on to a cheerleader who stinks of Bubble Yum. There are some teachers who think that guys like me and Tommy are cute—*endearing in the way that only the young can be*—that's what my homeroom teacher says. But it's easy to tell that Mevrouw Bergsma just thinks that we're a giant pain in her neck. Once she accused me of loitering in her classroom and impersonating somebody who gave a damn. This was her little joke I guess, but she said it all bitchy and I've never liked her since.

*Precise tvee jaheren geleden vandaag was ik thuis.* (Exactly two years ago today I was at home.)

I'm putting cans of Campbell's chunky soup at the bottom of a double bag. So chunky you could eat it with a fork. But use a spoon. You'll want to get every drop. Mrs. Gunderson looks at me and smiles. She's one of the women that called Dad at first, but she gave up without much of a fight, probably 'cause she's divorced and not widowed. She doesn't stop by the house all the time with ties or cuff links. She doesn't pump me for information about him at the supermarket. I feel sorry for her 'cause she had to take in her niece, Laurie Lindstrom, after Laurie's parents were killed up north. And I feel a little guilty 'cause I'm glad that her and my dad didn't get together. Not because of her, but 'cause Laurie is so very uncool.

Mrs. Gunderson winks and says, "I never have to worry about anything getting broken when you bag, Kevin. You take good care of me."

My boss doesn't want me to double-bag, but I like Mrs. Gunderson. She's always really nice to me. "No sweat," I tell her.

"How are you getting on at school now that you're a big senior?"

I mumble, "Okay."

"Have you made any plans for after graduation?"

"Going to the U, I guess."

She sighs. "My alma mater. So you're going to be a Golden Gopher, good for you. Are you going to live on campus?" Campus is maybe twenty blocks at the most from my house.

"No, ma'am." I'm about to say something else but I can tell by the look on her face that she's back at college, maybe with a boyfriend, maybe at a party. She's remembering something she hasn't thought about in a long time. When she snaps out of it, she blushes.

"You take care of yourself, young man," she says as she steers her cart toward the doors.

Next in line are three girls from school, all giggling and whispering. I know them from keggers and I got high with one of them once.

"Hiya, Kevin," the shortest one says. She has feathered hair like Farrah Fawcett-Majors and pink lipstick the same color as her nails. Her friends snigger, and one of them turns bright red like a stoplight.

"Hey," I say. They're buying two packs of Bubble Yum so there's nothing to bag. I can tell they're checking me out, so I run a hand through my hair 'cause I know I'm a fox.

"So," the little one says to me, "you going to Debbie Polanski's on Saturday?"

"Yeah, I guess so."

Lorraine, the checker, looks at me and rolls her eyes.

Feathered Hair says, "Allison was hoping you were."

The tallest one, with straight blond hair parted down the middle and a beet-red face, says, "Was not, shut up!"

They run out of the store, arguing and laughing, and Lorraine gives me a look. "Allison's looking forward to Saturday, I bet."

So am I. Jon Thompson will be there.

"The way these girls flirt with you, it's a wonder you can fit your head through the doorway."

I don't know what she means, so I say, "Yeah."


Floyd Anderson's scraping his sidewalk clear to the marrow when Tommy *blub-blub-blubs* up in his Challenger to pick me up for Debbie Polanski's party. For Mrs. Bartochevitz's sake, he honks twice, which gives Floyd a start, and his pyramid falls off his head and into a snowbank.

When I open the front door a blast of cold air hits me hard and I wheeze. It's supposed to get down between twenty and thirty below tonight and Dad's made me promise to call him if Tommy's car won't start. He pays attention to where I go and what I do since Mom died.

I have to sit in the back; Rick Foley's riding shotgun next to Tommy. "Hey, man," Rick Foley says, so I say, "Hey, man."

I see Tommy look at me in the rearview mirror. He nods and says, "Hey, man."

I say, "Hey, man."

And we're off, three men heading to Debbie Polanski's house, which turns out to be maybe all of four blocks from my own.

As soon as we're inside I see Allison and her friends. They see me too and scream and turn their heads. There's this cloud of cigarette and pot smoke that hurts my eyes and I'm afraid that I'm gonna reek like nothing else when I get home and Dad'll notice. They're blasting Aerosmith and everybody has to shout. Tommy yells in my ear. He tells me to drink the punch, not the beer, so I do.

It's one big plastic cup later and I'm already buzzed.

Two cups later and I'm drunk.

Three cups later and I've never been so smashed in my entire life.

Rick Foley finds me leaning against a wall, staring into my cup, trying not to fall over. He goes, "Whoa, man, you shit-faced?"

I just smile and nod at him. You know, he's kinda foxy, I never noticed before. I'm afraid to say anything 'cause I know I'll sound really blitzed. *Ja, Ik ben shit-faced.*

Rick Foley shouts over at Tommy, who's talking to Beth, who's wearing a tube top in the middle of January. You can see her nips from here. Beth used to go to Northeast, but now she goes to someplace near the U for kids who can't hack regular school. Rick Foley barely gets out, "Hey, man, Kevin's shit-faced," before he passes out, face first, on the floor in front of me. He's just lies there, maybe he's dead, I can't tell. I laugh as I step over him on my way to get some more punch.

"Man, Foley's wasted." This is Jon Thompson shouting at me. He's pointing at Rick Foley's body, right behind us. I get all warm. Jon Thompson! You're here! I love you! Do you love me?

"I know," I say and giggle again. Jon snickers too and I want to touch him really bad.

Now we're laughing so hard that we're not making any noise at all. We just, like, shake, and I'm kinda freaking 'cause I think I might be suffocating. I can't tell if I'm taking any air in or breathing any out. How long have I gone without breathing?

Jon finally makes sounds like "Ha, ha, ha" but then he grabs his stomach and pukes. Now the music stops and people are pointing at him, gagging and laughing at the same time. Oooh, gross, they all seem to say. I'm still laughing, but not 'cause Jon threw up. I'm still cracking up about Rick Foley.

Jon just stares at his own vomit, maybe a foot away from Rick Foley's head, and I can tell that he's not really sure if it came out of him. He sways as he looks at it, his mouth wide open. He looks up at me and I'm laughing really hard, but not at him, only I can't tell him that, 'cause I can't breathe. Next he looks at the people around us.

Somebody says, "Hey, Thompson, why don't you blow chow at your own house?"

He yells, "Shut up!"

I want to help, but my shoulders are jiggling and I think I might die laughing.

Some guy, who looks like he's thirty, shouts at Jon, "Don't drink with the big boys if you can't handle it, weak tit."

Jon screams, "Shut the hell up." He staggers past the gawkers and toward what I can only hope is the john.

I want to stop laughing but I can't and I notice Allison standing next to me. Her eyelids are heavy and her head's shaking, the way Mom-Mom's always did on account of the palsy.

She says to me like I just said something, "What?"

But I can't talk; I just gasp for air. Look at Rick Foley, I want to say. He's so funny.

"Do you have a girlfriend?" slurs out of Allison's mouth, and then her eyes close.

She's funny too. Knock, knock, anybody home? God, I need oxygen.

Finally my convulsions stop. I leave Allison standing where she is, like a bobblehead, and I work my way in what I think is the direction Jon's gone. I find a hallway and open the first door I see. Tommy's on top of Beth, only her tube top is off, and he's squeezing her little boobs.

"Sorry," I mutter, but they don't hear me, she's like moaning, and Tommy's grunting.

A second door and I stare at summer clothes stacked on shelves.

A third door and there's Jon on all fours, his head over the toilet.

"You poor bastard," I say, or maybe I only think it, I'm so drunk I can't tell.

He groans and his eyes are watering.

I kneel down beside him. I don't know what I'm doing so I put a hand on his ass. He's so out of it he doesn't notice.

"You okay?" I think I whisper, but he just keeps groaning, like he's got the dry heaves. I grab a cheek and squeeze it. It's round and it's firm and it feels like heaven. Oh, my God, I'm feeling Jon's ass!

He barfs nothing and I put my hands around his waist now, working my way up his chest. His stomach shudders under my fingers and when my hands reach his nipples I stroke them till they get hard. All the time I bite his ass through his jeans. Man, I can't believe I'm doing this. I am sooo fucked up. We fall over. I know this 'cause I feel the cold tiles of the floor on my skin.

I think I passed out for a little bit. Jon's curled up next to the bowl when I wake up. He's got all his clothes on, and I think about taking them off. I think, I'm stronger than he is. I can kick his ass. Maybe he's just waiting for me to do him. Shit. I am soooo fucked up. Gotta find Tommy and get home.

I leave Jon next to the toilet and I stumble over bodies in the hallway. I can't find Tommy. Dad'll be worried; he worries a lot since Mom died. Gotta get home. What time is it? A coat. I need a coat. And a hat. And gloves. A pile of the stuff is near the door and I can't tell what's mine. So I put on what I can, 'cause I know it's gonna be a motherfucker outside.

I open the front door and it's a thousand knives stabbing me at once. Isn't that from a book or a poem that Fey Hayes made

us read? Shit. Gotta get home. Only four blocks away, but I'm
lost. I don't recognize a goddamn thing.

Okay, I know it's cold. I get it. I know it's cold enough to kill
me, colder than when Mom hit the ice two years ago. Have to
find shelter. There's an apartment building. Gotta get in. Lobby
door's unlocked. I lay down on the floor, right by the mailboxes.
Can sleep in lobby. No, no good. Somebody will find me and
throw me outside and I'll freeze to death and I won't even know
that I'm freezing to death. Can't do that to Dad. He's already lost
Mom; he can't lose me too. I'm sorry, Dad. Jon, I love you. I
love you so much.

I'm outside and I'm moving my feet. They make a crunch
noise in the snow, like I'm walking on Styrofoam. I walk past
what I think is my house. I turn around and look at it closer. It's
small and covered in icicles and there is a duplex on one side and
a fourplex on the other. Oh, God! It's my house! I'm safe! Somehow I make it up the steps and to the front door. I struggle with
the key. Finally the bolt moves and I'm in, I feel the temperature
soar. I hear a voice—maybe mine—say, "Thank God. Thank
God."


I open my eyes. I'm in my own bed; I'm in my own house, the
one that used to smell like lemons. My head's royally fucked and
I look at my feet, my hiking boots still on. My jeans still on. My
flannel shirt still on. I don't remember much about last night, but
what I do makes me feel even worse. If that's possible.

From the hallway I hear: "Kevin?"

It's Dad. I throw a blanket over me. "Yeah," I croak.

"Can I come in?"

I check to make sure I'm covered. "Yeah."

From the other side of the door he leans in. "How are you?"

I lie. "Okay . . . kind of tired."

"You got in awful late."

"Sorry. Lost track of time."

He looks at me, a little smirk on his face. "Did you want to
go to mass today?"

I frown. "Uh, no." We never go to mass. Mom always had to go by herself. Dad tried to go after she died, but it didn't last too long.

Dad says, "You were thanking God quite a bit last night. I listened at your door for a while and counted each time you said 'Thank God.' I stopped counting at thirty and went back to bed."

*Fuck a duck.* "Well . . ."

"Why did you thank God thirty times?"

For getting me home alive. "I . . . I was grateful."

"What for?"

I don't say a thing; I know he's not buying it. The smirk's gone, replaced by a look that scares me.

He says, "Don't you ever do that to me again. Got it?"

I close my eyes. "Yes, sir."

He shakes his head and says, "You get away with a hell of a lot, Kevin. I let you get away with a lot 'cause we lost your mother. Your friends let you get away with a lot 'cause you're a good-looking kid. I know what that's like; I was young and handsome myself once. I know that people will forgive you almost anything if they like looking at you."

He stops and slaps the door with his hand, hard. He breathes in and out and then he says, "But you can't pull this crap with me; I'm your father. Do I make myself clear?"

"Yes, sir."

"Good."

I cry, or at least I make crying noises. There's no tears, 'cause I'm so hungover. I say, "I'm sorry."

He says, "It's okay. Just don't—"

But he doesn't finish 'cause I'm really sobbing; big old honking boo-hoos that make me shake. I'm sick 'cause I've had too much to drink and because I'm in love with a boy.

Dad says, like he's not sure he really wants to know, "Kevin, what's the matter?"

I say, 'cause he doesn't really want to know, "Nothing, I'm sorry."

He wasn't expecting this. He backs off, into the hallway. "Sleep it off," he grunts.

I hug a pillow; I tell Jon that I'm sorry, it wasn't supposed to happen that way. But part of me doesn't regret it. No matter what happens, my hands touched him, felt him, and nothing can take that away from me. There's always gonna be this one moment in time where I had my arms around him. For all eternity there's a moment when my fingers played with his nips, when my teeth bit into his ass. So we were both too drunk to know what I was doing. How else could it have happened?

I crawl out of my room every few hours for the john or the kitchen to try to rehydrate. Dad just watches TV; he doesn't call me down for lunch or dinner.

It's after midnight when I wake up. I'm starting to feel a little less miserable. I stand and head to the hallway when I stop and turn toward the bedroom window. Across the street, sitting on his front step, is Floyd Anderson. He rocks back and forth, the pyramid on top of him. Maybe he saw me stagger home last night and he's waiting for the hearse to come and haul my body away. Maybe he helped me inside. Yeah, maybe it was him who held me up while I put the key in the lock. Or maybe he was asleep in his bed, his pyramid next to him on the mattress, where his wife used to be.

# 2

# SINS

It's Monday morning. I've spent over twenty-four hours in bed. And today I'm eighteen years old. It's my birthday. I'm old enough to vote and die in a war.

Dad's left for work already. Either he's forgotten it's my birthday or he has a surprise for me tonight. One year he got me a goldfish bowl and two goldfish that I named Scooby and Shaggy. Scooby lived five years, Shaggy almost seven. Nobody could believe how long they lasted.

I look outside, waiting for Tommy. I pray for the first time in a long time: Dear God, don't let anybody have seen me feel up Jon Thompson.

I hear the *blub-blub-blub* of Tommy's Challenger and then the *beep! beep!*

I open the door and Mrs. Bartochevitz shouts, "Do you *have* to do that?"

I have five seconds to get in the car before she puts her hands on her hips and yells at me.

One—

I'm down the steps to the sidewalk.

Two—

I jump on top of a snowbank covering the curb.

Three—

I grab the door handle.

Four—

I open the door and throw myself in.

Five—

I slam the door shut.

Behind the wheel is Tommy, his dirty blond hair tied up in a ponytail. He has a pasty white face even for him and dark circles under his eyes. Like he could be Death's teenager. Grim Reaper Jr. He says, "Whoa, man, you must be feeling better than I do," his voice a pile of salt and sand. "I was still shit-faced yesterday afternoon. The hangover didn't start till last night."

"What was in that punch?" I ask him.

He coughs slightly. "Everclear. A shitload of Everclear. Vodka. Rum. Whiskey. Jesus Christ knows what else. How'd you get home?"

"I walked. How'd you get home?"

He pulls the car forward slowly. "I didn't. I crashed at Debbie Polanski's. With Beth." The one with the tank top. I almost laugh. He says, "Rick Foley crashed there too."

I try to sound really normal when I ask, "What about Jon?"

Tommy snorts. "Thompson? His old man showed up at three in the morning and carried him home. Fucking pussy spent the whole night worshiping the porcelain goddess. People had to puke in the bathtub and sinks and trash cans. Beth threw up in the washer 'cause somebody else was blowing chunks in the dryer."

"Jeez."

He clears his throat and says, "Happy birthday, man. I'm gonna give you your present later. It's a six-pack of Special Ex, but I couldn't even look at it this morning without wanting to heave."

"Thanks, man, that's extremely cool of you."

When we get to school I notice that almost half the kids who were at the party are home sick. I see Allison in homeroom, her head on her desk; too feeble even to blush when I look at her.

So of course today's our community service day, a tradition for Northeast's senior class ever since the blacks on the Northside rioted ten years ago. As head dweeb, Laurie Lindstrom got to choose our project for us. She's picked The Safe House, a crash pad on the West Bank for junkies trying to kick their habits. We're gonna help the junkies serve lunch to a bunch of bums and homeless people. When Laurie announced our project over the P.A. last week, she said that Sister Rita and Father Paul—the ones who run the place—had been the guest speakers at her church and had really inspired her.

We're all kind of quiet on the ride to The Safe House. The bus is colder than a witch's tit.

There's a line of people waiting for the doors of The Safe House to open. The house looks more like a dump, it needed to be painted maybe ten years ago and some of the broken windows have been stuffed with old pillows to keep out the windchill. The people in line for lunch aren't the junkies; they're just regular poor people and boozers and it's way too cold for them to be outside. Nobody in line budges and they don't really look at us when we get out of the buses. A bunch of kids coming to do a good deed must be a pretty regular thing.

A woman unlocks the door to let us in. She's short and skinny and doesn't wear a habit. Even though she's in jeans and a sweatshirt you can tell she's a nun, she's got that nun thing going on, peaceful and smug all at the same time. Her gray hair is cut short and she's wearing a big old honking crucifix around her neck. The people in line for lunch don't move; they know it's not their turn yet. She smiles like she's just been canonized and says, "Welcome, welcome to The Safe House! It's so wonderful that you chose to spend your day with us!"

We hem and haw, waiting for our teachers to say something for us.

The nun says, "You know, this is a place of hope for the hopeless. We're in the business of healing broken people, through Christ's love." Tommy and I look at each other and laugh. He whispers "Heal this" and slaps his ass.

As each of us enters the nun has to shake everyone's hand and whisper, "Bless you."

We're all crammed in the hallway and half of us are still waiting to get inside. That's when an old man—I'm guessing Father Paul—starts herding us to the kitchen. He says, "Come on, keep moving, kids, we can't afford to heat the entire neighborhood." He's tall and bald except for the long hair on the sides of his head that he has pulled back in a wispy ponytail. He's in jeans too and a ratty old brown sweater that looks like the secondhand crap the people outside are wearing.

Laurie Lindstrom says to him, "We're so excited to be here. You're so great—"

He flicks what's left of his hair behind his head and interrupts, "Oh, *no*, it's God who's great! I'm just his instrument, as are we all."

This is gonna be a big drag. I thought it was illegal to talk about God in front of public school students.

When most of us are jammed in a big old kitchen, the nun pushes her way into the room and joins Father Paul. They give each other a look and then she claps her hands just like Mevrouw Bergsma and says, "Let's form a big circle, everyone. Everyone, let's form a nice big circle. Let's hold hands and make a big circle of love and hope and *caring!*" We're packed too tightly to do anything but shuffle around a little and before anybody can do anything, the nun bows her head, scrunches up her face, and starts praying really loud.

"Thank you, Jesus, for bringing these fine young people to help us do your will. In your name, Jesus, we offer you another day, another chance to know your love and forgiveness, another opportunity to walk in your footsteps. The footsteps of the living, *activist* Christ who walked with the lepers and threw the money changers out of the temple. The God of *love*, not judgment. We ask your blessings, Lord Jesus, as we work together in community with our brothers and sisters recovering from the physical disease

of addiction. We live together, we learn together, we laugh together, we cry together. We *heal* together."

Now Father Paul claps his hands together really loud and
shouts: "Amen!" Then he puts his hands on his hips and yells,
like he's black and not white: "Can I get an amen?"

A few nerds mumble: "Amen."

He shakes his head and practically screams: "Can I get an amen,
*please!*"

A little louder this time, most of us say "Amen." To shut him
up.

"Again!"

"Amen!"

"Like you mean it!"

Tommy mumbles, "For Christ's sake," as we all yell "Amen!"

The nun says, "Now, who wants to serve our guests in the
dining hall and who wants to help prepare the food with Father
Paul and our residents here in the kitchen?"

Tommy, Rick Foley, and I bolt in the direction of the dining
hall as the nun counts us off. Jon Thompson is the last one to
make it out of the kitchen before she says, "I have enough servers,
thank you."

The dining hall is your basic cafeteria, a cinder-block box added
on to the original house. Along the pea-green walls the junkies
who live here are putting chairs next to washtubs full of soapy
water.

The nun says, "Jesus believes strongly in the dignity of all men
and women, rich or poor, black, red, brown, or white."

Laurie translates for us. "Before each meal the volunteers and
residents of The Safe House wash the feet of the poor. Just like
Christ did."

This isn't funny anymore.

Donnell White says, "I *know* you don't think I'm gonna wash
some bum's feet!"

Especially on my birthday, I say, but not out loud.

The nun repeats, even louder than before, "Jesus believes
strongly in the dignity of all. Count yourself so very fortunate to
be here, and not outside, waiting to get in. One day, you may

find yourself in a line, your stomach growling, hoping that someone will care enough to feed you. Someday you may be walking
in their shoes."

Nobody says anything for a minute or two, except Donnell
White who mutters, "I ain't doing it." Then our teachers point
at the plastic basins. I look at Fey Hayes, and before I can say
anything he tells me, "No, this isn't a joke." Tommy, Rick Foley,
and I stake out a tub at the far end of the cafeteria, hoping that
nobody will bother us.

Father Paul leads a line of people into the cafeteria. They shuffle
in slowly. They're white and black and Indian and all of them
seem to have bags full of crap that they carry around. Everybody
has to get a hug from Sister Rita. About every fifteen people or
so, she kicks somebody out of line. One of the rejects screams at
her, "Fuck you, bitch!"

"You're banned until you learn to treat women with respect,"
Sister Rita shouts back. A couple of the residents act as bouncers
and lead the guy back outside where we can hear him cursing for
another couple minutes.

All of us from Northeast High kind of tense up when the poor
people start walking toward us. Sort of like two armies staring at
each other on the battlefield right before the rebel yell.

But Tommy has an idea. He sits in a chair, takes off his shoes
and socks, and pulls his hair over his face. He sticks his feet in
our tub and says, "Start washing. I'll keep 'em in till lunch is
over."

But Fey Hayes is on to us and makes Tommy get out of the
water.

"Faggot," Tommy whispers.

Fey Hayes didn't hear him, but he knows what Tommy was
thinking so he shouts at the crowd of poor people, "No waiting
down at this tub!"

An old white man with a crusty red and gray beard staggers
toward us. His face is full of scabs and his eyes are watery and
bloodshot. He has maybe four or five dirty flannel shirts on and
it kind of looks like he shit his pants. He lands on the chair with
a grunt.

"Hey, man," Rick Foley says.

The old man doesn't say anything.

"You need to take your boots off," Rick Foley tells him. Tommy and I just stare.

Nothing.

"Fine," Rick Foley mutters, and reaches for the man's left foot.

"No!" the geezer screams. "No, no, no, no, no, no!"

All three of us jump back like he's pulled a knife.

Fey Hayes jogs over. "Is there a problem?"

Over the bum's screams, Rick Foley says, "We were just trying to wash his feet and he freaks out on us!"

Fey Hayes tries to calm the guy down, but he keeps shouting. Finally, Father Paul arrives on the scene. He shakes his head with a smile and says, "Jimmy, are you making trouble for these poor young men?"

Jimmy shuts up and looks at him, towering over with a crucifix hanging from his neck like an icicle.

The priest puts a hand on Rick Foley's back and says, "Jimmy's one of my regulars. I see him here each and every day, isn't that right, Jimmy?"

Jimmy doesn't speak, he just looks at him like he might take out a gun and blow his brains out.

Father Paul mustn't be afraid of anything 'cause he leans over Jimmy and hugs him tight. He says, "It's okay, Jimmy, Jesus loves you! He loves *you*, Jimmy! And you know what?"

Jimmy keeps his mouth shut.

Father Paul scrunches up his face and says, "*I* love you too, Jimmy. Yes I do!"

He's rocking him back and forth, maybe suffocating him in his arms. The stink of the bum's BO makes us gag.

Tommy whispers, "I didn't know people could reek this bad when it's so cold outside."

But Father Paul doesn't seem to mind. He lets Jimmy go and looks at Tommy, Rick Foley, and me. I can tell we're supposed to say something, but I don't know what. So he says, "I do it because I *care*."

Oh.

He moves on to the next group that's trying to get sneakers off a woman who keeps saying that she doesn't want her goddamn feet washed. In no time flat she finds herself in Father Paul's arms; this must be the cue to stop struggling.

We stare at our old man, wondering what he's gonna do next. He looks over at Father Paul rocking somebody new, gets up, keeps his head low, and tiptoes to the food line like he's sneaking over the border.

The next guy in the chair starts coughing, and then he throws up, missing Rick Foley by about an inch.

"Hey, look at me," Rick Foley shouts loud enough for Jon, two tubs over, to hear, "I'm washing Jon Thompson's feet!"

Everybody who was at Debbie Polanski's laughs, but I don't. I picture pouring warm water over Jon Thompson's feet and working my way up from there.


Floyd Anderson's inspecting his sidewalk carefully. If the wind doesn't pick up, it should stay clear of snow. I wonder how people end up like Floyd. This is the most important thing in his life. His lawn's weedy and overgrown in the summer, but his sidewalk is always perfect in the winter. Instead of heading in the house, I cross the street and join him. The Safe House has made me feel sorry for Floyd, who could wind up in the lunch line if he isn't careful.

"Looking good," I say.

He doesn't raise his eyes. "Youbetcha. So long it don't gust, we're A-okay. But that wind kicks up, I gotta shovel again. Last snow was powder; you blow on it, it goes halfway round the block, ya know."

I look across the street at my house, right at my bedroom window. You can't really see inside too well from here. There's glare from the streetlight that blocks the view.

Floyd says, "Happy birthday."

I smile at him and say, "Thanks, Mr. Anderson."

"Eighteen today, am I right?"

"Yeah."

He leans on his shovel like a sentry on his musket. "Big things start happening when you turn eighteen. Makes me wish I could do it over again, ya?"

"Yeah."

I leave him at his post.

On the front porch there's a widow, a pile of bills, and an envelope with Aunt Nora's handwriting on it. I tell the widow that Dad's not home and I open the envelope from Aunt Nora. Her card says, *To a Wonderful Young Man on His Birthday* and there's a picture of praying hands holding a rosary. Like I would ever do that. Inside she's written:

> *My darling one,*
>    *Do please ring with your new telephone number. It's been ages since we've spoken and I miss you very much. Your mother would be so proud of you, now that you've become such a fine young man. I hope you have a happy birthday.*
>                                        *All my love,*
>                                        *Aunt Nora*

That night Dad orders pizza. When the pizza guy comes Dad answers the door. Then he hands me the box and says, "Happy birthday." When I go to bed he says, "Good night."

I was kind of hoping for a hundred bucks.

When I'm under the covers, Jon snuggles up beside me. He says, Your dad blew off your birthday?

I guess. My birthday was always Mom's job.

This was your big one too, eighteen. You're a man now. You can vote. You can be sent off to war.

Vietnam's ancient history, I tell him.

I got you something, Jon says. His chocolate hair falls in his eyes as he reaches under the pillow. He pulls a small box out as he shakes the long Hershey strands off his face. He's kind of nervous when he says, Here, happy birthday.

I open it. Inside are two gold wedding rings. One for him and one for me.

Jon says, I love you and I want to spend the rest of my life with you. I wish we could get married for real, but these rings will let everybody know how much we love each other. So? Will you do it? Will you marry me?

He's smiling really wide because he already knows what I'm gonna say.

Oh, God, Jon. I love you so much. I hold him tight, I don't let go.


Dad's made me come with him to Jackie Shaw's for dinner. She lives in a little stucco house by Logan Park. I give her the bottle of wine Dad bought so he doesn't have to. She gushes, and then kisses him on the cheek, right in front of me.

"Oh, Pat, you shouldn't have," she says.

Dad shrugs and takes a giant step back.

Without asking *Mother, May I?* Jackie Shaw takes a giant step forward. She wraps an arm around Dad's waist and leads us to the sitting room where about a million candles are lit. She asks me, "And how are you, Kevin? Breaking all the girls' hearts, I bet, with that handsome mug of yours."

I start to say something but she's already back to Dad. "Pat, how did you know that red wine was my absolute favorite?"

Dad grunts. "Lucky guess?"

She pokes his shoulder with her finger. "Oh"—poke— "don't"—poke—"you"—poke—"be"—poke—"so"—poke— "modest. I bet you leave nothing to chance. Still waters run deep, they say."

Man, she doesn't know my dad *at all*.

"You two boys have a seat. I'll be back in a jiffy with the appetizers."

I sit in the La-Z-Boy, but Dad makes me get up. "You sit here," he says, pointing at the couch. I make a production of walking over to it, but he doesn't notice as he takes the chair for himself.

"Hey, Dad," I say, "this is one of those convertible couches. Pulls right out to a bed."

"Don't be smart," he tells me. When I was a kid he used to ask me: Kevin, why don't donkeys go to school? And I'd have to say: 'Cause nobody likes a smart-ass.

Jackie Shaw's put a record on, and we hear Patti Page singing the "Tennessee Waltz."

> *"I remember the night*
> *And the Tennessee Waltz*
> *Now I know just how much I have lost."*

I look at Dad; he's tired in advance. It's gonna be an early evening whatever Jackie Shaw might think. When she comes back she has a tray of pickles rolled up in cream cheese and ham slices, some green and black olives, and celery stalks with peanut butter smeared on them. Before she puts the platter down on a beat-up coffee table she stares at my dad in the La-Z-Boy. I guess that must have been her husband's chair. Men love their La-Z-Boys.

Still looking at him, she asks me, "What can I get you to drink?"

"A Coke."

Dad says, like I'm three years old, "A Coke *what?*"

I say all singsongy right back at him, "A Coke, *please.*"

"Your dad doesn't let you drink beer yet?" Jackie Shaw wants to know.

Dad, still looking at me, says, "Oh, no, Kevin goes for the hard stuff, don't you, son?"

Jackie Shaw smiles, confused, and says, "I'll be right back with your pop, Kevin. Pat, would you open that bottle of wine for me? I'm hopeless with corkscrews."

I look at the walls. One has a painting of a deer in the woods; another has a picture of a bunch of flowers in a vase. Everything's kinda old but really clean, like she dusts every ten minutes. Like she's got nothing better to do. Sitting on the wood cover on top of the radiator is a picture of Jackie Shaw with her husband on their wedding day. She's young and pretty and her husband's really good-looking, the kind of guy I'd like to practice on before I did it with Jon. I feel sorry for Jackie Shaw, you can tell from the photo that she thinks she's got it all figured out—a foxy husband, no worries for the rest of her life, never having to be alone ever. Then bam, cancer eats her husband alive and all she can do is watch. She has to start all over again. Like she has to go back to school, only she's as old as she is now and everybody else is my age. It must be really embarrassing. Maybe that's why she tries too hard. She wants to get this over with fast. She seems to say: Just hurry up and marry me. Just do it, will ya?

When they come back to the sitting room they've got glasses of red wine (Jackie Shaw's absolute favorite) and Dad reclaims the La-Z-Boy, which leaves Jackie Shaw no choice but to sit on the couch with me.

She says, "Pat, they must be working you all the hours the good Lord sends. Seems like you're always doing overtime these days."

Dad sighs. "Just keeping our heads above water. If this one"—pointing at me—"wants to go on to college, well, then, somebody's going to have to pay for it."

This gets Jackie Shaw's attention. She says to me, "So you're off to college in the fall? Oh, isn't that exciting. I always wanted to go."

I turn red. "I might go. I haven't really decided yet."

Dad says, "Oh, you're going." He says to Jackie Shaw, all proud-like: "He's the first generation of Doyles to go to college."

Jackie Shaw asks me, "What schools are you considering?"

"Ummm . . . the U. Maybe Dunwoody."

Dad says, "He's going to the U and living at home to save money."

Jackie Shaw slumps just a little; if you weren't looking for it you probably wouldn't even notice. You can tell she's thinking: No chance of getting the kid out of the house for another four years. She says, "I took a few classes at the U after Randy died, you know, from their evening program catalogue. I didn't take them for grades, I—oh, what's the word I'm looking for—I *audited* them. That's where you get to take the class without worrying about tests." She laughs. "I tried to learn Swedish, can you believe it?"

Yes. *Absolutely.*

Dad says, "The old guy across the street from us is a Swede. Say something in Swedish."

Jackie goes all red. "Oh, no, my pronunciation is just terrible. I couldn't, *really.*"

Dad says, "Kevin, say something in Dutch to get us started."

Dad can be really stupid, like there's only two languages, English and Foreign. I say, *"Ik wil te weg."* (I want to leave.)

"Oooooh," Jackie Shaw purrs, "what does that mean?"

"I like the food."

Jackie Shaw nods, all excited, like I'd just done something really cool. "Say something else."

*"Dat Thompson jounge is een lekker stuk."* (That Thompson boy is a delicious piece.)

Jackie Shaw claps her hands together. "Oh, he's good, Pat, he's very good!"

Dad says, "Fat lotta good Dutch'll do him. They all speak English over there, nobody needs to learn their language."

Jackie Shaw's fascinated. "Really? How do you know that?"

"When I was stationed in West Germany some of us would take a few days leave and spend it in Amsterdam. They all speak English. Really nice too, if they think you're Canadian. Canadians were the ones that liberated them from the Krauts."

Jackie Shaw finds her chance to change the subject to romance, or sex anyway. "Don't tell me you and your army buddies went to the red-light district. Is it true the women just sit in the window without a stitch on?"

Dad looks at me like I'm a virgin (I am) and back at Jackie Shaw. "Of course not! Honestly, Jackie, not in front of the boy."

"Sorry," she says quietly. She's telling herself to calm down, not to try so hard. I recognize the look.

It's awkward for a minute or two 'cause nobody says anything. If Mom were here, she would've called Jackie Shaw a *brazen article.* But on the car ride home, not to her face.

A buzzer goes off in the kitchen. Jackie Shaw jumps up and says, "Let me just go check on that. I'll be right back."

Dad's just staring into space like it's his job, something he's paid to do. So I grab a couple pickles wrapped in cream cheese and ham.

I say, "These are good. They look kind of gross, but they're scrump-dilly-icious."

Dad folds his arms across his chest. "How many times do I have to tell you not to say that? I hate it when you quote TV commercials."

I'd quote you if you'd ever say anything.

Jackie Shaw calls from the kitchen. "Oh, dear, it looks like the roast isn't quite done. I better give it another fifteen minutes or so."

Sure, it's not done. She just wants to drag this out for as long as possible. She's like the opposing team calling time out. Dad keeps doing his job, staring at nothing, like he's behind on his quota.

When Jackie Shaw comes back she's got her second glass of red wine in her hand. She says to Dad, "Why did you stop going to *To Live Again*? We miss you at our meetings."

Dad surprises me by telling the truth. "It's all gals 'cept for me. Made me uncomfortable."

"Oh," Jackie Shaw pouts, "you shouldn't feel that way! We're all in the same boat, you know! That's the whole reason for the group. Nobody knows better what it's like to lose a loved one than somebody that's lost theirs too. Oh, and that Carol Gunderson was asking after you at mass last Sunday. You know, I think it was the first time I've seen her at church in I don't know how long. She says she never sees you anymore. I told her you were doing well and that I'd be getting together with you tonight, so she didn't need to worry about a thing. She sends her best."

Dad nods but he doesn't say anything. Dad not talking to a woman is déjà vu; Jackie Shaw might as well be Mom.

Jackie Shaw says, "I feel sorry for her. Some of the parishioners aren't very nice to her, because she's divorced and all. I suppose that's why she stays away. But I say it's nineteen hundred and seventy-eight for goodness' sake! Divorced people have a place in today's church whether you like it or not."

Jackie Shaw's trying to keep the conversation going, but with

Dad that's like trying to figure out the square root of pi. So I say, "I bag Mrs. Gunderson's groceries at Red Owl."

Jackie Shaw says, "Oh, that's right, you work at the one over on Central. I used to go there all the time till I bought some moldy bread. Now I go to the Byerley's all the way out in St. Louis Park. That's where all the Jews live. You should see the deli! Oooh, you can get some yummy treats there. And the aisles are carpeted! Imagine."

Dad's watching nothing, so I say, "You can make good tips at Byerley's. But it's a long bus ride."

Jackie Shaw thinks it over. She says, "Yes, but I'd guess the best tips to be had would be at the Lund's in Edina."

"No way, they don't let you take tips at Lund's," I say. Actually, we're not supposed to accept tips at Red Owl either. Union rules. Probably can't take tips at Byerley's either. "Besides you gotta change buses twice to get to Lund's."

"Pat," Jackie Shaw says, "don't you get a discount on Fords working at that plant? You should get this young man a car!"

I know the strategy; some of the other widows have tried it before. Score points with the son to get to the father. I look at Dad and wonder why they even bother. This is as good as he gets, sitting there like a bag of trash on the curb. Maybe they just can't accept that. Or maybe it's enough for them. Poor saps.

Dad says, "If he wants a car, he can damn well save up for one himself. I'm not paying for his college *and* getting him a car. If anyone's getting a new car, it's me."

Jackie Shaw winks at me, to let me know she tried. I'm supposed to wink back but I don't. I'm not ready to hand over Dad just yet. This is probably my only chance to get to know him for real, before another woman hitches her wagon to him and I become part of the furniture again.

Somehow Aunt Nora's found out that Dad's started dating. When Dad got an unlisted number he made me swear not to give it to her. When he's really serious about something he makes me swear on Mom's grave. So even though Aunt Nora has written me almost once a week since we went unlisted, I've never called her with our number. That's why she's standing on our stoop looking like an old, big, and ugly version of Mom. Her big man arms are folded across her barrel chest and her dark hair sticks out from beneath her ski hat, not that she's ever been skiing. Nobody's sure how old she is 'cause she's always looked exactly like she does right now.

"Where's that worthless piece of shit you call Da?" she asks me. Aunt Nora talks like this all the time. You get used to it. She'll scold you if you curse, but it's okay when she does it. It used to really embarrass Mom. Mom always said, *I know Nora's my sister, but that woman mortifies me.*

I look at Aunt Nora. "He's at work," I tell her truthfully.

"Okay," she mutters. "Okay," she says again, like she's making up her mind about something. She looks me square in the eyes and barks, "It's cold as fuck out here, ask me in."

I step aside and she stamps into the house, struggling to take off what look to be about ten layers of coats and sweaters. She says, "I'd murder a cup of tea."

And that's just for a start.

I head to the little kitchen and put the kettle on. From the sitting room I hear Aunt Nora pacing. By the way that the floorboards creak I know she's stopped in front of the wedding photo of Mom and Dad. She shouts, "Your mother was a looker! She could have had any man, any man at tall."

"Yes, Aunt Nora." I look in the cupboard for tea bags. All we've got are the generic brand from Red Owl, which won't make Aunt Nora happy. She likes her tea strong, like her men. She's only had a couple of boyfriends that I knew about anyway, and they're either lying low or up the river. I look at the kettle and think: Hurry up and boil. If Dad comes home with Aunt Nora here there'll be one of those homicide-suicide deals.

"Any man!" Aunt Nora shouts.

"Yeah!" I shout back.

The floorboards moan again and she comes into the kitchen. "The state of this place, if your mother were alive she'd be pulling her hair out." She spots the tea bag on the kitchen table and says,

"Would it kill you to keep a decent tea in the house?"

"I'll get some Twinings for you next time I'm at work."

"It'll do," she sighs. She sits in a chair with ripped-up vinyl that's taped down, and grunts like an old man on the can.

The water won't boil. I pour some out in the sink and put the kettle back on the burner.

"It'll just be a second," I tell her.

She nods and then a minute or two later asks me, "Did you have a happy Christmas?"

I tell her it was okay.

"And the second anniversary?"

"It was okay."

Aunt Nora leans her round face on one of her big man hands. "What did you do for it?"

I shrug. "Not much. We had a pizza delivered."

She laughs bitterly. "More tomato pie in. Is that all you eat in this house anymore, take-away? Doesn't your da know how to cook you a proper meal?"

"He's too tired after work."

She says, real mean, "You sure it's his *work* what's wearing him out?"

She's starting to piss me off, cutting Dad all the time. I say, "We had a homemade pie."

This interests Aunt Nora. "You did? He baked you a pie? Was it a pecan?" Mom's favorite. She made it every Thanksgiving and Christmas.

"Yeah."

Aunt Nora thinks about this. "Well, there's something done right at least. He can still surprise you."

I don't think much before I open my mouth, so I say, "This lady made it for us."

Aunt Nora lifts her chin off her big man hand. "A lady made it for you? A *lady*?"

I nod, my eyes big, waiting for what's gonna happen next.

"He had a *lady* in this house on the second anniversary of losing my sister?"

I just stare at her. There's no right answer to that one.

Her face goes all red. "For fuck's sake! For fucking fuck's sake! He had that whore of his under this very roof on the second anniversary."

I try to make it better. "Jackie Shaw's okay. Mom knew her, she's been in our parish forever."

Aunt Nora frowns. "Jackie Shaw? Are you sure about that name?"

"Yeah."

"You're positive it wasn't Carol? Carol Gunderson?"

I frown. "No. I bag her groceries at Red Owl. It wasn't her."

Aunt Nora gasps. "Mother of God! You pack that woman's bags for her?"

There's no good answer for that one either. This happens a lot when you talk to Aunt Nora.

"That bloody bastard! Letting his own son carry his whore's bags! What a poor excuse for a man!"

I look right at her and say, "Please don't talk about Dad like that."

Aunt Nora stares at me, scowling. Then she looks around the kitchen before she shoots me another look. "Your da doesn't deserve any of this. Not this home, not you, and least of all my sister!"

I shout at her, "Jeez, can't you just leave the guy alone?"

"And why are you so loyal to him, eh? What's he ever done for you but give you a pat on the head every now and then? Don't you miss your poor mother at all? She's the one that brought you up! She's the one that loved you! Not that man of hers!"

"Aunt Nora, knock it off."

But she won't. The more she says, the angrier she gets, so she winds up saying stuff that she shouldn't. *Poor thing can't help herself,* Mom told me after one of her visits. *She's always getting herself in a tither about something or another.* Like now. She looks like she might cry.

She says, "Well, doesn't he have everything his heart desires, then? His obedient son, a grand home, and his trollop. It must be lovely, to sin and sin and never have to pay the piper."

"What's that supposed to mean?"

Aunt Nora says, "You're a grown man now, Kevin, and you need to know the truth."

I look at her, waiting, but she doesn't say anything. I can hear the water simmering. I say, "So tell me the truth. What's your goddamn problem?"

She doesn't like being talked to this way, it's, like, disrespectful. She hates that. "I will thank you to keep a civil tongue in your head."

So I ask again: "What's your goddamn problem?"

She pulls at her hair with her big man hands. "I'm off. It was a mistake to call."

"What's your goddamn problem?"

She gasps and looks at me like I just gave her one right in the gut. She says, "That bastard was cheating on your mother! He wanted a divorce, so he could be with his whore!"

I look at her like she just told me she was the Virgin Mary.

She says, "He'd been carrying on behind her back for years with that Carol Gunderson woman. Then he finally does your mother the great favor of telling the truth. About his 'overtime' at the plant. That's why she drove herself into the Mississippi! Because of him!"

No way.

*No fucking way.*

This is wrong.

She's lying.

She's always hated Dad.

My voice cracks as I say, "It was an accident."

She points a finger at me; her eyes watering, and she digs herself in deeper. "He drove her to it! She called me, shattered, when she found out they'd been carrying on behind her back. And for all that time! She couldn't bear it. She couldn't look at him anymore."

I pull at my arm. "It was an accident."

The kettle whines.

" 'Twas no accident! She did it because of your da. Because of him and his whore!"

It's whistling now.

"You've had it in for Dad since day one! Why are you doing this? Leave us the hell alone!"

But she goes on like I'm some goddamn idiot, too stupid to know that the sky's blue or shit stinks. She says, "Don't you dare defend that man to me—he killed her same as if he put a gun to her head. She tried to make him happy for years, but there's no pleasing Patrick Doyle, oh, no!"

The whistle screams and I pick up the kettle and throw it on the floor. I yell at the spilt water, "Fucking bitch!"

She slaps her big man hands against the table and it makes me jump. "You show me some *respect*—I'm all you have left of your poor mother."

The water's spreading under the oven and filling the cracks in the linoleum. I whisper, "It was an accident."

Aunt Nora stands up so fast that her chair falls over backward on the floor. "Why were there no skid marks? Why didn't she try to stop if she didn't want to die? He broke her heart and tossed it in the river!"

We glare at each other, our chests heaving, but nobody says anything. Aunt Nora never backs down when you look her in the eyes. She never looks away first; she doesn't even blink, like she's the alpha. There's so much going on in that face of hers. I can't tell if she's more pissed off or hurt. But I do know that she's kicking herself for opening her big, fat, fucking mouth. *That's what a temper will do*, Mom used to say, *open doors best left shut*. Open is too nice a word for it though. Aunt Nora's taken an ax and smashed them into little pieces.

Then, for some reason, I think: Carol Gunderson? I double-bag her groceries. She's always been really nice to me. And she had to take in her uncool niece, Laurie Lindstrom.

That's when I see him. Dad's standing in the doorway to the kitchen, his face raw from the cold, his hat and coat still on. He has that look people get when they drive by an accident on the highway. Aunt Nora pouts and then she follows my eyes and looks behind her, where Dad stands still as a statue. But he doesn't even seem to notice her; he's looking right at me. Without taking his eyes off me he says to Aunt Nora in a deep, even voice, "Get out of my house or so help me God I will not be responsible for what happens."

Her eyes go wide like she's seen Satan himself. She glances back at me and I know she's trying to say that she's really, really sorry, she didn't mean to blow up like that, it's just that her temper got the better of her. Next she walks by him, into the sitting room, where she struggles with a single sweater before she goes out into the freezing cold.

Dad doesn't move. I wonder if he's even breathing. Finally, he says, "Kevin Patrick Doyle, why the hell did you let *that* woman into *my* house?"

I ask him, "Is it true?"

I expect him to say, *Is what true?* or pretend he didn't hear me. But he says, like he's reading out loud in class, "Of course not, it was an accident. Your mother was a good Catholic; she'd never take her own life. End of story."

"I don't mean that, I mean Carol Gunderson. Is that part true?"

He doesn't answer, he just reminds me that he's my father.

I leave him standing there in his hat and coat and I go up to my room and hug Jon Thompson. Jon tells me that everything's gonna be all right, that I don't need to worry about a thing. I start to feel a little better in his arms. They're strong and smell like clean skin. I put a hand on Jon's face.

I ask him: Do you really think that my dad was fooling around with Carol Gunderson?

Yeah, I do, Jon tells me.

But why would he?

I don't know, Jon whispers.

I look at the ring Jon gave me for my birthday and I ask him if he would ever do something like that to me.

Not in a million years. You're stuck with me, baby.

I tell Jon that I love him so much.

I love you too, Kevin. Let me show you—

But then I hear the scraping of Floyd Anderson's goddamn shovel, and Jon's gone. And all I can think about is what Aunt Nora said.

FEBRUARY 1978

Dad's only coming home when I'm at school. It's been like this for almost a week. The only reason I know he's been home at all is 'cause he leaves little notes with cash taped to them. He writes things like *Study hard, Kevin* or *Make sure you eat a good supper tonight* or *I'm working the graveyard shift again tonight, put the chain on the door.*

I like not having him around. Not seeing him has made it all seem a little less real. I can pretend that it's just Jon and me who live here. Every night Jon's there, in my bed, waiting for me.

But then it's Thursday night and Carol Gunderson pushes a cart through the sliding doors at Red Owl like she does every Thursday. A blast of frozen air follows her in. She pretends to undo her scarf and take off her gloves, but I know she's really checking out the registers, looking for me. Our eyes meet for maybe a second; and then she dumps her gloves in the cart's basket and wheels it down the produce aisle.

Mom always used to say that stupid people have more nerve than brains.

Lorraine can tell that something's up. She says, "What's wrong with you? You've been acting strange all night."

"Nothing," I tell her.

"Some girl, I bet," she says.

How right you are.

Tommy's mother, Mrs. Grabowski, starts unloading her cart. She looks exhausted, but then she always does. It's like her thing to look half-dead. I like her, 'cause she has this really weird sense of humor, corny and funny at the same time. She says to me, "I don't suppose you've seen my pride and joy, have you, Kevin?"

"Yeah," I say.

She says, "And where was that?"

I lie. "At school."

She smirks. "Oh, so he *does* still make the occasional appearance at Northeast High! I'm so very relieved to hear it. I don't un- derstand *why* his teacher called me today and said that Tommy's

MIA. I mean, if *you* saw him today, there *must* be some mistake."

I open the bag and put cans of Green Giant corn and peas at the bottom. "Must be," I say.

Mrs. Grabowski and Lorraine look at each other and shake their heads; it's obvious I'm covering for Tommy. Then Mrs. Grabowski says, "And he was sober when you saw him?"

"Yes, ma'am." On top of the cans I put boxes of Hamburger Helper. Hamburger Helper helps you make a great meal.

"He's still alive, then."

"Yes, ma'am." On top of the Hamburger Helper I put a couple of those Stouffer's dinners that you boil in the bag.

"So I shouldn't call the cops and have them drag the—" but she stops and Lorraine nearly swallows her Juicy Fruit. Mrs. Grabowski was about to say "river."

She blushes and smiles at me. She says real fast: "I wish my Tommy was more like you, Kevin. Look at you! Going to school, holding down a job. You're a fine young man. Really, a very fine young man. And getting handsomer every day."

"Thanks." Next bag and I put a bottle of orange juice at the bottom. It's not just for breakfast anymore. Orange juice with natural vitamin C, from the Florida sunshine tree.

Lorraine says, like it's news, "Bitter, outside." She shivers to make her point. "Just bitter."

Mrs. Grabowski's eyes go big. "You know, every winter seems to get worse, or maybe I'm just getting too damn old. I can't take the cold like I used to."

Lorraine says, "Lots of folks are living in trailers down south during the winter. I wish I could be in one right now."

I'm done bagging and Mrs. Grabowski has paid up. I ask her, "Do you want me to help you out with those?"

She practically shouts, "Oh, no!" Then she says, more calmly, "I think I can handle these myself. Thank you so much, you really did a wonderful job."

Lorraine makes a big production out of saying, "He always does. It's a genuine pleasure to work with him."

Mrs. Grabowski says, "I bet it is," and she slips a dollar tip in my hand. Lorraine notices, and even though I'm not supposed to accept tips, she doesn't say anything.

After Mrs. Grabowski takes off, Lorraine says, "You know she didn't mean anything by that. She just forgot, that's all."

I stick my hands in my pockets. "Don't sweat it, it's no big deal."

I've known Mrs. Grabowski just about my whole life. When Mom died she put her arms around me and I cried really hard. I bet she's sitting in her car cursing herself out right now. I wish people would stop tiptoeing around Mom's death.

I wander over to the magazine rack. I want to look at *Tiger Beat* or *16* but I pick up *Sports Illustrated* and hope for some pictures of swimmers or divers or gymnasts doing their floor exercises. When they wear the real short shorts and do the splits. They've got, like, these thighs that are pure muscle. I don't even mind that they're only two feet tall. Red Owl won't carry *Playgirl*.

Mrs. Gunderson slithers by like the snake she is, doing a quick recon. We're still pretending that we don't see each other. I watch her as she heads down the baking goods aisle, where she acts like she's comparing the price of Shake 'n Bake to our Red Owl brand Baking Flakes.

Mom never used that shit on our chickens. She said they charged a fortune for crumbs. For something anyone with the sense the good Lord gave them could make themselves.

Lorraine pages me. "Kevin, register three."

I go back to Lorraine's register, and there's Fey Hayes, the faggiest teacher at Northeast High, another one of the Thursday night regulars. I say, "What's happening, Miss TerHaze?"

He looks up from his wallet like the absentminded professor. He says, "Hmmm? Oh, Mr. Doyle, good evening! Working hard, I see."

Lorraine says for about the millionth time, "Or hardly working!"

Fey Hayes says, "Now there's an original comment, I'll have to remember that one," and Lorraine goes tomato-red. Turning back to me, he says, like I'm in class, "Why would you stop by woods on a snowy evening?"

I say, "To watch the woods fill up with snow."

Fey Hayes smiles real bitchy, like everybody's so stupid except him. His face tells you, *Oh, why must I put up with this?* He's like Dr. Smith on *Lost in Space.* He says, "Why would you stop to watch the woods fill up with snow, Mr. Doyle?"

Without thinking I say, "To remember my mom. She loved how the snow covered up all the garbage and dirt. She'd sit for hours on the porch watching the snow fall. She grew up in Ireland and the snow doesn't last long there. She always said the snow was like a million fairy lights when the streetlamps caught the flakes just right."

I look up from the bag and Fey Hayes and Lorraine are looking at me weird. Finally, Fey Hayes says, "I believe that's the best reason I've ever heard for anyone to stop to watch the snow. Transformative, that's how your mother saw it. She must have had the soul of a poet."

I look back down at the groceries. "Yeah, I guess."

Fey Hayes smiles widely. "I *know*," he says.

I hand him his bag and he's beaming. Maybe he wants to get into my jeans, I can't tell.

When he's gone, Lorraine says, "I've never heard you talk about your mother before. I'm glad you said what you did."

Like it's a goddamn Kodak Moment. "Okay," I tell her.

That's when I see Mrs. Gunderson heading toward us. It's late and we're the only register open. She smiles at Lorraine. "Cold enough for you?" she asks.

Lorraine shivers and says, "Bitter, just bitter. Seems like the winters keep getting colder."

Mrs. Gunderson starts unloading her cart and says, "And darker. I get up for work in the morning and it's pitch-black. I come home from work and it's pitch-black. Honestly, I never see the sun between November and March. It's so depressing."

Lorraine tsk-tsks and I bag tomatoes, lettuce, peppers, oranges, and about twenty little containers of Dannon yogurt, the kind with the fruit on the bottom. Next comes ice cream, Mrs. Paul's Fried Clams, a couple of Totino's Pizzas, and twelve things of concentrated Minute Maid orange juice, the brand Bing Crosby does commercials for. His wife always says, *Are there Valencias in Minute Maid?* Finally, there's milk and pop and bottled water, the kind from France, which isn't a real big seller at Red Owl. I put her groceries into single bags without saying boo.

Mrs. Gunderson says to me, "Laurie tells me that she never sees you on the bus anymore."

I grunt.

Lorraine says, "That's right, your niece is still living with you, isn't she? She's a sweet girl. She comes in now and again to buy pop. Oh, and she loves the magazines about horses."

Mrs. Gunderson says, "Her parents would have been so proud of her. We just found out she's been awarded a full scholarship to St. Catherine's."

St. Kate's is an all-girl college in St. Paul. I guess Laurie figures there's no point bothering with a co-ed school.

"Oh," Lorraine says, a big impressed look on her face, "she must be very bright."

Mrs. Gunderson smiles and says, "Between the scholarship and the Social Security, she's set through college." Then she asks me, "Will you help me with my bags?"

I look at Lorraine who says, "It's dead in here," but then says, real fast, "I mean it's really quiet. Go on, help the lady with her groceries."

I throw on my coat and hat and we walk quietly to Mrs. Gunderson's car, a tan Cordoba with a dent in the driver's side door.

She purses her lips and says, "Your father called and told me about what happened the other day," her words a cloud of steam in the frigid air. They float above us and break apart into nothing.

"Mmmm," I say.

She opens the trunk that glitters with frost, like a million tiny camera flashes going off at the same time. Like when you watch a football game on TV and all those morons take pictures because they think a flash will work from the top rows. Glittering lights; that's what Mom loved best about winter, the way the snow and the frost sparkled. She hated March though, when the snow was old and covered with dirt and salt and sand. She said that it was like winter's hangover. It made her sad.

Mrs. Gunderson says, "I wanted to have a word with you, Kevin. At first, we thought maybe we should just stick with our lie. Tell you that your aunt is crazy, imagining things. But then I said to your father that you are eighteen years old now and deserve to know the truth, for better or worse."

She's warning me. Be mature, be a man. Real men don't freak out.

She says, "I'm so very sorry. I didn't mean for things to turn out the way they did."

"Yeah," I tell her. The first bag I put in the trunk is the cold bag. I pack all the frozen and refrigerated foods in the same bag so they won't melt or spoil. Not that that's gonna happen tonight.

Mrs. Gunderson says, "I know it's no excuse, but I fell in love with your father, and he fell in love with me. It's not something either of us wanted."

Mom used to call people who said stuff like that *brazen articles*. If a person didn't have the decency to let an awkward moment go without comment, Mom would say, *He's a brazen article*. Or if someone was rude or insensitive or just plain mean, then they were brazen articles too. My mom's life was full of brazen articles, from her husband on down to her only son.

The next bag's full of yogurt cups at the bottom and two loaves of bread near the top. Brown bread.

Mrs. Gunderson says, "The last thing we wanted to do was hurt her. I know that's easy to say, but you have to believe me, it's the truth. That's what makes this all so difficult. We didn't want you to get hurt either."

I shove the last bag in. It's full of discount pop, the local brands that cost half the price of Pepsi or Coke. I say, "She drove her car over the river bluff because of you." I drop the bag in the trunk and slam it shut.

Mrs. Gunderson stares at me. Her face goes all red, maybe from shame, maybe from the cold, I can't tell. "She hit a patch of ice and lost control of the car. It was an accident, Kevin; your Aunt Nora lied to you. She hates your father, she always has. She wants to turn you against him, can't you see that?"

I stare at her. Accident or on purpose, what's the difference?

"I don't understand. After what you've been through—the way you lost your sister—I don't understand how you could hurt somebody else so bad."

Her eyes fill and she whispers, "I didn't want to hurt anyone. When my sister and her husband were killed, life became so empty. And ugly . . . I fell in love; that's all. Love makes you do things you never thought yourself capable of. I was so very lonely. We both were."

I could punch this woman so hard she'd hit the ground and never get up. I could avenge Mom. I could be the guy who makes Laurie Lindstrom lose her aunt the same way she lost her parents. When Mrs. Gunderson looks at me she has this really weird expression on her face and I know that she sees my father. In me. She reaches out her hand and I take a step back, like she's a leper. She says, "I never wanted any of this to happen. We put a stop to it the day your mother died. We tried to be friends, but it was too painful . . . I know what it's like when someone you love dies."

"Leave me alone."

She closes her eyes and whispers, "How's your father?"

I decide to lie. "He's happy. He's going with Jackie Shaw now."

When she opens her eyes she shakes her head with a stupid little grin. Her way of letting me know that she doesn't believe a word of it. "How is he?"

"I'm freezing my ass off. I'm going back in."

She nods as she puts her key in the car door and says, like we've been talking about the weather, "I'll see you next Thursday, then. You take care of yourself, Kevin."

I look at her like she's nuts. "Don't come back here."

She turns and faces me. "What did you just say?"

"I don't want to see you back here. Get your goddamn groceries at Appelbaum's from now on."

She points her key at me and says, "I know you're upset, but you've no right to talk to me like this."

"I got no right? Eat me, lady! I've got every damn right and I'll talk to you any fucking way I want."

She gasps. "You watch your language, young man."

"You think I ever want to see your ugly ass again? You out of your gourd? Just get in your goddamn car and keep driving. Drive into the Mississippi for all I care."

"Stop it!"

"Get the hell out of here and don't come back."

She glares at me and opens her car door. As she gets in she says, "Just because your mother died doesn't mean that she was some kind of saint."

"You fucking cunt!" I shove the shopping cart hard, into the side of her car. She slams the door shut and jams the key in the ignition. She's freaking out.

I don't even think about it. Even though the cart weighs a ton, I pick it up and throw it at the rear windshield. The sound of shattering glass is muffled by her scream as the engine turns over. She's in tears when she hits the gas and flies out of the parking lot.

Lorraine runs out of the store and stares at the bent cart and broken glass. She hugs herself and says, "What the heck happened out here?"

"Mrs. Gunderson had an accident," I tell her.

Lorraine surveys the damage, her teeth chattering. "She's paying for that cart. Those things are expensive, you know."

3

# WHO KILLED KAREN
# SILKWOOD?

My mother's hair was red for as long as I can remember. Dad used to say that he married a brunette and was living in sin with a redhead. It was kind of a weird and unnatural shade, and even though the wake had to be closed casket, he made the funeral home guys dye her hair brown. He couldn't stand the thought of her having red hair for all eternity. I never knew how much he hated it. Did she toss the Miss Clairol in her shopping cart each week just to piss him off?

Sticking up for her wears me out. I stay mad at Dad out of respect for her. I scare the shit out of Mrs. Gunderson to prove how much I loved her. It's exhausting, and I don't know how much longer I can keep it up. Maybe you can only spend so much time feeling sorry for a victim before you start resenting them. But resenting her makes me feel guilty. I could sleep for a month and still be tired.

I know that Mrs. Gunderson called Dad and told him what I
did. I know because for the first time since Aunt Nora dropped
the bomb, he was waiting for me at home after I finished my shift
at Red Owl. He looks at me like he doesn't know who I am.
And I think, Good, now you know what it feels like. He doesn't
yell at me or get mad or even let me know that he knows. He
just watches me as I go upstairs and downstairs, in the front door
and back out again, as if some strange kid had found the key to
his house and decided to move in. It's like he can't quite believe
me. Not what I say or do, I mean he can't quite believe *me*. Who
I am.

I guess I should have seen this coming. Dad would tie one on
once or twice a month before Mom died, and sometimes he'd
cry. Everybody knows that men aren't supposed to cry. I'd creep
out of my room at night and listen to them in the sitting room,
Dad sniffing and Mom saying, "Calm yourself, it will all work
out, you'll see." But as I got older she stopped trying to make
him feel better; she'd just go for a walk, or watch the snow in
the winter.

Mom saw him in me since day one. She'd say, *Just like your
father*, at least three times a week, usually when I was being a
brazen article. But mostly I would catch her staring at Dad and
me at mealtime—it didn't matter which one, breakfast, supper,
dinner, it was always the same. She'd be looking at him and when
I stabbed something with my fork I'd feel her eyes on me. It got
worse as I got older. It began to piss Dad off so much that he'd
shoot her a look when it happened. He'd say, *For Christ's sake,
Eileen, do you have to do that?*

I think she did. She *had* to do it. I think there was some part
of her that couldn't believe that she had given birth to her own
husband. 'Cause I never really was me, I was always Dad or in
some stage of becoming him, especially once my voice changed.
She treated us the same, like we were interchangeable parts, both
made just to break her heart into little pieces. When Dad would
read his paper during supper she'd turn from him to me, like she
was saying, *See? This is what you're going to wind up doing to some
poor woman one day.*

I thought she could be a royal pain in Dad's ass. No wonder he wore the newspaper over his face like a mask. Staying on the other side of the *Minneapolis Star* was his only escape from her in our house. No matter what room you were in, you could feel her, in the way that her knickknacks were always arranged just so or by the smell of lemons that was everywhere.

It's kind of mental, but I know that some people think that a person's spirit stays in a place after they've died. You know, like they don't get that they're dead, so they hang out where they'd been happy. I've never felt like Mom's spirit was in the house after she died. Makes you wonder if it was ever here when she was alive. The smell of lemons is gone and the knickknacks covered with dust, but they sit there, facing the door, waiting for her to get back from the store.

At school I corner Jon Thompson. He smiles, on his guard. I know that he doesn't like me but he can't show it. I take advantage of this. I say, "You wanna see a flick this weekend?" I know it sounds like I'm asking him out on a date, 'cause I'm asking him out on a date. Only he doesn't get that, which is what I counted on.

He frowns, waiting for the punch line. "What flick?"

I shrug. "Got me."

He thinks about it for a second. "How 'bout *Close Encounters?*"

I've already seen it, but this is Jon, so I say, "Cool in the extreme. Can you drive?"

His eyes narrow. He thinks he's figured it out: I wanna go with him 'cause I don't have any wheels. Tommy and Rick Foley must have other plans this weekend. When he squints like that I want to kiss him real hard on the lips and suck his tongue down my throat. He says, "Cool. Gotta bolt, catch you later."

"Cool."

I love him so much I could puke my guts out all over the floor. If he was sitting across the dinner table from me, I'd never read the paper. See, Mom? Wrong on both counts. I'm not gonna wind up doing that one day, least of all to some poor woman.

I get to my Dutch class late and Mevrouw Bergsma says in plain English: "Kevin, you've been called down to the nurse's office."

Tommy's actually shown up for school today and he says: "Hey, Doyle, whatsthematter, got the clap?" Everybody starts laughing except for Mevrouw Bergsma and Cheryl Goldberg, an Orthodox Jew who probably doesn't even know what the clap is.

I say, "Yeah, from Beth."

Now everybody goes, *Ooooooooooh, what a cut.*

Mevrouw Bergsma says, *"Tommy, Kevin, hou op!"* (Tommy, Kevin, shut up!)

At the nurse's office, Aunt Nora ambushes me. She has the nurse leave us alone for a few minutes so we can talk *pressing family matters.* This is the same nurse that hugged me two years ago on my way out to Aunt Nora's car. She's a heavy Lakota woman with diabetes and the only one who's sent me a card on both of the anniversaries.

Neither Aunt Nora or me sit down in the cramped office. She says, "Sorry to trouble you at your school." Like getting out of class is something I would get mad about. She blows a strand of hair out of her eyes and says, "I'm sorry it came out the way it did. I was in a state when I found out your da was seeing other women, so soon after we lost your mother. I couldn't bear the thought that that . . . Carol Gunderson might be back in his life. You had to know the truth."

Well, Aunt Nora and Carol Gunderson agree on one thing, anyway.

She looks at her big man feet and back up at me. "So he denied it all, did he?"

I shrug.

"Tell me, what did he have to say for himself?"

I look at her clear white face that gets a little rounder every year. I tell her, "He didn't say anything. He hasn't been around all that much since you told me."

Aunt Nora looks up at the ceiling and then back at me. "I see." She clears her throat and says, "I think it's best that you come stay with me. Your da isn't fit to look after you."

"No way! I'm eighteen, Aunt Nora, not a little kid. I wish people would stop treating me like one, it pisses me off."

Aunt Nora looks at me like she never has before. Her face goes limp and she's about to cry. "I can see her every time I look at you, Kevin." She wipes her eyes. "I may not have been of any use when she was alive, but God help me . . ." She starts bawling. I've never seen her really cry before, not even at the funeral. She tries to get it together and says, "Sorry, sorry. It's just the idea of your beautiful mother . . ."

She starts up again and I ask her, "What? The idea of what?"

Aunt Nora chokes out, "Spending all eternity in hell."

"What are you talking about?"

Aunt Nora sobs, "Taking her own life . . . it's a mortal sin, Kevin! We had to lie to the priest so she could get a proper funeral mass, but all good Catholics know . . ."

It was an accident. She might of not been paying attention 'cause of Dad and everything he did to her, but she didn't kill herself. She was from Ireland, where the snow doesn't last long, she hit a patch of ice and she lost control of the car. End of story. I tell Aunt Nora, "Mom didn't kill herself. It was an accident."

Aunt Nora tries to clean herself up with a little travel pack of Kleenex she takes out of her purse. She dabs her eyes and blows her big man nose. She says like she doesn't mean it, "You're right, of course. She's up there in heaven having a right laugh at me for being such a fool. I'm sorry, Kevin, I hope you'll forgive me." She blushes, ashamed of herself or me, I can't tell.

I look at her. She's trying so hard to be strong that I say, "I'll stay with you for a couple of days, okay? How 'bout next weekend?"

She nods her head real fast and wipes her eyes again. "That'd be delightful. I think it would do us both a world of good."


It's finally Saturday night and I can't help myself; I'm giving off date vibes. Dad's picked up on it. He thinks we're back to normal, where he doesn't say anything and I don't care. I know that doesn't sound good, but I mean back to how we used to be, without bad feelings screwing things up or making us duck each other. This house has felt like it's gonna blow up ever since Aunt Nora told me the truth.

From his side of the bathroom door he asks me, "You two going to meet some gals tonight?"

Like it's any of his goddamn business what I do. I lie. "Maybe."

"Anyone special?"

I look in the mirror. Yeah, his name's Jon and I want to marry him. But first we're gonna live together for a few years. I say, "I dunno."

"You've got enough sense not to get gals in trouble, don't you?"

No sweat, Dad.

I part my hair down the middle, which I think makes me look really hot, but Dad will notice and Jon will notice and they'll wonder why I'm making an effort. I comb it back the way it was, a kind of Shaun Cassidy look, and experiment with different expressions, looking for one that has the double meaning I need tonight. One that says, "Let's make out," but in a crunch could also mean, "I wasn't coming on to you; what are ya, a retard?"

Dad says, "You know, I need to use the bathroom sometime this evening, if that's not asking too much."

'Tis, as Aunt Nora would say. 'Tis, indeed. "Just a sec," I tell him.

I put a hand on my arm and feel my bicep as I flex it. I try to imagine Jon's hand there. His fingers slip up my arm to my shoulder. He says, You feel so good, as his hand slides down to my pec and checks it out. I close my eyes as his hand feels its way over my stomach and down my waist.

"For Christ sake," Dad says and I hear him walk down the hallway to the stairs, down another set of stairs, and into the bathroom in the basement. It's not a real bathroom, just a toilet in a corner. Dad worked on it till Mom died. That's when all his home improvement projects stopped. Along with the toilet in the basement, we've got a stripped door that needs to be rehung, a new unconnected light fixture in the kitchen, and a hole in his bedroom wall. I don't know what that's for.

Jon's fingers unbutton my jeans. He says, Tonight, honey; let's go all the way tonight. Yeah, come on. Let me have you. You're soooo hot.

I go: uhhh.

The doorbell rings: *Jon's here*. I button back up, throw my T-shirt on, and bolt down the stairs as Dad flushes under the floor-boards. I wanna get out of here before Dad can meet Jon. It's important to me.

I yank the front door open and there *he* is. Jon's in an old army jacket with his hands stuffed in his pockets. I want him bad, very bad. "Jesus, it's cold as a witch's tit tonight," he says.

I throw on my down coat and my hunting cap and push him back out on the front stoop. "Come on, let's go."

He frowns and says, "Whoa, man, we got plenty of—"

I shove him again. "Cool. Move it."

I hear Dad's feet on the basement stairs, his pace quicker than normal. He wants to meet Jon. He knows and likes Tommy, he's knows and doesn't trust Rick Foley. I hear him shout, "What time will you—" and I slam the door behind us.

Jon looks at me and says, "I think your old man was calling you."

"Nah, he just talks to himself all the time." We head to Jon's dad's car, a brand-new Mustang II with the engine running. When we get in Glen Campbell's singing "Southern Nights." I thought he was pretty hot in *True Grit*. I cried when he died at the end. But then I was like nine or ten years old. I could shoot him myself right now for singing this shit.

Jon groans. "Sorry, man, "Hotel California" was on when I left."

We drive out to the big theater in Roseville but we're almost thirty minutes early for *Close Encounters* and there's nothing to do, so we stop at a 7-Eleven to get stuff to eat for the movie. Jon bolts for the magazine rack and picks up a copy of *Hustler*. I'm at the candy stand.

He whispers real loud, "Hey, man, come here. You gotta see this."

I join him and he shoves the magazine in my face. He says, "Look at her opening up her twat like that, jeez what a slut!"

"Yeah, gross," I say.

Jon says, "Yeah, nasty old slut," but he means it in a good way.

That's when I see a copy of *Playgirl* on the rack. A bare-chested guy is sneering at me from the cover.

Jon keeps flipping through *Hustler* thinking that I'm gawking over his shoulder, but I'm burning holes in the sneering guy's nipples. I want a nasty old slut like him. Goddamnit, I'm hard. I *have* to have that magazine. But first I have to think my way out of my boner.

"Hey, this isn't a library," the lady behind the counter yells at us.

"Relax," Jon tells her. He brings the copy of *Hustler* up to the register, drops it in front of her, and says, "I need a pack of Camel straights too."

She reaches behind her for the smokes and then tosses everything into a bag. "Anything else?"

Jon looks at my hands. He says, "Those can be on me."

I turn red. "Huh?"

"Your candy bars; I'll buy. Go on."

The candy bars I forgot I even had. The woman rings up two Hershey's with Almonds, a Pearson's Nut Goodie and some Milk Duds.

"Thanks," I tell him.

"No sweat," he says.

We still have time so we sit in his car. I eat my candy while he lights a cig and flips through his dirty magazine.

"Hey, Kevin, watch this," he says, and he opens it up to his nasty old slut and licks the picture of her you-know-what. The sight of him pretending to have sex turns me on. The way his tongue glides over the glossy page as he closes his eyes and moans. I pretend he's moaning because of me, 'cause I'm all over him and all he can do is lie back and enjoy it. He opens his eyes and says, "Oh, God, she's hot! Fuckin' A!"

"Very hot, fuckin' A." *Do it again.*

Jon blows out a cloud of smoke like he's just had sex. "I'm so fucking horny I could choke a chicken."

Cluck, cluck, bwaaaaaaaaak.

"Yeah, well, whatcha gonna do?" Have sex with me? Here? Now? In the backseat of your car? Over and over again till we trash the shock absorbers?

He inhales hard and the embers of his cigarette light up. He says in that voice people have when they're trying to keep down a hit off a joint, "You got a girlfriend?"

I shake my head; I'm swallowing half a Hershey bar.

He makes the smoke come out of his nose. "You should, you know, the girls are always checking you out. They always go, 'Oooh, he's *cute.*' Especially that Allison, man, I'd fuck her back to the Stone Age if I got the chance. She's got *tits!*"

Just like the guy on the cover of *Playgirl.*

We sit in silence for a little bit, and then I think to ask him, "You got a girlfriend?"

He laughs and points at the *Hustler.* "Just her," he says.


We have to sit near the front of the theater 'cause the movie's practically sold out. Dad and I saw *Close Encounters* over Christmas vacation. He took me downtown to the Nankin for dinner and let me have a few sips of his Wanderer's Punch. He had two glasses of the stuff and I had to drive us to the theater and back home again. He called in sick to work the next day, even though he wasn't really hungover. It was the first time I'd seen him drink much since Mom died.

Jon strains his neck to check out the crowd of people sitting behind us. "Man, there's a lot of fat chicks here tonight."

"Mmmm," I say.

"Big fat chicks with big fat asses. Their butt cheeks feel like Jell-O."

Who cares?

Even when the lights go down Jon's still checking out the women, looking for his target. He finally grunts and looks up at the screen. "Those all-you-can-eat joints would go broke if they had to feed the chicks in this place."

I don't bother to nod or say anything. Every time Jon opens his mouth it ruins my fantasy that we're out on a date. But of course we're not, since we live on planet Earth, where the only other guy like me is Fey Hayes, the faggiest teacher at Northeast High.

When the aliens steal the blond lady's kid all Jon can say is, "She's got legs up to her ass! I'd fuck her in a second!"

During the last scene, where the alien does the hand-sign thing with the French guy, Jon says, "Jeez, that's so fake. Looks like the Pillsbury Dough Boy."

The lights go up and I want to go home real bad to *my* Jon. 'Cause every second with this Jon is like reading a billboard over and over again that says: JON THOMPSON LIKES GIRLS. I was hoping that he'd drop these hints that he feels the same way about me as I do about him. You know, it'd start out kinda sly, like with all these double meanings, and then there'd be a really uncomfortable silence, and then he'd start crying and tell me that he loved me. Then I'd hold him and say that I loved him too. And then we'd do it in his car till we had to scrape off the frost from inside the windows.

Yeah, right. Mom always said, *That and a dime will get you a cup of coffee.* I wanna go home, he's messing tonight up for me. But he's got other ideas. In the parking lot he lights a smoke and says, "Let's hit the bars. I got a fake ID."

If I say no, I don't want to go to the bars, people would talk. They'd say, Whoa, Doyle passed up a chance to get shit-faced? He turning faggy on us? So I say yeah. Maybe getting drunk is just what I need. Maybe if Jon gets drunk he'll tell me that he loves me. Or at least be so out of it that I could bite him on the ass again.

We drive over to the West Bank of the U. The Viking won't let us in and neither will the 400 or Bullwinkle's. We wind up at Culla's Tavern, 'cause the woman behind the grimy bar can't see all that well. There's old kitchen tables in the little room with bunches of college guys sitting around them, drinking pitchers and talking loud. The group right next to us looks like they might be grad students; they're older and not as noisy.

Jon pours me a glass of Grain Belt from the plastic pitcher. "So Into You" is playing on the jukebox.

"What a dive," Jon says as he looks around the place. "But at least the beer's cheap."

I'm pissed that he likes girls so I say, "Just don't blow chunks my way."

That shuts him up.

A dog wanders out from behind the bar and licks up the spilt beer from the sticky linoleum.

I have no idea what to say to Jon, but I decide that we probably should be talking to each other or we'd be too much like Mom and Dad. So I tell him, "Look, a dog."

The guys at the next table are talking about divestiture and the U. I don't know what divestiture means.

One of them, a weird-looking guy with long brown hair, says, "The only way to change things in South Africa is to bankrupt their illegal government."

His friend, a blond with a big old ugly beard and John Denver glasses, says, "Yeah, right, that's not going to happen, not when the British, the French, and our own government veto sanctions."

The third guy in their group wears a T-shirt under a down vest. The curves of his arms are really hot and his face is tan, like he went to Florida for Christmas vacation or something. He has a weird haircut, short, like the Sex Pistols, and a pierced ear. That's supposed to mean you like guys if it's in the right ear. Or is it the left?

Jon says, "Hey, man, what about Allison, huh? She's really into you."

"You think so?" I ask, trying to listen to the guys at the next table.

"Fuck, yeah, she—"

But I hear the down vest guy saying, "I think constructive engagement is the only way to change things, whether it's South Africa, Northern Ireland, or Red China. You won't further the cause of human rights by walking away with your morals intact. Change is about getting your hands dirty."

"—and then the way she's always checking you out when—"

Ugly beard's saying, "When you engage with these regimes you simply postpone change, can't you see that? While we sit around the table with the apartheid government they're buying time, consolidating their power. But if you bankrupt them, make their domestic conditions such that reform or revolution become inevitable, then and only then—"

"I'm serious, she'd do it with you on the first date—"

Down vest says, "Give me a break! If you isolate these governments, you leave the common people at their mercy. If you engage, if you invest, and by that investment show everyday citizens different models, then you help the change process—"

"Hey, Kevin, you listening or what?"

Jon comes back into focus. Now I wish he'd just shut up and let me stare at his cow lashes and chocolate hair. "Yeah."

Jon laughs. "You're kidding me, you've really sucked her tits?"

What are you taking about? "No. Whose tits?"

"Man, one beer and you're out of it. That's truly feeble."

I tell him to shut up so he'll remember who's alpha and who's beta. The down vest guy folds his very fine arms across his chest and says, "That's so naive, I can't believe you just said it. Divestiture doesn't do anyone any good. All you do is leave people even more vulnerable to tyrants and dictators."

"Yeah," I say, loud enough so these guys know that I'm talking to them. Jon looks at me like I just cut one. Everybody's staring at me, so I go, "Divestiture doesn't do any good."

I can tell from the look on Jon's face that he doesn't know what divestiture means either.

Ugly beard looks at me and says, real snooty-like, "So you think we should follow Sullivan's Principles? All that does is alleviate the guilt of rich white capitalists. Why should they profit from the exploitation and political repression of the third world?"

They all wait for me to say something, but I don't, not for a good minute or two anyway. Now it's one of those deals where I *have* to say something, 'cause it's like I've been thinking it over and have an answer. I say, "You have to . . . get dirty, you know?"

"Exactly," down vest with the arms says. "Divestiture is like sitting in a corner with your eyes shut and your fingers in your ears, hoping that somehow it will all just work itself out on its own."

Ugly beard snorts and rolls his eyes. "You're just afraid of true revolution. That's dirty because it's real change at the cost of human life."

Jon says, "I gotta take a leak," and leaves me with the grad students.

Down vest says to me, "I'm glad you have some common sense, at least. My name's Chuck." He points at ugly beard and says, "And this is Pierce and this"—pointing now at the quiet guy with long hair—"is Loren."

I didn't know that Loren was a boy's name.

Ugly beard wants to know if I go to the U. I lie and say yeah. That's when Loren tells me that they all go to Macalester, a rich kids' school for brainiacs over in St. Paul.

"What are you doing here?" I ask them.

"Slumming," Pierce with the ugly beard says.

I don't know what slumming means either, but Pierce doesn't quiz me, he goes right on arguing with Chuck. When Jon gets back he says he's bored and wants to take off. That's when Chuck says that he can give me a ride if I need one. Chuck has an earring and Jon doesn't so even though I love Jon I decide to stay with the Macalester guys. Maybe Chuck likes boys. I could practice on Chuck and be ready just in case I'm wrong about Jon, that he likes guys after all.

"Cool," Jon says, and he's off to his dad's Mustang II with the *Hustler* inside.

Pierce lights up a clove cigarette that stinks like nothing else. He takes a long drag and says, "Investment in oppression is, in and of itself, oppression. However you may have deluded yourself that it was made with the very best of intentions. After all, the road to hell and all that . . ."

All what?

It goes on like this for another hour, and about halfway through a story about South African diamond mines and union organizing, I start to get what they're fighting about. Finally they all seem as bored with it as I do, so Loren asks me what I'm majoring in.

I decide on English. If they ask me who my favorite writer is, I can say Robert Frost and even quote a poem if I have to.

"English," Pierce says with a laugh, "that should get you about as far in life as my masters in art history is going to get me!"

I ask Chuck what he's studying. He just says, "Life."

That is *so* cool.

Loren grunts at his watch and says, "Gentlemen, I believe I have to call it a night."

"Me too," Pierce says.

"I should be going too," Chuck says. "Come on, Kevin, I'll drop you off at your dorm."

Oh, right, my dorm.

All three of them have their own cars and they separate outside the bar. Chuck and I cross Riverside Avenue, where a Pacer covered in bumper stickers is parked in front of a clinic. Chuck's car says NO NUKES and WHO KILLED KAREN SILKWOOD? and END APART-HEID NOW and there's one with little letters that I can't make out.

It takes three or four tries before the engine starts; it's about six below and I shiver in the passenger seat.

"Where am I going?" Chuck wants to know.

I head him down Washington Avenue, right through campus, like I go there, and then turn him northeast. I tell him that I share a house with a bunch of guys. On the ride over he tells me that Pierce isn't really all that bad. He's just an armchair revolutionary who's giving away his trust fund to the African National Congress and the Sandanistas.

I say, "Your earring's cool. Where'd you get your ear pierced?"

He laughs and says, "Oh, God, my girlfriend did that to me with a sewing needle and a piece of ice. I don't recommend that method. If you want to pierce your ear, have it done by a pro-fessional."

Man, it really is just me and Fey Hayes. I try to say, like it's just something people would say, "I thought an earring meant that you were into guys."

"Yeah, I've heard that too. Why, would it make a difference to you if I was?"

"Nah, I'm cool."

"Good, because homosexuals deserve the same rights as everyone else."

*They do?*

I say, "They do?"

Chuck looks over at me and says, "Of course they do. If you let the Anita Bryants of the world have their way, we'll all be ruled by a theocracy."

That would be bad. I wonder what he looks like without a shirt on. Or pants. Or underwear.

When we get to my house he says, "I'm having a party a week from Saturday. Stop by, I think you'd enjoy yourself."

He tells me his address, some street in St. Paul that I've never heard of, but I memorize it, knowing that I'll take out Dad's map of the Twin Cities tonight to find exactly where Chuck lives. And do a couple of practice runs on the bus so I won't be late a week from Saturday. He's so cool.


I've walked all the way to Roseville in a snowstorm 'cause I *have* to have that copy of *Playgirl* with the sneering guy on it. It's taken almost an hour to get here. I have a plan; I'm carrying a Sears bag with me, leftover from when Dad bought some new bits for his cordless drill. Inside there's a pair of gloves and a hat. That stuff isn't part of my plan, it's just there so that the bag isn't empty.

My face stings from the wind when I make it through the door, the kind that has measurements posted on the frame. So the clerk can tell the cops how tall the holdup man was. There's a couple of people in the store; one's fixing himself a cup of coffee and the other's paying for a bag of Doritos and a can of Rondo. *Lightly carbonated so you can slam it down fast.*

I decide on a Pearson's Nut Goodie. Next I go to the refrigerator case and pick up a can of RC.

A woman comes in the store now and shakes the snow out of her hair.

I stroll toward the counter. When I try to act real casual I stroll.

*Oh*, the look on my face seems to say, *what's that? A magazine rack? Might as well have a look.*

The guy with the coffee goes up to the counter. The guy with the Doritos and Rondo grabs his bag and heads out to his car to slam it down fast.

I smile at the magazine rack. Hmmm, what do we have here? *Time, Newsweek, National Enquirer, Sports Illustrated.* I pick up a copy of *Sports Illustrated* and flip through the pages, but there are no gymnasts or divers. Now my face says, *Nah, I really shouldn't buy it, it costs too much.* I put it back on the rack, but not where it's supposed to go. I put it in front of the *Playgirl.* Then I change my mind. *Why not*, my face asks everybody in the 7-Eleven. I pick up the *Sports Illustrated* again, with a copy of *Playgirl* behind it. I bend down to pick up my Sears bag and I slip the *Playgirl* inside.

At the counter I feel kind of faint, like I might blow chunks. The checker, a dweeby kid with zits who isn't much older than me, says, "That it for you today?"

I nod, waiting for a siren or an alarm. Then the call to my dad and the reporters. And then the newspaper with my picture on it and the headline *Kevin Doyle Steals* Playgirl, *Is He a Fag or What?* My one visitor at the prison will be Fey Hayes, who'll tell me that he's the only other one like me on the planet.

The woman joins me at the register. She puts a box of Kotex on the counter, along with a six-pack of Tab, a can of Aqua Net, and three bags of M&M's with peanuts.

The dweeb hands me a bag with my pop and candy bar and *Sports Illustrated.* He says, "Thank you, have a nice day."

I smile, trying not to look too friendly or too nervous. "You too," I say.

And then I'm out the door, back in the wind and the snow. But I feel warm. I can't believe it. The sneering *Playgirl* guy is all mine. I can stare right at him; I can lick him the way Jon licked his nasty old slut. I sneak a peak at the cover. Man, just wait till I get *you* home.

# 4

# ENJOY IN MODERATION

My Aunt Nora's house is on the west side of the Mississippi in South Minneapolis. She owns a duplex with another woman from her parish who lives with her boyfriend from Iran. Aunt Nora's place looks like any other in Powderhorn Park, but the inside might as well be a Catholic mission. Everywhere you look, there's Jesus, hanging from his cross, looking up at his father in heaven. There are times when I wish we were Lutheran like everybody else in this town; they don't have people nailed to crosses in their churches.

Or so I've been told.

Aunt Nora has four or five cats, I'm not sure of the exact number 'cause you never see them all at the same time. They're all toms and each one has a name ending in "an." There's Brendan and Aidan and Cian and Declan, those are the ones I can remember anyway. Her dinky sitting room is full of crucifixes and catnip toys, along with copies of *Catholic Bulletin, The Irish Voice, People,* and *TV Guide.*

She says as we walk up the stairs to the spare room, "Look at the state of this place, you must think I live like a pig."

This is gonna be a long weekend. I tell myself never to feel sorry for anyone ever again. You just wind up doing shit you don't wanna do.

"Here we are," she says, gasping as we reach the door. "I hope you'll be comfortable. This room does double duty as my office and the guest quarters."

There's a pile of papers on the little desk, most with letterhead from Catholic charities and pro-life groups.

What's there to say? "This'll be great, thanks."

She smiles. "You get yourself situated and I'll make us a cupper, that'll take the chill right off."

I'm really regretting this until close to midnight, when Aunt Nora pours me a tumbler full of whiskey and takes out a scrapbook. "Here we are," she grunts as she sits next to me on her couch that's covered with cat hair. "I've kept all the photographs of your mother here in this book. There's quite a few of her in Westport with our people there. Oh, you must get over to Mayo someday and visit your grandparents, they'd be over the moon."

The ones I've never met. The ones I've never talked to 'cause they don't have a phone. The ones who couldn't afford the plane tickets for their own daughter's funeral.

"Grand," she says as she opens the book. "Here's your mother at her first holy communion."

A little girl is smiling solemnly at the camera, dressed in white from head to toe. A lace veil covers her face and she holds a bunch of blossoms in her hands that wear white gloves. I laugh. "Jesus, look at what she's wearing."

"Language," Aunt Nora scolds. "Oh, there's none of them communion gowns like that anymore. Today it's all synthetic muck off the rack. Your grandmother made that for her, she was brilliant with a needle and thread, just brilliant."

I take a sip of whiskey and Aunt Nora shakes her head at the photo. I say, "It must have been hard to leave there."

Aunt Nora shrugs her big man shoulders. "Actually, it was much easier than any of us could have imagined. When we went to live with our cousins in Philly it was like we'd never left Ireland. All the Mayo people were on the same few blocks. You'd think they'd just dug up a piece of Westport and planted it in America. Oh, the crack was brilliant in those days."

Not like a crack in the sidewalk. Crack means that you had a time or something like that. Mom never said the crack was brilliant ever. Guess now I know why.

Aunt Nora points out other photos in her book. When we get to Mom and Dad's wedding picture, I find a dried and pressed autumn leaf over Dad's face. I smirk and say, "You never liked him, did you?"

She takes a shot from her tumbler. "You're dead right on that one. Look, my darling, are you having problems with your da? Is he treating you well?"

"He's okay. Could you tell that he was gonna cheat on Mom?"

"No, I didn't think that. I just took him for . . ."

For? For? "For what?"

She closes her eyes hard and opens them again. "Let's not quarrel."

"What did you take him for?"

She shuts her book and holds it close. "Peter Pan. I took him for Peter Pan, the little boy who never grows up. One day he says he wants to go to university, the next he enlists and they pack him off to West Germany. He wants a wife and a boy of his own but then he feels trapped. Oh, it was one crisis after another with your da, never knowing what he wanted to do when he grew up. How Eileen was able to stand it for as long as she did, I'll never know. She was a saint."

"He isn't that bad."

"Isn't he?" She sighs and pets the scrapbook. "Oh, maybe it isn't entirely his fault. The way the women in this country throw themselves at men, it's embarrassing to see. No respect for the holy sacrament of matrimony, that's the problem with the States. We don't have divorce in Ireland, of course."

"Dad's doing okay. He puts a roof over our heads and food on the table."

Aunt Nora makes a little "humph" sound. She says, "He hasn't evicted you and he shares his take-away pizza. Have I left anything out?"

"He's gonna pay for college."

Aunt Nora runs her big man fingers over her eyes and says, "Well, that's something I suppose. I hope that Carol Gunderson hasn't stopped by!"

I feel my face get hot. "No, I haven't seen her in a while."

"Whore," Aunt Nora grunts.

We don't say anything for a few minutes. But then I want to know: "What did Mom tell you about Mrs. Gunderson?"

Aunt Nora looks up at the ceiling and then back at me. "I shouldn't have said anything, that was my mistake. I lost my temper."

"What did Mom say?"

Aunt Nora frowns, like she can't decide if she should say any more. But then her face tells me that since she's already gone this far, she might as well go farther. "Your mother didn't tell me anything at tall, not straight away. Your da promised to end it with that . . . Gunderson woman, but he didn't of course. Your mother only told me after your da said he was going to leave her."

Aunt Nora takes one of my hands in her own and whispers, "Him and that Gunderson woman were planning to pack up and run off together, make a new start of it somewhere warm. You and your mother were coming to stay with me."

Oh. Dad was gonna leave both of us.


When Aunt Nora comes home she says, "Jesus, I'm dead." She plops down on the couch and moans. The church's pancake breakfast was a zoo, she tells me, she never got a second off her feet.

"Be a pet and fix us a cup of tea," she says.

The cats follow me into the kitchen. From the couch Aunt Nora says, "And how was your morning?"

"Kinda boring," I tell her as I turn on the tap.

Aunt Nora tsk-tsks and says, "It must be dull for you stuck here with your spinster aunt."

I say, "I'm not stuck here," because I'm stuck here.

She says, "Oh, yes you are. What do you say I let you have my car this evening? You can go and visit your little friends."

I turn off the water so I can hear her better. "Really? I can use your car?"

"It's all yours. Just don't be too late getting in, that's all I ask. And swear to me that you'll steer clear of the drink."


Aunt Nora's car is a Matador, a piece of crap AMC made for about twenty seconds. The first time she drove it over to show us, she said, just like in the commercial, "What's a Matador?"

Mom just smiled, not sure what she meant.

Aunt Nora said, "This is a Matador. My first brand-new car! Isn't it lovely? The cars in this country are so huge, you could live in them."

The back of the Matador is covered with pro-life bumper stickers, there's a rosary hanging off the rearview mirror, and a crucifix Krazy-Glued to the dash.

It's really embarrassing to drive. But I take it anyway.

I don't head over to Tommy's or Rick Foley's. I just drive, the radio blasting. I've only ever been in Minnesota and Wisconsin and the Badlands in South Dakota. I wanna drive to California or maybe New York or maybe all the way down to Mexico. If I had thought this through, I could have grabbed my money and took off, someplace where guys that like guys live, only I don't know where that is.

So I go down East River Road, the same route Mom was driving when she died. I stop the car right where it happened. At first I think that it'd be hard to drive over the embankment and down to the river. You'd have to build up speed; do it on purpose. But I know she didn't kill herself. The road's clear and dry tonight, thanks to about a million pounds of salt and sand. But she was driving in a snowfall. She was driving right after the January thaw, the three or four days before we go back into the deep freeze. The roads were like hockey rinks. It was an accident.

I wonder what she was thinking when she knew it was too late to do anything about it. When she knew that her car, doing what it was doing, would kill her. What do you say to yourself when you know you're gonna die? Do you talk to God? Does your life flash before your eyes? Do you think about the people you love, and cry 'cause you'll never see them again? Or does your mind go blank, and stay that way forever?

Aunt Nora said that Mom committed a mortal sin. But Mom didn't kill anybody. She wasn't a Nazi or anything. She was my mom, and her heart was broken. By my dad. And I don't believe, not even for a second, that she killed herself. She wouldn't do that to me. She wouldn't leave me with a man who wanted to skip town without me.

But then I wonder: What if she knew about me? I mean, did she figure out that I liked boys? Is that what drove her into the Mississippi? A no-good husband and a faggot for a son? Was it my fault?

I turn the engine off, so there's nothing to hear. No motor idling, no air blowing out the vents, just silence. And cold, bitter February cold, the month that kicks you when you're down. The kind of cold that makes you wonder why the Indians, let alone the whites, ever came to live here. Like nobody should have lived in Minnesota till they invented cars and central heating.

Mom, are you there? I'm like the family you left back in Ireland, who have to go to a gravestone or the exact place somebody died to talk to them. The family you said was ignorant and superstitious. The ones who left food out for the ancestors each year before America called it Halloween. Their blood's in me, whether you like it or not. Mom? Could you just tell me what happened? Could you just tell me, for Christ's sake? Or are you gonna let me go crazy, not knowing?

I hate you, you know? You get to leave without saying good-bye, and I'm stuck here. With nobody to believe. It must be nice. You get to be dead, and I have to live, wondering if I did something wrong. Wondering if you loved me or him. Wondering if not having his love was all it took for you to put your foot on the gas and fly into the ice. Not caring that I was left behind. With the man who made you kill yourself.

Did you say *Oh, shit* before you hit the ice? Are you just a bunch of bones buried in a hole in the ground? Maybe a corpse rotting in some landfill? Or are you looking down at me now? Are you holding my hand? That's the thing with the dead, they get to say nothing, forever. They get to keep you guessing. And we're stuck wondering what it all means. If anything. Did my mom fall over the edge, swearing at God? Did she call him a liar? A hoax? Or did she beg him to take her? Are there angels? Or is there nothing, just a bunch of arms and legs, preserved until the casement rots?

It's really cold. I turn the ignition, and the car snaps me back to the real world. The world where being dead happens to somebody else, not me. I laugh. Most people are dead. I mean think about it, everybody who has ever lived is dead, or gonna die. Like A follows B. It's the living who are the exceptions, not the dead. I mean, Lincoln, dead. Washington, dead. Jefferson, dead. Jesus, dead, maybe risen, but who the hell knows? Who knows if he lived at all?

So we sit in our Matadors, not knowing a goddamn thing, until we become dead too.

I drive back to Aunt Nora's house. I park her Matador in the garage, out in the alley behind the duplex.

She's asleep when I get inside. I lie down on the bed in her guest room. Just in case there is a heaven, and Mom's in it looking down on me, I say I'm sorry.


Jackie Shaw has come over to our house for dinner, 'cause Dad figures we should pay her back for the meal she made us. He's looking forward to this slightly more than he would a date with Aunt Nora. Earlier today he decided to call Jackie Shaw and cancel but I stopped him. Since I found out about him and Mrs. Gunderson I get to do just about anything I want, including making him go through with this. He gives me dirty looks a lot, but he doesn't take me on. He never lays down the law, it's like he's decided he's got no right to judge me anymore. He talks even less than before and he's stopped telling me that I should live at home and go to the U. His way of letting me know that he doesn't think it's a good idea anymore. I know he'll be glad to be rid of me, but only half as glad as I will to be rid of him. To think I used to like the guy; even felt sorry for him.

I haven't clued him in yet that I know he was gonna dump Mom and me. That ammo is stashed away for when I need it the most.

He's got the gas grill going on the back porch even though it's not much above zero. The only way he'll cook anything is on the grill, so he wears a *Genius At Work* apron over his down coat. I get the door for Jackie Shaw, and her usual smile's gone, traded for a bitter look. Bitter but a little hopeful. I recognize the look 'cause I've been wearing it a lot myself lately.

"Hey, Mrs. Shaw," I tell her.

She smiles for my sake. "Good evening, Kevin. Aren't you becoming quite the handsome young man."

"Yes. I am."

She snorts, and I can't tell if it's a ha-ha snort or a disgusted snort, the kind Mom used to make right before she told me that I was just like my father.

I take her coat and park her in our sitting room, just vacuumed for the occasion. I don't bother asking her what she wants to drink; instead, I bring her a big glass of red wine, her absolute favorite. When I hand it to her she just looks at it like she doesn't know what it is.

I frown. "You like red wine, right?"

She looks up from the glass at me and sighs. "I think I'll just stick to plain old water tonight, if you don't mind."

Hey, no skin off my ass. "Cool, be right back." Since she's in the front and Dad's out back, I drink the wine in a couple of gulps. Next I run the tap until the water gets cold. Come to think of it, red wine always gave Mom a headache.

When I give Jackie Shaw her water, she says, really soft, "Thank you."

"No sweat," I tell her.

We sit there watching her drink her water until I can't take the silence anymore so I say, "You have a good day today?"

She says, "It was a day just like the day before and probably just like tomorrow will be."

Jeez, glad I asked. Wish Dad would get the hell in here.


We're nearly through with dinner, the first meal we've had in the dining room since Mom died. Jackie Shaw hasn't gushed over Dad's cooking once. In fact, she's barely said a word. You'd never know that she's fought long and hard for a seat at our table. When she isn't looking down at her plate, she's checking out her nails. She frowns every once in a while when she sticks a forkful of rib in her mouth. I wish somebody would say something.

At last Dad says, "I got us some dessert. A pecan pie from Baker's Square."

Jackie Shaw just barely picks up the sides of her mouth. "No thanks, Pat, I need to make it an early evening, if it's all the same to you."

Oh, yeah, this has been a lot of fun. Let's do it again *real* soon.

But then Dad livens things up. "Jesus Christ, Jackie! Yes, it's all the same to me. You've been moping around all night. Honest to God, if you knew you were going to be like this I don't know why you even bothered coming over."

She looks at him like he just kicked her really hard, right in the ass. She gasps, and says, "You know what, Pat? Neither do I!"

He gets up and storms into the kitchen and then she's out the door without even stopping long enough to zip up her coat.

I join Dad, who's in the ripped-up chair, drumming his fingers on the table that needs to be cleared. His face is red and he's breathing hard. He wants a cig when he's pissed off, even though he gave up his Lucky Strikes almost five years ago. He sucks in the air and blows it out like he's smoking.

"What was that all about?" I ask him.

He grunts. "You see why I've been avoiding her? She's a moody one."

Just like Mom. Then I think, *Well, shit, Sherlock.* "You weren't working graveyard shifts that week you didn't come home. You were staying with her, weren't you?"

He doesn't say anything, just takes another drag of air.

Well, I'll be goddamned. He used that same line with Mom. And it's worked both times.


I'm on the school bus 'cause Tommy's gone missing again. Usually I just sit by myself in the back and space out, but today I'm next to Laurie Lindstrom. She's as surprised as I am.

"Hello," she just kind of says, her eyes on her books.

"Hey, Laurie," I tell her. The bus stops at a traffic light so I say, "I liked The Safe House. It was cool to feed poor people and stuff."

She believes me.

She smiles at the books in her lap. She says to them, "Oh, I'm so glad you said that! A lot of people were really mad about having to wash feet. Somebody wrote a swear word on my locker."

I say, "That's cold, people can really be big dicks. If they don't like it, screw 'em. The first gotta be last and visa versa, right?"

She turns bright red. Too loud and too fast, she says, "I-go-every-Saturday-if-you-want-to-go-with-me-sometime-we-could-go-together."

This isn't worth a Saturday, so I get to the point. "Yeah, maybe. What's it like living with your aunt?"

She smiles at me kind of weird. "She's fine. Why do you want to know?"

"I see her sometimes at Red Owl. She acts a little freaky, like something's bugging her all the time."

Laurie shrugs her shoulders. "Aunt Carol's okay. She shops at Appelbaum's now, though."

"So you guys weren't gonna take off down south a couple of years ago?"

Laurie frowns at her books. "What are you talking about?"

I say, real casual-like, "Your aunt told me that she was planning on moving a few years back, but then she changed her mind."

"Are you sure you don't have her mixed up with somebody else?"

The bus jerks forward. I say, "Carol Gunderson. Blond hair, brown eyes, always buys Perrier. That's her, right?"

Laurie nods. "Aunt Carol doesn't like tap water. She says it's full of germs. And she wants to go to France someday."

"Whatever happened to her husband?"

Laurie squints at her books. "Why are you asking me all these really personal questions? I don't know what happened to him after the divorce. He just left. I only met him once or twice."

"And you weren't gonna move south?"

"No. What a strange question."

She sits quietly for the rest of the ride, and when we make a sharp turn she leans into me like she's my girlfriend or something. When we reach the school, she says, "So you want to go on Saturday?"

"Saturday?"

She smiles and says, "You know, that's the day I volunteer at The Safe House. You can come, if you want. I have the car on Saturdays. We could go to McDonald's or something afterward."

Yeah, right. I'd rather roll around in my own puke. "Sorry, Laurie, I got something going on Saturdays."

"Oh," she says, like I just told her I didn't want to take her to the prom.

We get off the bus and I think, poor Laurie, her aunt was gonna bail on her just like Dad was gonna bail on me. When I hold the door open for her she whispers "Thanks" and walks in. The halls are full of kids, scrawny ones and fat ones, cool ones and uncool ones, freaks and jocks, cheerleaders and dogs, burnouts and nerds. It's like Berlin, divided, except there are more walls in this city, and they're better guarded.

Jon sneaks up behind me in the hall and slaps the back of my head just a little. "Hey," he says, a smile on that face of his.

*Why don't you like guys?* "Hey," I tell that face of his.

"What's happening," he wants to know.

My dad was gonna ditch me, my mom might have killed herself, and I'm in love with you. "Nada," I say.

He walks in front of me, backward, the way my old dog Rex used to when I came home from school. "A bunch of us are gonna play broom ball tonight at Van Cleve. Come with?"

My face gets hot. Maybe he does like guys. Maybe this is his way of asking me out on a date. I can't look him in those cowlash eyes. "Yeah, cool."

Jon punches me lightly on my shoulder. "Aw-right! Allison's gonna be there with some of her friends."

I stop midstep. "You setting me up?"

Jon laughs the way I pretend he does in bed. With me. On top of him. "No way, man, I'm setting myself up; you're just the bait. You don't mind, do ya?"

I think about it for all of half a second. "It's cool." I try to sound like I don't care when I say, "You want to go out with Allison?"

Jon winks at me. He says, "No, I want to go *out* with Deb Leavitt. I want to *fuck* Allison Minczeski," and then he jogs off to his next class.

I'm less hopeful that Jon likes guys.

When I get to Dutch class I see Tommy in his regular seat, his head on his desk. I say, "Hey, man, where the hell were you this morning? I had to take the bus again, like a goddamn dweeb."

Eyes shut he says, "Couldn't get out of the sack, man. I just got here."

"Your mom's been calling my house looking for you."

He yawns and then says, "Whaddya tell her?"

"I lie. I tell her I see you at school."

Tommy sighs, like he's a little kid saying good night to the grown-ups. "Cool."

I look at him, kind of foxy in his own way, and I say, "What's going on with you?"

But he's asleep. Mom used to say that I looked like an angel when I was asleep. Tommy looks like Tommy; nobody would ever mistake him for an angel. And they probably wouldn't think he was sleeping either. They'd probably figure he was passed out or overdosed or something.

Jon's brought a couple of bottles of Phillips peppermint schnapps to Van Cleve Park. The label says *Enjoy in Moderation*. Not much chance of that in this crowd.

It's a different clique from the guys I usually hang with. Tommy and I drink beer and talk about cars or the Vikings; Rick Foley and I get stoned, talk about music or go to concerts. Just this year we've seen Bruce Springsteen and Linda Ronstadt when we were high as kites. This bunch talks about sex and love and dating. It's all really dramatic and some of them won't talk to each other. I can tell that a lot of the girls want Jon as much as I do, maybe even more. They don't know how lucky they are. If I was a girl, I'd be all over Jon so fast he wouldn't know what hit him.

Allison's on me like Jackie Shaw used to be on Dad. She's not wearing a hat, none of the girls do, they don't like the way it flattens their hair. So they deep-freeze their heads. She says, "Hey, Kevin, it's really good to see you."

She's gone kind of mental with the blue eye shadow. "Hey, Allison."

Whenever I look at her, she blushes. She's a pretty girl, and I feel something for her, maybe like affection. Or gratitude. If she's so into me maybe we could get married and never have sex and she wouldn't mind 'cause she's so into me. Or maybe I could close my eyes and pretend it's Jon under me instead of Allison. That is, if she doesn't grunt or talk when we're doing it. But I don't think I could ever do it with a girl.

She says, "I'm really bad at broom ball. This one time somebody hit the ball really hard and it hit me in the face and gave me a bloody nose. Ever since, I've been afraid to play."

"Why are you here tonight, then?"

She has a dumb grin on her face, and like Fey Hayes always says, *I mean that literally*. It's a copyrighted look, like Goofy on the *Wonderful World of Disney*. You know, the way he goes *Aw, shucks*. Or is that the cowardly lion? I forget.

Finally she says, "Jon told me you'd be here."

Oh. If I don't come on to her, everybody's gonna think there's something *really* wrong with me. I'm trying to figure out a way to be some girl's boyfriend without always having to pretend that I want to have sex with her.

Allison says, "It's really good to see you."

So I say what I've heard Dad say a thousand times: "Thanks, it's good to be seen."

She laughs really loud. Ha, ha, ha. She's never heard anything so funny in her entire life.

One of her friends, the girl with Farrah Fawcett-Majors hair, passes us a bottle of schnapps. Allison takes a little mouthful, coughs, and hands it to me. I wink at her, because I can be so charming when I want to be. Mom always told me, *You can be so charming when you want to be.* And then she'd always add like it was the Amen at the end of a Hail Mary: *Just like your father.*

I guzzle the schnapps, nearly killing the bottle. When I give it to some kid I don't know, I have a warm buzz. Allison really is a nice girl. But I want Jon and bad. I just wish he wasn't such a jerk. If he could just keep his mouth shut and let me hold him, that'd be enough for me.

I ask Allison, "Where's Jon?"

She looks around and spots him over by the railroad tracks, alone. Waiting for me?

Jon does that come here thing with his arm. When we get there, he says, "Wanna cop a buzz, boys and girls?"

Allison looks at me and I can't tell whether it's because she really wants to get high or 'cause she really doesn't. I say what I always say, "Cool."

Jon pulls a joint out of his wallet. His wallet's the big kind that's hooked to a belt loop with a chain. Next, he grabs a lighter from his pocket and I wish he had asked me to get it for him.

He inhales and croaks at me, "Your turn, man."

I take off a glove and put the weed to my lips. I suck the end and close my eyes. When I open them I'm already stoned. I pass it to Allison, who looks at it like she's not quite sure what she should do with it.

She smiles at us, takes a drag, and starts coughing her guts out. Jon laughs. "Whoa, Allison, you okay?"

She tries to say she's fine, but she can't 'cause she's not.

Jon pats her back and says, "You never got high before?"

But Allison can't answer him, she's hack, hack, hacking.

Jon puts an arm around her and gives her a squeeze. "Take it easy, baby, take it easy, you're alright."

Wish I were the one coughing up a lung. He catches me staring at him and says, "You okay?"

I don't answer him, I just keep staring. *Give me a sign. Anything.*

Finally Allison stops, and wheezes softly. She wipes her eyes, which are watering and making her eye shadow smear all over the place. She says, "Oh, my God, I'm so embarrassed . . . it just went down the wrong way."

Jon's still holding her. He says, "That's okay, baby," and kisses the top of her head. Allison looks at me like she's apologizing. Then she finally clues in that Jon wants to get in her pants.

She slides out of Jon's arm and says, "Kevin, could you take me home? I really don't feel well."

Jon shoots me a look. I say, "I'm kinda buzzed and I don't have any wheels." And I might just stick my head on the railroad tracks if Jon kisses you again.

Jon says, "I'll take you home."

Allison says, "No, why don't you stay for the game? You play every week. I have my mom's car so Kevin can take me."

Jon stands behind Allison, shaking his head at me and mouthing *NO! NO!*

So I say, "It's cool, I'll take you home."

Jon's head slumps to his chest. Good. Now you know what it's like not to get something you want really bad. Maybe that should be my career. Taking people down a peg or two. Shit, I'm soooo stoned.

We leave Jon along the tracks by himself. All I hear is the crunching of the snow under our feet. Allison leads me to her car like I'm a little kid up past his bedtime.

• • •

Allison's driving. She never even offered me the keys. In spite of
the eye shadow all over her face, she's not as dumb as she looks.

"I'll drop you off," she tells me.

I roll my head back and forth on the headrest; it feels really
cool. "Hey, I'm supposed to be taking you home." At least I think
I say "supposed," but it sounds kind of like "sawmost."

She shakes her head, she thinks I'm funny. "I don't think that's
a good idea. You're pretty out of it, Kevin."

I'm really out of it so I say, "No, I'm not."

She turns her head to me and I can tell that she's in love with
me. Not with who I am, but with who she wants me to be. A
cute bad boy that just needs the love of a good woman. It's like
the number-one chick fantasy of all time. I blame it on the easy-
bake oven. You have this one thing, like this cup of gooey crap,
and you do something to it, and then it becomes something else,
something good enough to eat. That's why all girls think they
can change boys. 'Cause they all had easy-bake ovens when they
were little. God, I'm sooo stoned. What the hell did we toke,
Jamaican?

Allison stops the car. "That's your house, right?"

I look out the window. Yeah, she's right; that's my house. Hey,
how'd she know that? "Hey, how'd you know that?"

She says, "Come on, Kevin, you have to," but then she stops.
She starts again by saying, "Guess what? I saw your friend Tommy
Grabowski tonight. He's working at the Standard by my house."

"You sure it was Tommy?"

She looks out the windshield. "Yeah, it was him. I told him I
was going to see you tonight. He said to tell you 'hey.' "

"Cool." Everything's so very cool. Like when all your senses
are out of whack 'cause you're high.

Allison stares at the dashboard now and says, "You want to go
to a movie or something next weekend?"

"Cool." Everything's so very cool. Like when all your senses
are out of whack 'cause you're high.

She looks at me and her eyes are like crazed. "Really? You
mean it?"

"Yeah, it's cool."

She says really fast, or maybe it just seems fast 'cause I'm so stoned, "Okay, okay, so, we'll talk about it in school, right? We can pick a movie and figure out where it's showing. I can drive. Oh, my God, I can't believe it! Do you want to go to McDonald's or Burger King first? Or we could go someplace nice, like the Steak and Ale out in Roseville, after the movie."

"Cool," I say, but I don't reach for the door, I grab the back of her head 'cause I've never kissed anyone that I wasn't related to. And because the weed has put me in orbit over Earth, leaving Fey Hayes as the only fag left on the planet. I pull her toward me and it's kind of a shock 'cause she pushes her tongue into my mouth, and then my tongue does a little dance with hers.

She's making these weird noises, like she's eating something really good, a piece of cake or chocolate. Then I hear the scraping of Floyd Anderson's shovel on his walk. Next the Bartochevitzes' dog Max starts barking his head off. But Allison doesn't seem to care; she just wants seconds.


Now I'm like those sheep in Ireland, the ones with big paint spots on their fur or coat or whatever you call it. The color that marks them as somebody's property. Mom told me about it when I was a little kid. We were looking at pictures of County Mayo and I asked if the sheep's hair grew in that way and she laughed. No, she told me; that's paint. The ones with blue spots belonged to her neighbors down the way, she said.

Allison's dumped a whole bucket of the stuff on me. Everybody knows that we're going together, that I'm all hers. They see me coming down the hall and I hear the girls whisper and giggle. The guys that know me, and are cool enough to hang with, walk up and give me a high five, like I must have scored.

It's really immature. No wonder Jackie Shaw wants to get married so bad. I can't imagine having to do this when I'm forty.

I don't see Jon anywhere; he's probably pissed off that I didn't stick to the plan. But he was being a dick and Allison wanted me, and if I didn't want her back, people would start talking. So now I'm an Irish sheep with a big blue spot.

Allison spots me. She looks down like she's shy, but I know it's just for show, it's supposed to be cute and endearing and make me love her. Maybe it's even supposed to be sexy, I can't tell.

I walk up to her and I smile like I'm supposed to 'cause we're going together. I say, "Hey, Allison."

She looks up at me like she's a little girl and says, "Hey, Kevin." Now what do I do?

Rick Foley's walking down the hall with some burnouts so I lean down and kiss Allison right on the lips so that they can all see that I like girls. Allison kisses me back, hard, like she doesn't care who's watching or if they think that we've gone all the way. I hope they think that we've gone all the way.

I'm ready to stop kissing, but Allison isn't. Anytime I pull away she pushes her face against me. She must be standing on tiptoe-toes by now. She's making these little moaning noises too, like we're doing it right in the hall.

I finally get her off my face. "I'm gonna be late, Allison."

She looks at me all dreamy, like Betty in *Archie Comics* with little hearts floating all around her head. "Okay," and then she says, "*Honey*, I don't want to get you in trouble."

I stare at her. She said *honey*.

She turns red and says, "Sorry, Kevin, if that makes you un-comfortable, I won't say it."

Somebody just called me *honey*. I didn't think people really said stuff like that anymore; I thought it was like a fifties thing. Like daddy-o or cool cat. I say, " 'Sokay, Allison, no sweat."

She smiles at me. "You better get going, honey."

She did it again. So I say, "Okay, honey," and I know she wants to squeal like a pig in shit.

I hope she doesn't want to have sex after the movie.


Rick Foley and me are called down to the principal's office but we're not in trouble. Not yet, anyway.

Mr. Rogers (no joke), our principal, takes us into his office and points at two chairs. There's an American flag on the wall and a big black-and-white photo of Senator Hubert H. Humphrey, the happy warrior. He makes a big production out of sitting on his desk so that he can be like two feet taller than us. He goes, "Thomas Grabowski didn't come home last night. His mother's beside herself with worry, as you can imagine."

What does that mean, exactly?

Rick Foley says, way too fast, "I don't know where he is."

Mr. Rogers smiles at him. "Then we have a problem, Rick, because I don't believe you."

This is why Rick Foley bites the big one. All you have to do is look at him the wrong way and he narcs out his buds. He bites his lip and says, "Well, it's true, man, I don't know where he is."

Mr. Rogers says, "You may call me 'sir' or 'Mr. Rogers.' You may not call me 'man.' Do you understand?"

Rick Foley says, "Yes, sir."

Mr. Rogers, who you can't call a man, leans in, less than a foot from Rick Foley's face. "Where is Thomas Grabowski?"

Rick Foley whispers, "He's working at the Hennepin Standard. It's open twenty-four hours."

Way to go, Foley. Got anything else you wanna say? Somebody hiding Jews in their attic?

Mr. Rogers stands up now and looks down at us. "Let me make sure that I understand this. He's missing school and spending all night out so that he can pump gas?"

Rick Foley says, "It's good money."

Mr. Rogers looks at him like he's a retard. "Good money? Minimum wage is good money? What is wrong with you? Why is it you boys can't think beyond what you're going to watch on TV tonight?"

I give. Why can't we?

Rick Foley says, "Sorry, sir."

If we were countries, Rick Foley would be France, always ready to cave.

Mr. Rogers grunts, "Get back to class. I believe I'll go and get my car filled at the Hennepin Standard."

Man, Foley, you're *dead*.

•  •  •

So here's what happened today: Allison branded me and Mr. Rogers gave me an hour's detention for not spilling my guts like Rick Foley did. That made me late for work so Lorraine was pissed and my boss lectured me about responsibility. And now Dad's waiting for me when I get home from my shift where all I did was listen to Lorraine bitch about my generation. I can tell that Dad's been drinking 'cause all the lights are off. He can only get drunk in the dark, like it doesn't count if you can't see it. If it wasn't so fucking depressing it would almost be nostalgic—he hasn't done this in a long time. I suck in some cold air and open the door.

He flinches when I turn on the sitting-room light. There's a bottle of Southern Comfort next to him, no glass. That's his other thing, he never uses a glass when he drinks too much. That way there's not as much evidence to hide, one less thing to break or knock over.

Through squinted eyes he says, "What's that bitch been telling you?"

Of course he means Aunt Nora. Dad doesn't curse that much except where she's concerned.

"Nothing."

Dad shoots me his don't-give-me-that-crap look. He says, "Don't give me that crap! Carol called today. She told me her niece was asking her if she'd ever wanted to move down south. When Carol asked her what put that idea in her head, she said you did."

I roll my eyes at him. "Yeah, right, like I hang with somebody as uncool as Laurie Lindstrom."

Usually that'd be the end of it, 'cause Dad lets me get away with murder. Mom always said, *Your father lets you get away with murder.* I used to think it was 'cause I was his boy, but now I know that he couldn't be bothered or maybe he just didn't notice.

"So Laurie just made it all up, that's what you're saying?" he mutters.

Guess that's not the end of it. Dad's *really* shit-faced, his words are slurred. I look at him, sitting there wasted, pissed off at Aunt

Nora, pissed off at me, pissed off at the whole damn world. This used to happen a lot more often, but Mom's death has kept him sober for most of the last two years. He didn't even have a drink after her funeral, when everyone else was knocking 'em back, even Aunt Nora.

I fold my arms across my chest. "So you weren't gonna ditch me and Mom?"

His eyes go all big and his mouth drops open. He looks at me like I just wiped my ass with the flag. "Of course not! How could you . . . how could you? That old bitch Nora, she's filled your head with all this crap. I was never going to leave you and your mother." He shakes his head too fast to make his point. "Never, no way, no sir!" He looks at me again, this time like he's gonna cry. "I loved your mother! Eileen was everything to me. I love you too, Kevin."

He's only said that twice before. Both times he was *really, really* drunk.

"So you weren't going behind Mom's back with Mrs. Gunderson?"

This shuts him up.

I turn toward the stairs. "If I were you, I'd take two aspirin with about a gallon of water before I went to bed."

He says too loud, "I haven't had that much! Hey, you want pizza tonight?"

"Dad, it's almost ten."

When Dad staggered around the house Mom would say, *Never mind him, it's just the drink. He needs to remind himself every few weeks that he doesn't have the stomach for it.* See? Dad's failed at everything he's tried, even being a drunk.

Jon's waiting for me when I get to bed. He says how sorry he is. He's sorry that I have to pretend to like Allison, he's sorry he can't kiss me in the hall the way she can. But most of all, he's sorry about Dad.

It's nothing, I tell him.

No, it's not nothing, Kevin. You deserve a lot better than him. He's okay; he feels sorry for himself a lot. And Aunt Nora makes him homicidal. He doesn't mean anything by it.

Your father's a grown man. He can't go on blaming everybody else for his life.

You don't know my dad very well. I love you, Jon.

I love you, Kevin. I just wish I could tell the world what you mean to me. I wish we could go to the movies and hold hands like a real couple.

I kiss him, and I imagine his tongue in my mouth, but then he pulls away. He says: Tell me about your mother.

She was small and timid and scared of her own shadow.

Did you love her?

Yeah. She was a real quiet woman. But maybe we just weren't listening.

It must have been very hard for you, losing her the way you did.

Yeah, it was. But it's even harder now and getting harder all the time. 'Cause I'm ashamed of myself for not loving her more. For not being a better son. I'm sorry.

Don't be sorry, Jon says. It's good to cry. Healthy.

# 5

# HERE COMES THE BRIDE

Dad's embarrassed when he gets up with a bad hangover. He tries to pretend that he's fine, but he has all these different ways of not talking and I've learned how to read every one. Most of the time he doesn't talk 'cause there's nothing to say; this morning he doesn't talk because he wants to avoid anything to do with last night. So the only thing I ask him is, "You okay?"

"Yeah, sure," he says, like he's challenging me. He's really saying, *Why shouldn't I be okay? Huh? Are YOU okay?*

I leave it. I'm eating a bowl of Frosted Flakes and he just leans over the table, a glass of tap water in his shaking hand. The closer he tries to put it to his lips, the worse his hand shakes. So he sets it back on the table and grunts.

I finish my first bowl and pour myself another one. The doorbell rings. I'm supposed to get it, but I don't move. It rings again.

Dad croaks, "Would you answer that, *please?*"

"Why don't you? I always have to get it."

He puts a hand over his eyes and says through his tight mouth, "Do as I say, Kevin. Tell whoever it is that I'm at work."

I stand up. "Sure you're not gonna call in sick today?"

"I'm fine," he whispers.

And I like girls.

It's Jackie Shaw. She hasn't come by with warm cinnamon rolls with real cream icing or a homemade pecan pie. What she does have is a garbage bag full of Dad's shit, dirty clothes from his week at her place, most likely.

"These are your father's," she says, like I hadn't figured it out already.

"Come on in," I say, feeling sorry for her.

"Thank you, Kevin, but I can't. I'm going to be late for work as it is. With all the snow, traffic's really backed up. The roads are a mess."

That's when I notice it. The white flakes are falling without making a sound, millions and millions of them, like little pieces of diamonds. *Like fairy lights,* Mom used to say. In Ireland it doesn't snow much.

Jackie Shaw notices that I've spaced out. She says, "Well, I have to run. It was good to see you again."

I look at her. "Please come in. Dad's sick and I don't know how to make coffee."

I think she smiles, it's hard to tell. "How 'bout I show you how. Then you'll be able to make it whenever you want."

"Cool."

She leaves Dad's clothes on the porch and slides past me, stomping her feet and brushing the snow out of her hair. I guess women never wear hats, no matter how old they get.

She hands me her coat and I nod in the direction of the kitchen. I say real soft, so Dad can't hear, "He's hungover but he won't admit it."

Jackie Shaw laughs and joins Dad in the kitchen. By the time I get there he's sitting down with his head in his hands and Jackie Shaw is pouring water into the coffeepot. "Let's see," she says, "where do you hide the coffee?"

Dad doesn't call in sick to work and I don't call in sick to school. Jackie Shaw does it for us. Then she calls her boss and tells him that she won't be in today either. It's snowing, the roads are bad, and nobody feels like trying to get where they need to go.

We all sit around the table drinking coffee, not saying a word to each other. When Dad finally gets up he makes it as far as the living room, turns on the TV, and lies down on the couch.

Jackie Shaw says, "I think I'll join him, I never get to watch my stories since Randy died."

They spend the day together on the couch, quiet, except for the occasional question and answer: *Do you want something to eat? No, thanks. Can I get you something to drink? Some tea, please.* I spend the day in my bedroom, listening to tunes and looking out the window at the fairy lights.

When I come back downstairs, it's already dark again, and Dad and Jackie Shaw are watching the evening news. There's a pot of tea sitting on the radiator and Dad smiles at me from beneath a pile of blankets that Jackie Shaw has wrapped him up in.

Jackie walks into the kitchen, where I'm trying to find something to eat. She says, "Your father's been having a tough time at the plant, Kevin. You think they'd take it easy on him after all he's been through."

I go, "Hmmm."

"You must be starving. How 'bout I go out and pick us up some burgers and shakes?"

This gets my attention. "Very cool."

"Do me a favor and keep your dad company till I get back."

Make it quick. "Yeah, okay."

She laughs and musses up my hair, which makes me mad. "You're the picture of your father, including his moods, you know that?"

Yeah, I *know*. I get it. *Comprende.*

"A lot of women find that attractive."

This just keeps getting better and better.

She says, "I'm sorry, I wasn't poking fun. You two have had it rough, I know." She tries to smooth my hair back into place. "But I'm sure your mom would want to see you smile every once in a while."

I show her my teeth. "This okay?"

Jackie Shaw laughs and shakes her head. "It's a start. Remember, Kevin, smile and the world smiles with you, cry and you cry alone."

"Yeah, cool."


Dad and I are watching a show that we've already seen about the Israeli raid on Entebbe 'cause nobody will get up and change the channel. We haven't said anything since Jackie Shaw left to get dinner.

When she opens the front door we both start talking at the same time.

"How is it out there?" Dad wants to know, since he hasn't set foot outside all day.

"Do you need any help?" I ask 'cause I'm starving and want to grab my food and take it up to my room.

Jackie Shaw stamps her feet on the floor and says, "It's gotten even colder if you can believe it, I was afraid my car wouldn't start. I think I'll warm the burgers up in the oven for a few minutes. Do you boys want your shakes now?"

"Yeah," we say at the same time.

They eat on the couch 'cause Dad can't seem to move and I eat up in my room. It takes me all of maybe three minutes to finish my food. Mom used to say, *Chew like a civilized person, if you please. You're not a pig at the slop bucket.*

I reach under my mattress for dessert, the *Playgirl* I stole. The centerfold is twenty-five years old and has this really dark, dark tan except for his very fine ass, which is white as milk. He just lies there, on the other side of the photograph where I can't reach him, can't touch him, can't do anything but look. I wonder what a man's body feels like when it's not your own. I can check myself out whenever I want, but sometimes I want to put my hands on another guy so bad I could mess my jeans.

I run a finger down the guy's back when the doorbell rings and Dad shouts, "Kevin, get the door, will ya?"

Jackie Shaw must be in the kitchen making his lord and highness more tea. That's what Mom used to call Dad sometimes when she was fed up. She'd say things like, *His lord and highness wants you to shovel the walk* or *His lord and highness needs a bit of peace and quiet.* I shout, "Yeah, okay." My boyfriend's stashed back under my mattress. I make it to the door by the second ring. It's Tommy; his Challenger's parked in front of Floyd Anderson's house. I say, "What's happening, man?"

"A shitload. Gotta sec?"

Dad says real loud, "Close that door, you're letting all the cold air in!"

"Okay," I shout back at him. To Tommy I say, "Come on in, we can hang out in my room."

Tommy goes into the sitting room and says, "Hey, Mr. Doyle."

Dad says, like he's not hungover, "How's tricks, Tommy-boy?"

"I'm cool."

Jackie Shaw shows up with a fresh pot of tea and she smiles when she sees Tommy. "Kevin, aren't you going to introduce me to your friend?" She says it like Tommy's my date. Or maybe I take it that way 'cause I'm so paranoid.

I say, like it's no big deal, like I'm introducing her to a teacher or a priest or something, "Jackie Shaw, Tommy Grabowski."

Jackie Shaw puts the teapot on the radiator and holds out a hand for Tommy to shake. "Well," she says, all sunshine and puppy dogs and butterflies, "it's so nice to meet you, Tommy."

Tommy looks at me like *who the hell is this?* but he takes her hand and says, "Nice to meet you too, ma'am."

Jackie Shaw looks at him like he pissed on her leg. "Oh! Did you just call me *'ma'am'*? Did you hear that, Pat? You know you're over the hill when young men start calling you 'ma'am.' "

Jeez, get a clue, you *are* over the hill.

Dad laughs a little laugh and says, "Now, Jackie, you're still a young woman in her prime. Don't mind these two."

Tommy says, "My mom hates it too when people call her ma'am, and you look way better than she does."

Jackie Shaw laughs really loud and claps her hands together. She says, "I don't know your mother, but *thank you* so much, you've made my entire day!"

Dad says, "I thought I made your entire day, Jackie. Don't let this smooth-talker steal ya from me."

Yeah, a hungover guy in his forties who can't get off the couch all day is any woman's dream come true. But, hey, Jackie's thrilled. She mustn't get much attention. Plus Dad's acting like they're back together.

I say, "Well, we're gonna listen to some tunes."

Jackie says to our backs, "A pleasure to meet you, Tommy. Kevin, you can bring him over anytime!"

Dad shouts, "Keep that noise down!"

When I shut the door to my bedroom, Tommy says, "She's kinda weird. Do you like her?"

I shrug. "She makes good cinnamon rolls."

"So is your dad gonna marry her or something?"

I reach for a Linda Ronstadt album and put it on my record player. "He could do worse. A lot worse."

Tommy says, "I'm gonna beat the shit outta Rick Foley. He narced me out to Rogers."

"I know, Rogers made us both go down to his office. Why didn't you tell your mom you were working the night shift?"

Tommy lies down on the floor and stares up at the ceiling. "She made me quit my last gig because my grades were so piss poor. So I didn't tell her about this one, I didn't want the hassle. I need the bucks, man."

"Why?"

"You gotta promise me you won't tell anybody."

"I promise."

"I mean it, Kevin, this is important."

"Cool, jeez, relax will ya? I know how to keep a secret."

So Tommy just blurts out, "Beth's pregnant."

Beth is Tommy's sometimes girlfriend and the only one who

will go all the way with him. "You're shittin' me!"

Tommy closes his eyes and I think he isn't bad-looking, I could see how a girl would let him go all the way. He says, "I wish I was. We gotta take care of it fast."

"She's gonna have an abortion?"

"No, we're gonna buy a crib. What the fuck do you think we're gonna do?"

Years of Mom and Aunt Nora freaking out over the "abortionists" who murder babies come back to me. Tommy's upset, so I let the fact that betas aren't supposed to be smart-asses to alphas go. I say, "I dunno."

Tommy rolls over on his side and leans on his elbow. "I need your help, man. Mom made me quit my gig at the Standard and we're still like sixty bucks short. I know it's a lot of money, but can you loan it to me? You know I'm good for it. I'll pay you back as soon as I can."

The hundred bucks Dad gave me is still sitting in my sock drawer, along with a couple hundred more from Red Owl. It'd be easy to give him the money.

"You sure you don't want to have the kid? John Zurakowski and Michele Flanigan kept theirs." John and Michele graduated from Northeast last year and live in a trailer out in Forest Lake. Michele watches the kid all day and all night, and John goes out on dates with girls who think it's cool that he's a dad.

Tommy laughs, but not a ha-ha laugh, it's more of a boy-are-you-a-nimrod laugh. "I'm not having a kid now! Shit, I'm only seventeen. And I'm especially not having a kid with Beth."

I say, "Beth's okay," even though I've only partied with her a couple of times. She could be a skank for all I know.

Tommy laughs at me again. "Man, you don't know what the hell you're talking about. I'm not gonna marry Beth. I'm gonna get my mechanic's license and maybe have some kids in like ten years. Maybe. After I get a Harley and ride cross-country. We were supposed to do that together, remember? You and me and the open road."

"Yeah, it's cool, man, relax. I'll lend you the bucks."

Tommy sits up. "Yeah? Thanks, man, I owe you big time."

At the sock drawer I look at the bills carefully. I don't want to give Tommy any of the ones Dad gave me the day of Mom's funeral. It'd kill her to know they helped pay for an abortion.

When I give Tommy the money, he gets up and hugs me and slaps me on the back a couple of times, hard, to show he means it. "Thanks, man, I knew you'd come through for me. You're my main man, Kevin."

Mom's spinning in her grave.

## MARCH 1978

Jackie Shaw's over when Allison picks me up for our date. Jackie Shaw's making Dad a special dinner tonight, steak and fries, so she's in the kitchen when the doorbell rings.

Dad beats me to the door, he really wants to meet Allison, the first girl I've ever had over. I think he thinks I'm afraid of girls or something.

"Well, good evening, young lady," Dad says 'cause he can be so very charming when he wants to be.

"Good evening, Mr. Doyle, I'm Allison Minczeski."

Dad says, "Of course you are." Then he lies: "Kevin's told me all about you." Then he lies some more: "He's really been looking forward to your date tonight."

I just stand there in the sitting room looking at them. They're like really in love with who they think I am. I swear Dad is glowing, and Allison, well, she might as well be tripping out like the junkies at The Safe House.

Jackie Shaw practically stampedes into the sitting room. "So this is Allison!" To me she says, "Be a gentleman and take Allison's coat for her, Kevin. *Honestly!*"

I just hold my hands out and Allison has to walk over and give it to me. I can't believe it 'cause Dad walks right behind her and I catch him checking out her ass. It's really gross; she's young enough to be his daughter.

Jackie Shaw says, "Oh, don't you two make a handsome couple. Where are you going for dinner?"

Allison says, "We're going to the Nankin and then to the Sky-way for a movie."

Jackie Shaw says, "Oooh, Chinese food, that sounds yummy."

Dad says, "You keep away from that Wanderer's Punch, it packs a wallop."

Everyone laughs like Dad's some sort of comedian instead of a big dork, which is what he's acting like. Like he's a better person 'cause his son has a date. With a girl.

Jackie Shaw says, "You look absolutely stunning, Allison. Don't you think so, Kevin? Doesn't she look absolutely stunning?"

Okay, I give. "You look absolutely stunning, Allison. Absolutely."

Jackie Shaw snorts, "Oh, *you*, last of the great romantics, *just like your father.*"

Everybody laughs but me.

Jackie Shaw finishes by saying to Allison, "You have to watch out for these Doyle men, they're not the flowers-and-candy type."

And half of them aren't the I-like-girls type.

Allison says, "That's okay. I should have brought the flowers and candy, I'm the one who asked Kevin out."

Dad and Jackie Shaw look at each other and I can tell Dad's embarrassed. Then Jackie Shaw says, "Have a seat, everyone, I whipped up some appetizers to celebrate your big night out on the town." I can tell Jackie Shaw's loving this; she never had kids of her own and she's pretending I'm her son going out with the prom queen. Everybody seems to be really into it.

Dad smiles at Allison, waiting for Jackie Shaw to bring out her pickles rolled up in cream cheese and sliced ham. It's like he doesn't know what he's supposed to do when she isn't in the room to do it for him. Just like old times with Mom.

When Jackie Shaw comes back with her tray, she says, "So, Allison, have you had your eye on Kevin here for a while now?"

I say, "Jeez, knock it off."

But Jackie Shaw ignores me; she's having too much fun, and Allison can't wait to answer. I know jack about women, a lot less than the average guy, but I do know from experience that they love conspiracies. "Oh, you bet! Kevin's one of the cutest guys at school."

Dad says, "Kevin, you're a heartthrob? You never told me! My son, the dreamboat!" and then Dad goes "Ha, ha, ha."

Allison blushes and Jackie Shaw says, "Pat, stop teasing now. I think it's sweet that Allison took the bull by the horns. That's what I love about you young gals today. You do everything that only men were allowed to do." Jackie Shaw pretends she's my mom some more and asks Allison, "So, have you made plans for after graduation this June?"

Allison takes a bite of wrapped pickle. "Ooh, these are wonderful!" Jackie Shaw waves her hands, her way of saying it's nothing special, the least she could do, you're too kind. Allison wipes her lips and says between chews, "I've been accepted at the University of Wisconsin."

Jackie Shaw looks at me with her eyebrows way up and says, "That's not a bad drive. You could be there in four or five hours." Jackie Shaw turns back to Allison and says, "What are you planning on studying?"

Allison says, "Veterinary medicine. I'd like to be a vet and open my own clinic."

Dad says, "Kevin had a job at an animal hospital one summer, cleaning out the kennels."

We eat some more pickles with ham and Jackie Shaw and Dad beam at Allison and me. Finally, Jackie Shaw says, "I bet it must be very rewarding to save animals' lives."

Allison says, "Oh, yes. But the sad thing is that there are so many unwanted pets. The overpopulation of cats and dogs is a huge problem."

Dad says, "We had a mutt named Rex when Kevin was growing up. Boy did he love that dog! He used to kiss him right on the lips."

Jackie Shaw and Allison laugh.

Dad likes making Allison laugh. So he tells about the time I dressed Rex up in a sheet and made believe it was a wedding gown. "He was going to marry that dog. He had him all wrapped up in the white sheet and tried to walk him down the stairs like they were going down the aisle. Only Rex couldn't keep his footing in that sheet, and he slid down the stairs and crashed right into the landing! That was some wedding, eh?"

Jackie Shaw and Allison laugh so hard they can't talk.

Dad says, in between laughs, "Remember, Kevin? Remember how you used to play *Here Comes the Bride* with Rex?"

I stand up and say, "We gotta go."

Dad says, "He even sang a little song: *Here comes the bride, all dressed in pink, open the window and let out the stink!*"

Jackie Shaw grabs Dad's shoulder and practically blows pickles and ham all over him. She goes, "Pat, stop it!"

"We gotta go," I say again.

Dad pulls himself together, gets up, and slaps me on the back. To show Allison what a great guy he is, real father-in-law material, he says way too loud, "You be a gentleman tonight and treat this young lady right. And don't stay out too late."

If it were just us, he'd tell me not to knock her up.

We head toward the door and Dad says, "And *no* drinking."

Jackie Shaw says, "You two have fun tonight! Remember, you're only young once."

They scrunch up their faces and wave at us like we're their five-year-olds riding the merry-go-round all by ourselves for the first time. As soon as we're out the door I know they're gonna talk about us for the next hour. Glad we could give them something to do.

I finally notice what Allison has on, a short denim skirt with a white blouse. "Aren't you gonna freeze in that dress?"

She opens the passenger side door for me like she's the boy. "I prefer style to comfort."

We're on Hennepin Avenue heading downtown. There's all kind of bars downtown, places like Moby Dick's, the tough bar; and Augies, the strip bar; and Duffs, the dance bar. I haven't been in any of them.

At the Nankin I want to order the Wanderer's Punch, but I have a Pepsi, 'cause Allison's too young to be served. The place is full of white people; there's no Chinese people at all, except on the staff. This is Minnesota, after all.

Allison says, "Your folks are very nice," but then she remembers and says, "I mean your dad and his friend are very nice. Your dad's a real sweet talker."

"Yeah, it gets him in trouble all the time."

Allison looks at me like she's not sure if she should laugh, so she decides to smile sympathetically, like the people did at Mom's funeral. She says, "I hope I made a good impression on them."

Even though this is only one of a couple of dates I've ever been on, I'm a man, so I know when it's my cue to say: "Of course you did. You look beautiful tonight."

Besides, anything in a skirt would of made Dad happy. I could of brought Lorraine home and he would've danced a jig. He never said so, but I could tell he was worried about me never going out with girls. Maybe he thinks that I was afraid I'd end up like him, married and not in love. With my wife, I mean.

When our waiter comes, Allison waits for me to order for both of us.

"The sampler platter sounds good," I tell him.

Allison smiles at me. After a while she says, "You're always so quiet, Kevin. It makes me kind of nervous, I never know what you're thinking."

"Nothing. I'm thinking about nothing."

She reaches over the table, and after a second or two, I get that I'm supposed to give her my hand. Here, knock yourself out.

She squeezes my fingers and says, "You don't have to be shy with me."

This is the other thing I've noticed about girls. They think boys are just being shy when we don't say anything. They're wrong, we're not.

"Okay."

Allison's fingers are kind of feeling up my hand. "I mean it, you can tell me anything."

Wrong again.

"I'm fine."

She looks at me like I'm lying, 'cause I am. "Okay, I believe you. I just want you to know that if you ever need someone to talk to, I'm here for you."

Got it. Table 14, Nankin Restaurant, Minneapolis, Minnesota.
Sometimes I think girls flirt with me 'cause Mom died in a car
crash and they want to comfort me. But mostly I think it's because
I'm so hot.

She says, "Thanks for helping me out with Jon the other night.
He comes on way too strong."

"No sweat."

So that's the way it goes for the rest of the night. Me sitting
there like a lump, which is enough for her. My hand in hers is
enough for her. My arm around her shoulder when we walk back
to her car is enough for her. I kind of feel sorry for her, so happy
with so little. She reminds me of almost every other woman I've
known. And none of the men.


Tommy shows up during my shift at Red Owl. He looks kind of
strung out, like he's not sure where he is. I ask Lorraine if she'll
bag for a couple of minutes. I'm not like the other baggers who
ditch the checkers all the time for a smoke or to call their girlfriends, so Lorraine says, "Okay, but don't take all night." She's
kinda moody tonight 'cause her birthday's tomorrow and she still
doesn't have a man yet. She wants one even more than I do.

I catch up to Tommy at the dairy case. He's staring at the Old
Home brand cottage cheese. It's the freshest taste in the dairy
case, Old Home.

"Hey, man, what's happening? Wasn't today the day?" The day,
as Aunt Nora would say, that you were going to murder a poor
innocent and send its eternal soul to purgatory?

He remembers where he is. "Hey, Kevin. I was hoping you'd
be working tonight."

I say "Hey" again.

Tommy looks at his boots now. The snow and salt and sand he
tracked in is melting and making a brown puddle of slush in aisle
seven. He says, "Sorry."

"Don't worry, I don't have mop duty tonight."

He tries to smile but it looks all wrong. "Beth didn't do it."

*Holy shit!* "Holy shit!"

Tommy smiles again, this time like the losers on *Jeopardy* who get sent home with a bottle of Turtle Wax. He says, "We made it to the clinic. They called her in and everything. I sat in the waiting room and after five minutes she's back out telling me to take her home. I was such a fucking numskull, I go, 'Jeez, that was fast.' So she goes, 'I didn't do it, ya stupid prick.' So I take her home. She's gonna have it. She's gonna have the baby. It's this . . . thing, you know? It's this person I made. Jesus Christ, Kevin, what the hell am I gonna do?"

Lorraine pages me 'cause she can't go two seconds without needing help. Her voice is all over the store, "Kevin, register three, Kevin, register three."

I say, "I don't know."

He looks like he's gonna cry, something I've never seen him do, even when we were little kids and I gave him a bloody nose to let him know that I was alpha. He goes, "She said she's gonna put it up for adoption."

I try to sound helpful. "That's cool, right?"

Tommy smirks and does this little half-laugh thing. "I guess. Letting strangers raise my kid just . . . makes me feel so . . . I dunno. Like this kid is gonna grow up hating me. And I'll be all, 'Oh, I wonder what my son's up to now?' You know? If we went through with the abortion we'd be taking care of business, but giving it away is such a cop-out. It's like we can't handle it, so we pawn the kid off on somebody else, and he hates us for it."

For some reason I think, *It could be a girl, you know.*

Lorraine pages me again, and this time she sounds pissed off.

Tommy looks almost sweet, I want to hold him and tell him everything's gonna be all right, but that would freak him out worse than Beth having his baby. So my best friend since forever is having this big huge crisis, and I say, "I gotta go; my checker's freaking out. You want to come over to my house later? Dad's probably gonna be at his girlfriend's place."

Tommy sniffs and whispers, "Cool."

When I get back to register three, Lorraine's giving me her look. I give her one back. I shake a bag open and say, "I was doing something important, okay? Nobody's gonna die if I don't bag their shit. You don't have to get all bitchy on me."

The line of customers tense up and Lorraine says, "They don't pay you to take care of your personal business on work time. They pay you to do an honest day's work. You don't like it, go to Russia."

When I get home I pick up the pile of mail and store flyers off the front porch and tell a widow that's been camped out there that Dad's not home. Allison's sent me a card. When I saw the envelope addressed to me I was excited, I thought that maybe it was from Jon or Chuck, but then I saw the return address so now I'm like in this cloud of bogusness.

I open it, and there's Snoopy with a sweatshirt and sunglasses, his "Joe Cool" look. It says something feeble and then Allison writes:

> *Dear Kevin,*
>
> *Thanks so much for dinner at the Nankin! I had such a good time, it was a riot!!! I hope you had a good time too! Next time let's try a Mexican place over in West St. Paul, I bet you would love the food. Whenever you need a friend, I hope you know that you can count on me (in more ways than one)!!!!*
>
> *All my love,*
> *Allison*

I read it a couple of times. I think that this isn't fair to Allison, but then I think that planet Earth isn't very goddamn fair to me either. If she wants Jon, she's got him. If I want Jon, Christ Almighty only knows what would happen to me. And it'd be all my fault. For wanting him in the first place.

Given a choice, I'd rather be a slut than a fag.

I leave the card out on the kitchen table so Dad can find it later and be proud of me.

Upstairs, the sneering guy from *Playgirl* waits for me to play rock 'em, sock 'em robots. When he posed for the camera, maybe he thought, Oh, yeah, the chicks will dig this. Or maybe he thought, Easy money for a couple hours' work. But I doubt he thought, Oh, yeah, some eighteen-year-old kid in Minnesota is gonna shoot his wad when he sees my ass.

I'm about to cream when I hear the doorbell. It hurts, but I leave my boner for later and head downstairs.

When I look out the little glass window in the door I see Tommy.

I open up and say, "Hey, man."

He says, "Hey."

I point him at the couch. Hey, take a load off, I seem to say.

But he stands in the middle of the sitting room, like he doesn't deserve to sit.

I ask him, "You want a brew? Dad's got some Special Ex in the fridge."

He nods, and just stands there with his army coat wrapped around him tight.

When I get back with the beers he's on the couch, his arms hugging him, his knees glued together.

I pop a can and hand it to him. He whispers, "Thanks."

So we sit until we've killed our beers and I go back to the kitchen for a second round. Dad'll be pissed that we drank his beer, but sometimes you gotta do right by your buds.

We finish the next brews and Tommy says, "You know what's so fucking bizarre?"

I hold back a burp and say, "What?"

He leans his head over in my direction. "All it takes to make a new person is one night with some skank you hardly know. I mean, there I am, screwing her, and now there's somebody like you or me on the way. It's so fucking bizarre. You screw up one time and nine months later, bam! A new person."

Really? You have sex and then there's a baby? No shit?

He closes his eyes and says, "It's *waaay* too easy, you know? You do this thing you want to do so bad you'd kill your own mother to do it—*oh, sorry*—and then this happens. It's not fair, you know? It's way out of proportion. Say you're late for school one day, you think: Hey, no problem, I'll get detention. But no, they give you the fucking chair. They plug you in and fry you, just because you were late for homeroom. That's what it's like. You get your rocks off, and then there's a new person."

"But, it's not the same. Everybody knows that when you go all the way you might knock her up."

He snorts. "Yeah, we all *know* that, man. Like I know that gravity keeps us on the fucking ground. You know it, but so what, it doesn't seem real. I mean, I knew what could happen when we were doing it, but I wanted to do it so fucking bad, I've never wanted anything so bad in my life, you know? So I thought, Oh, yeah, nothing matters but now. Nothing matters but coming in her. Nothing fucking matters."

Oh, yeah, I know.

He belches and says, "It's so unfair. If I were God I wouldn't have made it so easy to make babies. I mean, you should have to do it a certain way or at certain times if you want to make a baby."

I keep my mouth shut.

He chokes. "You know? There should be this . . . thing you have to do, apart from the fucking, if you want to make a baby. You should have to say 'I want a baby' out loud before you do it, to get her pregnant. Or you should have to, you know, stop, do something that's not sexy, drink a glass of water or something, and then fuck. You should have to have one goddamn second where you have to do something other than fuck to make a baby. I wanna fuck all the time, I've never wanted a baby."

We sit there, drinking our beers until Dad comes home and wants to know who the hell we think we are.

I'm thinking about what I should wear to Chuck's party this weekend. I want something that makes me look hot, but not too faggy, like I'm trying too hard. That's when I see her walk through the doors of Red Owl. Carol Gunderson really does have more nerve than brains. She pulls a cart out of the stack and rolls it down the fresh produce aisle likes it's a Cadillac.

Lorraine spots her immediately. She's forgiven me for calling her bitchy because she needs somebody to gossip about the customers with. "She's paying for that cart she hit," she tells me.

Then again, maybe it's me that's got more nerve than brains.

It's quiet 'cause it's late; not many people come out on a Thursday night in the freezing cold to do their grocery shopping. Lorraine's working on a crossword puzzle, the kind that comes in the little booklets that we stock next to the register for impulse buyers, along with the *National Enquirer* and *The Star*. She's picked one about celebrities from the fifties, and every once in a while she asks me for help.

"Last name of the recording artist who had the number-one song of the decade. Four letters."

I think: E-l-v-i-s. No, that's five letters, and besides, it's his first name. "Sorry," I say.

Lorraine tsk-tsks. "You know, the fifties weren't the age of dinosaurs and cavemen. You should know these things."

I say, "Page. Patti Page, and the song was 'Tennessee Waltz.' "

She counts out loud, "One, two, three, four. I bet you're right, they played that one to death on *Your Hit Parade*. Of course, I'll take Les Paul and Mary Ford's version any day."

Whoever they are.

Lorraine sings in her squeaky voice, " 'I was dancing with my honey, to the Tennessee Waltz, when an old friend, I . . .' something, something, something."

When Mrs. Gunderson wheels up to register three, Lorraine puts down her crossword and says, "I'm so glad you're alright after that accident."

Mrs. Gunderson smiles at no one in particular and I open a bag as Lorraine's fingers fly over the register's keys. Lorraine's the best keyer at Red Owl. No one ever comes back to the store complaining that they've been overcharged.

Lorraine says, "I bet you were so shook up after hitting that cart you went straight home, not that I blame you one little bit."

Mrs. Gunderson nods as she puts her groceries on the belt.

Lorraine says, "Of course, I have to ask, you understand, when you intend to pay for the cart you hit. We really can't use it anymore, not with the frame all out of whack."

I put the Perrier at the bottom of a single bag and hold my

breath. It's my word against hers, and I've been a good employee for almost seven months now. I even work Saturday nights once in a while.

Mrs. Gunderson opens her purse and says, "I'd be happy to take care of it tonight. I know that it was rude of me to leave the way I did, but, as you said, I was shook up."

Lorraine stops keying and looks at her, all sympathy. "Of course you were! Who wouldn't be?"

Mrs. Gunderson says, "It was just the shock of it. I mean, one moment everything's fine, and suddenly it isn't. I should've been paying closer attention to what was going on around me, but I wasn't. My mind was somewhere else. What you must think!"

Lorraine hugs herself and says, "Oh, now, nobody thought anything, don't you worry about that. We were just concerned for you, that's all. We just wanted to make sure you weren't hurt."

Mrs. Gunderson says, "Thank you, that's very kind." But there's this thing in her voice, like what my mom called "doublespeak." Saying one thing and meaning another. Aunt Nora told me it was leftover from English rule. She said, "That's the only good thing to ever come of colonialism, Kevin. The Irish can tell you to go to hell in such a way that you look forward to the trip."

Mrs. Gunderson looks at me and says, "And how are you, Kevin? You seem awfully quiet this evening."

Yeah, like that's weird. You just wanna see me sweat.

Lorraine snorts and says, "Kevin hardly ever makes a peep. You'd think every word was taken out of his paycheck."

Mrs. Gunderson says, "Must run in the family. Your father's a man of few words and your mother was as quiet as a church mouse."

Lorraine glances at me as I bag and says, "Well, that's a sign of intelligence, they say. Must be why we yak-yak-yak all the time." You know, Lorraine's cool. She looks out for me. I can tell she thinks that Mrs. Gunderson's outta line.

Mrs. Gunderson says, with a coat of frost on every word, "They also say that actions speak louder than words."

Lorraine becomes like this other person in front of us, 'cause she thinks she's the only one who can give me shit. And I know that she feels sorry for me losing my mom the way I did, no matter how pissy she can get sometimes. She says like she's never met Mrs. Gunderson before, "That cart's sixty bucks per unit. I'll just add it to your total right now."

Mrs. Gunderson changes too because she gets that Lorraine's on my side, even if Lorraine doesn't know what that means, exactly. She smiles and says, sugary-sweet, "Yes, of course."

I put her goddamn Dannon yogurts in a single goddamn bag and put a finger through the bottom of it. I say, like it doesn't matter to me one good goddamn way or the other, "It's a freezing cold March this year. Bet you wish you were down south."

Lorraine says like I was talking to her, "Ooh, you know I do! My sister and I are thinking of buying a trailer in Arizona or Florida that we could stay in during the winter. I'd love to be a snowbird."

Mrs. Gunderson writes a check for her groceries and the cart that I threw through the rear windshield of her Cordoba. Then she says, "Kevin, would you help me take these bags out to my car?"

Okay, fine. If you want a rematch you can have one. "No sweat."

I throw a coat and hat on and push her cart out the sliding doors and into the twenty-below windchill that makes me gag. She's replaced the glass on her car. They did a good job; you'd never know what I had done to it.

She unlocks the trunk and says, "As I'm sure you've already gathered, I've decided it'd be best if we just forgot all about what happened. After I had calmed down, I realized that I had no business saying what I did to you. I had just hoped that we were friends, Kevin, and that I could be honest with you about what had happened. My mistake."

You mean it's my fault for being a dick. I love these apologies that shift the blame, that make it sound like the other person is so very and sincerely sorry that you're such an asshole. My fault you're an idiot. So sorry you're mental. My apologies for thinking you weren't a stupid motherfucker.

Then she goes, "So let's just leave all that in the past. Going forward, though, I have a few rules you'll have to respect. First, you don't drag my niece into this; she's had enough trauma to last her a lifetime. Second, you never speak to me like that again. Ever. And third, you never lose control like you did the other night. One time I can overlook, but I promise you I'll go straight to the police if you ever pull a stunt like that again. Do I make myself clear?"

She waits, her hands in her coat pockets, the trunk open and empty. This is the part where I'm supposed to look at my feet and say, *Aw, shucks, ma'am, I didn't mean nothing by it. You okay, Mrs. Gunderson.* So I say, "I told you not to come back here."

She shakes her head and says, "Kevin, you don't seem to—"

I pick a bag out of the cart and dump out the groceries onto the dirty ice beneath our feet, where the salt and sand make everything ugly. "*I* told *you* not to come back here. What are ya anyway, a retard?"

She gives me a dirty look and says, all gaspy-like, "You pick those up right now!"

I step on a cup of Dannon strawberry-on-the-bottom yogurt. "You were gonna dump Laurie, and you were gonna make my dad dump me and Mom. You might as well of pushed her car into the river yourself."

She says, in a real high voice, like she's gonna start crying any second, "I don't blame you for being upset, but you have it all wrong." She bends down and picks up her groceries so I won't see the tears.

"You know," I say, "you should have just left us the hell alone. Better yet, move south like you were going to."

She looks up at me, her face all wet and her nose running. "It wasn't me who wanted to leave, Kevin! It was your father; he wanted a clean break. We didn't leave because I wouldn't make a move without Laurie. And then, when the accident happened . . ."

I look down at her, all pink and miserable and I know that she's telling the truth.

She says, like a hundred times, "I'm sorry, I'm so sorry."

Then this really weird idea pops into my head. Did Mom do what she did so Dad wouldn't leave *me*? Did she think that she was that worthless?


It took me over an hour to dress for Chuck's party. I started out in a dress shirt, then a tight T-shirt, and then I finally put on one of my regular flannel shirts. I catch the 16A bus down University Avenue and transfer once to get to Chuck's house over in St. Paul. It's a small place near Macalester's campus and by the time I get there the party's pretty jammed. The whole U.N. seems to be in the house. There are Asians and Iranians and blacks and Africans (I know you aren't supposed to be able to tell the difference, but I can) and Puerto Ricans and even somebody from Iceland. They think I'm a party-crasher, and a guy who looks like he's maybe twenty-seven or twenty-eight asks me, "Hey, man, how old are you?"

He's acting like a dick, so I say, "Old enough to kick *your* ass."

He frowns at me and says, "Hey, there's no need for that macho bullshit here. All I meant is that you don't look like you're old enough to drink."

"I am," I tell him.

He mumbles, "Just asking, okay? You don't have to have a hissy fit."

"I wasn't having a hissy fit." Fags have hissy fits.

He moves on and I'm left by myself, pretending that I belong here. There's no one I know and the little groups yakking away don't look like they want my company. I walk around, looking for Chuck. I hear:

"Feminism is the ultimate liberation of *men*, I just don't understand why they don't appreciate that!"

"The Armenian holocaust was the inspiration for Hitler. He understood all too well how the world tolerates what it doesn't have the will to stop."

"Begin is the worst thing imaginable for Israel, just wait and see."

"London seems divided between punks and mods. It's a very

cool style, but they take it far too seriously and people wind up getting their heads bashed in. We didn't go to any of the clubs because of all the problems they've been having."

"Bhutto's arrest is really bad news for the region."

"My dad insists that I work at his firm over the summer, but I really want to spend it in Europe."

"Pornography is a violation of women's civil rights, it's violence against women, and if the mayor doesn't understand that—"

I finally find Chuck in the kitchen talking to a couple of what look to be Iranians. One of them is a woman; the other a guy dressed in a white shirt buttoned to the collar. He's, like, the desert fox. They're debating about how to get rid of the Shah when Chuck sees me and shouts, "Hey, Kevin, glad you could make it, little buddy!"

"Hey," I mumble at the floor.

Chuck puts his arm around me and I can tell that he's had way too much to drink. He says, "Kevin, Kevin, Kevin, you need to loosen up, you know? Cheer up, it may never happen! Come here, come here."

I come here.

Chuck opens a cabinet and says, "This'll put the spring back in your step. Here, on the house."

I know what it is, it's speed. I've seen it before, but never tried it. But it's Chuck handing it to me, and I want to have Chuck, like really, really bad, so I pop it in my mouth.

He hands me his beer. "Wash it down."

I down the whole cup while Chuck sings, "Just a spoonful of sugar makes the medicine go down." I like beer better than drugs. Beer I know how to do from all the keggers I go to.

Chuck's really out of it; he just smiles at me, his arm around my shoulder. I have my arm around his waist, he's tight and firm and feels like what I imagine the sneering *Playgirl* guy feels like. I want to check out his very fine ass, but then a new woman shows up, she's maybe thirty, I can't tell. She's really pretty, like she could be on the cover of the magazines we stock at Red Owl. Her blond hair's in a single braid down the back of her head, and she wears a big black pair of men's glasses, the kind that Mel

Cooley wore on *The Dick Van Dyke Show*. She says to Chuck, "I am so sorry."

Chuck lights up; almost floats out of my arm. He says, "Lisa, just seeing you is enough for me."

I watch them kiss, it starts slow and then becomes something humongous. She makes out with him the way I've imagined making out with Jon.

After a while, Chuck's able to talk again. He says, "Lisa, this is Kevin."

Lisa hugs me like she's known me all her life. She says, "Kevin, Chuck's told me so much about you!"

I'm just standing there, letting her squeeze me like a roll of Charmin. *Irresistibly soft.* "Cool."

She says, "It takes a lot to impress Chuck, but he's very impressed by you."

Why? I say, "Yeah, well, you know."

She laughs and kisses me on the cheek. "Oh, Chuck was right, you're too cute for words."

Chuck thinks I'm too cute for words? Then I think: She's like Dad, very charming, and she wants to be.

A new guy shows up and Chuck screams, "Hey! You made it, I can't believe it!"

Lisa puts her hand on my arm and whispers, "I know absolutely no one at this party, you have to stay right here with me. I'm a complete failure at small talk."

"Okay."

Chuck starts laughing really loud with the new guy. Lisa says to nobody but me, "That's Chuck's squash coach from the Minneapolis Athletic Club. He supplies Chuck with all the pot he wants."

I look at Lisa. I'm about to say something like, *uh-huh*, when I become, like . . . wired.

Man, speed is cool. Very, very cool. I start talking. About everything. I dump Lisa 'cause she's moving way too slow and I talk to everybody at the party. I smile, I'm charming; I have the *gift of gab* as Aunt Nora says. Yeah, I tell the Iranians, the best way to get rid of the Shah is divestiture. You gotta get your hands dirty. Yeah, I tell the woman from Iceland, I hear your country is a very beautiful place. I would love to go there someday. U.S. out of Iceland! Iceland for the Ice people! Yeah, I tell the women fighting about porn; you should've seen this copy of *Hustler* that my friend Jon was licking. There was a woman who opened up her twat and let them take pictures of it. Made him so horny he said he could choke a chicken. Now that should be illegal, you know what I mean? Yeah, I tell the Armenians, I don't know where your country is, but I think the U.S. should get the hell out of it. Yeah, I tell the Africans, I know you're not Americans 'cause you're too short and too skinny and too dark. Yeah, I tell some other women, feminism is okay by me. It's the true liberation of men. Yeah, I say to the American blacks, stick it to the man!

I talk to everybody on the bus ride home, but the only people who'll admit they hear me are drunk, and I'm talking way too fast for them. I forgot to say good night to Chuck. What a party! What a night!


Sunday I stay in bed.

# 6

# SACRED UNDERWEAR

I'm standing in front of my house after a short shift at Red Owl. The lights are out again and it's only maybe eight o'clock. I look over at Floyd Anderson, who sits on his front stoop, waiting for the sky to snow. He nods at me. His way of letting me know that he understands. He knows what a dark house with Dad's car parked out front means.

I shout, "Hey ya, Mr. Anderson."

He shouts, "How ya doin' there, Kevin?"

I smile at him but he knows it's a lie. I turn and face the house, my house, my father's house, where the man whose sperm fertilized my mom's egg waits inside, alone, in the dark, with a bottle of Southern Comfort next to him. Maybe he's even smoking again, who knows. Who cares? He's gonna be mad about something, maybe he's pissed off about last Thursday night with Mrs.

Gunderson, maybe somebody at the Ford plant talked down to him, maybe he's mad that he's not twenty years old anymore.

I don't need my key; he hasn't bothered to lock the door, or even shut it all the way.

"Leave 'em off," he says as soon as I'm in. He means the lights. He doesn't want them to hurt his eyes.

"I can't see anything," I tell him.

"Your eyes will adjust," he says, only it sounds like *Yoh eyes ell ahjus*.

"What's wrong?" This time?

My eyes get used to the dark and I can make out the sour look on his face. "You've been talking to Carol. Shouldn't talk to Carol, she'll say anything to make herself look good."

"She called you?"

"She told me what she said to you over at Red Owl last Thursday."

I turn on the lights and Dad swears, "Goddamnit, I *told* you not to do that."

I take off my cap and gloves and unzip my down coat.

Dad says, "Jesus Christ, Kevin, you can be a pain in the ass."

Just like Mom.

He's slumped on the couch. I sit in the chair across from him. He reaches beside him and I think he's going for his bottle, but instead he holds up the Snoopy card Allison sent me. He tries to smile and says, "She seems very nice."

"Allison's okay."

"She's more than okay, she's a looker and she's gonna get a good job. Won't leave all the providing up to you."

I look up at the ceiling. "What are you talking about?"

"You know, it's always been up to me to keep body and soul together—nobody else."

I look back down at him. "You're not making any sense."

He leans on an elbow and says, "I'm not working at the plant anymore."

The one thing in his life we thought—I thought—I could count on. "Why not?"

He looks like he's gonna cry. "It's sucking all the life outta me. I can't do it anymore, I can't do the same damn thing day in and day out till I die." He swipes at a tear.

I try to think what Mom would do when he got like this. Has he quit before? "What are you going to do?"

"God Almighty, when I think of all the years I've wasted there. I'm an old man before my time."

I ask him again: "What are you going to do?"

His voice cracks as he says, "I don't know. What should I do?"

"Maybe you could be a bagger at Red Owl with me. Huh? Wouldn't that be fun, working together at the grocery store? I can tell everybody, 'Yeah, that's my old man bagging at register six. Taught him everything he knows.' "

He curses me and reaches for his bottle. "You don't know what it's like to swallow your pride every single goddamn day to put food on the table. You think I wanted to be a nobody in some goddamn assembly plant? I did it for you and your mother! I went there every morning till my brain was so dead that I couldn't think for myself anymore! And this is the thanks I get! From my own son!"

I stand and start for the stairs but then I stop. I zip my coat back up and head for the door.

"Where the hell do you think you're going?"

And then the icy air slaps me hard across the face and I walk down the sidewalk in the snow. Floyd Anderson's shovel is echoing off the houses and across the street. The Bartochevitzes' dog Max barks a couple of times, but you can tell he doesn't really mean it, it's just for show.

I sit at the back of the bus, my head against the frozen window, and for only the second time in I don't know how long I cry. Not the way I used to cry when I was little, really loud and gulping for air; this time I just let all the energy leak out of me and the tears crawl down my face without a sound, like they're dying.

At Mom's funeral I didn't cry, but Dad did. He really embarrassed me, Tommy and Rick Foley were there, and Dad was slumped over with his shoulders shaking. Now I wonder if it was all for show. Aunt Nora wasn't impressed; she didn't lean over and put a hand on his arm or offer him her handkerchief. She just stared at Mom's coffin, a blank look on her face, like someone had just told her she only had a week to live. I sat between them, stiffly, every once in a while allowing myself a quick look behind me to see who had come and who had stayed away. A lot of women that I had never met, that I would soon hide Dad from, were there, including Jackie Shaw. And off by one of the stations of the cross was Mrs. Gunderson. She smiled sadly at me and nodded her head and I nodded mine back at her. Now I know that she was looking at Dad and caught my eyes by accident.

I sort of remember getting here. I'm in front of Chuck's house 'cause I don't know where else to go. Tommy's got enough shit of his own to deal with. I knock on the door.

The guy who answers the door looks at me funny. "Well, look who's here, it's Chatty Cathy." Then he looks at me kind of serious-like and says, "You okay, man? You don't look so hot."

"Is Chuck here?" I whisper in his direction.

He nods. "Yeah, come on in."

I make it in the house and he closes the door behind me. I can tell that he doesn't know what to do, 'cause there's this edge in his voice when he shouts up at the ceiling, "Chuck, that kid from the party's here to see you!"

He points to an old chair with the stuffing coming out, but I just look at it, I don't sit down.

Chuck's at the foot of the stairs. He needs a shave, but on him it looks good. He says, "Hey, Kevin, little buddy, what's happening? You were the hit of the party, my man! Or so I was told. I was kind of out of it myself."

"I was just, like, around . . . so I thought I'd see what you were up to."

He tilts his head like the RCA dog. "What's wrong?"

I look at the wall. "I just think that . . . maybe my mom killed herself. And I'm afraid, you know, that . . . I'm by myself." There's this choking sound that I'm making. "My dad quit his job today and I don't know what we're gonna do. I don't know what's gonna happen, you know? It just kind of getting to me."

He says, "Come here." He holds out his arms and I fall into them and I cry really, really hard, the kind of crying where you get them all snotty and wet, but Chuck doesn't notice or maybe he doesn't care.

"I'm sorry," I say while I'm humiliating myself.

Chuck takes me to the couch and we sit down, his arm around my shoulder. I think I'm sitting on somebody's *Rolling Stone* or something. His housemate's bolted. I would too, if some fag showed up at my door and started crying like a little girl.

Chuck tells me that it's okay, it'll be all right, the kind of things people tell you when they know for a fact that nothing's okay, that it probably won't be all right. I keep telling him how sorry I am when I can get the air to talk.

"Why don't you crash here tonight," he says.

So I just say it, for the first time in my life, I just say: "I love you."

I have to love somebody or I'll go crazy and Jon Thompson doesn't love me. Plus he can be a dick.

He doesn't skip a beat. "You don't love me, Kevin, you just haven't met anyone who could love you the way you want to be loved. It's cool, this has happened to me before."

I sniff, sniff, sob, sob, like a little girl. "It has?"

He reaches up and musses up my hair. "Yeah, when I was an undergrad my T.A. fell in love with me. You met him at the party, he's from Tehran."

I try to remember him but I can't. I hope he's a fox 'cause I'm so lonely right now that I'd do it with Fey Hayes.

We spend the rest of the night killing a bottle of rum and talking about everything there is to talk about. The fact that I'm a virgin, that maybe Mom killed herself, that Jon Thompson likes girls and I don't. Chuck tells me about growing up on Long Island and the first time he did it with a girl and why we're destroying the planet with plastic garbage bags and nuclear power. But he could talk about anything and I'd be into it, 'cause he's like nobody else I've ever met. He knows I like boys, and here he is talking to me like I like girls. I mean, it doesn't matter to him.

Dad's waiting for me when I get home the next day. At first I'm kind of touched, but then I remember he doesn't have a job anymore, so what difference does it make? He has to be somewhere. This is as good a place as any.

He's standing right on the other side of the door when I come in. He hasn't changed his clothes and I'm guessing he didn't sleep much. As his hangovers go, I would give this one a 5.5 on the Richter.

"Where were you, Kevin?"

I tell him, "I was working the graveyard shift."

He looks at me all serious-like. He says, like he's somebody else, somebody mature, somebody you might call Dad, "I suppose I deserved that. I was very worried about you. I even called your Aunt Nora but she hadn't seen you either. For all I know she's still out driving around looking for you."

I lean against the wall, exhausted, like I've just thrown up about a million times but feel better for having done it. "Why were you worried about me?"

He puts a hand on my shoulder and says with a straight face, "Because I didn't know where you were! For Christ's sake, Kevin, you could have been lying in a ditch somewhere."

Or at the bottom of the Mississippi.

I shove his hand off. "Why start worrying about me now? You were gonna leave me and Mom. If you were down south you'd never know where I was anyway."

He puts both hands on my shoulders now and holds them there, tight. "Kevin, listen to me, I mean it, listen to me! I'm your father and since we lost your mom you're the most important person in the world to me. You're all I have left of her, do you understand me?"

"Man, do I feel sorry for you."

His face gets all red, like he's gonna yell or ball. "God, you don't give up, do you? Must be nice to be perfect."

"Shut the hell up."

That's when he hits me right in the jaw. It doesn't hurt too bad 'cause he's too tired and too hungover to put any muscle behind it.

"Jesus Christ," he screams at me. "I've screwed up more times than I can count and yes, I was drunk as a skunk last night and I'm not proud of it! I'm paying for it today, believe me! But you're my son, and no matter what else has happened, I love you. Like the screw-up I am, I love you and you scared me half to death when you didn't come home all night."

I rub my cheek, pretending that he hurt me. "You just didn't want to get blamed for this one too. Do me a favor and love somebody else. I don't want your love, it's a big pain in the ass."

He slaps the wall really hard and I know his hand must sting like hell.

He breathes heavy and says, "If I had ever talked to my father the way you talk to me . . ."

We're stuck there, in the little entryway to our little house where we live our little lives. "Get outta my way," I tell him.

He doesn't budge. "No, you're going to stay right here and listen to me."

"Let me by," I tell him again.

He sticks his chin out like he's a big man and says, "You *are* going to listen to me."

No, I'm not. So I shove him really hard and he falls over. He's on the floor looking up at me like I just told him that I like boys. He's saying something like, "Oh no, oh no, no, this is . . . you spoiled little punk . . ."

He begins to get up but I push him back down again. That's when he grabs me around the knees and knocks me down and we're shouting and cursing and swearing and I finally twist his arm up behind his back and push the wrist toward his neck. He goes, "Aahhhhhh, stop it, stop it, ya little bastard!"

"You don't tell me what to do," I scream over and over again, at least I think I'm screaming 'cause I can't believe I'm doing this to my dad. I can't believe he quit his job and I can't believe he was just gonna pack up and leave me and Mom behind, and I can't believe that Mom drove herself into the river.

That's when I hear the pounding on the front door, right behind us. It's Floyd Anderson shouting, "Is everything okay in there? Kevin, you okay in there? What's going on? Tell me what's going on or I'm gonna go call the cops."

Dad and I are gasping and coughing and wheezing but I get out, "It's . . . okay, Mr. Anderson . . .'Sokay."

"Don't sound okay to me," he says. "Sounds like somebody's getting himself killed in there."

I huff, " 'Sokay . . . really . . . just . . . messing around."

It's quiet for a minute or two, but then I hear Floyd's boots crunching in the snow.

I get off Dad. He sits up against the wall and rubs his arm, panting like a bitch in heat. He says, all breathy-like, "Pack a bag and get the hell out of my house."

I look down at him and think: I used to like you. I used to feel sorry for you when Mom pissed and moaned about you. I used to feel proud when she said, *Just like your father.* I used to think you were cool for letting me keep the change from the pizza money. I used to think we were buds when I'd hide you from the widows like you were a secret I wouldn't tell them. I thought we were so cool.

And now I wish it was you who they had dragged out of the Mississippi.


My bag's easy to pack. I pull my rucksack off my dresser and put my money from the sock drawer in it. I lift my mattress and put my *Playgirl* in it and I see the little Charlie Brown doll with his orange baseball cap that Mom gave me when I was six, and I put him in. Some jeans, some T-shirts, some socks, some underwear. My whole life fits in a rucksack with room to spare.

Dad's down in the basement when I leave. He's not hiding from the widows; he's hiding from me, probably already ashamed of himself for throwing me out. Or maybe he's puking in that toilet he put in. Or maybe he's dead, who the hell cares?

Floyd Anderson's out on his front stoop, leaning on his shovel, waiting for the snow to fall or for me. He says, "Kevin, come over here why dontcha?"

I cross the street not looking either way, hoping a car will run me over. But none do and I'm facing Floyd Anderson with the pyramid on his head. Jesus, what a morning.

Floyd says, "That sounded pretty bad. You had a fight with your father, eh?"

I smile. "Yeah, you could say that."

"He kick you out then?" Floyd wants to know.

"Yeah."

Floyd shakes his head and sighs. "Oh, that's a shame. Tell ya what, you can stay here with me till you and your dad patch things up."

"Thanks, Mr. Anderson, but I can stay with my aunt." I'm lying; I'm gonna catch a bus to Chuck's.

Floyd says, "Your ma told me your aunt lives all the way over there in Powderhorn," like it's on the Canadian border. "No, you stay right here with me and I betcha you'll be back home before you know it. Me and my father fought like cats and dogs, but we always shook hands and made up."

I think about Floyd's offer. I'd rather stay with Chuck, but he likes girls, and I've gotta stop falling in love with these guys who like girls. But the only other people on the planet like me are Fey Hayes and some guy from Tehran that I don't remember meeting. It's about five degrees outside and is supposed to get to eighteen below tonight. "You sure you don't mind?"

Floyd laughs like I just asked him if farts smell. He says in his accent that lets you know he's never even made it as far as Wisconsin, "Oh, no, of course not! Dontcha even think that for a second!"

Floyd wound up at Fort Snelling during World War II making meals for the new recruits. After that he got a job at the U as a cook in the hospital kitchen. When his wife's mother died they bought their house with the money she left them. Floyd knows how to prep an industrial kitchen, cook for hundreds of people, and then clean up after them. But all he eats is cereal and pre-made puddings. If I want something different, I'm welcome to make it myself or order a pizza. I have refrigerator privileges, but I have to stay out of his big freezer in the basement, it's full of deer and duck for a family reunion up on the Iron Range.

After I put my rucksack in the spare room Floyd shakes my hand. He slips me two fives and winks, saying, "That's just a little something to help you out till you and your dad patch things up."

"Mr. Anderson, you don't have to—"

"I *want* to. You get yourself settled. If you need me, I'll be out front."

Waiting on the snow.

Being out of my house makes it easier to breathe. I don't have this tight feeling in my gut like I'm waiting for something bad to happen. I can inhale and exhale and it doesn't feel like it takes everything I've got to do it. I watch TV. I listen to the radio. I call Chuck, 'cause I want him to know where I am. Then I lie down on the guest bed. It takes me like two seconds to fall asleep, even though it's not even nine. I sleep right through to the morning.

Chuck picks me up in his Pacer 'cause he thinks a road trip will do me good. Floyd says, "Dontcha got school today?" I say no; it's the parent-teacher conference. Okay, so it's not really today, but when I say *parent* Floyd feels sorry for me and tells me to have a good time.

Chuck's decided I need to go up north to Duluth and look at Lake Superior. I haven't seen it since I was little. On the ride up we sing along with the radio; Chuck knows the words to every song ever written. He sings "Crazy on You" and "Year of the Cat" and "Ebony Eyes" and "Dust in the Wind" without flubbing up a single line. He's got a voice like Jackson Browne, but I don't care 'cause he looks as good as Jackson Browne.

I love sitting next to him in his car. When he doesn't talk, just stares out the windshield at the freeway, it's easy to pretend that he's my boyfriend. The other thing is this feeling like we're going somewhere, but not like a day trip. What I mean is we're leaving it all behind, for good. I know we're not, that in four or five hours we'll be on the other side of the freeway heading back to the Cities and Dad. But for now it's cool. For now Chuck's my boyfriend, and we're cruising on down the highway, starting our new life together. When we see someplace we like, we'll just stop and live there. People will wonder whatever happened to us, we'll be like this mystery for all time.

We stop about halfway between the Cities and Duluth at a place called Tobie's. Chuck orders the chili and I have a burger with fries. He talks about London, where he studied for a little while, and Greece, where his family goes on vacation every winter. But his favorite place in the world is New York City, and he tells me I should move there and live in Greenwich Village. "It's where all the homosexuals live."

I just about drop dead. He said *homosexuals* so loud that people might have heard.

"Don't say that," I whisper, looking around to see if anyone's staring at us.

He shakes his head and laughs. "London would be good for you too, Earl's Court has a very large and very active homosexual community. There's even a pub called The American Boy."

"Jesus, keep it down, will ya?"

He kind of snorts. "Relax, Kevin. You're wound far too tight."

Easy for you to say.

He finishes his bowl and puts his arms behind his head, which make his biceps flex. That's when he tells me that he's heading back east soon. For good.

"I've just been hanging around since last June working on my thesis. I can do that anywhere, so there's really no reason to live in Minnesota anymore. Besides, who knows if I'll ever actually finish it at this rate. I've just about had my fill of the weather up here."

I've never lived anyplace else so I don't get why everybody thinks the winter's so bad. "You can't go. Who am I gonna talk to? You're the only friend I've got."

He looks me in the eye and I look away first. "You've got a lot of friends. And a girlfriend. You're not alone, little buddy."

"You know what I mean."

"So talk to what's-his-face. The one who got his girlfriend pregnant."

I picture telling Tommy the truth. After he stops laughing—when he finally gets that I'm not bullshittin' him—his head explodes. His wake has to be closed casket, just like Mom's.

I try a different strategy. "You should stay here, and, you know, get a doctor's degree in something at Macalester."

Chuck smiles and shakes his head. "Nah, I need to give academia a rest for a little while. I'm going to travel."

"Where?"

"After I spend some time with my folks, I'm going to Alaska for a few weeks in the summer. Then I want to visit Australia and from there, I'm thinking of taking a few months in Europe and bumming around on a Eurail pass. I did it once before, I just hop a train every night and sleep onboard. Saves you a lot of money on hotels."

Take me with you.

"What about Lisa? I thought you two were pretty tight."

He says, "I do love her, but I'm not ready for the kind of relationship she wants. She's thirty, she wants a husband and she's desperate to start having children."

"You've told her you're taking off?"

He looks at me, embarrassed. "No, not yet. I haven't found the right way to tell her. I know she's going to be devastated."

I feel sorry for her. It's easier for me 'cause I can't have him. But she's had him and wants to keep him. "She's gonna be really bummed."

Chuck stares at his bowl and says, "This is something I have to do. Seeing the world is so much more of an education than any university. You arrive in a new city a stranger, and you can pretend to be anyone at all. You can try on all these different identities, a dozen different ways of being in the world, until you find the one best suited to you. I think that's at the core of your problems, Kevin. You're trapped in one small section of Minneapolis. But more to the point, you're tied up in the guise of who other people think you should be. It'll suffocate you in time, trust me. You need to make a clean break of it after you graduate from high school."

I've got a big chunk of cheeseburger in my mouth, but I say, "How'd you know I go to high school?"

He laughs and says, "You're such a rotten liar. I thought it was sort of sweet, the way you tried to pretend you were in college. I guessed that you were homosexual too."

"When?"

"When I met you at Culla's. You have this way about you, like you're wearing a suit that's the wrong size."

Take me around the world with you, Jon Thompson likes girls and I've got nothing going on here.

He looks at me, all serious. "I can see why all the girls are fascinated by you. You have this moody, pensive mystique about you. Makes you seem quite deep. Women adore that, it makes them crazy."

I may just be a high school senior and he may be getting a master's degree, but I know when I'm being talked down to, and it pisses me off. I say, "Why do you hang out with me?"

He frowns. "Because I'm genuinely fond of you, Kevin. I find you immanently likable, in spite of yourself. You're like an older, homosexual Charlie Brown."

I dab a French fry in ketchup. He was supposed to say, *Because I've never been with a guy and I want to know what it's like. Let's spend the night in Duluth.*

I say, "Or maybe you just wanna prove to yourself that you can have a faggot for a friend. I mean, that party of yours, it was like Noah's ark. Two of everything. And Lisa's thirty and you're twenty-three. I think you think it makes you look good or something."

Chuck starts to say something, but then he stops. After a second or two he says, "Yeah, maybe. So why do you hang out with me?"

Man, you *do* need some time in the real world.

• • •

"There it is," Chuck says like I don't know what I'm looking at. "Lake Superior, the greatest of the Great Lakes."

It's big, it's wet, it's freezing. "Yeah," I tell him. "Big wow."

He laughs at me. "I can see you're not impressed. Come on, let's find out what this port town has to offer two handsome young bucks like us."

Chuck takes me to a record store and blows like sixty bucks on albums for me. Along with the stuff I like, he gets me albums by the Sex Pistols and Talking Heads and The Clash to "expand my horizons." He says, "That burnout rock and roll you listen to is really lame." I keep telling him not to buy me stuff, but he's really into it, and the clerk probably thinks we're boyfriends, which, I guess, is what Chuck wants him to think.

Next we go to a humongous secondhand bookstore where he picks up a bunch of old paperbacks for his trip around the world. He says, "These are the best things for traveling because they don't take up much space. And you can leave them behind in cafés for someone else to find and read." For me he buys a copy of the *Advocate*—he tells me it's a newspaper for homosexuals—three old issues of *Playgirl* and a book of short stories by gay men. I spaz, I can't believe that he just takes them all up to the register like it's no big deal. The woman behind the counter rings them up like he's buying *Car and Driver* or *Heavy Metal* or something. I keep my distance. I'm not proud of it, but I don't want the other people in line to think we're together.

When we're outside again, he says, "Here's what I don't understand. We'll never see any of those people in that bookstore again for as long as we live. And yet you're terrified they may think you're a homosexual. Who cares what they think?"

I don't say anything; it's like I'm back at the principal's office.

He says, "Sorry, sorry, easy for me to say. Let's check out the used clothes store. We need to punk you out; you look like a cross between a burnout and a lumberjack all the time. You should get a short haircut too, like all the punkers in London and New York have."

"No way."

The clothes store has big bins of really weird shit, ugly plaid pants and wrinkled-up dress shirts and clip-on ties, but Chuck finds a pair of black jeans and a couple of T-shirts without sleeves. He gets real excited when he digs a beret out of a pile of crappy sweaters.

"Cool," he says. "You'll look like you're playing CBGB's in this."

I don't know what he means.

"Come on, try it on."

We stand in front of one of the mirrors, the kind where you see yourself three different ways at once. The beret does look very cool on me. And Chuck looks very cool next to me, like it's the coolest thing in the world when two guys are together. I don't know, like maybe it means more than a guy and a girl. Because nobody wants us to stand together. But we do anyway.


Dad's waiting for me at Floyd Anderson's house when Chuck drops me off.

Floyd squints at my beret, but he's still wearing his pyramid so he's got no room to talk. Floyd says, "Your dad's in the sitting room, there," only it sounds like, *Ya dad's in da sidding room, dare.*

Dad's not sidding in da sidding room, he's standing, with his hands in his pockets, looking out the window at our house. He doesn't turn around and look at me, he just says, "You might have let me know where you were."

I say, "I'm staying at Floyd Anderson's house."

Why don't donkeys go to school, Kevin?

He pretends he doesn't hear. He says, still looking across the street, "Aunt Nora called the police, your school said you didn't show up today, and Jackie took the day off to try and find you."

Oh.

He turns around and I swear to God he looks like he's been crying. "This can't go on. I don't know what to do with you anymore. I don't know how to get through to you. Everything

I say and do seems to be all wrong. I try my best, Kevin; I'm only human. When you have kids of your own one day, you'll understand."

"You act like it's my fault. You're the one who threw me out!"

He says like I'm a retard, "I lost my temper; I didn't mean it. You shouldn't have left."

I can't believe it. "Did you tell school and Aunt Nora and Jackie Shaw that you were the one who kicked me out? Or did you forget to tell them that part? Huh?"

"Kevin, I can't do this right now."

I laugh at him, 'cause he's the stupidest person I know. "What *can* you do?"

We just stand there not saying anything, either because he's so mad he can't talk or because he's trying to think of what it is that he can do. I make out a list: (1) he can screw around with Mrs. Gunderson; (2) he can get loaded about every couple weeks like he used to before Mom died; (3) he can quit his job, 'cause he's a big goddamn baby, and (4) he can make other people feel like it's all their fault. He's a talented guy; the world needs more like him.

Floyd Anderson comes in with two teacups full of his own special drink, hot whiskey with sugar, honey, and lemon juice. He says, "This'll warm you right up. Sid down dare, Patrick, and drink up. Kevin, you sid down and talk to your father dare. I'm going out to check the walk."

So we sit down on the furniture that Floyd's wife picked out about thirty years ago, Dad drinks his drink, I drink my drink, and I'm surprised because it tastes really scrump-dilly-icious. I down it and get a warm buzz and now I want another one, but Floyd's outside standing guard against the snow that's not falling.

Dad just sips his. If he wasn't so pissed at me, I'd ask him if I could finish it for him. He says, "Floyd was under the impression that you had told me you were staying here."

I look at him like it's none of his goddamn business what Floyd thinks.

"Maybe I should of done things differently after your mother died, but I thought you were doing okay. I thought we were

friends. But you've become a stranger. I don't know what to do
with you anymore."

"Yeah, well."

"I remember the day you were born. I remember holding you.
You were so tiny; I couldn't believe it. I thought that you'd never
stop loving me. I thought, Here's the one thing that I can always
count on, no matter what else happens to me. My son."

He looks at me. And then he reads my mind. "Here, you can
have the rest," he says, handing me his cup. "I don't much care
for it."

I'm supposed to say thanks, but I don't.

"I got a line on a job," he tells me, rubbing his neck. "Pays a
fortune, the only problem is that it's in Alaska, all the way up in
a place called Barrow."

"Where's that?" I ask, not as pissed as before I had the whiskey.

"The top of Alaska, right on the Arctic Ocean. One of the
guys I know from the plant moved up there last year and told me
he could get me a job at the airport. The place is swimming in
oil money. Couple of years up there and we'd make a mint."

I look at him. *We? We'd* make a mint? "Are you for real? I'm
eighteen; I'm not going anywhere! You can't make me."

He pulls out what he thinks is the ace up his sleeve. "Then
you'll have to move in with your Aunt Nora. I can't keep a house
here and pay rent up in Alaska too. Just come with us, I really
want you to, we need a fresh start."

I think I might be drunk. "No you don't! You just want to
make out like I'm the jerk. Fuck that, you know."

"Watch your language."

"I'm eighteen now, I can say whatever the hell I want."

"Not to *me*, you can't."

"They got a lot of widows up there in Barrow to take care of
you? Or is Mrs. Gunderson going with you? Huh? You and her
and Laurie moving up together? Get a goddamn map, Dad,
Alaska's north, not south."

Now Dad looks at me all serious. "I wish, for just one goddamn
second, you would cut me some slack. And no, they're not moving to Alaska. Kevin, I asked Jackie to come with me. And she's

said yes. She's really hoping you'll come too. We could start over, all three of us. She cares a lot about you, she wants you to be happy."

Okay. This is some kind of lesson I'm supposed to learn. First, when your dad kicks your ass out of the house, don't leave. Second, never cut school and go to Duluth or some very weird shit will happen. I say, *"Godverdamme."*

Even in Dutch, Dad knows I'm swearing. "What did I just say?"

"Why can't I stay in the house?"

He sighs. "Kevin, I just told you. I can't pay a mortgage and rent too. I'm sorry. How many times do you want me to say I'm sorry?"

"Mom loved that house. She said it was the nicest home she ever lived in. It'd kill her to have strangers living there."

"Come to Barrow with Jackie and me. It'll be an adventure. A new beginning."

"I'm gonna move to Greenwich Village," I tell him, 'cause I guess I'm drunk 'cause I don't think I would say that if I was sober.

Dad says, "Did you know that the sun never sets in Barrow for months? They call it the land of the midnight sun." Then he says, like I'm a little kid, "There's polar bears and seals and whales up there. You'll love it. Remember when you were in the sixth grade and wrote a letter to the governor to save the wolves? In Alaska they have hundreds and hundreds of wolves. And you'll make Eskimo friends."

"Dad, I'm not a little kid."

He sighs. "No, I guess you're not."

We don't say anything for a while, just stare at nothing. Then I ask him: "When are you gonna leave?"

"As soon as the house is sold."

"Oh."

Dad puts a hand on my knee and pats it. "Come on, get your stuff, say your good-byes to Floyd, and let's go home. Jackie's making a nice big dinner for us tonight so we can plan out everything we need to do before we leave."

"I'm gonna stay here."

He gets up; he's in no mood for another fight. "You know, Kevin, you're right. You're eighteen; you're an adult. Do what you damn well please, you always do anyway. I just hope you can make it on your own without having me to kick around."

He's supposed to stop and say he's sorry. He's supposed to beg me to forgive him for being such a dick. But he just walks out the door. And I'm here in Floyd's house. I thank God for Floyd; otherwise I'd be at the The Safe House with Laurie Lindstrom washing my feet.


That night Floyd and I eat chocolate pudding. He's reading *The Second Ring of Power* and I'm watching *Donny and Marie*, 'cause I think Donny's kind of hot. Floyd only makes it through a page about once every fifteen minutes.

He says, "Those are them singing Mormons, eh? They wear the sacred underwear, ya know."

Maybe Floyd's senile. I laugh and say, "There's no such thing as sacred underwear. Jeez, how dumb do you think I am?"

Floyd's so sincere you almost wanna believe him. "Them Mormons believe in sacred underwear. They got to wear this special kind."

"Yeah, right. Well, they mustn't wear it much 'cause there's about a million Osmonds running around."

Floyd has to think about it for a minute, but then he laughs and says, "Ya, that's a good one dare! If I could have a buncha wives, I wouldn't be wearing no underwear either."

I shake my head.

"Those two married then?" Floyd says as he points at the dusty screen.

"Nah, they're brother and sister."

Floyd says, "He looks like my boy."

Floyd has a foxy son? How come I've never seen him? "Where's he live?"

Floyd says, "Oh, we lost Stevie back in Korea."

Somebody pounds on the door and before Floyd can even get

up to answer it, I know it's Aunt Nora. Beating her big man hands against the house.

I say, "Don't worry, I'll get it."

Floyd says, "Tell 'em to stop trying to break my door down!"

The second she sees me, Aunt Nora grabs me and hugs me real hard. I mean really, really hard. She could be one of those lady wrestlers. *And here she is, the champ-eee-on, the killing machine from the Isle of Green, the bonnie lassie who's plenty nasty, the pretty colleen who'll make you scream, Noooooraaaaah!*

"My darling boy," she says. "My poor, poor darling boy! What's that bastard done to you?"

I'm strong, which is good, 'cause you gotta be to get out of one of Aunt Nora's hugs.

"I'm okay, it's no big deal."

Aunt Nora says really loud, even for her, "No big deal? No big deal! Mother of God! It most certainly is a big deal. He told me you left home! Pack your bag, you're coming to stay with me."

"It's cool, Aunt Nora, I can stay here tonight."

She gasps. "You'll do no such thing. You're coming home with me."

I just look at her and she grunts. I'm at that awkward age where she thinks that she should still be able to order me around, but she gets that I'm too old for that. "Okay, you're staying the night here. But I'll be around tomorrow after work to collect you."

I cave. "Cool."

She looks around. "Is there somewhere private where we can have a chat?"

I take her into the dining room, which looks like it hasn't been used in years. It's very neat, except that there's a coat of dust covering everything. Aunt Nora brushes off the tabletop with her hands and frowns.

"How did you end up here?" she wants to know.

Why lie? "Dad quit his job, got shit-faced, and kicked me out of the house."

She sucks up all the air in the room. "Mother of God! He threw you out of your own home?"

She stands up and the chair she was sitting in nearly falls over backward. I know she's about to march across the street, like a storm trooper, kick the front door open, and kill Dad with her bare man hands. I hold on to her arms. She pulls, really hard, and I have to brace myself against the table to keep her there. She pulls for a good minute or more, but then she sits back down.

She says, "I'll murder him," like she was saying the Earth revolves around the sun.

"He's not worth it," I tell her.

But Dad's right about one thing. On Mom's side of the family they let nothing go. They hold it tight, the more painful the better; the more it hurts, the closer they are to God. "He's a dead man," she says.

We sit there, not saying much. Then Aunt Nora puts a big man hand on my cheek and says, "I'd murder a bit of whiskey."

Floyd makes his special drink for us, and has one himself. He sits right next to me; this is the most excitement he's had since his wife walked out on him.

Aunt Nora finishes hers in all of ten seconds and says to Floyd, "Once more, if you would be so kind."

This time he brings the bottle. Aunt Nora helps herself, and then puts a head on mine. She says, "Tell me what the world's coming to when a man's unfaithful to his wife and turns out his only child."

Floyd says, "They had a fight, dat's all."

Aunt Nora looks at him like he's the village idiot. That's an expression she taught me. She'd say, *Look at him, if he isn't the village idiot then I don't know who is.* "That bastard you call neighbor has been fornicating for years with a woman who's not his wife. I call that wrong. So does the good book, not that he's ever read it."

Floyd thinks about it, you can practically smell the rubber burning. He says, "Cheating, yeah, dat's wrong, dare's no forgivin' dat. But when love dies, well, dat's a different story."

Aunt Nora and I look at him. She says, "Whatever do you mean?"

Floyd looks at his drink and says, "I'm just saying, is all, dat it's not so simple as one's wrong and one's right. Take me and my missus. We're still married, have been almost fifty years. But sometimes one of ya changes, ya know? Sometimes, ya think to yourself, you're not getting any younger dare, time's running out. You don't have forever to figure tings out, ya know. And dat's something ya got to do on your own, but ya know that the other one won't understand. So ya stay. Ya never find out who ya might have been. Me and my missus got used to each other though. Even though I don't love her no more, ya know, like a man's supposed to love his wife, I don't know what I'd do without her. She's been a good friend to me. She keeps my feet on the ground."

You're without her now. Jeez, Floyd's lost it.

Aunt Nora says, "So you're defending him?"

Floyd doesn't look at us. He says, "Ya know, all I'm trying to say is dat maybe tings change. When you promised that you'd love each other forever you were young, and the years go by, and tings change. Ya start tinking dat maybe ya made a mistake. Dat maybe ya got married because you were old enough to, and ya wanted to please everybody else. They're all married so they want you to get married too. So they can feel good about what they did, even if they're not so sure about it themselves anymore."

Aunt Nora rests her chin on one of her big man hands. She says, "So people fall out of love, so what? You think that calling it a day is nobler than staying the course? People fall in and out of love all the time. What matters is what lasts, through the good times *and* the bad. That's what matters." Aunt Nora warms to the subject, sticking out her finger and pointing it at Floyd. "You can think what you please about a stranger, but the one who shares your bed, now, that's the one you know inside and out. 'Tis a child that dreams there's something better 'round the corner. It's a grown man who knows it's right there in front of him." She nods her head like it's the period at the end of a sentence.

Floyd says, "So ya should just say this is as good as it gets? Dare's nothing more? Okay, I don't believe dat. I don't believe dat da one ya said 'I do' to is always gonna be da one dat ya spend da rest of your life with. Tings change. Ya can admit it or ya can deny it, but what's in your heart, dat's da truth."

Aunt Nora holds up her little glass and says, in her fake Swedish accent: "O-tay, den. If ya sleep wit a whore, ya just bein' honest, dare. En dat's good, ja? Everybody loves da honesty, dare."

Floyd turns red. Then Aunt Nora says, "And what in Jesus' name is that thing on your head? You look ridiculous. Take it off before they toss you in the booby hatch."

Floyd excuses himself and goes up to bed, pyramid in place. And I think: You're right, Floyd. Things change. But screw it, it sucks the big one.

Aunt Nora points at the bottle and says, "Be a pet and top us off."


Chuck leaves for New York tomorrow so I invite myself over to say good-bye. His room is full of garbage bags—the plastic kind that he says are destroying our planet—and I don't think he's too happy to see me. He keeps saying that he's way behind and has all this shit to do before he leaves. It hurts to hear him say that.

I say, "Well, I just wanted to see you before you take off."

He looks up from a pile of papers that he can't decide what to do with. "Hey, I'm sorry, Kevin, I'm being rude. It was very thoughtful of you to stop by. I'm just on edge because I've left everything until the last minute. Typical of me."

" 'Sokay."

He comes over to where I stand by his bedroom door and gives me a hug. And I hug him back and it's like nothing else, even better than when I was biting Jon's ass at Debbie Polanski's. I put my head on his shoulder, which is really hard to do since he's only like five-ten.

He doesn't let go of me. He says, real quiet, "What's wrong?"

"I'm gonna miss you. You're the only one I can really talk to about . . . everything, you know? Will you write me?"

He slaps me on the back and says, "I'm not much of a corre-spondent, little buddy. Sorry."

" 'Sokay, I won't have an address soon anyway. Dad's moving to Alaska with his girlfriend."

Chuck puts his hands on my shoulders and looks up at me. "I'm sorry. You know, I was wrong about you. You're not like Charlie Brown at all. I'd say you're more like Eeyore from Winnie the Pooh."

I pull away. "Thanks a lot."

He laughs and says, "Don't get mad, I was just kidding. I didn't mean it, I'm just trying to get you to lighten up a bit."

But I'm mad, 'cause I know he wasn't kidding. Easy for you to bounce all over the world like Tigger when you're rich and like girls. Easy for you to try to lighten me up when your mother's alive and married to your father. Fuck you, you know, and not in a good way.

"Don't sulk, Kevin. Here, I have a farewell gift for you." He puts his hands behind my head and pulls me toward him. "Your first kiss from a man. Like Junior Walker said, pucker up, buttercup."

He kisses me right on the lips. It takes me a second to realize what he's doing. Then he slides his mouth over to my cheek and gives another kiss, a peck like Aunt Nora does. But I'm still living that first kiss, the one where his lips touched mine. I say, "Oh, God," and I pull him back to me 'cause that's where he belongs and I plant my lips on his face and shove my tongue down his throat. Like I wanted to do the first night I met him, the night that Jon Thompson let me know that he likes girls.

He kisses me back for maybe five or ten seconds and then he waits for me to finish, but I don't and he comes up for air. He gasps and wipes his mouth, "Jesus, it's really weird to be kissed by a guy. It's kind of bellicose. Like a competition."

I say real fast, "Yeah, can we do it again?"

He says okay and now he's really pushing his mouth into mine, like it's a demolition derby and he's the defending champ. He shoves his tongue into my mouth, but I push back, 'cause it feels so right. I want him to know that he's all mine, that I'll take care of him. I hold him tight and run my hands down his back and grab that very fine ass of his and squeeze.

He pulls back and says, "Hey, don't do that." He pants a little bit and says, "This was a really bad idea, I got you all hot and bothered, I'm sorry."

I say, all desperate-like 'cause I am desperate, "Don't stop, please." I grab his wrist and pull him back to me. He's struggling hard, but I'm way stronger than he is. I say, "Come on," and I pull on the waist of his jeans, I want to see his ass for myself.

He yells, "Stop it!"

I let go of him and he backs away, kinda freaked out. He says, "Kevin, I'm really sorry, I shouldn't have done that. It was my mistake."

"Just once more, please, I'll do anything."

He looks at me differently now, like he's scared of what I'm gonna do. "No, I'm sorry, I thought I was doing you a favor but I can see that I wasn't. I wondered if kissing a guy was any different than kissing a girl. I was curious."

"Is it different?"

He says, all serious, "Yeah, it is. Very different. Maybe it's like the way you feel when Allison is kissing you."

"Maybe. But everybody wants me to kiss Allison. Everybody thinks it's cool when I kiss Allison. But I want to kiss you, and nobody thinks that's cool. I want you, Chuck; I wanna kiss you. I wanna take off your shirt and your pants and your underwear. I wanna do it with you. Wanna see if being with a guy is different from being with a girl? Huh?"

He takes a deep breath and says all calm-like, "I didn't mean to lead you on. I'm sorry. You have every right to be angry with me."

He apologizes about a million times as he leads me out the front door. Like I'm his experiment gone wrong, a big bad Fagenstein monster that can't be controlled.

Instead of good-bye, I say, "You might like it if you tried it."

He looks at me, just outside his front door. He rolls his eyes and says, "I think you're the one who should get used to hearing that."

On the bus ride home I realize Chuck's gone for good, even if he lived right next door.

# 7

# MY BIGGEST PROBLEM

There's a FOR SALE sign in our front yard. The ground's too hard to dig, so a pile of old snow keeps it up. Inside, Jackie Shaw and Dad are taking inventory. Jackie Shaw smiles when she sees me, like I'm her kid. She's the reason I'm here, she said she really wanted to see me before they took off for Alaska. "Kevin! I haven't seen you since the big news! Now make my day and tell me that you're going to come with us."

I like Jackie Shaw, and I feel sorry for her when I think of the two of them stuck on the shores of the Arctic together. "Thanks, but I'm gonna stay here."

Jackie Shaw bargains with me. She says, "Why not finish up the school year in Barrow? Then you can decide what's next for you. You might even love it up there."

Dad says, "Don't waste your time, Jackie. Kevin's stubborn as a mule; the more you ask him to do something, the more he won't do it."

His tone's nasty, and it stops the conversation dead for a few minutes. To smooth things over, Jackie Shaw says, "So you'll live with your Aunt Nora? I haven't met her, is she nice?"

"She's cool."

Dad says, "She's a big pain in the ass is what she is. Never has a good word to say about anyone."

Jackie Shaw says, "Pat, please don't talk like that. You two don't want to fight now, not when you won't be seeing each other again for a long time."

Dad shoots Jackie Shaw a look, his don't-tell-me-how-to-run-my-life look. She shoots him one right back, her don't-you-dare-give-me-that-look look.

Better get used to his looks, Jackie Shaw, he's got plenty more where that came from.

Then I think: They go weeks up in Barrow with it always being dark. Dad can get really drunk in the dark, and stay drunk a lot longer.

Jackie Shaw stands right next to me and whispers in my ear, "I think your dad has the jitters, that's all."

I whisper back to her, "I think my dad's a big dick, that's all."

She pulls back and looks at me, like she doesn't know what to do. Then she laughs. She says, "Come with me, Kevin, I've got a little something I want to give you."

We leave Dad in the kitchen staring at dishes. Jackie Shaw grabs her purse and tells me to sit down on the couch. She sits right next to me and says, "Pat told me that you don't want to go. I can understand that you don't want to leave your girlfriend—"

I cringe.

"—and you don't want to miss out on the rest of your senior year. But I just worry about you. You're so young to have so many changes in your life."

I shrug.

She sits next to me. "When I was your age I had two parents who loved each other and the future seemed very bright. I wish you had that."

"I'm okay," I tell her, a little pissed that she thinks I'm such a loser.

"You're better than okay, Kevin. I just wish things were easier for you, that's all I mean. It's not much, but maybe this will help."

She hands me a card. I look at her, not sure if she wants me to open it in front of her. She smiles and nods at me.

It's Snoopy and Woodstock on his doghouse. Snoopy's in his Joe Cool outfit. It says something stupid, but then I open it and two one-hundred-dollar bills fall out. Cash in my hands, just like on my birthday, the one when we buried Mom.

I look at her.

"It's not as much as I wish it could be, but it should help a little when you break out on your own."

I look at the money again, and then back at her.

She puts a hand on my knee. "You know, I wish you were my own son, Kevin. I understand that I'll never take the place of your mother, and I'd never try to. This is just my way of saying thanks for being so wonderful about me and your dad. And if you ever need anything, anything at all, you just ask, it's yours."

I say, "I can't take your money," but I think: She's gonna let me keep it.

"You're not taking anything, I want you to have it. Think of it as a late birthday present and early graduation present all wrapped up in one."

"How did you know about my birthday?"

She shakes her head and looks at her hand on my knee. "Your dad told me. He had had a miserable day at work and nearly forgot all about it. He told me he gave you a pizza on your eighteenth birthday. He was sick about it."

I don't say anything.

"There's one more thing I have for you." She reaches in her purse again, and this time she pulls out a set of car keys and puts them in my hand. "It was my husband's car, I never had the heart to get rid of it. We aren't going to haul three cars up to Barrow; we won't even need two. So I thought you could have this one. It's nothing special, just an old Dodge Dart, but it runs okay."

I stare at the keys. "I dunno what to say. This is way too much."

She winks at me. "You're a good boy—excuse me, a good young man. Your mom isn't here to help you get started, so I'm happy to pinch-hit. It's the least I can do."

I hug her, hard. And she hugs me back and says, "You're going to be fine, just you wait and see. Now do me a favor and move back into this house and be with your father while you can."

I groan. "Okay." Then I ask her, real quiet, "Are you sure you're doing the right thing?" She knows I mean going to Barrow with Dad, not giving me the gifts.

She whispers, "I know it must seem crazy, your dad and I have only been together a short while. But if Randy's death taught me anything, it's that life's short. I know it's nuts, it's impulsive, I haven't thought it through at all. But sometimes, Kevin, you just have to say 'what the heck?' and take a chance."

She pulls away and looks at me. I say, "And what if it doesn't work out? What if you're wrong about him?"

She says, like she couldn't possibly be wrong about him, "Then I'll know I tried. I won't be an old woman wondering 'what if.' I won't regret what I didn't do. That's important too. Not second-guessing yourself. Because you can make up this whole life based on what you didn't do. And it's always a wonderful life, better than the one you have."

I think about it for a couple of seconds. Then I say, "Yeah, but it's my dad we're talking about."

I honk the horn outside of Tommy's house. Mrs. Grabowski makes it outside before he does. She's got a sweater over her shoulders and she's hugging herself, shivering in the cold. I roll down the window and wave my hand over the car like I'm Carol Merrill on *Let's Make a Deal*. She smiles and says, "So this is the new chariot, huh? Very sharp, Kevin, very sharp."

"Wanna peel some rubber, Mrs. Gee?"

She laughs and says, "Oh, now, you don't want to be seen with some fat old broad like me."

"Jeez, Mrs. Gee, you're not old."

She laughs again and says, "That mouth of yours is going to get you in trouble."

Tommy shows up in his army jacket and flap hat. "What's the matter, Mom, never seen a car before?"

She says, "Just showing an interest in my son and his friends. I'll stay in my room from now on so nobody will have to see you with your unhip mother."

He gets in the car and says, "Promise?"

Mrs. Grabowski tells me, "You don't have to bring him back. In fact, I'd rather you didn't."

We drive up to Central Avenue and Tommy says, "Not bad for a Dart. Sounds like the carburetor needs adjusting, but nothing major."

I say, "Your mom's cool."

Tommy pretends he didn't hear me, but then he says, "Yeah, I know."

"You tell her she's gonna be a grandmother?"

Tommy says, "Of course not, what do I look like, the world's biggest fucking moron?"

"Relax, just asking."

He looks at me, all serious-like. "She doesn't know, and you're not gonna tell her, all right?"

I don't answer right away; I want him to remember that I'm alpha. So I say, like I'm doing him a huge favor, "Cool, I'll keep it shut."

We drive to Shinders, a store downtown that sells papers and magazines and stuff. Shinders also has these really cool posters; it's where I buy all of mine. Tommy and I are flipping through the racks when he says, "How's Allison?"

She's one of those things I would forget about, except that I see her every day at school and we make out by her locker. She keeps waiting for me to ask her out someplace, but I never do. So she has to. I go 'cause people would think it was weird if I said no.

I tell Tommy, "She's cool."

He says, "Jon Thompson's making out like you stole her from him."

I look at the poster of Peter Frampton without his shirt on. "That's his problem."

Tommy looks at Frampton and says, "If I hear 'Baby I Love Your Way' one more time, I'm gonna blow my brains out."

The next poster is Adrienne Barbeau and her boobs. Tommy says, "Flip to the next one, it hurts just to look at her tits."

I move on, but Tommy flips it back to Adrienne Barbeau. "Man, she's got tits! Fuck! I could suck her tits all day and night and still want more."

There's this thing that guys do. Maybe girls talk about guys this way too; I don't hang with any so I don't know. Guys talk about tits in this really weird way that makes them sound so goddamn desperate. It's like they think if they talk about tits enough, they've had some. Tommy does the squeezy-squeezy thing with his hands. His face gets all red.

He says, like saying it means he's doing it, "Jesus, I wanna squeeze her fucking tits . . ."

There was this nature film we had to watch in biology class about birds and how they mate. This one kind of bird does a funky dance for the female. He hops all over the place like he's mental. You could make the same exact film right now with Tommy bouncing around Shinders on his dick like it's a pogo stick. This stuff must be in the blood; nobody in their right mind could have thought it up. It's like God has this really sick sense of humor. And I'm not just talking about boys who like girls; I mean everybody.

Tommy's going nuts over a couple of boobs with the nips covered up, so I say, "Think she'd have your baby too?"

Tommy says, "You know, fuck you, alright?"

I smack him lightly on the side of his head. "Just kidding, jeez. Kind of touchy there, pops."

Tommy flips to the next poster, one of Jackson Browne playing a guitar in concert. Tommy says, "I like his stuff, but he really can't sing very good."

He could sing like a cat on fire and I'd buy tickets. He's got this thing going on with his lips that makes me want to jump around like Tommy just did.

Tommy says, "You heard Cheap Trick's coming to the civic center?"

"We're there."

"Cool."

Tommy looks at a poster of Dolly Parton in a pile of hay like she's Daisy Mae. He says, "You know—"

I say, "Yeah, I know."


Lorraine's kind of bummed out when I show up for my shift, but it's not like that's anything new. I say, "What's the problem?"

She says, "Not a thing."

So I leave it at that. She reads *People* and *Time* and the *Enquirer* while I check out the people coming through the sliding doors, waiting for that one foxy guy who sees me and smiles.

But just like every other night, he doesn't show up. There's couples, men and women, who rush in out of the cold, laughing. They can kiss and hug each other, and people smile. They can hold hands, and people will say, "Isn't that sweet." I wonder what it would be like if I ever found the man of my dreams. I wonder what would happen if I walked down Central Avenue hand in hand with my boyfriend. I wonder how long it would take the people in their cars to stop and scream at us. I wonder what we would do when the men and women ran out of the bars and stood in our way, screaming "Faggots!" like they were screaming "Rape!"

I wonder what it'd be like to walk down the aisle with a man. It's not that different, you know? Instead of a woman, there's a man, and you promise to love him, to honor him, to cherish him, in sickness and in health, till death do you part. I mean, it's been done a million times, right? So what would be so weird about a man saying all the same stuff to another man?

Everything. Everything would be weird. And that's just the way it is.

Lorraine puts down the *Enquirer* and asks me, "You ever get lonesome?"

I laugh 'cause it's an embarrassing question and besides, she's hit a nerve. But she's dead serious, so I say, "Yeah, I guess."

She smirks and closes her eyes. "Of course you don't get lonesome. You're young and have all the girls after you. Must be tough."

Lorraine's blue. It happens a lot. I have a bunch of stuff I usually say to her, like, *Any man would be lucky to get you* or *There's somebody out there for you, you just haven't met him yet.* Tonight I say, "Are you afraid of winding up by yourself?"

Her eyes open and she frowns, surprised that I haven't whipped out one of my standard clichés. "Yes, it scares me half to death. I'm scared that I've run out of time. I'm forty-three years old."

She's old. "That's not old."

"Oh, Kevin, yes it is. If you're a single woman, forty-three is pretty darn old. Any day now I won't be able to have babies. And the men out there, well, don't get me started."

"All the good ones are taken," I say for her.

"That's right, they are." She's quiet for a minute, but then she decides she has to let me know again how unfair life is. "You'll always have women coming round. If you were plain, you'd have to wait till you were older to get the ladies. But you're handsome, so they'll be there for the taking your entire life. When you're older you can lose all your hair and gain a ton of weight, but the women will still want you, 'cause they're older too. And that's the worst thing that can happen to a woman."

Lorraine's really blue. "There are worse things that can happen to a person," I say.

"Like what?"

I leave it at that.

When I get home from my shift at Red Owl I see Mrs. Gunderson's Cordoba parked in front of our house. I park the Dart right behind it and check for the dent just to make sure it's really hers. Then I run inside and find Dad and Mrs. Gunderson on the couch, holding hands. Mrs. Gunderson's been crying and wipes her nose with a Kleenex.

She looks up at me and says, "Good evening, Kevin."

She's inside our house. She's sitting on the same couch Mom sat on. "What the hell are *you* doing here?"

Dad says, "Don't be like that, Kevin. Be polite for once in your life."

Mrs. Gunderson says, 'cause she's a brazen article, "Pat and I have been talking about his move to Alaska. And about us."

I glare at her, sitting on the couch that Mom used to sit on. "Jackie Shaw's going to Alaska with Dad, not you. They leave on Saturday."

Dad looks at me all timid and says, "Nobody's going anywhere. Barrow's off."

He *is* the stupidest person I know. Guess what, Kevin, I'm moving to Alaska. Guess what, Kevin, I'm not moving to Alaska. Guess what, Kevin, I don't fucking know what I'm fucking doing. "What are you talking about? You just sold the house! You bought plane tickets. You've shipped half your shit up there already!"

Dad says, "You'll still need to move in with Aunt Nora. I'm going to live with Carol."

That's what you got to love about Dad, he's got a million of 'em. He's killing me. "What the hell?"

He stands up and puts his hand on Mrs. Gunderson's shoulder. "Carol and I have had a long talk about everything that's happened. We've decided we're going to try again. We're going to make a fresh start of it."

*Jesus Christ.* "What about Jackie Shaw?"

Dad says softly, like he's telling his best friend a secret, "I'm going to talk to Jackie tomorrow. I know this is going to hurt her, but I'm going to do what I want for a change."

Mom used to say, *You're the only person who can't smell your own stink.* "What do you mean 'for a change'? You always do what you want! You gotta be kidding me, this is a joke, right?"

Mrs. Gunderson pats my dad's hand and has the balls to say, "It's not a joke, Kevin. Your father and I still love each other, and we're not going to apologize for it anymore. We broke up for all the wrong reasons—what other people would think, guilt over your mother's accident—but we're not going to make that mistake twice. I'm sorry that you find this upsetting. In time I hope you'll understand; maybe even be happy for us."

I laugh. "Yeah, *that's* gonna happen. You just love being the other woman, don't you? You can't stand to see him with anybody else!"

Dad looks at Mrs. Gunderson and his face changes, becomes all lovey-dovey like. He says, "Don't speak to her like that. Carol's going to be your stepmother. You two are going to have to bury the hatchet. If she's willing to give it a try after what you did to her, then I think you should be man enough to try too."

I should be man enough? What, now I gotta love this . . . Mrs. Gunderson to prove I'm a man? "*She* is not gonna be my stepmother. Even if you get married she won't be my stepmother 'cause you were never a real father to me anyway."

Mrs. Gunderson's really stupid, almost as stupid as he is, so she says, "You know that's not true. Your father loves you very much. You have no idea the sacrifices he's made for you over the years."

My voice cracks, which pisses me off, I don't want them to think I'm gonna cry or anything. "He was no father, just a big lump of nothing that sat on the couch and fucked you once a week."

I think Dad's gonna get up and hit me, but he doesn't, maybe 'cause he knows I can take him now. Or maybe 'cause Mrs. Gunderson's here going on and on about what a great father he is. Dad says, "A good father goes to a job he hates every day for eighteen years because he has to feed his family. A good father tries to stick it out with a woman he doesn't love anymore for his son's sake. A good father almost walked away from the best thing that ever happened to him just so his son wouldn't get upset. Eileen was a good mother, but I was a good father too. You want to know why I tied one on so often? To kill the pain, that's why. So don't you ever tell me that I wasn't a good father to you."

I feel like I'm choking on fire. "You were gonna leave us. You were just gonna take off with . . . her."

Dad uses his let's-be-adults tone and says, "I was desperate, I was at the end of my rope. You should thank Carol; she's the one who made me see sense. I was panicking, alright? I was getting older and nothing was changing for me. I wanted out. But you know what? I didn't leave. I stayed right here. And you know why? Because Carol had a responsibility to her niece and she helped me remember mine."

Oh, yeah, you can even lie to yourself now. You believe what you just said. "So we're giving up the house for nothing. Jackie Shaw quit her job for nothing. She turned herself upside down so you could go back to *her*?"

Dad says, "I can't keep up with a mortgage when I'm out of work, you know that. And you wanted to move out anyway, so what's the problem?"

"What about Jackie Shaw? What about the promises you made her?"

Mrs. Gunderson says, like she belongs here, like she's the wise and loving mother, "Pat, he needs time to get used to this. We're not going to work it out tonight."

I mutter, "No shit, Sherlock."

They stand up and she hugs him right in front of me, in our house, the house my mom lived in. "I should really get home and explain things to Laurie." She kisses him, like she owns the place, and says, "Kevin, I know you're very fond of Jackie, but in the long run, you'll see that we're actually doing her a favor."

"Christ, I can see that right now. She's too good for him."

She smiles sadly at me like she's some sort of Christian martyr suffering for the one true faith. When she walks past me I say, "You should have stayed the hell away from us."

Dad barks, "Kevin, shut it."

Oooh, protecting his woman like he's a big man.

But she's such a goddamn saint, she closes her eyes and says, "Pat, please. He needs time."

"This isn't over," I tell her, and I mean it, I'm not done, not by a long shot.

She shakes her dumb-ass head and she's out the door, on her way to have her little talk with Laurie Lindstrom. Guess what, honey, she'll tell her, a dumb fucking loser without a job is moving in with us. He likes to get shit-faced and screw around. Won't that be fun?

I sit down in the big chair, the one Mom used to sit in when she did her knitting or watched her stories.

I say, "I'm moving to Aunt Nora's tomorrow. I'm not hanging around here."

Dad sits back down on the couch. "Someday you'll understand that this is for the best."

"Why did you take the job in Barrow? Why did you lead Jackie Shaw on?"

"I was going to go through with it because we needed the money, and I didn't want to go by myself. But then Carol called me after she heard the news. Barrow was the wake-up call we both needed to get back together. I wish you could be happy for me."

I close my eyes. "Yeah, right."

"You know, punishing me every second of every hour won't bring your mother back."

"Leave me alone."

He says, "You get this stubborn streak from your mother's side of the family. They all hang on to their grudges like they're diamonds. It makes you very immature for your age."

I open my eyes again and look at him, so smug, so sure he's doing the right thing. "You can't believe that it was an accident. Did you ever really think it was?"

He says, without missing a beat, "I don't know that it wasn't an accident, Kevin, honest to God, I do not know. But I gotta tell you, if she did do it on purpose, then it was her decision. Hers and hers alone, nobody made her do it, it was her choice. I'd like to think it was an accident because I can't believe she would do that to you. To me, maybe. But not to you."

I look at him, not like I hate him, I'm too zonked for that. I'm about to say that maybe she felt she didn't have a choice. Maybe she needed help but we were too goddamn stupid to know it. But instead I say, "Good night."

"Good night, Kevin."

Jon's not waiting for me in my bedroom.

So I say to myself, Your father's a dick.

And I say to myself, This is gonna kill Jackie Shaw.

And I think, I should give the car back. And the money. And I should tell her that he's not worth crying about, I don't.

That's when Jon finally shows and says, *Of course you do. You're such a rotten liar.*


Tommy's followed me over to Jackie Shaw's house. He waits outside in the Challenger while I go up to the door. I ring the bell about a million times, but there's no answer. I know she's home; her other car, a Duster, is parked out back in the alley. I checked.

Tommy honks the horn twice. He rolls down the window and shouts, "She's not home, man! Just toss the keys down the mail slot. I don't wanna wait out here all day."

I put the keys through first and then push an envelope with two one-hundred-dollar bills inside. One of the bills is the one Dad gave me the day of Mom's funeral.

When I'm halfway down her walk, I hear the front door open. I turn around and see her in a bathrobe, a weird look on her face, like maybe she's dead but doesn't know it. I say, "Hey, Mrs. Shaw. I didn't think you were home."

She has the keys to the Dart in one hand and the money in the other. She says, "You shouldn't have bothered."

The way she says it you know that she doesn't care. I mean she *really* doesn't give a shit, it makes absolutely no difference to her if I kept the car or gave it back, if I returned her money or used it to wipe my ass. It's kind of freaky.

Tommy's out of his car and standing next to me. He asks her, "You okay? You don't look so good."

She kind of sways there in the wind. She knows she's met him but she can't quite place him.

I say, "Mrs. Shaw, can I come in for a minute?"

She doesn't say anything, just goes back in the house, leaving the front door open.

Tommy says, "Let's bolt, she's pretty out of it, man. Give her a couple of days, she'll bounce back."

"Wait for me, okay?"

Tommy just nods like I'm the slow cousin.

I stamp my feet in the entryway and pull off my boots so I won't track in snow. I expect her house to be a mess 'cause Dad dumped her, but it isn't, it's clean, cleaner than our house has ever been. Even when Mom was alive. The only mess is Jackie Shaw, who sits on her couch with a blanket pulled over her.

"Heard any good jokes lately?" I ask her.

She tries to smile at me but it doesn't look right.

"I'm really sorry my dad's a dick."

Now she smiles.

"A really big dick," I say, hoping for a laugh.

But the smile's gone, and she has this kind of glazed look like she's made of wax or something.

"Can I sit down?"

She nods a little bit.

I sit on the couch with her, and we're both staring straight ahead, at nothing. She says, real quiet, "I've made a big fool of myself. If Randy were alive I'd still be able to look myself in the mirror. But Randy's gone and this is what I do. Throw myself at some bastard who can't hold a candle to him. I've betrayed Randy, you know? I've spit on what he and I had. Your dad asks me to quit my job and move up to the north pole with him, and I say, Okey-dokey. Here, let me pay for our tickets. Here, let me sell your house for you. Here, take everything I have. And then dump me for the one you were cheating on your wife with."

She looks over at me now, like I've just come into focus. She says in a normal voice, "I'm so ashamed of myself. I used to be one smart cookie. I can't believe I let this happen. Now I'm back at zero. And it's all my fault."

I feel my eyes water 'cause I really like this woman. "It's not your fault, it's my dad's. He lies all the time. Well, maybe not lie exactly, I guess he means it when he says it. He just doesn't know what he wants, and it screws everything up for everybody else."

"Well, you're right about that," Jackie Shaw says. "You're right about that."

I look around the room. "You didn't sell your house too, did you?"

She smiles and says, "I had it on the market, but nobody was interested. Story of my life since Randy died."

"Can you get your job back?"

"Even if I could, I don't want it back. I made such a big deal of going off with your father that I couldn't face those people again. I was really going on, letting everybody know that I had found love not just once, but twice. Vanity. I was vain. I'll find something else. Eventually. In the meantime I'm going to be the world's oldest Kelly Girl."

I laugh 'cause even when she's bummed out, she's funny. "You're too good for Dad. I bet you twenty bucks that he dumps Mrs. Gunderson in less than a year."

Jackie Shaw sighs, musses up my hair, and says, "Tell you what. If he lasts a year with her then you have to give the car back. And the two hundred bucks. If he leaves her before a year is up, you keep it all."

I like those odds.


Laurie Lindstrom has decided it would be a good idea for all of us to have dinner together—her aunt, my dad, me, and her. I think it's a real dumb-ass idea, but she nags me about it every day at school until I finally say yeah, I'll come to your goddamn dinner, shut the hell up about it already.

Allison gets weird 'cause she thinks it's like a date. I tell her that: (1) it's Laurie Lindstrom, for Christ's sake, and (2) my dad's shacking up with her aunt. Laurie's like a step-cousin or something, that is, if Dad and Mrs. Gunderson were actually married, which they're not, thank you, baby Jesus.

The night of the dinner, Aunt Nora paces in front of the window like a caged bear. She mutters, "Shameless! Completely shameless! That fuck, I'll end his miserable life myself."

Jackie Shaw would buy tickets to that.

I look at the clock, next to the glow-in-the-dark Jesus. Dad's late; he must be circling, trying to figure out how to duck Aunt Nora. But he winds up being smarter than that. It isn't him that honks the horn outside. It's Mrs. Gunderson, sitting in her Cordoba with her niece, Laurie, who she's brought along as protection, I guess, or maybe as a witness, in case the cops are called. She probably thinks that Aunt Nora will behave herself in front of Laurie. She doesn't know Aunt Nora.

Before I can even grab my coat, Aunt Nora's out the door. "Ya cheap whore! How dare you show your painted face here!"

I make it to the front stoop and see Laurie, who looks like she's just seen Sister Rita take a dump in a big pot of homeless soup. Mrs. Gunderson drives away before Aunt Nora can reach the car so now I don't have a ride to dinner. Yeah, I could take the Dart, but driving Jackie Shaw's dead husband's car over to Mrs. Gunderson's house seems really wrong. Besides, it might pull a *Christine* and run Dad over.

Aunt Nora's doing a little victory dance. "That's right, run, ya coward! Murderer! Whore! You just wait till I get my hands on ya! Then you'll know what it means to be sorry! I'll make you sorry you were ever born!"

But Mrs. Gunderson fools us; she's only gone around the block. When her car comes round again, she's honking the horn and pointing straight ahead, like I should run up to the intersection and jump in before Aunt Nora can catch us. Aunt Nora is even more pissed off somehow, like steam-coming-out-of-her-ears pissed off, the kind you see in cartoons.

"Mother of God, you aren't taking this poor lad to your whorehouse," she screams at the Cordoba.

I stay put; I wouldn't run after Laurie Lindstrom and Mrs. Gunderson even if you paid me cash money.

Laurie waves like a spaz as they pass, but I just shrug my shoulders like I'm saying, *What can I do?*

Aunt Nora screams, "That's right, keep going, if you want to save your worthless hide!"

Aunt Nora's Iranian neighbor is looking out his window. He sees me and taps on the glass but I can't figure out what he's trying to tell me. Keep it down? I've called the police? Don't worry, she always does this?

Aunt Nora heads back up the walk. "That's the last we'll see of her, I reckon."

But she's wrong again. The Cordoba comes round a third time, so Aunt Nora grabs a snow shovel and runs out into the street. "Go on, leave, before I kill the lot of ya!"

Mrs. Gunderson rolls down her window and screams, "Kevin, you get in this car right now! Laurie's scared half to death!"

Oh, yeah, some psychos murdered Laurie's parents. By beating them to death.

Aunt Nora manages to get in a few licks with the shovel on the car's rear bumper. "Shaggin' bitch, peddle your wares somewhere else!"

Carol Gunderson's honking the horn and screaming at Aunt Nora and Laurie's hands are over her ears. She looks like she's praying.

Aunt Nora hits the rear windshield with the shovel and I think, Wouldn't it be funny if Mrs. Gunderson had to have it replaced again? But then I think, Aunt Nora doesn't deserve this. She doesn't deserve to see the woman her brother-in-law was screwing around with drive away with her sister's only child.

I run over to Aunt Nora and hug her from behind. "It's cool, calm down, okay, calm down, please."

Aunt Nora speaks in tongues for a minute, maybe more, but then she's too beat to go on, like she's just had really great sex, not that I would know what that's like.

The Cordoba pulls ahead and sits idling halfway up the block; Aunt Nora idles in my arms.

"I probably should go," I tell her. "Don't worry, I'll make it miserable for everybody."

But Aunt Nora doesn't laugh. She drops her shovel and starts crying, really hard, and it surprises me. "She thinks she can just come here and . . . after what she did to my poor little Eileen . . . oh, God, there's no justice, there's no justice at tall."

I kiss her on the back of her man head and say, "Aunt Nora, come on, it's okay."

She's sobbing as she says, "Do you remember when your mother sat out on the porch in the freezing cold, looking at the snow?"

"Yeah."

She gasps, trying to catch her breath. "She was waiting for him. To come back to her. To leave that woman and come home. He was gone for an entire week once, that week she told you he was on a business trip. *A business trip!* Since when do they send the plant lackey on a business trip?"

She collapses but she doesn't fall over, 'cause I'm holding on to her really tight. It's like her body just gives up. She moans real quiet-like and says, "What does it matter? The damage is done. What does anything matter anymore?"

I whisper in her ear something she's said to me whenever I was really mad. "Offer it up."

Aunt Nora stands straight, wipes her eyes, and pulls my arms off her. She sniffs and says, "You go, then. I need a mass."

Aunt Nora says *I need a mass* like other people say *I need a drink.*

I leave her there, standing on the curb, staring at the dirty snow. I know what she feels like, she feels like there's nothing she can do. She feels powerless.

I get in Mrs. Gunderson's Cordoba and Laurie's going mental. "Ohmigod, that was your aunt? Is she crazy? Was she really trying to kill us?"

I stretch out over the backseat, my boots on the upholstery. "Yeah, that's my aunt. No, she's not crazy. She wasn't trying to kill you." I nod in Mrs. Gunderson's direction and say, "She was trying to kill her."

Laurie's going nuts the whole ride over to the Gunderson place, and her aunt is trying to get her to take deep breaths.

Laurie keeps asking, "Why? Why is she so mad at Aunt Carol?"

So I tell her. " 'Cause your Aunt Carol was screwing my dad while my mom was still alive, that's why. She thinks my mom's death was no accident, that it was all your aunt's fault."

Mrs. Gunderson slams the brakes and Laurie almost smashes her head on the dashboard. I fall in between the seats and bang my arm on an ice scraper. Mrs. Gunderson turns her head all the way around like Linda Blair in *The Exorcist* and screams, "That's enough, do you understand me?"

Laurie starts crying.

"What? Am I lying? Tell me I'm lying!" I grab my arm and climb back up on the seat.

Mrs. Gunderson screams so loud that Laurie puts her hands over her ears and sobs. "I am not going to spend the rest of my life hearing about this! The only one who knows what happened to Eileen Doyle is Eileen Doyle! Nobody else! If she made up her mind to do it, then don't blame me!"

I flip her the bird and shout, "Shut the hell up! You don't talk about my mom!"

Laurie's whimpering, "Please stop! Please!"

Mrs. Gunderson takes a swipe at my finger, but I move too fast and she misses by a mile. I say, "Don't touch me, I don't want the clap."

Now she's even more pissed off than Aunt Nora was. "You may think you're a big man but you're just a petty little boy! A nasty, petty, ungrateful, spoiled little boy! Do you hear me?"

Laurie's crying hard now, she says, "Stop," sob-sob-sob, "please, stop it."

Every once in a while Aunt Nora calls other women cows. There are selfish cows and mean cows and bitter cows. So I say to Mrs. Gunderson what Aunt Nora would say if she were here, "Shut your ugly hole, ya miserable old cow!"

That's when we notice the cars behind us leaning on their horns. The miserable old cow and I eye each other, but then she turns around and starts driving again. You can almost see the steam coming off the top of her head. She says to herself, loud enough for me to hear, "I don't know why your father even bothers."

The rest of the ride's quiet, except for Laurie's little whimpers. Oh, and once in a while I go, "Moo."

When we get to the cow's house Laurie shoves past me, bolts up the stairs, and slams her door.

Dad puts down the paper. "What's the matter with her?"

That's when the miserable old cow comes in and answers for me: "*He's* what's the matter with her! He told her that I killed Eileen!"

Dad drops his paper on the floor and stands up. "For Christ's sake, I knew this dinner was a stupid idea! I need a drink."

The miserable old cow shouts at his back, "So do I."

"Me too," I say.

The miserable old cow sits in an ugly worn chair with her coat still on, like it's armor. I sit on the nasty old couch where they've probably had sex a million times. I keep my coat on, 'cause I don't want any part of me touching any part of the couch that touched any part of them while they were doing it.

When Dad comes back he's carrying three little glasses of whiskey, no ice. He gives one to the heifer, one to me, and then he sits down next to me on the couch with his own glass.

The cow downs hers like a sailor and says to Dad, "Your sister-in-law's a lunatic, they should put her in an institution."

Dad takes a sip and says real low, "Tell me something I don't know."

Mrs. Gunderson goes "Ahhh" and leans her head back against her gross, rotting chair like she's gone twenty rounds with Mohammed Ali.

Dad and I finish our whiskey and I want more. But Dad says, "That's more than enough for you. Go upstairs and apologize to Laurie. And tell her to come down for dinner."

It's then that I notice the smell of spaghetti sauce. I'm hungry so I take off my coat, head up the steps that need sweeping, and pound on the first door I see.

From behind a wall, I hear Laurie say real loud, "That's a closet. I'm the next door over."

I fold my arms and look at the floor. "Come out and eat dinner."

Her muffled voice tells me, "Your aunt's a maniac."

"And yours is a slut. Come on, I'm starving."

A few seconds pass before I hear, "Just give me a minute."

I don't. I open the door to her room and that's when I see them, Jesus Christs all over the place, like wallpaper. "Christ Almighty, you got enough of those or what?"

Laurie's sitting on her bed with a box of Kleenex. "You don't have to take the Lord's name in vain."

I roll my eyes. "Give me a break, okay?"

Laurie blows her little pink nose and says, "Jesus Christ is my Lord and personal savior."

I make a face. "I thought only Protestants went in for that born-again bullshit."

I might as well of been the one who killed her parents for the look she gives me. "It is not BS, and Catholics can be born again in Christ too, you know."

Yeah, right. "Fine, let's eat."

She wipes her eyes with her palms and clears her throat a little. "Okay."

I follow her down to the sitting room where the cow's still in her coat, stuffed in her chair like the corpse at a wake.

Laurie kneels down beside her and takes her free hand, the one without the empty whiskey glass in it. She says, her voice hushed, "Aunt Carol, are you all right?"

The cow says with her eyes closed, "I'm fine, honey, please don't worry about me."

Yeah. Aunt Nora always says, *You need only worry about the clever ones, God looks after the ignorant.*

Dad yells from the kitchen, like we're the Brady Bunch instead of the Manson family, "Come and get it."

The cow barely manages to lift her lazy old ass off the chair and shuffle into the kitchen behind her niece who loves Jesus the way other girls love Shaun Cassidy.

We sit around a little table with a green Formica top. Dad puts a pot full of noodles on a little cutting board and says, "Dig in."

Laurie says, "We have to give thanks first."

"Oh, right," Dad says, like he's still getting used to this whole religion thing.

Laurie closes her eyes and holds up her hands. Dad takes one and looks at me, nodding toward Laurie's other hand. I shake my head, but then he makes his eyes really big so I cave. Just when you think things can't get any worse, you're holding hands with Laurie Lindstrom. To pray. To God.

The miserable old cow reaches for my other hand with her free hoof but I pull away. She doesn't bother trying again.

Laurie says, "In your name, Jesus, we offer you another day, another opportunity to know your love and forgiveness, another chance to walk in your footsteps. We ask for your blessings, Jesus, the *activist* Jesus who walked with the lepers. The Jesus who affirms the dignity of all men and women of all races and colors."

Jeez, she's become Sister Rita Junior too. Like her life wasn't mental enough already. I sneak a look at Dad who's trying not to laugh.

"Amen," the cow moos, like she isn't an adulterer or a murderer.

Dad says, "Let's dig in," like he isn't the biggest dick who ever lived.

We pile pasta and sauce on our plates in silence. Next we eat in silence, and then we just sit there in silence.

The cow finally moos, "That was delicious, Pat."

I choke. "*You* made dinner?"

Dad smiles a little bit and says—pretending like he's said it a hundred times before—"Yep, my world-famous spaghetti and meatballs."

I tell the cow and Sister Rita Jr., "He never made it for us."

Then we're quiet again until Laurie says, "I made dessert. Are folks ready for it now or do you want to let your food settle first?"

I say to Dad, 'cause I still can't believe it, "You cooked something that wasn't grilled?"

Dad says for Laurie's and the cow's sake, "Kevin's always teasing me."

The cow says, "Oh, he's quite the kidder, isn't he?"

I snort and say, like Aunt Nora would if she were here, "And you're quite the—"

But I don't get to finish 'cause Dad smacks me on the back of my head.


Living at Aunt Nora's isn't as bad as I thought it would be. She's scared shitless that I won't like it here, so she goes out of her way to be extra nice to me. Basically, I can do whatever I want, which, if you think about it, is the way it should be, since I'm eighteen now and old enough to die in a war.

My biggest problem is where to hide my *Playgirls*. I tossed the *Advocate* that Chuck bought me; it was boring. I decide to stash the *Playgirls* in my locker at school.

Aunt Nora always asks me what I'd like for dinner, something Dad never did. She's happy to drive over to McDonald's and get me a couple of Big Macs with large fries and a chocolate shake that I wash down with a large coke.

She tells me, "Someday you won't be able to eat whatever you please. You'll be worried about getting big and fat. It seems everyone in this country is big and fat. Not like back in Ireland."

I just chew and look at her.

She always tells me, "Ironic, isn't it? So many Irish came here because of the famine, and now every Yank you see is the size of a house! Soon the whole country won't be big enough for them."

There's this thing about people from another generation. They resent you, whether they admit it or not. They're jealous 'cause things seem so much easier today than when they were young. Like I wanted them all to die in Ireland, or Korea, or Vietnam. Stupid, 'cause all I want is to be left the hell alone.

She takes a bite out of her fish sandwich and says, "You're very lucky to be young now. There was a time when a lad your age didn't stand much of a chance."

Because Aunt Nora will do just about anything to please me, I listen to her tirades. She seems better after she rants and raves about abortion, Dad, the filthy English, and cheap American women. After she calms down, she looks at me, winks, and says, "Ah, I do go on. You're lovely for putting up with me."

Aunt Nora has a sad little life, I think. She works at the Northwest Bank downtown, the one with the globe out front that changes colors to let you know what the weather's gonna do. She's been there forever, auditing each day's deposits and withdrawals, and scaring the shit out of the tellers. What money she makes pays the bills and then is divvied up between the missions and the orders and the pro-life groups. She goes to church every holy day of obligation, and sometimes twice on Sundays. And she watches TV when she isn't at work, at church, or asleep. She can tell you who the guest stars are this week on *Carol Burnett*, or why they changed cast members on *Barney Miller*. She'll tell you that she won't watch *All in the Family* 'cause all they do on that show is shout, and she's had enough of that to last her a lifetime.

And then she talks about her sister, Eileen, my mom.

Like the time Eileen choked on the heavenly host and had to spit it out. Everybody was afraid she'd go to hell.

Or the time Eileen fainted in the confessional. Everybody thought it was a judgment.

Or how angry Eileen got when she found out she couldn't be an altar boy 'cause she was a girl.

Aunt Nora has all these stories, but they don't really tell me anything new about Mom. That's what I want, almost as much as I want a guy. I want Mom to tell me something new.

The snow and ice are old, covered in rotting layers of salt and sand and dog shit and garbage. March is the ugliest month in this city, the time when the trees are bare, the ground a dirty mess of thawing and freezing and thawing and freezing. You know the worst of it is over, but so what? Yeah, the sun shines brighter and longer every day, but winter hangs on like a son of a bitch. Tighter than a drowning man trying to pull you under with him. Aunt Nora sits numb in front of her television till eleven each night, complaining that there's nothing on worth watching and why did they ever cancel *Lawrence Welk*?

I suppose you could say I'm unhappy. I swear to God that time's standing still, or maybe it just seems that way when all you can do is wait around for something good to happen. Nothing is changing for me; I still go out with Allison, praying she won't want to go all the way. I still get way too drunk with Tommy and Rick Foley and we say "fuck" a lot and talk about tits until I feel like I've grown some myself. I want to talk about something else, anything else, but cars and beer and tits are all that's on the menu. I want to talk about leaving for a place where a guy like me might stand a chance. Weird, huh? Mom came to the U.S. from Ireland for a better life and now I want to leave here for exactly the same reason.

When I shoot the shit with Tommy and Rick Foley I hope that we'll talk about something new. Like is there life on Mars, or how weird Jimmy Carter's family is. But everybody knows that real men don't talk about stuff like that, real men are dumb and proud of it. Guys who talk about the Milky Way or politics or cities they've never been to are faggots, even if they do it with girls.

So I'm already bumming when I find out that Dad and the miserable old cow are gonna get married. He tells me over the phone, right after Aunt Nora curses him out when she realizes who's on the other end of the line.

When I manage to get the phone away from her, Dad tells me, "We're not having a church wedding, since Carol's divorced and all. We're just going to go down to city hall, keep it simple, since it's the second time round for both of us. But we want you to be there."

Yeah, right. *She* wants me to be there.

"You can be my best man. Afterward we'll go someplace nice to eat. Maybe one of those fancy outdoor places on the Bloomington four-ninety-four strip if it's warm enough."

I don't say anything.

He says, "Laurie's going to be maid of honor. Come on, it'll be fun."

There's this part of me that doesn't know what I should do. Dad's alive and Mom's dead, so I'm probably gonna say okay to the one who can actually pick up a phone and call me. But lately I don't know if I should hate Dad more for being a dick, or if I should hate Mom more for trying to cross the Mississippi in a Ford Galaxy. I know that neither of them were perfect. I know that I'm a part of both of them. But, like, is the fact that they're my mom and dad enough to make me honor them? Like in the Bible? Maybe parents were different back then. Maybe they stayed together and loved each other. Maybe they were proud of their kids and paid attention to them. Or maybe the Bible days were

like March in Minnesota, a bunch of Jews and Romans and Sa-
maritans sitting around waiting for better times.

"Kevin, still there?"

"Yeah, yeah."

"So you'll do it? You'll be my best man?"

"I don't know."

"Come on, for your old man?"

As Mom would say, *You're not helping your case.*

I groan. "Okay."

"I guess I can't expect you to be excited about the wedding.
But thanks for standing up for me."

When I don't say anything, he says, "What's new with you?"

I say, "Not much."

"We want you to come over on Sunday to talk over some of
the details. And I want you to tell your Aunt Nora."

"Why me? You tell her."

"It would be better coming from you, don't you think?"

"No way. You want her to know, you tell her. I have to live
with her."

Allison thinks that Dad getting married is a good idea. She's hint-
ing around that she wants to be my date for the wedding. I tell
her, "They're not going to get married till May sometime."

She pouts. "I wish it were sooner, weddings are so much fun.
My sister's wedding was an absolute blast! I can't believe they
haven't set the date yet."

I pull the Dart in front of Allison's house. They live on the
first floor of a duplex and her parents rent the upstairs to a couple
of old ladies who play the TV too loud 'cause they're both deaf
as a post. "This isn't going to be a real wedding, they're just going
to have a judge do it. The only thing you can count on is that it
won't happen during *Baa Baa Black Sheep*." Dad's favorite show.

I lean in to kiss Allison good night but she says, "Come on in,
we've got the house to ourselves."

*Oh, crap.*

Our feet crunch on the ice that's melted and refrozen. She's at the door, putting her key in the lock, and I'm scared shitless that tonight's the night I'm going to have to try to go all the way.

The TV blares *M\*A\*S\*H* from upstairs so Allison plays a Fleetwood Mac album loud enough to drown out Hawkeye and Radar. She asks me, "Do you want something to drink?"

"A beer."

She shakes her head. "How about something different? I'm bored with beer and pop. I could make a pot of hot tea. Or maybe a glass of wine."

"Wine."

"Okay, I'll be right back. Take off your coat and stay awhile."

She saunters into the kitchen like she's a fox (she is) and I look down at my boots and the puddle of dirty water that grows beneath them. I shout, "Where are your parents?"

She shouts back to me, "They went up to Mille Lacs to take in the icehouse."

Gone all night, most likely. Her brothers are long gone, one in the army, the other in the navy.

She's back with some white wine in water glasses. I reach for one but she pulls back, frowning. "Are you cold or something?"

Oh, yeah, my coat. I take it off and the boots while I'm at it and I'm worried that my feet smell bad.

Allison hands me a glass. "Here's to us," she says, and she clinks hers against mine.

I take a gulp and crinkle my nose. "Tastes like grape juice with a bunch of sugar thrown in."

Allison sits on the couch, which her mother just had reupholstered. I've never seen the fabric, it's always covered up in blankets and sheets to keep it nice. Allison pats a cushion hidden by a comforter and says, "Have a seat, Kevin. You look like you just lost your best friend."

I sit next to her and put my arm around her shoulder, a little ritual of ours. She curls up against me, the top of her head pressed against my neck. She says, "You make me feel safe."

I take a sip of the sugar wine. "Yeah?"

She sighs. "Yeah. Sometimes I have dreams that we're doing exactly this, just sitting here holding each other. It's peaceful."

If it weren't for wondering how far I'm going to have to go, I wouldn't mind. Since Mom died, nobody touches me. I miss being touched. I give Allison a little squeeze and kiss her on the top of her head.

She puts an arm over my chest and says, "Have you decided for sure on the U?"

"I guess."

"You know, Wisconsin and Minnesota have residency reciprocity. You wouldn't have to pay any more to go to Madison."

I snicker. "I don't have the grades for Madison. And I bombed the SAT."

She thinks about it for a moment. I expect her to say: *Well, then, I'll just have to stay here and go to the U.* But she says, "I'm going to miss you. I'm going to miss this. And I'm going to miss all my friends. I'm kind of scared to leave Northeast, it's been such a blast. I wish it didn't have to end."

Do we live on the same planet? I should have guessed what was coming next. She says, in a real quiet voice, "Are you going to miss me?"

"Yeah." Sure, why not?

She giggles. I whisper, "What's so funny?"

She squeezes my arm. "You. I asked my mom how to get you to open up and talk more, but she told me not to bother, that you're doing me a favor."

I rub her hair with my cheek. "Why'd she say that?"

"She thinks that most women aren't really all that interested in what most men have to say."

Now I laugh. "Yeah?"

"She was having a bad day. She hates fishing and only went up to Mille Lacs to spend time with Dad. She wishes he'd talk about something other than his 'damn old rod and reel.' "

"Your mom's pretty smart."

She sighs and says with a straight face, "Tell me what you love."

I cringe; I'm mortified. "What?"

"Don't worry, I'm not waiting to hear that you love me. I want to know what you love. If it's cars or football, that's fine. You can talk to me about that stuff, I don't mind."

"I'm not in love with cars or football."

"What, then?"

"I loved my mom. It's harder to love her now, but I still do."

"Because she's dead?"

"That too."

Allison looks up at me, a serious look on her face. "What do you mean?"

"Nothing, forget it."

"No, come on. What did you mean?"

I want to say: *Because she left me with him.* Because the more I get to know him, the less I like him. I wish I had a real father. I wish Mom was still alive. I wish I liked girls. I wish I liked you the way you like me. I'm bumming all the time anymore and I don't know how to make it stop.

Allison runs a hand through my hair, something she loves to do. She says, "You don't have to be the strong silent type with me, honey."

I kiss her hard and hug her tight. We have a marathon make-out session on her couch and the feel of a human body holding me is really kind of nice. I get a boner just from all the hugging and kissing, which I'm really happy about. We don't go all the way, 'cause when I open my eyes I lose my hard-on. Even so, I hope she'll tell all her friends I had a woodie.

## April 1978

Tommy's helping me take out Aunt Nora's storm windows. It's only April, still plenty of time left for a good, deep snowfall, but Aunt Nora says she's fed up with her house being shut tight as a drum. She wants fresh cold air to circulate, to breathe some life into the rooms and rid the place of the stink of way too many cats.

For the most part, we work quietly and I remember how weird Mom always was about spring. She was the only person I knew who wouldn't go on and on about how we all survived another winter. And I know the neighbors wondered why she would sit outside on the front steps in the coldest windchill, the kind that could frostbite your skin in minutes, but stayed indoors on the hottest days. She seemed bummed when the windows were finally open again and the noise of outside—Mrs. Bartochevitz, Max, the birds, the tunes cranked out of cars and apartments, the little kids screaming and playing in the street—was all over the house. She loved the silence, I guess. She missed *the absolute stillness of the white.*

I like spring 'cause guys stop wearing shirts. I mean, most guys should probably keep their shirts on, but when you see the other ones, it makes it all worthwhile.

Tommy likes spring 'cause he can work on engines outside. And he likes the way girls' boobs bounce up and down when they jog. Cars and boobs, boobs and cars. If there were a pair of boobs big enough to ride around town in, that went from zero to sixty in under half a minute, Tommy would think he'd died and gone to heaven.

He smirks 'cause maybe he knows what I'm thinking. He looks over at me and tells me that I'll knock Allison up and marry her.

Before I remember who I'm talking to, I say, "We're both too smart for that." He goes all quiet and I say, "Sorry, man, I forgot."

He shrugs and wipes his dirty hands on his jeans. "No sweat. I *was* stupid."

We work in silence until Aunt Nora calls us in for sweet coffee and sandwiches. She says to Tommy, "You're a saint for helping me get the house set for spring."

Tommy says, "Do they have Irish Spring soap in Ireland?"

Aunt Nora laughs. "Of course not. That stuff smells like cheap perfume."

Aunt Nora curses when she sees the Irish Spring ads on TV. *Do they think all we do is stand around and cut up perfectly good bars of soap?*

For some reason Tommy likes Aunt Nora and gives her shit all the time. She loves the attention and sometimes I wonder if she's flirting with him. He asks her, "So why did the Irish get their asses kicked so bad by the English?"

She doesn't miss a beat. "I reckon for the same reason Poland fell like a house of cards to the Nazis."

They laugh.

Tommy says, "So, are you after me Lucky Charms, Miss O'Connor? Do you think I'm magically delicious?"

"You've not a single charm, my boy, let alone a lucky one."

They laugh.

Every once in a while I catch Aunt Nora looking at Tommy. She likes *charming rogues* and the only time Tommy's charming is when he's around her.

She asks him, "What are your plans for after graduation?"

He wipes the crumbs off his lips and tells her, "Going to Dunwoody to become an auto mechanic."

This makes her smile. "Oh, you'll be staying close to your family, that's brilliant. I don't suppose you could give my poor old Matador the once-over for me?"

Tommy laughs. "No offense, Miss O'Connor, but I don't know why you bought that piece of shit. All AMC makes is crap."

She smirks. "Well, so long as no offense is intended, I'll forgive you your language."

"Sorry," he says.

She sighs. "It's lovely to have big strapping men around again. I hope you two will only go with nice girls, not the common ones."

I stare at my cup. "Aunt Nora, jeez . . ."

She defends herself. "You need to learn about women from women. You're both too fine to bother with all the painted hussies trolloping around. I just worry you'll be tempted to do something you'll regret."

Tommy says, "Too late," and I almost blow coffee all over both of them.

Aunt Nora frowns. "Whatever do you mean by that remark? Is there something the matter?"

Tommy says, "Promise you won't tell anybody, especially not my mom."

Her face lights up and she leans in. "I'll take it to my grave."

So Tommy tells her, "I got a girl pregnant."

This is when I expect Aunt Nora to beat Tommy to death with her Bible. But all she does is put her big man hands on her cheeks and gasp, "No! Oh, is it that Allison that comes round for Kevin?"

No wonder Mom always called Aunt Nora *mortifying*. I say, "Jesus Christ, of course not!"

Aunt Nora, still looking at Tommy and waiting for more, says to me, "Language."

Tommy says, "It wasn't Allison. Man, I wish it was. Her name's Beth, I met her at a kegger."

Aunt Nora hasn't blinked. "Oh, I say, does she attend your school?"

"Nah, she goes to an alternative school."

"You mean for the delinquents?" Aunt Nora says.

Tommy looks like he just smelled something bad. "No way, it's for kids who can't hack regular school. And delinquents, I guess."

Aunt Nora reaches her hand across the table and Tommy puts it in his own. She says, "Are you getting married?"

"No way."

"Putting it up for adoption, then?"

Tommy nods.

Aunt Nora says, "Good for you, Tommy, good for you. A pregnant bride is no way to start a marriage."

We finish our lunch listening to Aunt Nora yak and yak. Be sure it's adopted by a good Catholic couple. Make sure it's baptized. When we finally head back outside to hose down the windows, I look at Tommy like he's somebody else. "I can't believe you told her."

He shrugs. "Your Aunt Nora's cool. You need to give her a break, Kev." Then he says, "We need to start checking out apartments."

"We've got time," I tell him.

"I don't want to wait till fall to move out. We should get a place in June."

I look at him. After graduation I was thinking about moving to New York. Or San Francisco. Or Earl's Court in London. "I need to save money, man. Why pay rent all summer when I can live here and work full-time at Red Owl?"

"I need to get out. My little brothers are a pain in the ass. And my mom's been all over me about working too many hours. Come on, Kev, we'll be able to do whatever the hell we want, it'll be so cool. It's freedom, man."

I look at him, a strong wind blowing his long dirty blond hair all over his face. Somewhere underneath it is his smile, the one he uses to get me to do something I don't want to do. The one that dares me.

"July."

He's about to argue, but then he changes his mind. "Cool."

Here's what I think about when Allison's kissing me: I tell myself that I got to get my application together for the U. I wonder what Chuck's doing. I wish Jon Thompson wasn't such a dick. I pretend that Allison is Bruce Springsteen. Or Jackson Browne. I remind myself to stop and put gas in the Dart. Then I always open my eyes a crack to see who's walking by, watching us make out, 'cause this is why I do this, so people can see.

Today it's Tommy and Rick Foley. They're practically standing right on top of us; probably have been for a couple of minutes.

"Jesus," I shout, Allison's spit all over my lips. "How the hell long have you been there?"

Rick Foley says, "Only about five hours." They think it's funny and start laughing like a couple of nimrods. Allison's blushing, but she always does when we make out, so I don't think she's embarrassed.

Tommy says, almost like he's singing, "How are you this morning, Allison?"

She wipes her lips and says, "I *was* doing just fine."

Rick Foley says, "Yeah, we could see that."

I say, "What do you want?"

Rick Foley says, "The kegger tonight. You're coming, right? 'Cause Tommy's car is dead again and we need the Dart. Whaddya say?"

Allison looks up at me, real urgent-like. She says, "Tell them."

Tommy raises an eyebrow and shakes his head. "Tell us what, man? And it better not be feeble."

Allison answers for me. "We're watching *Holocaust* tonight."

Rick Foley says, "Jeez, that sounds like a lot more fun than a kegger."

Tommy sticks his pinky out and with a finger on his other hand, runs little circles around it. Then he says, "At least let us use the Dart."

I mumble, "Cool."

They take off and Allison watches them as they disappear. She says, "You know, I think you need some new friends. There's more to life than getting blasted all the time."

"They're cool."

She rolls her eyes, but then she reaches up to my neck and pulls my face into hers. And we go at it again. Now I wonder how I'm gonna get to Allison's tonight to watch *Holocaust* 'cause I just gave my car away. Maybe Aunt Nora will let me use the Matador. She's not going anywhere; she's already watched the first couple of episodes with a big box of Kleenex in her lap. During the commercials, she says the rosary. I know, because she made me watch it with her. She said, "It's important for you to understand what people are capable of."

In the miniseries, when the younger sister stormed off and ripped the Star of David off her coat, Aunt Nora practically screamed at the set: "Get back to your house straightaway!" When the sister was raped by a couple of Germans, Aunt Nora put her head in her hands and rocked back and forth, mumbling, "Nazi bastards, no better than the English!"

There was a scene, in the camp, when one of the actors is told what all the symbols on the uniforms mean. I knew what the Star of David meant already, but then they went on to explain what a pink triangle meant. It was for homosexuals.

I just sat there. Homosexuals? There were homosexuals back then?

But they didn't show any.

Aunt Nora sucked in her lips and hugged herself during all the camp scenes. She said, "Oh, they put the Jehovah's Witnesses in there too. Oh, remind me to be more pleasant when they come round."

Frankly, it'll be a relief to watch it with Allison tonight. Aunt Nora's little comments are mortifying. Plus, I want to see how it turns out. I mean, I know how it turns out in history, the Nazis lose and what's left of the Jews go back to Israel and kick ass like nobody else. But I want to know how it turns out for the people in the show, especially the younger brother. I know it's like a tragedy, like the famine was in Ireland, but he's really foxy and I can't help it.

I hear a little *ahem* and a finger tapping me on the shoulder.

I pull Allison off my face and there's Fey Hayes.

Allison says, "Good morning, Mr. Hayes."

I say, "What's happening, Miss TerHaze?"

He puts his fey hands on his fey hips. "Your very public display has made you late. I assume you did not hear the bell for home-room?"

Allison's off faster than a bullet.

Fey Hayes looks at me. Finally he says, "Are you waiting for an engraved invitation, Mr. Doyle?"

So I head to homeroom, hoping that the younger brother makes it out of Nazi Germany alive.

## MAY 1978

I'm supposed to drive over to the Gunderson place and pick everybody up 'cause I'm the best man. Then I have to haul our sorry asses to city hall and watch my dad do something really fucking stupid, even for him.

Aunt Nora's sitting on the couch, her cats around her like mourners at a funeral. She says, "So you're going to go through with it," like I'm the one who's gonna marry the miserable old cow instead of Dad.

"What do you want me to do about it?"

Aunt Nora says, "That woman already has one husband. What does she need with two?"

I keep forgetting that they don't have divorce in Ireland. "Well, I gotta go. They have an appointment for three o'clock."

She says, like I'm spitting on Mom's grave, "Go on then, I'm not going to stop you."

"He's gonna marry her whether I'm there or not. Don't blame me."

She pets one of the cats, Declan or Brendan or Kieran. "You don't have to be a party to it, though, do you now?"

This is a waste of time. "I'll bring a piece of cake back for you."

"Don't you dare make jokes! Do you hear me? If your mother—"

That's what she's saying when I close the front door and head to Jackie Shaw's dead husband's Dart. The one I might have to give back to her if this thing doesn't blow up within a year.

I drive to the Mississippi and take the River Road to northeast Minneapolis. When I drive by the place where it happened I stop the car and get out.

We've had a storm, so the land is soft, as Mom used to say. Down on the riverbank a woman is walking her dog, a golden retriever that can't seem to stay out of the water, no matter how cold it is. It loves to splash and bark, and it begs her to throw the stick in the river just one more time.

I miss Rex. Then I think: Mom didn't drown; it was the impact that killed her. That's why the casket had to be closed for the wake. I wonder if she looked like the cow did when I threw the shopping cart through her rear windshield. I wonder if she had the same look of panic, and regret. Like she knew that she had gone too far but there was no way to stop. There was no turning back.

The more I look out at the river, the less likely it seems to me that Mom would have driven herself off the edge. It just doesn't seem like something she would do. Kill herself? Maybe. But like this? No way. Unless the car began to spin out of control, and she just decided to see what would happen. That would make more sense. That she didn't do anything to stop it.


I haven't seen the miserable cow in a couple of months. She's smiling at me, asking if I'm excited.

I shake my head. "Why should I be excited?"

She frowns at me. "I know you don't care much for me at the moment, Kevin, but can't you at least be happy for your little brother or sister's sake?"

I laugh at her and say, "I don't have a—" Then I damn near drop dead. "Jesus Christ! You're pregnant?!"

She screams at Dad as he comes down the stairs. "You didn't tell him?"

He screams at her. "You tell me how I'm supposed to tell him!"

I scream at her. "You're pregnant? How old are you? How can you even get pregnant?"

She screams at me. "None of your business! And how do you think women become pregnant, Kevin?"

Dad screams at both of us. "Stop screaming, everybody just calm the hell down!"

I scream at him. "Is it even yours?"

Laurie Lindstrom comes in carrying some flowers. "Stop it," she screams.

"Why didn't you tell me he knocked her up?" I scream at her.

"Because I knew you'd freak out," she screams at me.

Nobody screams now. We all just look at each other, panting like a wolf pack.

Finally the cow says to Dad, "I can't believe you let him get away with asking me if the baby's yours. I can't believe you let him get away with half the things you let him get away with."

Dad says, "He's upset, he'll get over it."

She says, "That's what you always say. He needs to grow up. I can *not* believe you didn't tell him that we're going to have a baby."

Dad just rubs his neck, like she's a big pain in it.

Laurie Lindstrom says to me, "This should be a joyful occasion.

You're going to have a little brother or sister. And I'm going to have a little cousin. We should be celebrating." But she doesn't sound like she means it.

Oh, man, this isn't happening. No way I'm related to Laurie Lindstrom.

Dad says, "Everybody calm down."

We all look at him.

He says, "Everything's going to be fine, if we all just take deep breaths and count to ten. This isn't Bloody Sunday, nobody's gotten killed."

Yet.

So we just stand there, with nobody getting killed.

The miserable old cow finally says, "We're going to be late if we don't leave right away."

She has the nerve to wear white. On the day she's marrying a second husband and her belly is beginning to stick out, she wears white. Except for Laurie, I'm the only one in the room who can wear white without lying about it.

We head out to Jackie Shaw's dead husband's Dart, and Dad says, "Maybe we should take my car, it has air-conditioning."

The cow says, "Please, I'm going to wilt in this heat."

We wait by the curb for Dad to pull his car around from the back alley. He has the windows down and the air going full blast when he stops in front of us.

He gets out of the driver's side and says to me, "Kevin, will you do the honors?"

I shoot him a look and get behind the wheel. Mrs. Gunderson makes a big production of getting into the car, like she's nine months along.

Laurie sits behind me. She says to her aunt, "I can't believe it. Today's your wedding day." But she seems about as excited about it as I am.

The cow says, "We've been waiting for this day for a long time now."

How thoughtful of Mom to die.

When we get to city hall we can't find a place to park right away and the cow's going mental. Dad tells her we have plenty of time, no need to get upset, but I say, "Looks like we're not gonna make it." Then I say what Aunt Nora would say: "It's a judgment."

But we do make it. We get to the clerk's office and Laurie whips out an Instamatic and starts snapping anything that moves. She takes a shot of the cow putting on more lipstick, another one of my hands in front of my face, and one of Dad looking like he has no idea where the hell he is.

It takes no time at all. One minute they're single, the next, they're married.

Dad says, "Aren't you gonna congratulate your old man?"

I look at him, all serious-like. "No."

The plastic smile falls off his face and he whispers, "If not for me, then you're going to be happy for your little brother or sister's sake. You got that? I've had all the scenes I'm gonna take, Kevin. Try and act like an adult for a change."

I just look at him.

He says, "Only ladies and sissies pout."

Take a wild guess, Dad, which one am I?

That's when Laurie takes a picture of us. She says, "That will make an interesting shot."

They shove us out in the corridor 'cause another couple's waiting to get hitched.

Dad says, "Let's have a meal to celebrate."

The cow nods but then she says, all panicky, "Where's a rest room? I *need* a rest room."


We're a miserable little group when we get to the Mud Pie restaurant on Lyndale Avenue.

My mood doesn't get any better when Laurie tells me it's a vegetarian restaurant. The cow let her choose the place, and this is where we wind up, granola-land. We sit out on the patio with the leftover hippies.

"Why did you wanna come here?" I ask Laurie.

She says, "Do you have any idea how they breed and slaughter the animals we eat?"

So I choke on a veggie burger with organic fries served by a waitress with pit hair.

Dad's kind of pissed that they don't serve booze. "I wanted to propose a toast," he says, all pouty. Like a lady or a sissy.

Laurie says, "The best man is supposed to make the toast."

*You'll pay for that.*

The cow says, "She's right, Pat. It's traditional for the best man to toast the newlyweds."

All three of them lift a glass of iced tea and look at me. Dad's face says: Please don't make another scene.

I think about screwing it up for him, but then I say, "If it makes you happy, then, well. Toast."

We clink glasses and the cow says, "Well, that was inspired. Are you a poet, Kevin?"

I say, "Yeah, want to hear one? 'There once was a bitchy old cow—' "

Dad says, "Shut it."

Laurie asks Dad and the cow, "Are you hoping for a boy or a girl?"

Dad's about to say a boy but the cow interrupts and says, "We just want a healthy, happy baby, we don't care about the sex."

The waitress with the pits wants to know if we want any dessert.

Dad knows we need time in our separate corners. He says, "Just the check, please."

We sit there, staring at each other. I've only been to a couple of wedding receptions in my life, but none of them were like this. There were always people laughing and clinking their glasses and yakking and drinking. The old people would be all over the dance floor 'cause they'd play big band music and the kids would sneak booze. The women would gossip and the men would suck on their stogies, 'cause you always have stogies for special occasions.

We just sit waiting for the bill.

# 8

# THINGS IN THE FREEZER

Aunt Nora doesn't gush over Allison the way Dad and Jackie Shaw did. She's suspicious of her, 'cause Allison's a Yank, and she's told me about a million times what she thinks about American women. But just in case I forgot, she says, "Prancing around with their noses in the air, too grand to give you the steam off their piss. But they'll spread their legs for a man at the drop of a hat."

When Allison called she asked me to just wait for her outside. She's afraid of Aunt Nora, like all women and most men are. But I told her she has to come inside. Aunt Nora has been known to come out to the car, and you don't want that.

When the doorbell rings, Aunt Nora says to me, "Sit, I'll answer my own door, if you please."

Allison's first mistake is not wearing enough clothes, even though it's like a swamp outside.

Aunt Nora says, "Shouldn't you have finished getting dressed?"
Her next mistake is her makeup.

"You must buy eye shadow by the drum."

Her final mistake is not having any Irish blood. Aunt Nora explains everything to her like Allison's retarded.

Allison just smiles, that's all she does when Aunt Nora's around. When we're in the car she'll imitate Aunt Nora's Irish accent. Last time we pulled away from Aunt Nora's house, Allison said, *'Tis the common tart what's not fit to wipe my lovely nephew's arse.*

When we make it to her car, she just says, "Well, don't I boil that old bat's potatoes?"

I tell Allison, "She doesn't mean anything by it."

But Allison says, "Of course she does. She doesn't think I'm good enough for you. I don't know how you can stand living with her."

We pull out into traffic and I say, "It's not like I've got much choice."

Tonight we're gonna see *The Deer Hunter*, which sounds really boring. There's like all these movies about Vietnam vets anymore.

When we get to Roseville, the movie's sold out. We stand in the lobby for a minute, not sure what's next; we've never done anything that wasn't planned out ahead of time.

I say, "We could grab a couple of Big Macs."

Allison looks at me like I'm five. She says, "It's a beautiful evening, let's go for a drive."

She heads out to Stillwater, on the Wisconsin border, with the radio cranked. She doesn't sing along with the tunes like Chuck, she doesn't nod her head in time like Rick Foley, she just listens. There's a park near the border she wants to check out, and I'm like, oh, great, now we're gonna have to make out the whole time. I like holding each other, but making out is starting to get on my nerves.

When Allison stops the car, she says, "When are you going to ask me to the prom? It's next week, in case you hadn't noticed."

I say, "Do you want to go to the prom?"

She says, "Yeah," like she was saying, *Just how thick are you?*

"Cool, we'll go to the prom. We can triple with Tommy and

Rick Foley." Tommy and Beth are history; he's been hanging with a sophomore who thinks it's too cool that he's a senior.

Allison makes a little tired sound. "Can't we go with my friends? All Tommy talks about is cars, and Rick can barely string three words together, he's such a pothead. You're a lot like him."

"Jeez, thanks."

She slides over next to me and takes my hand in both of hers. "I didn't mean you were some inarticulate burnout, I meant that you never say anything. I wish you would tell me what you're thinking once in a while."

"Not much."

She squeezes my hand. "You always say that. You have to think about something sometime."

Jon's ass. Chuck's ass. The guy's nipples on the cover of *Playgirl*. My mom. My dad.

I say, "No, I don't."

She puts a hand on my cheek and I know where this is going. Marathon make-out session. I don't know if I can do another one.

One kiss and she knows it too. She pulls away and says, "Are you getting tired of me or something?"

Yeah. "No." I mean, I'm tired of this, not you.

"That kiss was . . . Don't you think I'm pretty?"

Oh, God, here we go. I say kinda pissed off, "You're beautiful."

"You say that, but I don't know. The reason I broke up with my last boyfriend was because he was always all over me. But at least I knew that he found me attractive."

Oh, shit.

"I mean, I'm not ugly or anything. I know I'm no Jaclyn Smith, but I'm not repulsive either. At least with Dan I knew that I was wanted."

Oh, man. Okay, just blow some shit. "I want you, Allison."

She looks me right in the eye to see if I'll freak when she says, "Show me. I have my pride too, you know. I'm tired of throwing myself at you, Kevin."

My heart's pounding. I don't know what to do.

She says, "I'm sorry, it's just that, sometimes I feel so . . . nuts

when I'm around you, like you're just going through the motions
or something because you can't be bothered to break up with me.
Are you seeing someone else?"

She won't shut up so I kiss her hard. I shove my tongue all the
back to her tonsils and try to yank them out without anesthesia.

She goes, "Hmmmph! Humph! Mmmmm. Mmmmm."

I just stay stuck on her face; she's gonna have to be the first
one to pull away tonight.

Now she's kinda grabbing my hair and it sort of hurts. She's
still going, "Hmmmph! Hmmph! Mmmmm. Mmmmm," like
she's having a seizure.

She pulls me down until I'm lying on top of her, sort of, with
my legs all crunched up under the dashboard. The seat belt's dig-
ging in my hip and I want to sit up, but she just lies there, spazzing
out.

That's when she grabs my hand by the wrist and puts it on a
boob.

*Jesus Christ! Don't do that!*

She's like, Take me, I'm yours. I don't know what to do with
her. But if I stop? I close my eyes real hard and squeeze her boob
a little.

Finally she stops kissing me; she's all "Oh! Oh! Oh!" She puts
her hands behind her head and I'm like, Jesus Christ, I have to
do more shit with her boobs. Her eyes are closed, so I turn my
head and make a face, I can't help it, and I put both hands on
her boobs and squeeze them. It's like when Dad made me put a
worm on a hook for the first time.

Now she's going, "Ooooooooh, ooooooooh," and I'm wondering how the hell I can get out of this. I'm about as hard as a
wet noodle and there is no way I can stick it in her without it
popping back out again.

But now she takes my hands and puts them under her shirt,
and I'm gonna have to touch boobs for the first time in my life
and I really, really don't want to but I don't know how I can't
not do it.

Her nipples are like all big and hard, I think I'm gonna pass
out 'cause all the blood's rushing out of my head and I'm seeing

spots in front of my eyes and she won't stop spazzing. Why the hell do I have to do this? I squeeze, I cringe. She's like *oh, oh,* and I'm like *eeeew, eeeew.*

I take my hands off her boobs and sit up, pissed off.

She opens her eyes. She's looking at me weird. Her face is bright red, like it was that night months ago at Red Owl when her friend asked me if I was going to Debbie Polanski's party. She says, "What's wrong?"

I don't say anything.

She asks me again. "What's wrong?"

"Nothing's wrong, okay? I wanna go home."

"Honey, did I do something to make you mad? What did I do? Tell me, I won't do it again."

My eyes start to water. I bark, "You didn't do anything, Jesus Christ! Can we just leave? Is that okay with you? I don't feel good."

Now she looks like she's gonna cry and she pulls her shirt down and starts the car. She's wiping her eyes on the ride back and she stops at a gas station and gets me a ginger ale. She tells me it's to settle my stomach. But when I open the can it sprays all over me, and I just wanna be alone. Why can't I be alone?

When Allison drops me off, she says that she hopes I'm feeling better. I hope I drop dead, 'cause then people will think something was really wrong with me instead of what's really wrong with me.

I whisper, "Yeah, thanks."

She says, "Ummm, Jon Thompson asked me to the prom."

She wants me to say, *No, don't go with him, I love you!* But I just sit there, my shirt sticking to my chest 'cause of the ginger ale.

"Well," Allison says, "I better take off, it's late and I don't want my folks to freak out."

I just get out of her car and watch from the curb as she drives away.

Aunt Nora must have been looking out the window, watching

for us. She opens the front door and says, "You should have rang, I was out of my mind."

I say, "It's still early."

She's about to say something else until she sees the big wet spot. "Mother of God, did you spill your drink? What's that all over you?"

"I got too fresh and Allison dumped her pop on me."

Aunt Nora's mouth drops open, but then she starts laughing. "Oh, my, good for her! I didn't think she had it in her! Oh, you look like a clown!"

I run past her and up the stairs to the spare room so I can be the hell alone.

She says, "Oh, now, don't be like that, I was just having some fun."

But I'm upstairs and in the bedroom, lying on the mattress with the lights out.

Jon's there too, for the first time in a long time. He doesn't lie next to me, just sits on the edge of the bed, staring at the floor.

I made a fool of myself tonight, I tell him.

He nods.

What's gonna happen if Allison tells everybody?

She won't.

But what if she does?

Maybe she's more embarrassed about it than you are. Maybe everything isn't about you.

I just roll over, leaving him there, alone, awake.


I drive myself to school on Monday, after spending the day before locked in the spare room. Rick Foley called, and Tommy called, but I had Aunt Nora take messages. I asked her: Did they sound funny to you? Funny how, she wanted to know. Funny like there's a rumor going round that I don't like boobs.

Aunt Nora's caught on that Allison and me are history. Now she likes her. Any American girl who actually defends her virtue can't be all bad.

I stop the Dart and look at the school. There are gangs of kids hanging out in front of Northeast, but none of them are carrying signs that say I'm a big faggot. When I walk down the hallway, people are screaming and laughing and yakking. I try to catch what they're talking about, but it's hard to make out one conversation from another. So far I haven't heard my name though. I hear "Fag" a lot, but that's just how people talk. Boys are fags, girls are sluts. It's all about sex; I'm beginning to think that everything is.

I can do this. Northeast will only last a couple of more weeks and then it's behind me. I'll never have to walk down these halls again. I'll never have to be anywhere again if I don't want to. I should have dropped out, but Dad wouldn't let me. But *he* gets to quit *his* job.

When I open my locker, Rick Foley walks up behind me and smacks the back of my head. He says, "Hey, man, what happened to you?"

I say really loud, "What? Nothing happened!"

He smirks and says, "Jeez, don't shit your pants, man. We were supposed to hang out at Tommy's yesterday. His mom took his brothers up to Brainerd to visit the old lady in the nursing home. We got loaded."

"Oh, yeah, I forgot."

Rick Foley says, "Your loss, my man." He folds his arms across his chest and says, "Does Tommy seem weird to you?"

"No."

"He just seemed kind of bummed out, like something was bugging him. He wouldn't tell me what it was."

Either Allison called him and told him I'm a big faggot, or something else is going on with Beth. Come on, God, let it be Beth. Let her have found out she's gonna have twins.

Rick Foley looks around. "Aren't you usually swapping spit with Allison right around now?"

Guess I might as well get my version out there. "We broke up."

Rick Foley bugs his eyes out. "You gotta be shittin' me! You let her get away? Man, if I had a girl with tits like hers I'd hang on with both hands, you know what I mean?"

Everybody knows what you mean, 'cause this is the third planet in orbit around the sun. I say, "Maybe she doesn't want me to."

Rick Foley punches me in the arm just a little and says, "That's harsh, man. Sorry, I didn't know she dumped you."

"Yeah, well . . ."

"Look, let's grab some brews and hang out at my house after school. You and Tommy both need to loosen up."

"Cool, thanks."

"No problemo, man."

Rick Foley walks away and for the first time since I've known him, I wonder why we never just call him Rick.

Tommy's sitting aggressively in our Dutch class when I show up. As soon as I sit down he goes, "So where the hell were you? We were supposed to hang out yesterday."

"Sorry, man, I forgot. Allison dumped me."

Tommy shakes his head. "That's why Thompson was sniffing her butt like a dog. That guy's such a dweeb, he can't wait two fucking seconds before he tries to get in her jeans."

"When was he doing that?"

"This morning. He's hanging all over that chick. I feel sorry for her."

I shiver like I've got the flu.

Tommy says, "You cold?"

"I'm fine."

Mevrouw Bergsma claps her hands and says, *"Eidereen, komt nu, alstubleift."*

Tommy grunts, "Here we go again. I'm so fucking tired of school. I just wanna get my mechanic's license. Like I need fucking Dutch to rebuild an engine."

"It's June, we only got two more weeks left."

Tommy puts his hands behind his head and spreads his legs even wider to take up as much room as possible. Like when dogs try to make themselves look bigger by sticking their fur up. He says, "Beth made me sign the papers, you know, where I give up my rights as the father."

"That's cool with you, right?"

"I guess."

Mevrouw Bergsma says, *"Hoe gaat het met jouw, Meneer Doyle?"*
(How goes it with you, Mr. Doyle?)

*"Het gaat."* (It goes.)

## June 1978

When I get home from my shift, Aunt Nora says, "That lovely
neighbor fellow of yours died. Mr. Anderson. His parish just rang
for you."

"Floyd's dead?"

Aunt Nora scrunches up her big man face. "Yes, and what a
pity. His heart gave out on him, poor darling. There he was,
watching the telly, and his heart stops dead. They say he was
sitting there for almost a fortnight before anyone found him. And
in this heat, oh, it's terrible, just terrible."

The cats are mewing for dinner and rubbing Aunt Nora's big
man ankles. She says, "His priest says that you are to be a pallbearer. Wasn't that thoughtful of Mr. Anderson to remember
you?"

"Floyd made *me* a pallbearer?"

Aunt Nora picks up three cats at once. "Yes, I imagine the
poor old thing didn't have anyone at the end. He must of thought
the world of you to make you a pallbearer."

Who knows what Floyd thought.


It's nowhere near time to get up, but Aunt Nora's pounding on
my door like a banshee. Banshee is Irish for mental.

"Wake up and look at this," she screams.

I sit up and rub my eyes. "Jeez, what's wrong?"

"Mother of God, you won't believe your own eyes!"

I stand up and scratch my ass, looking for my jeans somewhere
on the floor.

"Come on then, open up!"

I shout at the door, "Will you relax? I gotta put some clothes
on."

"Manners," she says.

When I open the door, Aunt Nora turns her head and shuts her eyes, but not before she checks out my chest. "You're not decent," she says.

"I can't find a clean shirt," I tell her. "What's wrong?"

With her eyes closed, she holds out the paper. "Look, it's right there on the front page for the entire world to see."

*Body of Dead Man's Missing Wife Discovered in Freezer*

There's a picture of Floyd and his wife underneath the head-line.

Holy shit; there's a picture of Floyd and his wife underneath the headline.

I drop the paper on the floor and say to Aunt Nora, who has her back to me, "He killed his wife and stuck her in the freezer?"

"They don't know that he killed her, but yes, it seems he put her in the freezer."

"Jesus Christ!"

"Language."


They don't know yet whether Floyd snuffed his wife or not, but I've already figured it out. Floyd wasn't in love with her anymore, but he didn't kill her. I mean, they were married forty years; if he was gonna kill her, he would have done it a long time ago.

No, what happened is that Floyd lost a son in Korea and after so long with his wife, he couldn't let some guys from a funeral home cart her away in a pine box. He knew exactly what he wanted. He wanted to spend what was left of the rest of his life with her. It was a comfort to have her there with him.

You gotta hand it to Floyd.

Jon Thompson's at my locker. He says, "Hey, did that old guy really kill his wife?"

Jon looks like sex on legs. I wanna touch him so damn bad, but if I did, the Earth would fall into the sun. I say, "No, he didn't kill her. He just put her in the freezer after she died 'cause he didn't want to be by himself."

Jon whistles. "That's fucking weird. What a nutcase."

I say, "Floyd Anderson wasn't a nutcase, he was one of the nicest guys I knew."

Jon says, "Sorr-ree, didn't know he was your boyfriend."

*Did Allison tell him?* I shove Jon. "What was that?"

Jon mutters, "Nothing, man, it's cool."

"What did you say to me? Say it again, I wanna hear it."

Jon goes, "Relax, man, it was just a stupid joke."

Fuck you. You don't know Floyd. He lost a kid who looked like Donny Osmond. His wife died in his own home. He took me in after Dad told me to get the hell out of the house.

So I hit Jon hard and fast right in the gut and he falls over. Aunt Nora always says, *If you throw the first punch, make sure it counts.* He's coughing and wheezing and he can't catch his breath.

I say, "Fuck you, Thompson, you know? You want me to kick your ass for you, huh? Fucking pussy piece of shit."

He just curls up in a ball, gasping.

I kick his ass with my foot, really hard, like I'm kicking a football. "Want another one, faggot? Huh, ya fucking cunt?"

He's all, "Uhhhhh, uhhhhh, uhhhh."

"Motherfucking cocksucker! You wanna suck my dick, faggot? You want me to come in your mouth?"

"Uhhhhh, uhhhhh, uhhhhh."

I grab my crotch. "This what you want, faggot?"

It's like this . . . thing. Like I'm the exorcist getting all this shit outta Linda Blair.

That's when I see a bunch of kids staring at us. Traffic in the hall has stopped dead, and Fey Hayes is pushing his way past the gawkers.

"What happened here?" he screams at me.

I look at everybody standing around. They all look at the floor. I look too, and that's when I see Jon Thompson, the guy I'm in love with, holding himself and trying to breathe and not cry at the same time.

Fey Hayes grabs me by the shoulders and shakes me. "Did you do this?"

I look at him, I'm kind of mixed up, if I did do it, I didn't mean to. I just nod at him.

Mevrouw Bergsma is kneeling over Jon now, rubbing his back. She says, in her South African accent, "It's all right, you're going to be just fine. Slow your breathing down, easy, easy, now."

Fey Hayes pulls me by the arm; he's a lot stronger than he looks. I think he's taking me to Mr. Rogers' office but he doesn't, he shoves me in his classroom and shuts the door. He points at a desk. "Sit."

I sit.

He leans down, his hands on the desk, and says, "What just happened out there?"

I whisper, "I don't know, I guess I kind of lost it."

He says so loud that spit flies out of his mouth and hits me in the face, "You don't know? You guess you just lost it? Is that what I'm hearing you say?"

I mumble, "Yes, sir."

He stands up straight and folds his arms across his chest. A little calmer, but not much, he says, "Well, that's one theory. Would you like to hear my theory? Hmmmm?"

"Yes, sir."

"Good. Here's my theory. You attacked a fellow student and called him hateful names. Names like faggot and cocksucker. Does that sound right so far?"

"Yes, sir."

"And now you sit here and claim that you don't know how it happened. Is that correct?"

"Yes, sir."

He breathes in and out, real heavy-like, and then he says, "What provoked you, Mr. Doyle? In four years I've seen you in your fair share of fights, but I've never seen anything quite as vicious as what I saw just now out in the hallway."

I frown 'cause it feels like I'm gonna cry. This is so damn stupid. He asks me again, "What provoked you?"

And then I start crying. It's so goddamn humiliating.

Fey Hayes says all gentle-like, which makes me cry harder, "What's wrong, Kevin? Please, help me to understand."

I say, like one syllable at a time, 'cause my breathing's all screwed up, 'cause I'm crying like a little girl, "He—was—making—fun—of—Floyd—and—it—made—me—mad."

Fey Hayes frowns. "You mean the man who put his wife's corpse in a freezer?"

I gulp and say, "Yeah."

At first Fey Hayes doesn't say anything. But then he starts laughing. I wipe my eyes and look at him like he's finally lost it. He says, "Forgive me, Mr. Doyle"—ha, ha, ha—"it's just that"—ha, ha, ha—"I find it hard to believe that you were defending the honor"—ha, ha, ha—"of some poor old lunatic!"

I stare at him. But then I start to laugh too.

Now we're both laughing, really hard, and I think I might keel over 'cause I'm still crying too.

Fey Hayes says, one syllable at a time, 'cause he's laughing so hard, "You—know—I—have—to—punish—you—for—hitting—that—boy."

Ha, ha, ha. "Yeah."

"What—kind—of—punishment—do—you—think—you—deserve?" Ha, ha, ha.

I breathe in easier, 'cause I've kind of got it back together. I wanna tell Fey Hayes that I like boys. I wanna ask Fey Hayes to help me 'cause there's only three people on the planet like us, and I don't know where to find the TA from Tehran.

But I say, "I dunno."

He dabs his eyes with a handkerchief. "Detention. You just bought yourself six hours of detention."

Jeez, you think he'd just let this one go after I made him laugh for the first time in his life. I rub my eyes and say, "You know, Miss TerHaze, I'm eighteen. In a couple days and I'm outta here for good. So why should I bother with detention?"

"Let me put it to you this way, Mr. Doyle. Do you want to receive your diploma or not?"

They always have something on you.

"And don't let me ever hear you say faggot or cocksucker again."

Don't sweat it, I was yelling at myself, Jon Thompson just got in the way.

•  •  •

That night, in bed, I try to apologize to Jon for what I did. But
he's not beside me, he never is anymore. I miss him, my Jon. I
miss talking to him before I go to sleep. I miss how I used to
think that any day he would tell me he was just like me. That he
was in love with me. I wonder if I'll ever meet anybody like me,
I wonder if I'll ever really fall in love. Floyd said *things change* and
I pray to God that he's right, 'cause things have gotta change.


Dad brings the miserable old cow with him to Aunt Nora's house.
Aunt Nora agreed not to be here when they showed up, so she
*won't do something I'll regret.* Dad's in his one and only suit, the
cow's dressed in a black maternity dress, not that she needs it, she
doesn't show at all. But she has to tell the whole goddamn world,
Look at me, I'm pregnant. Like it's never happened before.

I say, "Where's Laurie?"

The black cow moos, "She's at The Safe House. She's always
there on Saturday, like clockwork."

Dad says, "Well, almost like clockwork."

The cow says, "What's that supposed to mean?"

Dad stretches and says, "She told me she's having her doubts,
that's all."

The cow wants to know, "Doubts about what?"

"She's wondering if handing out bowls of soup will change the
world. She's young, she's idealistic, and she wants to make the
world a better place. Remember what that felt like?"

The cow says, with an edge in her voice, "Do you?"

Dad smiles at her. Then he winks at me like I'm his son. He
says, "Yep, I remember. When I was stationed over in West Germany, I felt like I was keeping everyone back home safe. I got
up before the sun rose and I ate Spam and I marched until I
thought I was gonna drop dead. But, yeah, I thought I was making
the world a better place. A safer place."

The cow rubs her belly and says, "Well, kudos. Kudos to you,
Patrick Doyle. While you were over in Europe, seeing all the

sights, I was living on the Northside trying to figure out how to make a dime stretch into a dollar. I was calculating how long ten gallons of heating oil would keep a shack above freezing. I stayed with my mother and my sister and managed the household. I kept us out of the poorhouse." She could go on, but she doesn't. She could have said, *And I put myself through college* and *I raised my niece on my own,* and *I've held down a job at Pillsbury for twenty years.*

Dad doesn't say anything. He just stands there, pissed off by her one-upmanship.

At least I've never tried to make the world a better place. I say, "We're gonna be late."

The ride over to the church is quiet. Floyd's funeral mass is being held at St. Stephen's, a hike from the old neighborhood. It's the parish where he and his wife first started out, before the freeways carved up South Minneapolis and made nice homes worthless. Decades before he stopped loving her like a husband's supposed to love a wife. Decades before he stuffed her in a freezer 'cause he didn't want to be by himself.

Reporters are outside; they still think that Floyd killed his wife.

The church's packed, but it's full of gawkers and people who'd never heard of Floyd before they read the article in the paper. We were supposed to have a rehearsal before the funeral mass, but there was no way to keep anything private.

A big fat lady in a maxi-skirt says, "Kevin Doyle? Come with me please, the pallbearers are assembling in the rectory."

The other pallbearers are all in American Legion caps. They've come down from Ely, up on the iron range, Floyd's hometown almost fifty years ago. I've never seen any of them before in the old neighborhood and none of them look like they can carry a coffin without winding up in one themselves. I guess that's why Floyd wanted me as a pallbearer.

One of the old guys puts a hand on my shoulder and says, "You don't think that Floyd did in his missus, do ya?"

I say, "No, sir."

He looks at me, kind of relieved, kind of disappointed. Like Floyd didn't have the nerve to do it.

The priest tells us we're just gonna walk alongside the casket;

two guys from the funeral home will roll it down the aisle. Then he looks me over and says, "I didn't know Floyd had a grandson."

"I'm his neighbor. Was his neighbor."

The priest smiles, like he didn't know that Floyd had any neighbors either. Like Floyd lived on his own planet all by himself, only coming back to Earth to die.

We walk down the aisle and the only people I recognize are Dad and the cow. You'd think I'd see somebody I knew, the church is packed, but I guess they're all tourists here to see the freezer murderer. When we make it to the front of the church, one of the funeral home guys point us to a pew.

People cough, and there's a lot of creaking noise as people shift their asses in the wood pews.

The priest says something and I start to space. At Mom's funeral I was sitting up front too, wondering if she was really in the casket or in some Dumpster somewhere, on top of a pile of dead cats. She never made a will so everything went to Dad. Aunt Nora was really pissed. She'd wanted some things that her parents had given Mom, but Dad wouldn't let her have them. They were really vicious to each other and Aunt Nora said that Dad was poison in my system and only she had the cure. But he always kept her from giving it to me.

One time she came over to the house when he was at work and just took whatever she could find that Mom had brought over from Ireland. When Dad got home he hit the roof. He put his fist through a wall and told me to never, ever, let that woman in his house again. He made me swear on Mom's grave. He drove straight over to Aunt Nora's house and pounded on her door. When she wouldn't let him in he threw a rock through her front window. That's when she called the police and had him arrested. He had her arrested for stealing.

The priest says the eulogy. It's all about not rushing to judgment, and he who is without sin casting the first stone, and shit like that. But if he knew Floyd like he's pretending to, he'd know that Floyd didn't kill his wife. But everybody listens to him, like he's Moses down from the mount.

If it were me up there, I'd say: Floyd was one weird guy. He loved his wife like a pal, his son who looked like Donny Osmond, shoveling snow, whiskey with sugar in it, pudding and cereal. He cooked army food for four years and then hospital food for the next thirty. And his last days were spent with a pyramid on his head, freaking everybody out. But as Floyd would say, *Ya don't know what you're missing.*


The *Minneapolis Tribune* runs a front-page article on the coroner's report on Floyd's wife. Cause of death was a heart attack, no evidence of foul play. She died of natural causes. The article said the body was well preserved even though she had been dead for a while. Thanks to the freezer.

I wonder if Floyd sat down in the basement and talked to her. Or maybe the pyramid was his way of staying in touch. It's kind of freaky to think that she was down in the basement the whole time I was staying at his place.

Anyway, now that she's thawed out, they're burying her right next to Floyd.

When I tell Aunt Nora, she says, "Oh, isn't that sweet?"

I feel sorry for Aunt Nora. She doesn't have anybody to stuff her in a freezer when her time comes.


Dad's taken about a million pictures, and we haven't even left the miserable old cow's house yet. The cow makes Laurie and me pose together like we're a couple, and you can tell that Laurie's embarrassed but kind of into it, and as Mom used to say, I'm mortified.

Laurie says, "Come on, we're going to be late."

The cow says, "Calm down, we've got scads of time and they're not going to begin the commencement ceremony without the class valedictorian. Do you have your speech?"

Laurie nods.

Dad—who still hasn't found a job—says, "And what pearls of wisdom are you going to share?"

Laurie doesn't answer and the cow says, "She wouldn't let me anywhere near her speech."

Laurie says, "I've got to go to the bathroom."

Dad says, "Again? Whaddya do, kill a six-pack?"

Once Laurie's upstairs, the cow says, "I hope I don't cry. She isn't letting me read her speech because it's a tribute to me. For raising her after her parents died."

Dad says, "Really? Did you sneak a peek?"

The cow says, "No, she made me give her my word that I wouldn't read it. And I haven't. Call it women's intuition, I just know."

On the ride over we try not to sweat, and then not to freeze. I don't want anyone to see me in the same car with Laurie Lindstrom so I jump out while Dad's still parking. He yells, "Jesus Christ, Kevin, whatya trying to do, get yourself killed?"

As I walk away, I wonder why the hell I should care if the class of '78 sees me with Laurie Lindstrom. I need to grow the hell up. I take off for the gym. In the hallway Allison and Jon Thompson are fighting. He's calling her a bitch. She's telling him to leave her alone.

When they see me they both shut up. I say, "Hey, Allison, is he giving you problems?"

Allison looks at Jon and says, "No, it's no big deal."

Jon wants to tell me to mind my own damn business, but he can't 'cause I'm alpha and he's beta. He's found out the hard way how fast I can kick his ass for him. I mean, I'd still do it with him, but I don't feel like I used to about him. I don't feel about anybody like I used to.

He says, "It's cool, don't worry about it."

That's too close to the line, so I say, "Maybe I *should* worry about it, tough guy."

Jon looks at the floor, a guy's way of rolling on his back, and says, "It's cool, man, it's cool."

I walk away and Allison says, "Thanks, Kevin."

A couple of minutes later I meet Tommy and Mrs. Grabowski. Tommy's little brothers are here, but his dad's a no-show 'cause he can't be in the same place at the same time as his ex-wife. And she swore she'd break his girlfriend's neck if he ever had the nerve to bring her to a family gathering.

Tommy's dad and his girlfriend are engaged. Tommy's stepmom will be maybe ten years older than him.

Mrs. Grabowski gives me a shopping bag and says, "Congratulations, Kevin. I thought you and my boy weren't going to make it, but that just shows you how much this old broad knows."

"Jeez, Mrs. Grabowski, thanks."

Tommy says, "Wait till you open it before you thank her."

It's a T-shirt. It says, *Hi Skool Gradyouate.*

Mrs. Grabowski laughs and says, "Isn't that a hoot? I saw them and I just had to get you one. I got Tommy one too."

Tommy says, "Other parents get their kids a stereo or a TV when they graduate."

She grabs his cheeks in one hand, which makes his lips pucker. "Aww, poor baby. Consider eighteen years of keeping you out of jail my present."

Tommy's brothers are pouting. I ask them, "What's happening?"

Timmy, who's ten and was held back a grade, says, "We can't go camping with Dad 'cause stupid Tommy has his stupid graduation."

Tommy says, "Don't be a crybaby, ya little shit."

Mrs. Grabowski unbuttons her blouse and says, "Kevin, look!" She has her own T-shirt on. It says *Prowd Mudder of da Gradyouate.*

I say, "Jesus, that's retarded."

But Mrs. Grabowski thinks it's the funniest thing ever.


We have to sit in alphabetical order, so I'm between two dweebs that I've never talked to my entire time at Northeast. It's about eight million degrees in the gym and I'm sweating like a pig. Everybody's fanning themselves with programs and the square hats they made us wear. When Laurie Lindstrom gets to the microphone, the teachers and parents clap, but nobody else does.

She looks at her speech, all typed up and in a three-ring binder. So that in case she drops it, the pages won't get out of order. This is the kind of thing she thinks about. She says, "Thank you, Mr. Rogers," and some people laugh. Fey Hayes's up on stage too, wiping his face with a handkerchief. Actually, he doesn't wipe, he dabs. Laurie looks kind of different up on stage.

Without looking up from her notebook, Laurie begins. "Welcome, teachers, parents, fellow students, friends, and family. I am honored to have this opportunity. We, the Northeast High School class of nineteen-seventy-eight, face a future full of challenges and opportunities. We live in a world where there are enough nuclear bombs to destroy the planet hundreds of times over."

The people who were talking shut up. Nobody saw this coming.

"It's going to be up to the class of 'seventy-eight to put an end to this waste of resources, resources that would be better utilized feeding the poor, finding a cure for cancer, and cleaning up the environment. It's going to be up to us to end the arms race and to make good on the promise of détente with the Soviet Union."

Mr. Rogers sits behind Laurie on the stage, a freaked-out look on his face.

"There are signs that a brighter tomorrow may be within our reach. We have established relations with Red China; we have pardoned the courageous men who said no to the war in Vietnam. These are just the small steps that have been taken. Bold ones will be necessary if mankind is to survive into the next century. We are the generation that must take them."

Holy shit.

"Our generation has been accused of cynicism and of only thinking of ourselves. Perhaps that is true. But what is also true is that our generation saw our older brothers killed halfway around the world for no reason. We saw our president break the law and then lie about it to the American people. We saw the Supreme Court rule that the death penalty is not cruel or unusual punishment. The Rockefeller Commission told us that the CIA doesn't respect the laws of the country it's supposed to protect, and we ignore human rights atrocities because they're being carried out by 'governments friendly to the United States.' And at home, we grew up seeing four college students murdered by our own soldiers at Kent State."

It's really quiet. Nobody's even coughing or sneezing or anything.

"It's up to us, the class of 'seventy-eight, to make this world a better, safer, and freer place for the generations that will follow. We can't fight war after war until no one even remembers what we're supposed to be fighting for. Does anyone know or care why the ancient Athenians fought and died? Thousands of years from now they'll be asking the same question about us. That is, if we don't blow up the planet first.

"When my parents were viciously murdered, it wasn't just a crime. It was history repeating itself; it was some men thinking that other people's lives were of less value than their own. This has happened since the first man and it is up to us to break the chain of violence and ignorance and hatred. We kill each other because of borders. We kill each other because of religion. We kill each other because of color. We kill each other because our ancestors killed each other. It has to end if mankind is to survive. Each of us has to make this happen, in our everyday lives. I want to break the chain. I want the killing to stop; I want to live in a world where we don't have to be afraid of each other, where we don't feel like we need a gun to protect ourselves. Or more locks on our doors.

"So, class of 'seventy-eight, tomorrow is calling. What kind of tomorrow it will be depends on us and the decisions we make today. It is up to us to leave our children a better world than the one our parents left us. Because if we won't do it, who will?"

There are different kinds of quiet. Bored quiet. Embarrassed quiet. The quiet after you first smell a fart but nobody's been accused of cutting it yet. This quiet is dead quiet. Edge of your seat dead quiet. The something's gotta happen soon, but nobody knows what it's gonna be quiet.

I hear somebody in the bleachers clapping. Everybody turns around, and there's the miserable old cow, and she's up on her feet, clapping her hands together so hard they must sting like hell.

I thought she'd be pissed that she didn't get her tribute, but as Aunt Nora says, *People can still surprise you.*

In like a nanosecond, the class of '78 is up on its feet, clapping, screaming, and hollering. People throw their square hats in the air even though we were warned that anybody who did wouldn't get a diploma.

Some people in the bleachers join us; others look like they wanna puke.

Mr. Rogers is at the microphone. "Okay, let's settle down, everyone, that's enough. Thank you, Laurie, for your thought-provoking comments. Let's sit down now, quiet please."

But it's pretty hopeless. Some people are cheering 'cause they liked what Laurie said, some people are screaming 'cause we're graduating, other people are going mental 'cause it's fun to go mental, especially in a crowd of people who are all going mental with you.

Laurie just sits on her chair on the stage, staring at her notebook. Fey Hayes gets up and shakes her hand, but you can tell Mr. Rogers wants to pop her one.

We nickname her Laurie Fonda.


We've turned in our caps and gowns so now it's time to get shit-faced. Rick Foley is having a kegger tonight, our final blowout as the class of '78. In keeping with the spirit of our class, there are separate and unequal parties for each clique. Laurie invited me to a brainiac party where they'll drink wine and listen to music and play board games like Risk or Monopoly. I told her that I liked her speech and to celebrate, I was gonna get smashed at Rick Foley's house. She kind of cringed but then she told me to enjoy myself.

Rick Foley's parents are at the party so it's hard to find a place to get high. But leave it to Rick Foley; he's thought of everything, and there's a stash of brownies in the basement. It's kinda weird with magic brownies 'cause you get high, then you get the munchies, so then you eat more brownies, and then you're stoned to the gills. That's what Tommy said anyway, right before he crashed beneath the Ping-Pong table.

I'm only a little high when I see Jon Thompson come down the stairs by himself. He sees me too and stops, and I can tell he's wondering if he should go back upstairs. But finally he comes all the way down and grunts, "Hey."

I nod. I expect him to avoid me, but he stands right next to me. I look at his chocolate hair and I still want to touch it. He's afraid of me, but he's like the omega wolf who crawls to the alpha, getting his permission to hang with the pack. He must think that a good strategy is a common enemy, so he says, "Now I know why you broke up with Allison. Stupid cunt won't put out."

"She's not a cunt and she broke up with me, I didn't break up with her."

He looks at me funny. I was supposed to agree with him and then stand around bitching all night about Allison or maybe girls in general. He says, "You still like her?"

"Yeah."

He shakes his head. " 'Cause you can have her, man. Good luck, you'll fucking need it."

What is it about this guy? I don't know whether to kick his ass or grab it with both hands. I say, "She has a mind of her own, you know, and she's not yours to give to anybody. Jeez, you can say some really stupid shit, you know that?"

He mumbles, "Sorry." His attempt at détente a bust, he walks away, looking for the brownies that are almost all gone. I see Tommy's feet move a little under the Ping-Pong table so I fill up my cup with beer and sit down next to where he lies on the floor. It's kinda uncomfortable 'cause I'm all stooped over.

Tommy says, real soft, "I'm so stoned, Jesus, I am so stoned."

I take a sip and spill a little on my shirt; I filled the cup up too much. I wipe myself and ask Tommy, "Have you seen Rick Foley anywhere?"

Tommy rolls his head back and forth. "He's passed out in the backyard. We stashed him in the garage so his parents won't find out."

I laugh.

Tommy says, "You're my best friend, you know that? You're my main man, Kev."

"Thanks. You're pretty fucked up, aren't you?"

He giggles and rolls onto his side, pulling his knees up to his chest. "Yeah. But I'm telling the truth, you know, you're the best friend I ever had. You're like my brother, Kev."

"You're like my brother too."

He closes his eyes. "That's cool. We're brothers. We gotta find a place to live or I'm gonna kill my mom." He opens his eyes back up. "Oh, sorry! I'm sorry. Your mom's dead. I'm sorry."

I smirk. "It's cool, don't freak."

He's looking right at me. "But I'm really, really sorry, Kev. Your mom was so cool."

I look at my beer. "She was?"

Tommy's gushing. "Oh, yeah, yeah, she was so cool. I really liked her. Remember when I slept over when we were ten and I broke a window? She didn't yell or anything. She never even told my mom about it. That was cool."

I nod.

Now he says, "And when my folks split up, I was practically living at your house. I'd talk to her about stuff and she'd listen to me, you know, really listen."

"Why do you get along with my family so much better than I do?"

He giggles again. " 'Cause they're so cool. Yeah. So very cool."

We're quiet for a while and every couple of minutes somebody sticks their head under the table, wanting to know what's going on. Some jock says, "What, you guys making out or something?"

Before I can tell him to fuck off, Tommy says, "Yeah." He pats the floor. "Come on down so I can fuck that tight little pussy of yours."

Oh, my God. I laugh really hard and say to the guy, "I can fuck you better than he can." I grab my crotch and I say, like I'm stuck behind one of those stupid free sample tables at Red Owl, "Taste and compare!"

His mouth drops open and then he says, "You guys are sick."

I say, "Aw, don't be such a priss. I bet you're a screamer."

The guy's there one second and gone the next. Tommy's still giggling and rolling around on the floor. Then he says, "Kev, I don't feel so good." That's when the brownies and about a six-pack of beer come out of his mouth.

"Oh, man, Tommy, you just spewed all over. Jesus."

He just says, "Ohhhhhh."

I crawl around him and pull him out from under the table by his armpits. "Do you think you can stand up?"

He moans. Now I almost puke because there's like strings of spit hanging off his lips. I look around at the gawkers, but nobody's laughing at Tommy 'cause he looks so gross. I whisper, "Come on, let's find a bathroom," as I yank him up off the floor. He leans into me hard and says, "I'm sorry, Kev, I'm really sorry."

Then I think about what he said to the jock and I laugh. "Don't be," I tell him. "This is the most fun I've had in weeks."

Tommy smiles at me with his eyes closed.

## July 1978

Aunt Nora runs into the sitting room, a big man smile on her big man face. I can hardly move. Red Owl is out of control right before the Fourth of July holiday and I've just come off a twelve-hour shift. I barely hear her when she says, "It's Allison on the phone for you!"

When I don't jump straight up in the air, she looks disappointed. She says, "Hurry along, you might not get another chance."

She's hovering around in the kitchen when I pick up the phone. I give her a look and she goes back in the sitting room, but just barely. She turns off the TV so she won't miss anything.

I say, "Hey."

Allison says, "Hi, Kevin."

And?

She says, "I feel bad that I've been avoiding you."

"It's cool."

She says, "No, it's not, it was a really immature thing to do. I was just embarrassed."

"I'm the one who should be embarrassed. I'm just glad you didn't tell anybody that I couldn't get it up."

From the silence on her end I know she's blushing. Finally, she's able to say, "I would never do that. You guys make too big a deal out of stuff like that. You know that I like you a lot, Kevin, I still do."

I hear Aunt Nora inching toward the kitchen. I say, "Hold on a second." I put my hand over the phone and say, "Would you give me two seconds of privacy, for Christ's sake?"

Aunt Nora says, "Language," and heads upstairs.

"Sorry about that. My aunt has to stick it in everything."

Allison laughs and says, "I almost miss her. I bet she's thrilled that we've stopped seeing each other."

"She likes you now that you dumped me."

"I didn't dump you, Kevin. I just thought that . . . you didn't want me. That I wasn't pretty enough or something."

"Girls worry too much about that. Anyway, you're going with Jon Thompson now."

She makes a snort noise and says, "Not anymore, I'm not. He's such an asshole, pardon my French."

"Yeah, well, he knows what he wants."

"Let's not waste time talking about him. Are you doing alright?"

"Working my ass off."

"I've thought about dropping by to see you but I wasn't sure it was a good idea."

When I don't say anything, she says, "I know it's late, but I was wondering if you wanted to get a burger tonight. I have the car."

"I don't know, Allison, I'm pretty beat."

The way she says it tells me that she's starting to cry. "I miss being with you. I miss calling you honey. I miss the way you used to hold me. I'm sorry, Kevin, it's just I was so embarrassed. I felt humiliated, you know? Like there was something wrong with me. And then you never called."

I look at the phone. High school is finally over, and I lived through it. I don't have to do this if I don't want to, nobody will talk, but if they do, I don't have to see them ever again, so what does it matter? I don't wanna do this. I could lie, like Dad does, but I decide to tell her the truth. I say, "I think you're really cool and pretty and everything, Allison. You mean a lot to me. But, you know, I've got something else going on now. I'm really sorry."

She's quiet for a second, and then she says, "Okay. It's my fault, I should have known you'd be going with somebody else by now. Maybe I'll catch you later?"

"Cool. See ya around."

She says in short hard breaths, "Bye, Kevin. Take care of yourself."

I put the phone down and rub my eyes. I just want to go to bed. I just want to be left alone.


Lorraine's reading the *Enquirer*. It's Thursday night and nobody's shopping 'cause the weather's so nice. In the winter they don't shop, 'cause the weather's so bad. It gives Lorraine a lot of free time at register three.

"Mmmm, look at this, John-John Kennedy is breaking with the family tradition and going to Brown. How do you like that?"

How am I supposed to like it?

Lorraine says, "He's turned out to be so handsome. I remember when he was a little boy and saluted his father's casket. It just broke my heart. Poor little boy."

In my family, the Kennedys are saints. Aunt Nora and Mom used to talk about them all the time. I remember how Aunt Nora spent a week in bed after Bobby was shot. How neither of them ever forgave Jackie for marrying again. Aunt Nora has a shrine to the Kennedys and Martin Luther King, Jr.—another one of her heroes—in her tiny dining room. Whenever I walk by it, she says, "Stop and say a prayer for the greatest men of our time." Whenever she said it, I felt guilty for fantasizing about John-John.

Lorraine says, "Hello? Anybody home?"

"What?"

Lorraine tsk-tsks. "Honestly, Kevin, you're always a million miles away."

I shrug.

"Isn't it a shame you're not going to Brown? You and John-John would be classmates."

Yeah, Brown was beating down my door to get me to enroll. The recruiter said, *We need more homosexuals with C averages who can't afford our tuition. Wanna bunk with John-John?*

Lorraine says, "The U is a good school though. Plus you get to stay in Minneapolis, so I don't have to lose my star bagger."

Lorraine's trying to cheer me up. So I say, "Lorraine, are you sweet on me?"

She snorts and says, "Oh, you!"

So we're enjoying ourselves when the miserable old cow walks through the sliding doors in a maternity dress. She doesn't stop to grab a cart. Instead, she walks straight over to us and says, "Good evening, Kevin."

Lorraine almost chokes. "Well, look at you, back after all this time! And expecting, to boot! Congratulations, you must be thrilled."

The miserable old cow says, "Oh, I am, I am. But I suppose Kevin's already told you all about it."

Lorraine smiles way too big and says, "About what?"

The cow looks at me and says in a voice that's borderline pissed off. "About becoming my stepson. He did tell you that his father and I got married, didn't he?"

Lorraine puts her hands on her cheeks and sucks all the air out of the place. "Oh, no! Not a word! Oh, my God, you snagged Patrick Doyle! Good for you, honey, good for you!"

The cow and I just shoot each other looks.

Then Lorraine figures it out. She says, "That means you're going to have a little brother or sister, Kevin! Oh, my! Isn't this exciting? Kevin's going to be a big brother, oh, how wonderful."

The cow says, "I suppose Kevin wanted me to break the news to you myself."

Yeah, a checker at a store you never go to anymore shouldn't have to hear it on the street.

Lorraine says, "So when are you due?"

"December. It looks like I'll have an extra-special Christmas this year."

Lorraine coos, "Oh, isn't that marvelous? You must have to pinch yourself."

How 'bout a right cross?

The cow moos, "If you had told me even six months ago that I'd be an old married lady again with a baby on the way, I would have said, 'You're crazy!' It just goes to show you how life can change like that." She snaps her fingers.

Lorraine says, "So, do you want a little girl or a little boy?"

"Oh, it doesn't make any difference to me at all. I'm already in love with my baby, I couldn't love it more if I tried."

Lorraine claps her hands and squeals like she's the one who knocked the cow up. "Have you decided on names yet?"

The cow says, "Well, Pat likes James for a boy, but I'm not sure how I feel about it. Sarah if it's a girl."

"Oh, how thrilling."

The cow leans in and whispers loud enough for me to hear, "Pat wanted to name it Eileen if it's a girl, but I said I didn't think that that was such a good idea."

Lorraine nods. She says, all quiet, "I can understand him wanting that, but I suppose you're right."

"Well," the miserable cow moos, "I better get started on my shopping before my ankles swell up."

Lorraine laughs and says, "If you need the ladies, just let me know, I'll take you back to the employees' rest room, it's much nicer than the public one."

As soon as the cow's gone, Lorraine turns on me. "Why didn't you tell me that your father got remarried? I didn't know he had started dating. And now you're going to have a little sister or brother!"

I shift to my right leg and say, "What's the big deal?"

"*What's the big deal?* Is that what you just said? Honestly, Kevin, sometimes I wonder what goes on in that head of yours. This is big news."

Then Lorraine frowns and says all mushy, "Are you happy about it? Did they have to get married?"

I could tell her the truth, I'm not happy about it, that cow killed my mom, but what's the point? "If she makes him happy, it's okay, I guess."

Lorraine shakes her head and says, "Boy, if I had known your dad was finally ready to start dating . . . you tell me, how many single Catholic men my age are there who aren't divorced? I bet ya she knew what she was doing, all right. It just kills me, she could have gone with a divorced man, being divorced herself, but no, she has to snap up a widower." She sighs and says, "Oh, well, good for her," like she's saying, *Hope that bitch rots in hell.*

Tommy's got the top down on the Challenger, this is the time of year he lives for. His mother thought he was an idiot for getting a convertible in Minnesota 'cause the summer's so short. But he says that's exactly why you gotta have a convertible in Minnesota. He's honking the horn, he can't wait to find an apartment. I said we should wait till August, but he can't take living at home even one minute more, so we're gonna look at mid-month leases.

I can't find my sneakers so Aunt Nora goes out front to keep Tommy company. When I join them, she says, "Why doesn't Tommy just move in here, you two can share your room. I won't even charge you rent. You're going to need every penny for college."

Before I can tell her why that idea bites the big one, Tommy says, "I can't be under the same roof with you, Miss O'Connor. I won't be able to control myself. I already got one girl pregnant."

She slaps his hand really hard and he goes, "Owww! Jeez, that hurt."

"Serves you right," she says, but then she smiles.

I jump in the shotgun seat and say, "Let's peel some rub-bah."

Aunt Nora shakes her head. "So you'd rather make a check out to some landlord every month than live with your own flesh and blood."

I say, "That's a big ten-four, good buddy."

Now she looks hurt, so I say, "Come on, Aunt Nora, we're eighteen now. We want to be out on our own."

She says, "I suppose."

Tommy blows her a kiss, which she really doesn't think is funny, and we're off. All we can afford are one-bedrooms with shared baths. The first place we look at has mouse shit all over the kitchen counters. The second place has a bunch of holes in the wall that the caretaker tells us we can cover up with posters. But one of the holes is so big that I don't think that even Adrienne Barbeau's boobs could hide it. The third one isn't much better, but it's got more room. The guy who shows it to us says we can have it today if we give him a deposit and the first month's rent. Tommy tells him he'll change the guy's oil and flush out the radiator in the fall if he doesn't make us put a deposit down. He thinks it over, and bargains Tommy up to two oil changes, a flush, and a new air filter. They shake and we've got ourselves a new home. When we're back out on the street, Tommy grabs me by the shoulders and hugs me. "We're free, Kev! We're free men! Man, this is so cool."

I say, "I guess I should tell Dad I'm moving."

Tommy wants to haul our shit over right away, but I can't move in tonight, I gotta work at Red Owl. Tommy's kind of bummed, but he decides to move in today anyway. He's so psyched that it's kinda cute. He says, "It's right on a bus route to the U so you won't have to fuck with trying to park on campus."

I sit in my bucket seat and almost jump out of my skin. "Jeez, Tommy, why'd ya get a convertible with a black interior?"

" 'Cause it looks cool."

Tommy puts the key in the ignition. First try and the engine won't turn over.

Tommy mutters "Fuck," and gives it another go.

Second try and we hear *blub-blub* and then the engine goes dead.

Tommy says "Fuck," again. We're both starting to sweat, stuck to the seats like flies on No-Pest Strips.

Third try and the engine turns over and stays over. But I go, "Fuck!"

Tommy looks at me. "What's wrong?"

I smack the dashboard. "I forgot to apply to the U. Jesus!"

Tommy's quiet for a second or two, but then he starts laughing. So I smack him one.

• • •

When I get to Red Owl for my shift, I got maybe an hour to call the Admissions Office at General College before they close for the day. Lorraine hates it when I ditch her even for my designated breaks, but she says I'm acting so squirrelly that she can handle things without me for a few minutes. I bolt for the phone in the break room—local calls only, no more than two minutes per call—and I grab the beat-up directory underneath it and search for General College. I look under the University of Minnesota, but there's about ten million numbers to choose from and I don't have time to look through them all. So I pick one and dial and I wind up with the School of Agriculture, Department of Animal Husbandry. Jesus.

Whoever answers the phone is a friendly hick and connects me to the Admissions Office. As I hear the phone ringing, I think up excuses for why I'm calling so late. *My mom died.* True, and so long as they don't ask me when she died, it oughtta work. What else? *My dad kicked me out of the house.* True again. What else . . . why the hell do I even want to go to college? What's so great about being the first Doyle man to enroll in a university?

It's a guy who picks up and he sounds old. "General College Admissions, may I help you?"

"Uh, hi. I wanna enroll. You know, in college?"

"Are you a high school graduate? Do you have a G.E.D.?"

"I graduated in June from Northeast."

It sounds like he's wiping his nose. "All right then, just drop off a completed application and we'll get you processed. Did you want to start fall term?"

"Yeah."

"All right then. Do you need directions?"

*Jesus. I'm going to college.* "You mean I'm accepted?"

"You graduated, right?"

"Yeah."

"You're accepted."

Jesus! I mean, I know it's open enrollment, but Jesus! I'm a Golden Gopher! Me, Kevin Doyle!

Lorraine's looking at me funny when I get back to our register. "What was that all about? You're looking awfully pleased with yourself."

I look at my nails like a man's supposed to, palm toward your face and fingers folded over. "Just talking with the folks at the U. I'm gonna be a freshman there, you know."

"This is news? I already knew that."

I smile at her 'cause I can be so charming when I want to be. "Just reminding you, Lorraine. I'm a college man now."

She shakes her head. "You'll be a little fish in a big pond. It's not going to be like high school where you know everyone and everyone knows you."

"Thank God for that."

She laughs and says, "You'll need to learn the rouser."

"The what?"

"The rouser. For the football games. I dated a college boy for a while when I was a girl. He took me to all the Gopher games and we sang the rouser."

I look around. "Nobody's here. Sing it."

Lorraine gets all giggly and says no, she couldn't possibly sing it, my cue to beg her. So I do and finally she clears her throat with a little *ahem*.

"It's been years," she tells me.

"Go on."

She puts a hand on top of the register and the other on her hip. In a voice that sounds like slamming on the brakes, she sings:

> "Minnesota, hats off to thee
> To thy colors true we shall ever be
> Firm and brave, united are we
> Rah Rah Rah for Ski U Mah
> Rah, Rah, Rah, Rah
> Rah for the U of M!"

Jeez, no wonder they need an open enrollment program.

• • •

Beth's standing in front of our building. It's muggy, like it always is in late July, on account of all the lakes in this city. And the Mississippi. She looks like she's dying from the humidity. Her stomach's swollen and her face is pink and wet. When she sees me get off the bus—I had to loan Tommy the Dart again—she says, "Will Tommy be back soon?"

Her legs are skinny and her maternity dress doesn't come down much farther than her thighs. Over in England they just had a test tube baby, which I thought was cool until I found out that it was born the same way Beth's baby is gonna be. I had kinda thought that it grew in the test tube. Aunt Nora's upset about it, not because it's against God's will, but because she says there's enough English in the world already without having to manufacture more. I look Beth over and say, "He's over at the Standard."

She laughs, but it's a mean laugh. "I thought his mom made him quit that job months ago."

Tommy did quit. He said to his mom, *I quit*, but he didn't say it to his boss. He just called in sick till things blew over. I say, "Well, yeah, but he's back."

She pulls on the hem of her dress, embarrassed it's so short. "Can you tell him I stopped by . . . nah, forget it. Don't say anything."

She takes a step but I block her way. "Come on upstairs, I'll get you something cold to drink."

She doesn't look me in the eyes, just nods her head. Our apartment is over a Laundromat and Beth struggles on the steep stairs, hanging on to the railing for all she's worth. By the time we make the landing she's breathing hard and wiping the sweat from her eyes. It takes a minute to open the door; there's three locks to keep out the drunks who wander up from the Laundromat, looking for a place to piss. We enter and Beth looks around, disappointed. The walls needed a fresh coat like ten years ago and the ceiling is brown from water stains. The place is like a furnace 'cause we can't open the windows more than a couple of inches; nails stick out of the frames to keep burglars out. A little portable

TV sits on the floor by itself. There are two other rooms, a kitchen and a bedroom. We share a bathroom with another apartment down the hall. When Beth sees the poster of Adrienne Barbeau she rolls her eyes.

"Nice pad," she says.

I open the fridge with the fan on top. "You want a Coke or a Special Ex?"

"Just a glass of ice water."

I look in the freezer, thick with frost. The frigid air feels good so I keep the door open as I say, "Sorry, Tommy forgot to fill up the tray."

"Just water then."

"Cool."

I run the tap and grab a plastic cup from the stack I stole from Red Owl. When the water feels a little less warm, I fill the cup. I hand it to her and she says, "Yeah, thanks."

I watch her drink it down. When she's nearly finished she puts a couple of fingers in the cup and flicks some water on her face.

"So how you been?" I ask her.

She finishes her water. "Pretty shitty. How have you been?"

I lie. "Okay."

She looks back and forth and says, "Is there anyplace to sit down?"

"We don't have any chairs yet. We're gonna go Dumpster diving on Sunday."

Slowly, she lowers herself down to the floor, grunting the whole way, and sits, her legs spread out in front of her, her arms behind her. "How has Tommy been?"

I sit across from her, cross-legged. "He's cool. He's excited about Dunwoody."

She says, "Yeah, he would be."

We sit there for a while. I say, "Is it a boy or a girl?"

"Boy."

"Cool."

"They've picked out the parents already. I haven't met them, but my case worker says they're very nice. They live out in Minnetonka."

I lie down on the floor and look up at the rotting ceiling. "Minnetonka? Never been there. They must be loaded."

"Yeah."

"That's good."

"Yeah."

"Do you get any money from the deal?"

She sighs. "Medical and living expenses until the baby's born." She lets her head drop back and stares at the ceiling with me. "I think I'm doing the right thing."

I say, "So do I."

## AUGUST 1978

It's about a million degrees in the shade. Pope Paul VI died two weeks ago and Aunt Nora is still upset about it. She calls me every day to tell me what a wonderful man he was and how she can't believe he's gone. It's like when Elvis died for other people. When Tommy answers the phone he doesn't kid her, he just tells her how sorry he is for her loss, like she's a widow.

I'm at the U for freshman orientation. I have to be herded around campus with the rest of the new General College students. Actually, they call it GC, not General College. GC's open admission, which is why my group looks more like a gang than a class. When we pass the Institute of Technology geeks on the mall it's like a reunion of bullies and victims.

One of the Institute guys looks at us and says, "Those guys from county corrections?"

Donnell White, who is black, is in my group, but he hangs with the other black guys. I hang with a short guy who's got really big pecs, you can tell 'cause his T-shirt's tight as skin. He's built like those Olympic gymnasts who get me all hot and bothered. His name's Jack and he's from the Iron Range. I was checking him out when he caught me looking at him.

He came right up next to me and said, "I don't know if I can hack college."

I said, "Me neither."

Now he's saying, "Those Institute guys look pretty wimpy."

I say, "Kicking their asses would be doing them a favor."

He laughs even though it's not really funny. He says, "I'll get lunch during the break. My treat."

I blush. "You don't have to do that, man."

He smiles and keeps looking me right in the eyes. He says, "I know I don't *have* to. I *want* to."

I look stupid and say, "Cool, thanks."

We go to the campus health service where we listen to a talk about rape, the clap, alcohol, and drugs. The speaker is part of what she calls a "peer education group." We're her peers, being educated. She's like the girls who were in pep club, the ones who didn't make the cut for the cheerleading squad.

Jack's sitting next to me, and our arms are touching, but he doesn't pull his away. It feels so cool. I concentrate on the sensation of his skin against mine. It's like a current running between us.

For lunch he buys us a couple of slices and pop from a lunch truck. We're sitting on Northrop Mall. There are little picnics everywhere. Guys are playing Frisbee; a girl is strumming her guitar. It's like this whole different world, and it's so close to where I grew up I can't believe it.

When Jack sits down he takes off his shirt. He does it all slow and sexy like he knows I'm staring. I almost drop my slice in my lap. He rubs his neck with both hands and his biceps flex.

He says, "Have to catch the rays while we can."

"Yeah."

He knows he looks scrump-dilly-icious without a shirt. He acts like he's tired and stretches his arms behind his head and sticks his very fine chest right out at me. I try not to stare at his tits, but I can't help myself. I've never touched a guy in my life, apart from slapping or hitting and occasionally shaking a hand. I want to put my hands on his skin and know what it feels like. It's like I've been waiting my whole life to do it. I'm afraid I won't be able to control myself, that I'll just reach over and grab him.

He says, "You oughtta catch some rays too." He says it like it's an order: "Take off your shirt."

I pull my green T over my head. It's kind of pitted out from the heat and from being with him.

Jack checks me out like he doesn't give a shit that I might think he's a fag and says, "You must bench-press, you got a really excellent build."

*Holy shit.* "Nah, it must be from hauling kegs around."

Jack laughs. "You gotta invite me to your next party."

"Cool."

He pulls out his wallet and writes his name and number on a sales receipt from the U bookstore. "I'm sharing a place over on the West Bank with a couple of guys from Silver Bay. Give me a call, we can hang out sometime."

"Cool."

He frowns as he runs his index finger over my stomach and then slides it up my chest and flicks a nipple. He says, "Man, you sweat a lot. It's like you got a river running down your chest."

I open my mouth but nothing comes out. What I want to say is, *Can I do that to you?* But what I do say is, "Uh."

He wipes his hand off on my thigh. "What are you gonna major in?"

"I dunno."

He says, "I was thinking that I'd transfer from GC to the College of Liberal Arts. Get a history degree or something."

I'm still feeling his finger on my nip. His hand on my thigh. I want him to touch me again.

He says, "You don't talk much, do you?"

I smile at him. I want to reach over and squeeze his tits so bad. Now I know what Tommy felt like when he was freaking out over Adrienne Barbeau. Jack's tits are, like, all I can think about. I want to do the squeezy squeezy thing with my hands. I wanna talk about his tits to anybody who'll listen.

He finishes his pizza and puts his shirt back on slower than he took it off. He stands up and holds out his hand, saying, "Come on, man, we gotta bolt or we're gonna be late."

His grip is strong. He pulls me up and when I'm next to him, he doesn't let go right away, it's like we're holding hands. He squeezes my fingers and says, "Next time, you can buy."

# YOU SHOULD SEE WHAT
# GOES ON IN THERE

I'm giving off *love* vibes. At Red Owl Lorraine looks at me funny. Then she says, "You got lucky, didn't you?"

I blush. I giggle. I actually go like *tee hee hee.* I tell her, "Jeez, knock it off."

She says, smiling really big, "That's why you've been acting so strange tonight. Are you and Allison back together? Oh, that's wonderful!"

I say, "Customer."

Fey Hayes wheels his cart up to register three and says, "Good evening, Mr. Doyle."

I say, "What's happening, Miss TerHaze?"

"Just a little under the weather. This heat is oppressive."

Lorraine says, "Well, you know what they say, it's not the heat, it's the humidity."

Fey Hayes puts a box of Creamette pasta shells on the belt and says, "Are you certain that is what they do indeed say?"

She doesn't get his sarcasm 'cause she never had him for English Lit. She says, "Sure I am. They have these heat indexes now, just like the windchill in winter? Tells you what the temperature is and then what it feels like on your skin."

Fey Hayes stops unloading and leans against his cart. I say, "You okay?"

He looks at me and lets out a gasp. He almost whispers, "I believe I need to sit down."

Lorraine looks at me and back at him. "Kevin, you take him back to the break room and get him a cold can of pop."

Fey Hayes says, a little stronger now, "Thank you, I think that would be a good idea."

I walk around and put an arm around his shoulders. He puts an arm around my waist and teeters a little. I say, "Are you gonna make it? Do you wanna sit on the floor for a minute?"

He shakes his head and says, real slow, "I'm—just—a—bit—light—headed."

We weave our way to the break room, stopping every few steps to let him catch his breath. He sits on one of the ugly yellow plastic chairs. There's ashtrays everywhere and he almost puts his elbow in a pile of butts. I say, "Is there somebody you want me to call?"

He says, real fast, "No! No, I'll be fine." He fakes a smile and says, "Just need to get off my feet for a few minutes. It's the heat that does me in, that's all."

I get him a Coke, not one of the discount brands. When I get back with the pop, he looks a little better. As I snap it open and hand it to him, he says, "Thank you, I think the sugar will do me good."

I stand there looking at him. He takes a little sip, wheezes, and then takes another. He says, "You can get back to work, Mr. Doyle, I promise not to have a stroke on your shift."

I smile. "No sweat, if Lorraine needs me she can page me. Thursdays are never that busy."

He closes his eyes and runs the side of the can over his face.

"I know, that's why I do all the shopping on Thursday evenings. I'm not too keen on crowds."

I sit down at the table across from him. His breathing's steadier, and some of the color's back on his face. He says, "How have you been faring since graduation?"

"Really cool. I'm going to go to the U and keep my hours here. I like the U a lot." Jack goes to the U. I think Jack was flirting with me, but I'm not sure, 'cause I don't know how a guy is supposed to flirt with a guy. I wanna find out, but I don't know how. Can you tell? Is there something guys do to let each other know they're into guys? 'Cause nobody's told me and I need to know pretty fucking bad.

He takes another sip of pop, holding the can with a pinky sticking out, like it's a cup of tea. "I remember my college days," he says. "To paraphrase Dickens, they were the best of times, they were the worst of times."

I never read *A Christmas Carol.* "What do you mean?"

"The war, of course. My education was interrupted for several years."

"That bites."

He grins a little and says, "Yes, it did bite. They sent me to the Philippines. The Japanese kept me there as their guest."

My mouth drops. "You were a prisoner of war?"

He takes out his handkerchief and dabs his forehead, just at the corners. "Yes. It's not a time I care to dredge up very often, but yes, I was a prisoner of the Japanese. Their hospitality left something to be desired."

I look at him. He wouldn't be telling me all this unless he was afraid that he almost dropped dead. I say, "So you were a war hero. Did they give you a medal?"

He laughs a nasty kind of laugh. "No, they didn't give me a medal. You'd be very surprised by what they did give me." He closes his eyes and runs his handkerchief over his lips. "Well," he says, eyes open, "you don't need to hear an old man ramble on about the bad old days."

Beats working.

"Please, go back to your register, I'd hate to get you into trouble. Although you're quite familiar with what that's like."

"You're okay?"

He says, "I'm fine."

I'm almost at the door when he says, "Oh, and Mr. Doyle, why would you stop by woods on a snowy evening?"

I say, " 'cause I was in love." *L-O-V-E.*


I'm over at Aunt Nora's 'cause there's still some of my stuff over there and I need to use her phone. Our apartment is so small that you can hear every word when somebody's talking on the phone and I don't want Tommy listening to this call. I wait for Aunt Nora to go to church so I can talk freely. But she just sits on the cat hair couch, fanning herself with *The Catholic Bulletin.*

"Aren't you gonna go to mass tonight?"

She can hardly lift her big man head. She says, "This heat is murder, the good Lord will have to let me take a pass. I'm gasping, Kevin. Be a pet and get us a cold beer. Have one yourself."

She's at church every single night except when I wanna make a personal call. I grab a couple of Blue Ribbons and put them under my pits for a second or two. Then I go back in the sitting room and give her a bottle.

"Ta," she says. She takes a big man swig. "Cold as ice in the winter and an inferno in the summer. It's days like this that I miss Westport. Even in the summertime it was cool. Nothing like here."

I suck on my beer.

She says, "You don't have much to say for yourself."

I empty the bottle in about thirty seconds and get up. "I'm going for a walk. I'll pack my shit in the Dart when I get back."

Aunt Nora frowns. "Did I say something to upset you?"

I pull up my T-shirt and wipe my face with it. "You didn't do anything, I'm just in a funky mood."

I have to walk around the cats, which are laid out like a minefield.

It's a little cooler outside and I take off my shirt and stick it in the waist of my cutoffs. There's a Tom Thumb two blocks down on Thirty-eighth that has a phone.

On the way over I start freakin'. What do I say when he picks up?

Hey, Jack, it's Kevin. What's happening?

Hey, man, it's Kev. What are you up to tonight?

Hey, Jack, I wanna pour Southern Comfort all over your tits and lick it off again.

Some kids are hanging out in front of the store on their bikes. They're like twelve or thirteen, but they curse like sailors and they're smoking. Of course they've parked themselves right next to the phone.

I tell the one leaning against the booth, "Move it or lose it, pee-wee."

He looks up at me. He's about to tell me to fuck off, but I'm a good foot taller than he is and his expression changes from tough to sulky. But then it changes again, and I can tell he's checking me out. When he reaches my face, he can tell that I can tell that he's just looked me over like I was a girl.

He moves his bike and I stick a dime in the slot, still looking at him. So there's me, Fey Hayes, the Iranian T.A., this twelve-year-old kid, and maybe, if I'm lucky, Jack. It was like he was flirting with me at lunch, right? And when he touched me, he had to know what he was doing, didn't he?

Maybe he was just being friendly.

I should of called him right away; maybe he thinks I'm not interested. But I didn't want him to think I was a fag. I should of given him my number. He's probably like Chuck, just cool with it but into girls. *Jesus.*

I dial.

It rings.

The guy who answers tells me that Jack took off after his rent check bounced.

When I get back to Aunt Nora's, she can tell I'm really pissed.

## September 1978

I look for Jack on campus, hoping that he didn't skip town, that he had just bailed on his roomies. But I don't see him and Lorraine says that my mood swings are getting out of control. When Tommy asks what's wrong I lie and say I miss my mom instead of telling the truth, that Jack's gone and it kills me. It's not like I even knew the guy, but it kills me just the same. When I go to classes I look at the guys and I get sad. In every class there's at least one guy who's so good-looking it hurts. Some are scrawny but beautiful, others are big and built and their asses fill out their jeans like bowling balls. I don't really make friends 'cause I don't know what to say to people. I don't know what to say to the girls and I don't know what to say to the guys. So Tommy and I watch TV a lot on the little black-and-white set his mom wound up buying for him when he moved out. Sometimes Rick Foley comes by with a couple six-packs or some weed, but now that he finally has a girlfriend we don't see him every weekend like we used to.

Tommy's getting kind of desperate. There's hardly any girls at Dunwoody and he wants us to go barhopping every night to meet some. But after classes and my shift at Red Owl, all I want to do is go to bed. Tommy's trying to be patient, but I can tell that he's wondering if sharing an apartment with me was such a good idea after all. Can't say I blame him.

Aunt Nora calls to tell me the new pope is already dead. And after she had just gotten pictures of him up in her house. I tell her, "We all gotta go sometime," and she hangs up on me.

My mood doesn't improve when Dad finally calls. We haven't said boo to each other since I graduated. He wants to get together and talk *man to man*, but I think we're one short and I don't mean me. I meet him at Grumpy's, his favorite bar in Northeast and an appropriate choice since it's us, after all.

When he sees me he gets off his bar stool and shakes my hand, like he's meeting a friend. I just let my hand sit in his, waiting for when he's done with it. He sounds like he means it when he says, "It's good to see you, son."

I nod.

He smiles and shakes his head. "You're getting kind of old for the sullen kid routine."

He's right, so I ask him, "How are you?"

We pull our stools up to the bar and Dad waves at the bartender as he asks me, "What can I get you?"

"Special Ex."

He doesn't argue. He tells the bartender as he holds up a glass, "Once more and a Special Ex for my pride and joy, here."

The bartender doesn't smile, he takes the bar's name seriously. Dad winks at me and says, "I'm fine, I'm fine, thanks for asking."

"You got work yet?"

He laughs. "Odd jobs here and there. Nothing permanent, but I know something will come along."

"How's"—the cow? The bitch? The woman who murdered my mother?—"your wife?"

"Getting bigger every day. That's why I wanted to talk to you."

I frown and the bartender sets two mugs down in front of us. Dad lifts his, waiting for me to join him in a toast. We clink our glasses as he says, "Better days."

"Better days," I tell him and suck down maybe half my beer.

Dad wants to smoke. The index finger and middle finger on his right hand separate a little, holding a phantom cigarette. He says, "How's school going? Are you the big man on campus?"

I roll my eyes. "Yeah, I'm the big man on campus. There're fifty thousand students, but I'm the big man on campus."

Dad smirks. "Getting good grades?"

"We just started classes. But I'm kind of worried, you know. Maybe I should cut back on my hours at Red Owl so I can study more."

"Maybe." Dad takes a sip of foam. "You know, Carol's due in December."

"Yeah."

"So you're going to have a little brother or sister."

"Yeah."

He puts a hand on my shoulder and says, "So I'm counting on you to act like a big brother. I want you to look out for your little brother or sister."

I shrug.

His grip on my shoulder tightens. "I mean it. Just because this baby isn't your mother's doesn't mean it's not a member of the family. Don't hold a grudge against your brother or sister because you're mad at Carol and me. I won't have you acting like your Aunt Nora around this kid."

I shake my head and laugh a little. "I wouldn't do *that* to anybody."

Dad laughs too and his grip relaxes. He pats me twice on the arm and returns to his beer and his invisible cig. "Good boy," he says. "You're a good boy, Kevin."


If I don't do it with a guy soon I'll lose my fucking mind. Last week I hid an article in the *Tribune* under my bed. It's about this big old bar downtown called The Gay 90's. It used to be a strip joint a long time ago, but now it's for guys who like guys. The reporter went in and interviewed a bunch of the customers about Anita Bryant and the referendum coming up in St. Paul. I can't believe it 'cause I've gone past the 90's about a million times. It's right on Hennepin, the main drag through downtown Minneapolis, but I've never seen anybody go in or out of the place. I don't think a bar could make it with just Fey Hayes, the Iranian T.A., and a twelve-year-old kid for customers, so there's gotta be a lot more guys like me in this city.

So I decide that tonight's the night I'm gonna find out. Tommy's gotta baby-sit his brothers 'cause even his mom has a date. It's like the last straw, everybody's on the hunt for somebody except me. And Aunt Nora. 'Cause she's been dumped so many times she gave up on men. She always says, *I wasted my prime years on lowlifes. And now I'm past it.*

Tommy's getting ready to leave. He asks me, "You wanna watch my brothers with me? I gotta case of Bud."

I can't look at him; I'm scared he'll figure out what I'm up to. "Uh, no thanks."

"Come on, they think you're really cool. They'd love to see you."

I look at Tommy, his hair pulled back tight in a ponytail, a pack of Camels in the pocket of his flannel shirt. "Sorry, man, gotta hit the books. Tell them I say hey."

He watches me, trying to figure out what my problem is today. But then he says, "Cool, do what ya gotta do," and he's gone. I feel kinda bad, if I wasn't so goddamn horny, I'd of baby-sat with him. I listen for the Challenger to start; if he has to borrow the Dart again my plans are screwed. It takes three tries, but the engine turns over and his car *blub-blub-blubs* down the street.

I walk down the hall to the bathroom, but one of the guys from the other apartment beats me to it. I pound on the door. "Hey, I gotta use the john."

"Hang on, I'm almost done."

It takes like maybe five minutes, so I'm pretty pissed when the door finally opens. As he passes by me he says "Sorry" so softly that I almost don't hear him. I watch him walk to the other apartment, and then I remember where I've seen him before; he was one of the addicts at The Safe House. Great, I got junkies living next door.

The bathroom, like everything else in this building, needs a ton of work. The tiles are cracked; the mirror's all scratched up. I miss my house. I take my comb off an old shelf with maybe its twentieth coat of white paint cracking and peeling. I try out different parts in my hair and I think: Fuck all, if only Jon Thompson had told me that he loved me, I wouldn't have to do this. If only Chuck had kissed me harder instead of pulling away like I was some kind of freak. If only. I put the comb back down and look at my face, hard. If I look as good as I think I do, where are all the guys who should be asking me out? Why is this so fucking impossible? *Jesus.*

I walk down the stairs, careful not to trip over an old drunk on the landing. The Dart waits for me on the street, Jackie Shaw's dead husband's car. Jackie Shaw. I should really call her and find out how she's doing, but tonight I gotta get laid. I put the key in the ignition. It starts with no problem and as I drive downtown, I tell myself that tonight is gonna be the night that I meet somebody just like me. He's gonna be my age, and tonight will be his first night in a gay bar too, and we'll see each other, and we'll leave right away and go to his place and have sex and talk about everything. He'll tell me how lonely he's been and I'll tell him how lonely I've been. He'll be my new best friend. I gotta be careful though, so Tommy doesn't get wise. But Jesus, *I gotta get laid*. I gotta meet this guy, whoever he is.

So of course I drive right past the 90's. I don't want the people in the other cars to think that I'm going there, so I don't slow down at all, I don't look for a place to park. *Fuck*. Calm the hell down.

Now I turn right and head back to the 90's. There's a spot near the Army Surplus and I pull in. People will think that I'm going to the Army Surplus, which is a cool thing to do. Except it's closed. Goddamn it. Okay, so I'm window shopping at the Army Surplus. But why would I be in this neighborhood? There's a topless bar next to the 90's; I could pretend I'm heading there. Okay, so that's my story if I see somebody I know: I'm going to the topless bar to get shit-faced and stare at boobs. Also a cool thing to do. I turn off the engine, the lights; I put on the emergency brake. Then I just sit there. I look up and down the sidewalks, waiting for the lynch mob or for the guy I'm gonna meet tonight, the one who's gonna save me. The one who'll tell me that he loves me, that he will always love me. The one I run away with.

But there's no one on the sidewalks. I pull the door open and barely manage to get out of the car before I slam the door shut again. I lock it and pull up on the handle to make sure I've done it right. All that's left to do now is walk to the 90's. So I just stand there, looking in the window of the Army Surplus. Knives, canteens, coats, old medals, helmets, caps, backpacks, camouflage jackets. That's what I need, camouflage. A big fucking bush to hide behind as I sneak into the 90's. I put my hands in my pockets and walk fast, deliberate, like I'm late for a surprise party. Now shapes appear and I walk past men, alone and in pairs, and I can't tell if they are like me or if they hate me, I don't know if they're coming out of the 90's or the strip joint. Some are foxy, some are dogs. A few look at me, their faces asking questions. But I don't dare lose my pace; there's somewhere I pretend I have to go.

I walk by what I think is the front door of the 90's. No one enters or leaves, so I stroll past. I go around the block and every few steps I see a man or men out of the corner of my eye. The ones who walk in little groups smile and talk to each other; they laugh out loud. They ignore me as they share a joke or a secret. I wanna say hello. I wanna say *My name is Kevin and I am so fucking lonely.* But they have no idea who I am any more than I think I know who they are.

The door of the 90's is a few yards ahead of me. Again. I've gone around the block so many times now that I've lost count. The traffic on Hennepin Avenue stops for a red light. I'm scared that the class of '78 is in each car, staring at me, wondering why I'm circling the 90's like a big faggy vulture. I'm scared that they'll figure it out, mouths wide open, faces turning to each other. *Oh, my God, did you see that? Kevin Doyle is a cocksucker!*

I wanna go inside, but I can't make myself do it. So I head to the Dart and stick the key in the lock. I sit inside for a minute or two before I turn the ignition, before I snap the lights on. I drive home, alone, cursing myself. I wanna cry. 'Cause the guy I love was waiting for me in the 90's, but I didn't have the balls to walk through the door and say hello.

I'm back to the apartment and I decide to have a beer and start work on my first essay for freshman composition. So when Tommy gets home I can pretend that I didn't go anywhere, that I was here all night. Besides, I can't flunk out of freshman comp. That's the class that you have to take 'cause they want you to be able to write at the college level. So I snap open a Special Ex and sit on the floor, some paper and a pencil in front of me, still pissed off at myself for not going into the 90's. The essay has to begin with "when I was ten" and has to be between five hundred and five hundred and fifty words.

*When I was ten I was in fifth grade. My best friend was Tommy and he is still my best friend. Our favorite things to do were to watch TV and play baseball.*

Jesus, only thirty-three words. That leaves four hundred and sixty-seven. What else?

*We had to be in the chorus of Huck Finn because everyone was required to be in the play. We wore straw hats and my mom had to buy me a pair of overalls. Our song was "Drat That Boy." We had to sing it three nights in a row.*

Cool, that was fifty words. Four hundred and seventeen left.

*We got really sick of the song because in addition to singing it every night, we had to sing it every day for two weeks in rehearsals. When everyone else would sing "Drat," we would sing "Smack." We thought we were really funny and we would start to crack up. Then we would get in trouble because we were laughing and not singing.*

Sixty-three words. I keep getting better and better at this. Three hundred and fifty-four more and I'm done.

*Our teacher told us if we had the audacity to laugh during the performance, in front of the entire school and all the parents, she would give us ten hours of detention. So even though we stood next to each other, we did not look at each other, because we were afraid that if we did, we would start laughing. The first night my mom and dad and aunt and Tommy's parents came and saw us in the show. We didn't laugh and everybody said we did a good job. That night Dad kept singing "Drat That Boy" and looking at me like he was being really funny.*

*The next night Tommy didn't look at me but he did sing "Smack" instead of "Drat" and I smiled really hard but I didn't laugh. My dad came that night too and asked me why I had a big grin on my face during the song. I lied and told him because I was happy that he was there.*

One hundred and sixty-seven words this time. I deserve another beer.

*The last night I knew that Tommy was going to try and get me in trouble by singing "Smack" and making me laugh. I decided I would one-up him and make him laugh instead. When everybody began to sing*

*"Drat," I came in early and shouted "Smack" and hit Tommy so hard on the back of his head that his straw hat flew into the audience. He shouted "Ow" and people started laughing except for our teacher. She looked like she was going to kill me. She grabbed me while everybody else was still singing and the audience laughed again. She dragged me into the hallway and shook me by the shoulders. She asked me why I had to spoil things for everyone else. How could I be so selfish? Didn't I ever think of anyone but myself? She told me I was a spoiled little boy who needed to grow up.*

*That's when Dad showed up because he was there that night too. You could tell he had been laughing really hard because his eyes were still watery. He told her to leave me alone, I was just a little kid having some fun. He asked her if she had ever been young once. She told him he was setting a bad example and if he didn't take discipline seriously, I would wind up a juvenile delinquent. He thought that was funny.*

Jeez, five hundred and forty-six words. Cool.

Then I think: Jesus, Dad was there every night.

## OCTOBER 1978

You know, every year it's the same deal. You blink and summer's gone. And if you're on the can during fall you miss the leaves changing and falling off the trees. Lots of things happen when you're not looking. There are still over three weeks left till Halloween, but the apartment building's caretaker has taped cardboard ghosts and skeletons on the walls. Some kid has already taken a Magic Marker and written *bite me* on one of the ghosts.

Anytime I see a Halloween ghost I think of Mom. I hope she isn't watching me when I jerk off with my *Playgirls* or take a dump.

This is what I'm thinking about when the phone rings. Tommy picks it up. It's Aunt Nora, but she hasn't called for me, she's still pissed that I didn't offer her my condolences when the last pope bought the farm. She's called to congratulate Tommy on the first Polish pope and tells him she can only imagine how excited he must be.

He says, "Yeah, you can only imagine."

They talk for a while, giving each other shit. As soon as he puts the phone down, it rings again.

I say, "That's probably her again. I bet this pope just kicked the bucket too."

Tommy picks up the phone as he says, "No way, Pollocks live forever." Then he says, "Hello? Yeah, Kev's here. Hang on."

He covers the receiver with his hand and whispers, "It's your stepmother. She sounds kinda freaked."

I get up from where I sit on the floor, sorting albums; Tommy's gotten them all messed up again. He hands me the phone and I say, "Didn't you ever learn your ABCs?"

He smacks me on the back of the head and takes his turn with the stack of LPs. I say to my wicked stepmother, "Yeah, what's happening?"

She says, real fast, like she's on fire: "Is your father there?"

"No." He's never been over here. "What's going on?"

I hear her breaths, short and fast, the kind of sounds an obscene caller makes. I can hear her swallow, which is kinda weird. She says, "He wasn't here when I got home from work. All his clothes are gone. I think he's left me."

Now she starts crying and hyperventilating at the same time. I look over at Tommy and point at the phone, shaking my head. He looks at me, his face asking *What gives?* I say to the phone, "Calm down, I can't understand you."

She's gasping, "I think he's left me. Oh, God!"

I tell her, "He's gone missing before and he's always come back. He's probably drunk and sleeping it off in his car."

She's sobbing for all she's worth, and I make out: "Do you think he's with Jackie?"

I can't help myself, I laugh. "Not unless he wants a pan of cinnamon rolls shoved up his ass."

She screams, "Be serious! Oh, God! Where is he?"

"I'm sorry, okay? Don't scream in my ear, *Jesus.*"

"Will you call her? Will you find out if he's contacted her?"

"Jeez, I don't think I have her number."

"Look it up!"

Tommy's staring at me now. I look at him and roll my eyes. "We don't have a phone book."

"Go over there!"

For Christ's sake. "He's not gonna be at Jackie Shaw's, all right? Just give him a couple days and he'll come crawling back like nothing's happened."

"I can't wait that long. I need him here to help me. God, I'm in my last trimester and the doctor says I'm supposed to stay off my feet."

"Okay, okay, I'll go over to Jackie Shaw's."

"Now?"

"Yeah, now. Give me your number again, I think I lost it."

After I hang up, Tommy says, "What's her problem?"

"My dad. I promised her I'd try and find him."

"He's gone?"

"He did a runner. I gotta find him before she shits her pants."

"Want some help?"

We split up. Tommy takes his Challenger and checks out the bars, starting at Grumpy's. I head over to Jackie Shaw's even though I know it's a big waste of time. As I pull up in her dead husband's Dart I don't see a single light on in her house. I get out of the car and ring the front doorbell. Then I knock. Then I look in some of the ground-floor windows. No sign of Jackie Shaw, let alone Dad.

Maybe he's gone back to the house. Our house. Then I think, That's stupid, somebody else lives there now. But I head over anyway. On the way over I turn the dials on the radio; all the stations play anymore is the BeeGees.

I park the Dart in front of what used to be my house, where I lived for more than eighteen years. The lights are on and as I walk up the front steps I notice that they've rescreened the porch and replaced the rotted floorboards. I ring the doorbell and wait.

I hear an adult yell at a kid, a kid yell at another kid, and then the adult yell again. As the door opens the man is shouting, "Do I have to do everything myself?" Then he turns to me and smiles. "Kids," he says.

Mrs. Bartochevitz must have had a stroke when she found out

that Dad sold the house to a black family. I say, "My name's Kevin
Doyle. You guys bought this house from my dad, Patrick."

The man says, "Actually, I only met him at the closing. We
always dealt with Jackie." Then he says, a little annoyed, "By the
way, women are always stopping by looking for your father. They
want to know where he's living now."

"Trust me, they're happier not knowing. Look, this is gonna
sound weird, but have you seen my dad?"

The man frowns. "No. If there's a problem with the sale, you'll
need to talk to our lawyer. We bought title insurance."

"It's nothing like that. I just don't know where he is."

"Oh."

"I thought he might be drunk off his ass and come round here."

"Oh," the man says again, but deeper and softer this time.

He gets a notebook and a pen so I can leave my name and
number. Before I leave he says, "If it's all the same to you, I think
I'll call the police first and you second if he does show up."

"Good plan." I turn to leave, but I stop myself. "How's the
house working out for you?"

"Great. We love it here."

When I'm back in the Dart I sit and think. I think that Dad's
gone for good.


The phone rings and Tommy asks me to get it. He's studying an
engine diagram. I tell him to get it; it's never for me, it's always
some burnout from Dunwoody. He mutters and answers it. After
he hangs up, he smacks me on the back of my head. He says,
"Your stepmom's had it. Premature, but she's had it. She wants
you to come visit. She's at St. Mary's till Tuesday."

"Cool," I tell him. I'm watching *Saturday Night Live.*

Tommy sits on the floor next to me. "She really wants you
there. Laurie can't get in until late tomorrow. You got a little
sister, man."

I take another bite of my Swanson Hungry-Man salisbury
steak. "I'll go, I'll go, don't sweat it." There are peas in the cob-

bler section of the tray, which pisses me off 'cause I hate peas. Then I get it. Tommy never got to see his own son before Catholic Social Services took him away. I pick a pea out of the mashed potato compartment. I say, "You wanna go over with me now?"

Tommy says, "Cool."

We take the Dart; the Challenger has died again. It's the class project at Dunwoody right now.

We drive and Tommy says, "Aren't you kind of psyched? You're a big brother. When Mom had Timmy I was really psyched. He's a pain in the ass now, but when he was little, it was really cool."

I'm not psyched. "Yeah, I'm psyched."

Okay, now that we're almost there, I'm kind of excited. The hospital is on the West Bank, not far from the leftover hippie shops that sell the pyramids like the one Floyd wore. There are slogans painted on the New Riverside Café and as we pass the People's Center, the phone poles and streetlights get thick with layers of flyers. Finally, we drive by Culla's before we make the turn into St. Mary's. The place is quiet, it's late and visiting hours are over. But when we get to the miserable old cow's floor, a nurse leads us to a double room. The nurse whispers just outside the door, "Hardly anyone's been by since she was admitted, poor dear." Inside is the cow, lying in the shadows like she's had the shit kicked out of her and then stuffed back in again.

When she see us she says, all hoarse, "Thank you for coming."

I say, "Where's the baby?"

She swallows and it must be painful to do, 'cause she scrunches up her face. "The intensive care unit."

Tommy looks at me and frowns. I say, "Cool. Can I go see her, or do I need permission or something?"

She closes her eyes and says, "Just tell them you're her brother. Kevin, you should know that she isn't doing well. There were a lot of complications."

I look at Tommy and back at her. "What do you mean? Is she gonna die?"

Eyes shut, her voice cracks as she says, "They don't know."

Tommy nods toward the doorway and leaves us alone. I sit in the chair next to her bed and say, "I'm sorry."

She puts a hand over her face and says, "I don't suppose you've heard from your father."

I could lie, but what would be the point? "No." To be helpful I tell her what I always tell her when she asks: "He's taken off before and come back."

She sighs. "I guess I shouldn't have expected anything different. We knew the baby was going to have some problems, the doctor told us."

I look at her. "When did you find that out?"

"The day before he vanished."

Oh.

She lies there, quiet, and I sit there, with nothing to say. I try to get mad at her for Mom's sake, but I can't. I should feel like a traitor but I don't. I get to keep the Dart and the two hundred bucks, which I've already used for rent money anyway. Well, not just the rent. I bought some records, to tell the truth. And a couple of them just because the guy on the album cover was really hot.

Whenever she called me after Dad took off, the miserable old cow sounded mental; here, lying on the hospital bed, she's too tired to do much of anything, except talk softly. I expected there to be some flowers or balloons or candy, but the room's empty. A gust of wind pounds on the window. Winter's already on its way.

After a while I say, "Laurie's getting in tomorrow night?"

She nods.

I make conversation. "Kind of weird that she didn't go to St. Kate's. NYU is the last place I thought she'd wind up."

The cow, I mean Mrs. Gunderson, I mean Mrs. Doyle, screw it, Carol says, "It suits her new political outlook."

I say, "You mean like her speech at graduation?"

Carol smiles a little and says, "Yes, but as I learned, pretty speeches aren't enough. You must act for justice, not just talk about it. You see, Laurie has evolved to a higher level of con- sciousness than the rest of us. 'If you want peace, work for justice.'

Oh, and let's not forget her other mantra, 'If you're not part of the solution, you're part of the problem.' I couldn't wait for her to move out. She had become a holier-than-thou pain in the neck."

I laugh.

Carol says, "My guess? In five years she'll be a radical nun doing 'social justice work' in some third-world backwater."

Carol's kind of funny. I never noticed before.

She sighs and says, "I could never understand why she didn't have a sense of humor. Her mother loved to laugh; so did her father. And they both could stay out all night long on the dance floor. Then they had her, this glum little girl. I just didn't get it. But her 'political awakening,' that was what finally pushed me over the edge. You want to go to New York, I said to her, be my guest."

We're quiet again until Carol says, "You know, I'm just feeling sorry for myself, pay no attention to me. You should go visit your new sister. Her name's Sarah."

"That's a pretty name."

She runs a hand through her messy hair and says, "It was my sister's name."

Tommy goes to intensive care with me. A nurse in blue scrubs makes us wash our hands, and then we have to put on masks and gowns.

"Ten minutes, no more, and then you'll both have to leave," she tells us.

She leads us to a big glass box with tubes and wires sticking out of it. There's a *beep-beep-beep* noise and another sound, like Darth Vader breathing.

Tommy says, "God, she's so tiny. There's nothing to her."

I squat down for a closer look. "Is this stuff helping her breathe, do you think?"

"Yeah, I guess so."

She doesn't even look like a human being; she's more of a kitten without any fur. People say that babies look like the father or the mother, but this one's got a look all her own.

Tommy asks me, "Do they think she's gonna live?"

"They're not sure. I didn't think she'd be this bad off."

Tommy says, "We should say a prayer."

I look up at him. I'm gonna say that that's not funny, but then I get that he's not kidding. I say, "Okay."

"Cool."

I wait for him to start. "Go ahead."

He says, "I don't remember any."

I shake my head at Sarah. "Jeez, Tommy, what were you, a pagan baby? I'll say a Hail Mary."

"Cool. You start, I'm sure it'll come back to me."

So I say, "Hail Mary full of grace, the Lord is with thee, blessed is thee among virgins and blessed is the . . . something of something, something Jesus. Holy Mary, mother of God, please pray for us sinners, now and at the hour of our death, amen."

Tommy says, "Amen." Then he says, "Man, that was really feeble."

"Shut up."


I pick Laurie up at the airport. Her flight's late and she's the last one off the plane.

"I thought you'd missed it," I tell her when she finally gets through the gate.

She shakes her head. "You don't want to know how close I came."

She looks like somebody else. I mean she looks the same, it's just like, the way she comes off is really different from what I'm used to. I say, "Give me your bag."

She hands it over and says, "Your father's sense of timing is impeccable. I could have told you this was going to happen."

"It's not my fault."

Laurie says, "Sorry, he just pisses me the hell off."

If it were anyone else who had said that I wouldn't be so shocked. But it was Laurie Lindstrom.

We walk down the concourse without talking, until she tells me she has to stop at the bathroom.

I wait for her with the other men whose wives or girlfriends are in the can. Some of them have babies or little kids with them, cranky and whiny after sitting in a plane. It's kind of freaky, how much Laurie has changed. Or maybe she's always been like this, only she never showed it, 'cause she was afraid what other people would think. She doesn't seem afraid of anything anymore.

When she makes it out of the bathroom, she says, "You should see what goes on in there. Some of these women won't get out of your way so you can wash your hands, they're too busy reapplying their makeup and touching up their hair. It's ludicrous. You know, sometimes I think we're our own worst enemy."

I laugh. From dweeb to Sister Rita Jr. to whoever she is now in less than a year.

She pulls her hair behind her shoulders and asks me, "Did Aunt Carol seem okay to you?"

"No, not really."

Laurie nods and picks up the pace. "We weren't exactly getting along when I left for NYU. Your father had gotten really weird about the pregnancy. You could tell that he couldn't deal with it. I told her he was going to dump her and she'd have to raise the baby by herself, but she wouldn't listen to me."

I don't say anything; I just try to keep up with her.

"And having a child at her age, she had to know how risky it was. When she called me with the news that there was something wrong, I told her she should have terminated the pregnancy. I told her that there were way too many people on the planet anyway, more than what's sustainable, but she wouldn't hear of it. No way, suddenly she's Catholic-of-the-Year, not that she went to church once the whole time I was growing up."

Even if I wanted to say anything, I'm afraid to. She's like Aunt Nora, except in reverse.

The more she talks, the faster she walks, till we're practically jogging. "Well, if she wants to be the world's oldest single mother, that's up to her. It's the baby I feel sorry for, you know? No father, a list of handicaps longer than your arm, what kind of quality of life is she going to have? It was very selfish of Aunt Carol to get pregnant, like one of the most selfish things anybody has ever done. Did she tell you the baby has Down's syndrome on top of everything else?"

*Jesus Christ.* I shake my head, my eyes big.

Laurie grunts. "Why would she? Why tell the brother that his sister's retarded? Why think about anyone else at all? And your father, acting like his sperm just got up and crawled into her uterus on its own, like he had nothing to do with it. Typical man. No offense, but you have to admit, it's typical."

I'm starting to breathe heavy. I say, "Laurie, could you slow down a little?"

She stops and says, "Sorry. I do this when I'm upset." Then she's speed-walking again. "They deserved each other, you know? She couldn't keep away from a married man, and he can't keep it in his pants. It's a match made in heaven. They lied to both of us, you know, pretending that nothing was going on. Your poor mother. It just makes me so damn mad. I mean, sure I'm grateful she took me in after I lost my parents, but come on, she could have tried a little harder to set a good example. If she thinks I'm dropping out of school to sit around and take care of her kid— no offense, I know she's your sister—she's my cousin too, after all—well, she's got another thing coming. She made this mess, she can damn well clean it up."

Laurie stops in her tracks. She asks me, "Where am I going?"

"Huh?"

"Where did you park the car?"


The reunion at St. Mary's is like when two boxers enter the ring and have the rules of the match explained to them. Both Carol and Laurie are waiting to see who's gonna throw the first punch. I'm hoping for a good, clean fight.

Carol's sitting up in bed. She says, "Thanks for coming," like she's saying *Wipe your feet.*

Laurie says, "No problem," but you can tell that it *is* a problem, maybe the biggest one in history.

Carol says to Laurie, "Have you seen her yet?"

"No, not yet. I'm going to look in on her in a few minutes."

Carol says, like it's a warning, "She's a beautiful little girl." She might as well add: *Anybody says different gets their ass kicked.*

"I'm sure she is. Has the prognosis improved?"

Carol says, "They've upgraded her condition to serious. She's off the critical list."

Laurie says, "So she's going to pull through?"

Carol says, "Of course she is. She's my daughter, isn't she?"

Laurie says quietly, "So you're going to keep her?"

An upper cut.

Carol frowns and says, "Why on earth would you ask me something like that?"

Laurie crosses her legs and folds her arms. Louder now, she says, "Do you have any idea what it's going to be like raising a special-needs child? And on your own?"

Carol gasps, but recovers. "I raised you, didn't I?"

Oooh, one right to the gut.

"Barely."

*Ouch!* Ya know dat one's gotta hurt.

"Oh, so now it all comes out when I'm lying in my hospital bed. You think I was a rotten mother, is that it? I'd like to see how well you'd have done if you'd been single and free one day, and parenting a six-year-old the next."

Laurie says, "All right, calm down. The only point I'm trying to make is that this is going to be so much harder than you can possibly imagine. And where's my 'Uncle Pat' in all this?" When she says Uncle Pat, she does that quotation marks thing with her fingers. "Any chance of him coming back into the picture, or is he gone for good?"

Carol looks at me, like I'm the expert on this one. So I just tell the truth. "I don't know what he'll do."

We sit for a few minutes until Laurie says, "Well, I'm going to see the baby. Do you want to come with me, Kevin?"

"Yeah, you bet."

We leave Carol on her bed, steaming. Part of me feels like I should stay with her, but I want to see Sarah.

We're getting ready to enter the intensive care nursery. Laurie scrubs, telling me, "She can't admit what a mess she's made of everything."

I dry my own hands with paper towels. "You're being kind of hard on her. She just had a baby, you know."

Laurie puts on a mask. "That's what I love, somebody gave birth, so they're better than the rest of us. Just because we can reproduce doesn't mean that we should."

I fumble with a gown. "All I meant was she's really wiped. Give her a break."

"Since when do you stick up for Aunt Carol? All a woman has to do is crank out a baby to win your approval? That makes women a-okay in your book?"

"Sorry I said anything."

Laurie laughs and says, "And now you're thinking that I must be having my period. Am I right?"

She is, but I just shoot her a look, which doesn't work really well since I have my mask on.

She says, "You know, Kevin, you're lucky you're so cute. Ugly people can't get away with being this stupid. I know."

"I'm not stupid."

Her voice softens. "You're right, I'm sorry, I didn't mean it. It was the only way I could think of to tell you that you're very attractive. I've always thought so."

I stare at her.

She says, "Don't worry, I'm not flirting, I'm over my crush on you. It's just kind of fun to say it; that's all. I wanted to a million times at school."

The nurse takes us to the incubator and tells us to make it quick, there's a lot that needs to get done, and we'd just be in the way.

I can tell by the way Laurie's eyes get big that Sarah breaks her heart.

I say, "It's kind of a shock when you see her for the first time."

She doesn't say anything, just kneels down and puts a gloved hand on the glass.

I say, "Do you want to be alone with her?"

Laurie shakes her head. Finally, she says, "Poor little thing. She's beautiful. I'm afraid that just looking at her could hurt her."

Our ten minutes go by without talking. When the nurse comes back, pointing at the clock on the wall, I nod. I put my hand on Laurie's shoulder and say, "We gotta leave now."

Laurie stands up slowly and says, "I know this is going to sound weird, but I don't like leaving her here by herself. I mean, I know she's not by herself, but none of these people are related to her, what do they care? She needs her family."


When I go back to the hospital the next day, Laurie's sitting in Carol's room reading a book about Red China and Carol's asleep.

Laurie whispers, "She's been out for a couple of hours. They had to give her some more painkillers."

I stare at Carol, who looks like what's left after they knock down an old building. She lies there in a pile. I say, "I feel sorry for her."

Laurie doesn't argue. "So do I. It makes it hard to stay mad at her. I still hate your father though."

I shrug. "He is who he is. He just doesn't know what he wants to be when he grows up."

Laurie thinks about this.

I ask, "How's Sarah doing?"

Laurie smiles at me. "Better, she's stable. She's going to make it." Laurie looks around and says, "There's only one chair. Do you want to sit down?"

"Nah, that's okay."

She stands up. "Please, I've been sitting all day. I really should stretch my legs."

So we both stand there.

I can't think of anything new to say, so I tell her, "I think I'll go see Sarah."

Laurie nods.

Back in the hallway, I'm thinking that maybe I should have brought Carol a card or flowers or something. That's when I see Aunt Nora at the nurses' station.

*Holy shit.*

The nurse behind the counter points in my direction and Aunt Nora looks right at me. She doesn't smile, just winks.

I run up to her and grab her by the arm. "What are you doing here?"

Aunt Nora says, "And hello to you too. Tommy called me with the news. At least *he* has the good manners to keep me informed. I'm here to see the baby. She may not be my niece, but she's your sister."

I tug at her arm. "The baby's up in the intensive care nursery. Let's go."

Aunt Nora frowns. "Intensive care nursery? Mother of God, what's the matter with her?"

There's a long list of things, but none that I can remember with Aunt Nora looking at me the way she is. "She's getting better."

Aunt Nora sighs and says, "That woman can't even give birth without disaster striking." Then she sees the look on my face and says, "I didn't mean to upset you."

"Just give it a rest, will ya?"

She raises an eyebrow. "Done. And you remember who you're talking to."

"Done."

She makes a face and says, "These places all smell so nasty. I suppose I should stop and call on . . . the new mother. Then we can see your sister."

When we get back to Carol's room, Laurie looks up and smiles at me. But then she sees Aunt Nora and drops her book on the floor. She whispers really loud, "What's *she* doing here?"

Before I can open my mouth, Aunt Nora says, "*She* is Kevin's Aunt Nora. *You* may call me Miss O'Connor."

Laurie says, "I know who you are. Last time I saw you, you were swinging a shovel. You're the last person Aunt Carol wants to see."

Aunt Nora says, "No, my sister *Eileen* is the last person your Aunt Carol wants to see."

Laurie says, "Kevin, please get her out of here before Aunt Carol wakes up."

Aunt Nora says, "I've come to see Kevin's baby sister. Don't fret, now that there's a little one involved I won't be upsetting . . . the new mother. We're all family now, after all."

Laurie doesn't like the sound of that.

Aunt Nora looks over at Carol and says, "What's the matter with her? She looks stone cold."

Laurie says, "It was a difficult birth. She's on painkillers."

I say to Aunt Nora, "Let's go see Sarah."

She says, "All right, then." She points at Carol and says to Laurie, "You might want to call the doctor and make sure she's still among the living. Mind you, a comfortable bed is a much nicer way to go than the way my poor Eileen did."

# PEOPLE CAN STILL SURPRISE YOU

NOVEMBER 1978

Lorraine sucks air through her teeth and says, "Oh, you don't mean it. He just left her and she had to have the baby all by herself?"

I can tell that she's enjoying this so I say, "The baby's my sister and she's gotta lot of problems."

Lorraine shakes her head and says, "Oh, I'm so sorry." Then, like two seconds later she says, "So, you *really* don't know where your father is, or you're just not supposed to tell her?"

"I really don't know where he is. Maybe he took the job in Barrow after all, who knows?"

Lorraine thinks about it and says, "Imagine going farther north. As if it doesn't get cold enough here."

A man pushes his cart up to register three. He's maybe fifty and I can tell that Lorraine's never seen him at Red Owl before. She takes her gum out and sticks it in the trash can. You can tell that she wishes she'd had a good twenty minutes in the ladies to get her makeup just right for this guy.

"And how are you tonight?" she says, sap sticking to every word.

He doesn't look up at her, just concentrates on putting his groceries on the belt. "Good, and yourself?"

She says, "Oh, with winter knocking on the door I'm just waiting for some millionaire to take me away from it all."

Jeez, that's bold. The guy looks up, a can of Le Sueur peas in his hand. "Really?"

Lorraine nods.

He puts the can on the belt and grabs a frozen pizza, saying, "Well, I certainly hope your Prince Charming shows up soon, we're supposed to get three inches this weekend."

Lorraine says, "Oh, noooo! You don't mean it. Snow already?"

The guy puts two Swanson Hungry-Man dinners on the belt. They're salisbury steak, the kind that I rip off for Tommy and me. He says, "That's what they're forecasting."

I open a bag and put the peas at the bottom.

Lorraine says, "Well, I bet you're happy you're just passing through then. Visiting family? I've never seen you in here before."

"I'm originally from Iowa, but I've lived in Minneapolis for almost twenty-five years now. I don't usually do the shopping."

Lorraine's already checked out the guy's ring finger, which is free and clear. She's keying slowly, dragging this out. She says, "Oh, the missus sick tonight?"

The guy smiles and says, "There is no missus."

Lorraine whistles. "Living in sin, then?"

He laughs. "I guess that would depend on who you ask. Or is it whom you ask? If he was here right now, he'd be correcting my grammar."

I look up from the bag and Lorraine loses her place on the keys. After a second she picks up a box of Total cereal and asks me, "Did I ring this up already?"

I say, real stiff, "I dunno." Neither of us can remember what to do next. Then I say, "Why don't you check the tape?"

She smiles at the guy. "Sorry, sorry. This won't take any time at all."

He looks at her and then at me. My face says, *What can ya do?*

Lorraine says, "There's the Total." Then she laughs real nervous-like and says, "The Total cereal, not the total total."

That's when I figure it out. Thursdays are when Fey Hayes does his shopping. This guy's his boyfriend. So there are five of us on earth: me, Fey Hayes, the Iranian TA, the kid on his bike, and this guy. Six if you count Jack, but he's MIA and I'll never know for sure.

When Fey Hayes's boyfriend is out the doors, Lorraine says, "How do you like that? He's one of them."

"One of what?"

She whispers, "A gay. He's a gay. That's what they all call themselves, gay. And he's a brash one too; he doesn't care if the whole world knows. Oh, what a shame, he can't be happy like that."

I'm desperate to meet a guy, so I pick up a copy of *The Reader, the Twin Cities Alternative Weekly.* Mostly it's articles about why everybody is so stupid and lots of ads for bands appearing at the local clubs. You can see Lamont Cranston or Willie and the Bees at the Cabooze almost every weekend. There's a buncha ads for the record stores and head shops too, like the Wax Museum and the Electric Fetus. But the ads I'm checking out are the personals in the back 'cause there are some from guys who are into guys. Here's what I've figured out so far: GWM means Gay White Male. GBM means Gay Black Male. That's about it, there are a lot of other letters that don't make sense 'cause I haven't cracked the code yet. And I don't know what top and bottom are supposed to mean.

I'm too paranoid to actually answer an ad, but I try to write one of my own. My first one says:

GWM, 18, *looking for somebody like me. Nobody knows about me.*

I read it and think: that's not much information. I try again.

GWM, *college student, wants to meet same. Please be discreet* (I got that from some of the other ads). *I like music and partying and high times.*

That makes me sound like a burnout.

I try one more.

GWM, 18. *I want to fall in love.*

That sounds faggy.

I rip my ads up into little pieces 'cause I know I don't have the guts to send one in. There might be somebody who works at the paper who'll see my name—you have to give your name to buy an ad—and tell everybody about me.

You don't want people to know about you. Or to think that they know about you. That's what I remember most about growing up, the kids who were always picked on. If they were skinny or weak or smart or weren't good at sports, they'd get called names like faggot and queer and sissy. And they'd get the shit kicked out of them daily. I remember one kid in fourth grade who liked to read and always got good grades. Like four or five kids would wait for him every morning when he got off the bus and drag him into the bushes. Every single morning. He'd come out crying, blood on his face, his clothes all ripped up and his lunch money gone. I should have helped him, but I was afraid of what people would say about me if I did. Some of the girls would tell a teacher, but nobody ever did anything to stop it. The teachers would always say shit like, *He's got to learn to stand up for himself* or *As soon as he fights back they'll leave him alone.* I remember thinking even back then that adults were so fucking stupid. I wondered what they would do if four guys showed up at their houses to kick their asses. They'd run to the phone, peeing their pants, and call the cops. Or they'd whip out a gun and start shooting anything that moved. But if you're nine, you just get the crap knocked out of you and it's a game. It's called smear the queer.

I close my eyes and try to remember if I was ever one of the kids who dragged him into the bushes. All the boys in my class did something to him to prove that they hated him too. Even some of the girls were mean to him. Sometimes a boy would knock his books out of his hands or trip him in the hall. Sometimes one of those little milk cartons would hit him hard, on the face, from across the cafeteria. And now I remember that sometimes the kid who sat behind him would punch him in the back during class, but he would never tell. He'd just sit there, in front of me, not making a sound, letting me punch him.

I put the little pieces of paper in the toilet and flush them down.

Here's what I think is really weird. I've got the hots for the guy who plays Apollo on *Battlestar Galactica*. So when I found out he was gonna be on the "Battle of the Network Stars," I got really excited, 'cause I wanted to see him in a swimming suit or shorts or something. And then I find out that while I was watching "Battle of the Network Stars," hundreds of Americans in Guyana killed themselves by drinking poisoned Kool-Aid. That is what I think is really weird, that you can be getting all worked up watching Apollo on "Battle of the Network Stars" and at the same time, all these people decide to off themselves. It makes you wonder if we really live on the same planet.

So now there's all these Jonestown jokes that I hear on campus. *Did you hear the one about Jonestown? I'd tell you, but the punch line's too long.* Stuff like that.

As for me, I spend a lot of time trying to figure out how to pay rent and go to school on $2.75 an hour. And if I hear "Hot Child in the City" one more time, I really will have to kill somebody.

But not today. It's Thanksgiving. Tommy's invited me to his house, but I told Aunt Nora I would spend the day with her, even though she's not much of a cook. She's so excited that she gives a turkey with all the trimmings her best shot, but no matter how long she bakes it, it won't get done.

So I don't embarrass her, I leave her alone in the kitchen and watch the snow fall.

After another hour I hear Aunt Nora shout, "I give up. This bird wouldn't be ready for the second coming. Oh, Kevin, I'm so sorry, I've made a mess of it."

I touch one of the window's panes and feel the cool glass on my skin. I yell, "No prob, we can make sandwiches."

Aunt Nora shuffles out of the kitchen, wiping her hands on her apron, the first one I think I've ever seen her wear. "Sandwiches on Thanksgiving, oh what you must think of me."

"Don't sweat it."

She puts her hands on her hips and arches her back, like a bear just coming out of hibernation. "Let's not have cold sandwiches on a cold day. How 'bout I boil up some spuds and make us a pot of tea? The good Lord knows I ate that for my meal hundreds of times when I was a girl."

"Cool."

So we're in the dining room eating potatoes off the good dishes and drinking tea out of the good cups with Jack and Bobby and Martin looking down on us from their places of honor. Aunt Nora closes her eyes after she puts a bit of potato in her mouth, but she doesn't chew, she sucks all the butter and salt out of it and then swallows the mush. She says, "Is there anything better than a spud swimming in butter?"

The other thing she does is stick her face maybe an inch or two away from the steaming potatoes. It makes her skin pink and moist and she says, "That always takes the chill off. When we were girls we practically wore our spuds when they were nice and hot."

For dessert there's pecan pie (from the store) and whiskey in little glasses.

After two glasses, Aunt Nora asks me what I'm thankful for.

I duck her question. I say, "You go first."

She doesn't mind. She says without having to think about it, "I'm very thankful for you, my darling one. Look at you, you turned out grand. You've become a real steady-Eddie, holding down a job and doing a degree. There's a brilliant future waiting for you."

"You really think so?"

She leans her big man face against a big man hand. "I'm certain of it! You'll get a good, solid position and before you know it, they'll be a wife and little ones. Oh, it breaks my heart, your children will never know their grandmother."

I can feel myself getting hot. "I'm only eighteen."

Aunt Nora laughs. "I'm not talking right this minute! There's time enough for all that. Finish your degree, start a career, and then they'll be lining up around the block for you." She takes a sip of her whiskey and then she cuts herself another piece of pie.

"Is that all you're thankful for? Me?"

She looks up at me and stops chewing. Then she swallows hard and says, "That's more than enough to be thankful for. Don't you sell yourself short."

"I just meant that there's gotta be other stuff too."

She wipes her mouth with a lace napkin and clears her throat. "Of course there's more. I'm thankful for Eileen, may she rest in peace. I'm thankful for my cats. But above all, I'm thankful for the many mercies of my Lord Jesus and the Virgin Mother."

"What about the new pope?"

She sniffs and says, "Let's wait and see."


Rick Foley's girlfriend had to spend Thanksgiving weekend with her family in Mankato so he's invited Tommy and me to hang out at his house and crack some brews. Rick Foley's really in love, he won't shut up about his girlfriend and when we ask him if she's a good lay he gets all huffy. So we knock it off, but listening to him go on and on about her is starting to piss me off. The guy's gone totally ape-shit over some girl we've never even met, it's like he's embarrassed by us or something. Then he tells us he's gonna ask her to marry him.

Tommy says, "You're shittin' me."

Rick Foley says, "I'm getting her a ring for Christmas."

"Jesus," I say, "what's the rush? You knock her up?"

Rick Foley looks really mad, but then he remembers that that's exactly what Tommy did, so he says all matter-of-fact, "No, she's not pregnant. We'll have kids later."

"What's the rush?" I ask him again.

Rick Foley says, real quiet, "I don't want to lose her."

He never really had any serious girlfriends the whole time we were in high school. Mostly he just tried to score with drunk girls at parties. Once in a while he succeeded and then we'd have to hear every last detail, including how he *ditched the slut* after he shot his wad.

"Don't do it," Tommy says. "My parents got married right out of high school and look at them. When they split up they almost killed each other. My mom's dating and it's really embarrassing to see her throw on the war paint."

Rick Foley says, "That won't happen to us."

I snap open a beer, my third in an hour, and I'm not even keeping up. "You remember the old guy who died, the guy who . . ."

Tommy burps really loud. Then he says, "That was a good one!"

". . . the guy who stuck his wife in the freezer?"

Rick Foley says, "Yeah."

"Well, he didn't love his wife like you love this girl. He was just used to having her around and he didn't want to be alone, but he didn't love her. Not like he did when he married her. You know what he told me?"

Rick Foley says, like he doesn't care, "What?"

"He told me that things change."

Tommy and Rick Foley look at each other and start laughing. Tommy says, "Wait! Wait! Back up! I wanna write that down!"

Rick Foley says, "Is that what he said to the missus before he stuck her in the freezer?"

I get all red. "Shut up!"

They quiet down, but they're still kind of giggling. And they won't look at each other 'cause they know if they do, they'll crack up again.

I say, real slow, "What he meant was . . ."

Tommy burps again, but this time he doesn't say anything.

". . . that people fall out of love."

Rick Foley says something smart, which kinda surprises me. "So what? That can happen to anybody, no matter when they get married." Then he adds, "It could happen to your Aunt Nora if anybody had the nerve to marry her."

They laugh again.

So I say, "Eat me," and take a sip of my beer.

Rick Foley says, "I'm sorry, Kev, I didn't mean to cut your aunt. I just want to get married. Nothing says I'm gonna turn out all fucked up like Tommy's parents."

Tommy says, "Thanks a lot, dickweed."

Rick Foley says, "You know what I mean."

I say, "My dad was screwing around on my mom."

Rick Foley says, "We know. But I'm not gonna screw around on my wife."

Maybe it's the beer—no, it's definitely the beer—that makes me say, "I hope to hell you mean that, 'cause my mom didn't care if she lived or died after she found out. That's why she didn't bother to try and save herself when her car started skidding off the road."

Tommy looks right at me and says, "Your mom didn't kill herself."

I say, "I know. But I think part of her was dead already. 'Cause of what he did. And look at Carol Gunderson, on her own with a baby 'cause of him."

Nobody says anything for a while, but then Rick Foley crushes his beer can and says, "You guys are bumming me the hell out. Can't you be happy for me? This is a big deal. *Jesus.*"

Now it's Tommy and me who look at each other and start laughing. At the same time we say, "Sorry, man."

Rick Foley says, "And you're both gonna be in the wedding."

Tommy says, "Can we at least meet her first?"

Rick Foley says, "After she says yes. I don't want you blowing this for me."

I say, "You mean by telling her what you're really like?"

Tommy says, "Or all the weed you've smoked?"

I say, "Or all the other dumb-ass shit you've done?"

Rick Foley says, "Yeah."

Tommy says, "So how are you gonna ask her? You gonna take her out for dinner?"

Rick Foley says, "Nah. She's coming over for Christmas Eve so I'm gonna wait till everybody's gone to bed and then ask her. When we're sitting in front of the tree with only the Christmas lights on. And we're listening to our song."

Tommy raises his eyebrows and I'm kinda shocked too, 'cause Rick Foley has really thought this out. And it's kinda romantic. Tommy says, "Jeez." Then he asks, "What's your song?"

Rick Foley blushes and says, " 'Evergreen' by Barbra Streisand."

Tommy and I scream and nearly fall off our chairs. I'm laughing so hard I think I'm gonna wet my pants.

Rick Foley's shouting, "Shut the hell up!"

When Tommy can speak, he says, "Oh! Oh, Jesus! 'Evergreen'? I'm gonna spew!"

## DECEMBER 1978

Tommy wants to go barhopping a lot, he says it's easier to pick up girls around the holidays 'cause nobody wants to be alone at Christmastime. He goes out almost every night. On Wednesday he asked me to go with him, but that's the night that "Rudolph" was on, and besides, Steve Martin was gonna be on the "Johnny Cash Christmas Special." So he asked me to go out again on Saturday, but I didn't 'cause that was the night that "Rudolph's Shiny New Year" was on. He asked again on Monday, but then I would of missed "The Flintstones' Christmas."

So now he's started hanging out more with guys from Dunwoody 'cause they all want to meet girls too.

The one thing we always do together is our Christmas shopping. We go shopping once a year, the week before Christmas. We start at Dayton's—the one that Mary Tyler Moore was in front of when she threw her hat up in the air—and if we have to, we go to Donaldson's. That's for the nice stuff; for the cheaper stuff we go to the Montgomery Ward's on University Avenue or the Target in Roseville.

At Dayton's we'd always buy perfume for our moms. After my mom died we just bought some for Tommy's mom, but this year I decided I'd get some for Aunt Nora, she could really use it. Not that she smells bad or anything, it's just that she needs all the help she can get when it comes to other people.

Tommy's sniffing all the bottles on the display case.

I say, "Don't you always get her Charlie?"

He grunts, "Yeah, but this year I want to get her old-lady perfume. She needs to tone it down."

I hold up a blue bottle that smells like every other perfume. "Has she met somebody?"

Tommy scrunches up his face after he sniffs a nozzle. "I wish she would. She's started going to bars, it's really gross. I ran into her over at the Cabooze last week."

"You didn't tell me that!"

"You think I wanna advertise it? I walk in with some guys from school and there she is on a bar stool talking to a goddamn biker."

"Whaddya do?"

"Just walked up and said, 'Hi, Mom.' Then I said to the biker, 'Better take off, my dad's in the parking lot and he's got his gun.' "

"No, way!"

"Yes, way. Mom and I had a big fight. Jesus, I just wish she'd give up trying to find a boyfriend. What does she need one for at her age, anyway?"

I pick out a perfume for Aunt Nora not because it smells any different from the others, but because the bottle is fancy. I say, "She's just lonely. Give her a break."

Tommy says, "I guess. She's gotta stop hanging out in bars, though."

Now Tommy holds up a box with a label that says *Chaste*. "Found one," he tells me.

We go up the escalators 'cause the other thing I need to get this year is baby toys for Sarah. I wanna get her something really big and soft, like a stuffed bear. In the toy department, Tommy just picks up a toy every once in a while, looks at it, and then puts it back on the shelf.

I say, "You could get your brothers something here."

He says, "Why, they sell stink bombs?"

I decide on a huge stuffed brown bear. I'm ready to go to the register, but now Tommy's staring at a mobile, the kind you hang over the crib. I look at him as he touches it, making it spin slowly in a circle. He bends down and looks up at the moving shapes, trying to figure out what it would look like to a baby.

I say, "You ready?"

He looks over at me and says, "Yeah. Let's make a move."

We're walking through the skyways with businessmen in suits rushing past in every direction. Tommy says, "Do you think you should get something for your dad, you know, just in case?"

Jeez, he's like a mind reader. I say, "I was thinking about it, but I'm pretty sure he won't be back for Christmas."

Tommy says, "Ya never know."

But I think I do. He was only gone one other Christmas. I was twelve and Mom was calling everyone she could think of, just like Carol Gunderson did when he left her. Aunt Nora came over and when I asked her what was going on, she said I shouldn't worry. Worry about what, I wanted to know. About your da, she told me. He'll turn up.

But he didn't make it home at all that day. To try and cheer us up, Aunt Nora said we should open our presents. Then Mom said that was a good idea, we shouldn't let Dad being called in for the holiday shift upset our celebrations. I said I thought you couldn't find him. She said, Oh, I was just mixed up with my dates, he's at the plant. So I said: You just forgot he wouldn't be here for Christmas? Yes, she said, it slipped my mind. I told her she was a rotten liar and Aunt Nora told me to shut my hole and show my mother some respect. She said my mother would never lie to me and I should apologize. But I asked Mom, Is he really at the plant. Mom said, Yes, he really is, I'm sorry for getting us all in such a state. So I said I was sorry and Aunt Nora said, Good lad. I never thought of that until today. Weird.

Tommy says, "Hey, Kev, tune in, man."

"Sorry," I mumble. When Aunt Nora spaces out she always says, *You'll have to forgive me, I was miles away*. Just like Dad must be right now.

It's Christmas Eve and Mrs. Grabowski's invited me to spend it with her and Tommy. Tommy's little brothers are at his father's apartment with his new wife 'cause they're not old enough to choose where they go for the holidays.

Laurie's back in town for the break and she wanted to know what I was doing. When I told her, she asked if she could come too. Mrs. Grabowski said sure, the more the merrier. So Laurie's here. Carol and Sarah came with her 'cause Carol needed to get out of the house.

Aunt Nora felt left out so she's here too.

You really have to feel sorry for Mrs. Grabowski. She's in the kitchen cooking for seven people, four of them she's just met.

Aunt Nora has Sarah on her lap. When Carol came the first thing Aunt Nora did was take the baby from her. She told Carol, "Give me the little darling, you look dead."

Carol just handed Sarah over and fell on the couch, where she sits now watching them. She wants to fall asleep, but with Aunt Nora in charge, she doesn't dare.

Laurie and Tommy and I are down in the basement to see if there are any good records left around the house that we should take back to the apartment. I find an Eagles album and Laurie rolls her eyes. She's kind of punked-out. She's dressed in the same kind of clothes that Chuck tried to buy me in Duluth and she wears a safety pin as an earring now. Laurie goes to all these really cool clubs in New York and she says the days of the Mellow Mafia are over. She's seen the Ramones and the Talking Heads and Blondie. She says, "The scene out there is so far ahead of anything in the Cities. I mean, Minneapolis has First Avenue, but that's it. And St. Paul's got nothing going on. I feel sorry for you, it's like you're stuck in a time warp out here."

Tommy says, "Rub it in, why don't you?" But if Minneapolis

is behind the curve, Tommy's even further back. He thinks rock reached perfection when Pink Floyd released *Dark Side of the Moon*.

Laurie asks me how the U is going. I tell her I'm taking next semester off 'cause I need to make more money.

She says, "And that's how it begins."

I say, "That's how what begins?"

"Dropping out."

I say, "I'm not dropping out, I'm saving up some bucks, that's all."

She looks me right in the eyes and says, "If money's a problem, I can lend you some. I have a full scholarship and I get Social Security. I could let you have forty bucks a month."

Tommy says, "I might have to drop out too."

I say, "You don't have to give me money, I'll be okay. Thanks, though."

She blushes and I can tell that she still has a little crush on me.

Tommy says, "I might have to drop out too."

Laurie laughs and says, "Nice try. If you had kept your baby, then I could see how going to Dunwoody would break the bank."

*Oh, shit.*

Tommy turns his head and says very quietly, to nobody but me, "You told her."

Laurie says, "Oh, my God, I'm sorry, Kevin, I thought he knew that I knew."

Tommy says, "You told her. I can't fucking believe you, man."

I say, "I'm sorry. It just came out when we were at the hospital, right after Sarah was born. We were talking about babies and shit."

Next, Tommy looks at Laurie and says, "Have you told anybody?"

She reverts back to the old Laurie and squeaks, "No."

He says, "We take this to our coffins, got it? No way my mom finds out."

We nod, like he's our dad and not some baby's. Some baby that Catholic Social Services gave away for him. He says, "I'm serious."

We nod again. I don't even care that he might think he's the alpha.

From upstairs, Mrs. Grabowski shouts, "Come and get it." She's made a buffet on the kitchen table and we help ourselves. Tommy's still pissed so he says, "Hey, Laurie, you wanna wash our feet first?"

Mrs. Grabowski doesn't get the joke, but she says, "Don't be rude to our guests, ya brat-kid."

Aunt Nora won't let go of Sarah so Carol has to fix a plate for her. She puts a little bit of everything on it, but when she gets to the jar of fish, she asks me, "Does your aunt eat herring?"

I say, "We never had herring at her house. That's like, Swedish."

Carol stares at the jar. Then she says, "That's convenient. She'll just assume that it's supposed to taste like rat poison."

We all laugh.

Mrs. Grabowski says, "That's terrible, don't even joke about it. It's Christmas, after all. Just spit on her food."

We all laugh again, but quieter this time, so Aunt Nora won't hear.

We've spread out in the small sitting room. Laurie's on the floor, cross-legged, like she's protesting or meditating or doing something else deep. Tommy's already done with his first plate and heads to the kitchen for seconds. Aunt Nora and Carol gush over Mrs. Grabowski's cooking and she blushes. I've never seen her turn red before, except when she's yelling at Tommy or one of his brothers or when she's talking about her ex and his slut of a wife. Carol asks Mrs. Grabowski for her chicken recipe and I get up off the radiator that's burning my ass. I pick up the baby that lies at Aunt Nora's feet on top of a pile of blankets, a caterpillar in its cocoon.

"Where are you going with her?" Aunt Nora wants to know.

"I'm gonna show her the snowfall."

Aunt Nora swallows and says, "Wrap her up good and tight, it's bitter out there."

Carol keeps a careful eye on me as I bundle up her baby. She's stopped paying attention to ingredients and temperatures and cooking time, but Mrs. Grabowski hasn't noticed. She's still talking as I open the front door with Sarah in my arms.

Outside, the snow falls in small, tiny pieces, glistening in the glow of the streetlights like bits of broken glass. When the snow is this fresh and white, before the car exhaust and salt and sand have left their marks, it can almost seem as bright as sunset even in the middle of the night. I hold Sarah tight with one arm and brush off a place on the steps with the other. If she's noticed that sixty degrees have disappeared in a few seconds, she doesn't let on. I sit on the frozen cement and prop her up, my hands on either side of her tiny body. I point her face out toward the street. I whisper, "Look. Do you see the fairy lights?"

Behind me I hear the front door opening with a frigid creak. I turn my head and see Laurie and Tommy, their huge coats making them look like football players. Tommy pushes the door shut carefully, afraid he might disturb Sarah.

I say, "What's happening?"

Laurie brushes the snow off a step and sits down beside me. She says, "We got tired of swapping recipes."

Tommy sits on the other side of me but he doesn't say a word.

Laurie asks, "What are you two doing out here?"

I squeeze Sarah, but not enough to hurt her. I look at Laurie, the flakes piling up on her hair. Then I turn and look at Tommy, a headband making his ponytail stick almost straight out. I tell Laurie, "Nothing." Then out of the blue I ask her, "Have you ever been to Greenwich Village?"

She looks at me. "Yes. It's a lovely little section of Manhattan. Why do you ask?"

I stare at a streetlight. " 'Cause I've been wondering what it's like."

She follows my gaze, like something down the block must of prompted my question. Then she's silent, and I can tell she's afraid I'll be pissed off if she tells me that the Village is full of fags. But now she grunts, figuring it out all by herself. You can practically see the lightbulb go on over her head. She frowns, not a mad frown, more of an uncertain frown. She says, "I think you'd like it. I guess."

I say, "Cool." I should tell Laurie what Aunt Nora always says—*People can still surprise you*—but I don't, I just let it go at that.

Tommy's shivering. He says, "Let's go back inside. We can hide out in the basement."

Laurie stands up and says, "Good idea. I think I just froze my buns off." Then she says, but not in a mean way, "And I think I could use a drink."

Tommy's cold, he's slapping his arms with his mittens. He says, "Jesus, Kev, it's like an icebox out here. Come on."

I hand him my sister. I say, "Go on, I'm right behind you."

He smiles at Sarah and Laurie opens the door for them. He says, "Don't stay out too long, you'll get frostbite."

I nod.

Tomorrow is Christmas so the city won't declare a snow emergency till the twenty-sixth. People will shovel out their cars and move them from one side of the street to the other. The plows will dig a trail that allows us to get to our jobs and the lives we lead, the lives that won't wait for snow to melt or car engines to turn over.

But for now, all is absolutely still.